By the same author, TERRIBLE WITH RAISINS

JIGSAW ISLAND

Lynne McVernon

This novel is entirely a work of fiction. The names, characters, and incidents portrayed in it are the work of the author's imagination. Any resemblance to actual persons, living or dead, events or localities, is entirely coincidental.

Publisher: Independent Publishing Network
Publication date: June 2020
ISBN 978-1-83853-343-4
Author: Lynne McVernon
Email: lynne@lynnemcvernon.com
Website: www.lynnemcvernon.com
Please direct all enquiries to the author

This book is dedicated to all refugees who have
arrived and are arriving on the shores of the
Greek islands and to the people who
give them aid and sanctuary.

ONE

ANNIE – Harkin Croft, Kilachlan, Scotland

'You broke his nose, Jude.'

'I know.' He gives me such a wicked look of triumph I nearly let go. But I conjure myself a whiff of mindfulness and go on.

'OK, I'm struggling to know how I can help you. Give me a heads up.'

'Get off my case, Mum.'

'Come on, you know the rules. One, talk about your issues honestly. Two, give other people the respect you expect yourself.'

'Yeah, right. How about three?'

'What's three?' I'm sensing an adolescent 180° slew.

'Get off my fu –'

He's slewed too far. My cue to be a traditional parent.

'Hold it right there, buster. I'll tell you what three is. Three is what you'd say if Maggie was in the room.'

His face twists, his voice is low. 'That's no' fair. Using Maggie.'

Just turned thirteen, he's learnt boys don't cry, especially not mixed-race boys in small Scottish coastal towns. Even to their mothers. He's also right. I am out of order. Two years on, both of us still feel the pain of losing Maggie. Just thinking her name makes my insides contract, like I'm staring into the bottomless hole she's left in our lives. In the life of anyone who knew her. She was such a blissful human being, the friend who took Jude and me in, loved us and let us love her. Now, she watches over us from a canvas photo print on the wall opposite, Jack – or is it Tatty?– on her lap, the other Westie on the back of her armchair, snuffling into her neck. Eight-year-old Jude is on the floor, arm resting over her knee, dead cool, like he owns her. Dimitte diem, she was saying, let the day go.

'Fair game, Jude, I'm sorry. We all miss her.'

I wait while he absorbs my apology. The room is quiet and white, the furniture old and beloved. Maggie *is* the room, still comforting, still reassuring.

Summer breathes flowers, grass, and new leaves through the open window, bringing me back. Time for me to shift focus, use his language.

'Problem for me, pal, is they're on my case. Schools don't like dudes going around punching other dudes and they blame the –'

'Mum – he called me "the half-blood arsepiece".'

'Could you not just have called him something back?'

'I did, I said, "Shut yer puss, fannybaws". But it didn't feel like enough, so I thumped him.'

He's caught me off guard. We both honk with laughter. He throws himself on the lumpy old sofa and slings his endless legs across my lap. I am pinioned by a young giraffe. One with his hair shaved in a straight line across his forehead and nearly scalped down the sides in a 'taper fade'. A young giraffe called Bolshy.

It's getting to be quite a menagerie in here because there's also an elephant called 'Exclusion' in the room, and it has elephant relatives called 'Petty Theft', 'Provoking the Teacher', 'Occasional Truanting', and 'Smoking', amongst others. Quite a herd. Jude's eye contact says we're solid, though.

'He was being racist, Mum, and that's not acceptable. You said.'

'No, it's not, pet, but smashing people's faces isn't acceptable either. We have to work out how to move forward.'

Jude sets his mouth. 'OK. But no more psycho-speak, deal?'

That's a dig at me and my Degree and MSc in Psychology.

'Deal. No more psycho-speak.'

Not from me, anyway.

Jude's behaviour of late is symptomatic of his situation; grieving *and* being bullied. The Children and Adolescents Mental Health Service is so short on funds there's no knowing when we'll get an appointment. I ring Peter, my old uni tutor. A colleague of his may lever in a couple of free sessions for Jude under the cover of an EU research programme into the effects of 9/11 on racism in Britain. Or similar. Better than nothing.

Problem is, how to introduce a therapist to Jude and stay within the 'no psycho-speak' deal? He'll put up the Berlin Wall if he knows she's a 'mind-y woman'. Might take it better from a man but we don't have that choice. I offer it up gently, emphasising the 9/11 aspect. He's suspicious, but excited by the possibility that kids at school might think he's a terrorist. I swallow his hair-raising misconstruction, anything to get him there. I've had to keep the whole problem away from my parents; it's outside their emotional limits.

A couple of weeks later we're waiting at the therapist's consulting room up by the Botanical Gardens in Glasgow. She comes out, says 'Hello', and in he goes. Fruit fly into the collecting jar. Good mother that I am, I sit in the waiting room listening to the traffic stopping and starting on the Great Western Road with no *Hello* magazines to distract me. I glance at a *Homes and Interiors Scotland* and decide against a two-hundred grand, four-bedroom detached villa in Banff and having my hair ripped out by the Arctic wind. Besides, it's a bit of a stretch on a care worker's wages.

I want to share this unsettling experience with someone. Maggie would have been my first 'go to'. But if she'd been around, none of the nightmare would have happened. Could have happened. I run through other possibilities but either their work commitments or lack of signal rule out most of them. So it'll have to be Shona, whom I've known since Jude wasn't much more than a collection of cells. Shona belongs to my time in London. Apart from Maggie and one other, I've never mentioned her to anyone. But if ever I told the story of how we met, I might begin with:

1) As I was going into The Ritz Hotel – or,
2) As I was having tea at The Savoy – or,
3) As I was being thrown out of Grosvenor House – or,
4) – the real story, which is. 'As I hung about on the pavement outside the Langham Hotel, pissed off for being sent there –'

The brilliant green vision who swept past me on her way to the theatre then into my life belonged more to myth than my pathetic little tale. But, long story short, we've been in touch, on and off, ever since. I message her, now:

'Hi Shona – your favourite street urchin, here – currently awaiting urchin son who's closeted with child psychologist. She's going to tell me what I know already. Jude being bullied at school makes him feel isolated and angry. He's grieving for Maggie and could be at the anger stage of bereavement. He's also an adolescent trying to cope with new physical, mental, and emotional changes – which makes him angry. Consequently his terms of reference are shifting and he has no security. Which makes him, guess what? Angry. She'll say it isn't a reflection on me and it's nothing to do with needing a male role model. Don't know why we've bothered coming – gimme strength! A x'

Apart from losing Maggie, the one great hole in Jude's life is a guy on hand to convince him he's not a wimp. I can hear the need inside of him, see it. Of course he's angry and hitting out, who wouldn't? But is he too angry? Is he reacting too extremely? Is there anything about his father I should have known – should know? Or about my birth father – or mother? Poor Jude, most of his background is a series of blanks. He's not sure where he really belongs. A feeling I know myself.

It's Jude's luck that the two main men in his life are so distant, one in age, the other in miles. His Grandpa's fifty-plus years away and a couple of centuries in mindset. They have Rangers and PlayStation in common. He dotes on Jude and Jude tolerates him as a lesser, male version of Maggie. As if.

The other's my brother, Fraser who, on the rare occasion he's back from his Greek island, rocks up, spoils Jude rotten, and rolls out again. They Skype pretty often, but you can't get that close with two screens and two thousand miles between you. Would a sustained period of contact with his uncle help Jude? On the pro side, Fraser is generous, supportive, and has a heart of warm mush. But his con side is he's inconsistent, unreliable and has a growing drink problem. Like our mother. One thing I do know is, he behaves better when he's around his ex-partner, who lives on the same island, Symi, most of the year. Face it, in terms of accessible men, Fraser's the best I've got right now.

Jude and I are due to fly out there in July. Right now, it's nearly a month since the exclusion, halfway into June; Jude should really be back at school next Monday. If I can negotiate another week or so away, the pair of us can take off now. Thanks to Maggie and my father, there's enough in the bank to cover the time away from work. Maybe Jude could stay there on Symi until school starts in August? If he behaves well enough for his Uncle Fraser… or Uncle Puke as he's become. I'm searching for flights on my phone when the consulting room door opens and Jude shuffles out, hands rammed deep in hoodie pockets. His eyes bore holes through me into the classy beige wallpaper, indicating I've been sussed. It'll take the patience of a tree sloth to make him come here again.

Back in Kilachlan, I ring Fraser.

'Me and the we'an's coming over Wednesday.'

'But I thought –'

'All changed. We fly this Wednesday, the twenty-second.'

'Ye what?! You could've given me a bit more warning. I mean there's –
'

'Too late, oh brother of mine. Jude's climbing the walls by his toenails. I've got to sort his school, my work, my proxy vote for the referendum, pack, muck out the croft, get the dogs to the Scrymgeours, sort Jude's haircut, and explain it all to his grandma and grandpa – so I need your input.'

'But you can't just –'

'We're on the flight from Glasgow, stopover in Rhodes and first ferry the next morning. Book us into somewhere for Wednesday night, OK? Mates' rates. And could you email the times of the ferries or whatever for Thursday morning?'

I imagine Fraser on his bar stool, frothing at the mouth because I've asked him to *do* something. Without doubt it'll be his ex who organises it all. Want stuff sorted? Give it to a busy woman. Feminist bias, my perfect flaw.

I confiscate both phone and tablet from a high-octane Jude, do not give in to the flak, then revise my two special subjects – anxiety and insomnia. Mindfulness is not up to this one. Or I'm not up to mindfulness. Ridiculous challenge I've set myself, achieving all this in six days. And healing my son in the eight weeks away. See me? Susie Orbach meets Lara Croft.

A text from Shona appears filled with sympathy and questions. I don't feel up to replying, just sit staring at the empty fireplace. Out in the midnight dusk there is a squeal from some creature. Either a bad ending or great beginning.

TWO

ANNIE – June

'Finding out where we come from helps us know where we want to go.'

Jude's with the Westies on the strand. The needle cries of gulls wheeling against a blinding white sky, salt breeze buffing his skin, the slosh of a rogue wave drenching his trainers. Accidentally on purpose. Off the lead, Jack will stick close by him but Tatty will rush barking into the water regardless of the temperature or swell. He'll dry the worst off her then slap the sodden towel against the fence on the way back up the lane. Jack trotting obediently at his side, and naughty Tatty back on the lead. She's an old lady now, should know better.

So, too, should Jude. Exclusion isn't intended as a holiday at the seaside, even if it's your home. I'm the one doing a detention, keeping an eye on him, going to work, running the house and, not least, starting the search. I return to the screen, hoping he's remembered to put the dogs' muzzles on when they leave the beach, and re-read the advice. The words lunge back at me.

'...while people are not legally required to have a Counselling Interview, many adopted people have found it helpful and useful to meet with an adoption social worker.'

I have a personal dilemma over the Counselling Interview. To be honest, more of an internal fist fight. My polar positions are these: if I don't go for counselling, I'll be Annie Mega-Ego for being a know-all. If I do go, I could well start telling the counsellor her – or his – own job.

'You're a cocky besom, Annie,' is what Granny Buchanan used to say to me, often followed by, 'You take after your –' Then she'd stop, and I'd wonder why. She knew, you see, genetically anyway, I couldn't take after anyone in the family. But before she and I could have the nature versus nurture discussion, Granny did a bunk to that great distillery in the sky.

I was eleven, younger than Jude now, when Rosemary – Mum – told me I was adopted. It was just after my not-adopted brother, Fraser, found his courage and took off to points global. Thoughtful of her, what with me adoring the very guitar strings he plucked. He said, later, he'd been on pain of his life not to tell me I was adopted. Helluva big secret for a boy to keep, especially with me being as annoying as I'm sure I was. I was angry with him for not saying, though, I thought we were closer than that. Even so, I still missed him every nanosecond. It was around then I started calling my parents Rosemary and George, like he did, neither of us to their faces, though. Later, when *The Truman Show* came out, it was like watching the story of my life; nothing Truman and I had relied on was true.

Current thinking is that telling a child about their adoption should happen much earlier than I was, pre-school being the preferred age. What could I have told Jude when he was pre-school? There was certainly nothing appropriate I could have said about his father. And I was still in education myself. Bearing all this in mind, the least I can do, now, is give him some certainty. First there's my tracing my birth family, then, if he wants, a DNA test on him to find out whether his daddy really did come from Zanzibar (ha!) or was just an Ali G impersonator from Tower Hamlets. All he knows now is that his father did a disappearing act. He accepts it because he knows he isn't the only kid without a dad.

I had a WhatsApp chat with Shona, about it. She's not adopted, definitely would have mentioned it, so she can't really know what it's like. One of her gems was: 'Knowing where you come from wouldn't change who or what you are now'. She's right in a way, it wouldn't, but it would give me the past that was taken from me. And it would mean Jude had at least *some* roots, given his father was a tacky question mark.

As for me, his mother? I'm an unfinished puzzle of some kind: my own birth parents – missing; true identity of Jude's father – missing; reason for failed relationship – missing; any kind of relationship – missing; any reason for all the dire bits of my life – missing. Would finding those pieces make me feel whole? It's inconvenient I'm not a celebrity or the BBC would swoop in and do a *Who do you think you are?* programme on me. I'd insist it was narrated by my childhood imaginary friend, Bill Paterson, the actor. I believed Mr Paterson was real, he'd been on telly so he had to be. He wouldn't have known me from a Tunnock's Wafer. For now, I imagine his voiceover to this scenario:

'We follow Annie to the Public Records Office in Glasgow where we discover that she is the secret lovechild of David Bowie and Chrissie Hynde'.

Like I'd get *that* lucky.

I'll initiate the birth parent search before Jude and I escape to Symi. With everything to get done before flying off to my brother's Greek idyll, now is a hell of a time to start agonising. I should be loading washing, making lists, unearthing suitcases, turning the place upside down for the passports, making more lists, emptying the fridge, sorting the dogs, letting relevant people know – ah, yes, first of all Rosemary and George – about the holiday *and* about the birth parent search. Only polite.

So, the search is definite, but what to do on the counselling? It's a damned if I do, damned if I don't situation. No Maggie to help me go over my doubts again.

It's late. We've had dinner, Jude's argued about bedtime, having a wash, switching off the telly, and removing socks and underpants before going to bed. I check on him now and he's well asleep, so lift the guitar and strum a few random chords. 'Dreadlock Holiday', a favourite of my mother's from before I was born, would be inappropriate, maybe 'Summer Holiday'– from before Fraser was born? He hates it but he drops it in occasionally at Angelina's Music Bar on Symi, to indulge the British tourists who enjoy a little singalong and may tip well. Bit of a musical snob, my bro. Anyhow, tonight, I find myself sinking into Simon and Garfunkel's 'I Am a Rock'– must have been thinking of Symi and the *'being an island'* line. The lyrics confirm my aloneness, depressing the hell out of me. Still, it's not a deep and dark December, it's June and soft rain is freckling the window with elf pebbles. So I stop.

Deep breath, and another – and another. Wipe face off on a tissue, blow nose disgustingly, breathe again, do piano fingers, and back to the main question. Do I need counselling before I initiate the adoption thing? Peter would listen and ask the odd, dead annoying, totally relevant question. At least two female friends would say, 'Offload on someone else for free? Absolutely!'. Don't know about Fraser. None of this is any help. So while the mood's on me, I just do it, email the Adoption Advice Service. Yes, start the search. Yes, I'll have counselling.

OK, that's that. Now I have to gut the croft, sort the dogs, dah di dah di dah. But first, I cheer myself up with Jude's favourite ditty, *'Aunty Mary had a canary up the leg of her drawers...'*

THREE

FRASER – June 2016. Symi, Dodecanese Islands, Greece

In case you hadn't noticed, this is me, Fraser, standing in the shadow of Annie while trying to work out a local trader's eccentric impression of double entry bookkeeping. Dearie me, my glass is empty. Maybe a wee shot to help with the calculations – and the thought of imminent kin.

Typically, my sister has decided what will suit her best and expected everyone to fall in line. Which we've done, as we always do. This time it's bringing forward her trip to Symi to tomorrow. Doesn't occur to her I've got work to do, it's just 'Sort it, Fraser'. Don't get me wrong, I've been looking forward to seeing her and Jude, it's just her new time frame's carried forward – 'carried forward', an accountant joke, apologies – the period of sensible behaviour required of me. Ach, well.

Luckily, Clair was on hand to talk me down after I got the call. Nothing fazes her. Make a room free early? No bother. Ferry options? She'll forward them to Annie. All I had to do was book the hotel in Rhodes town. From being my, what, significant other?…Clair's becoming uncomfortably like a mother figure. Mercifully, with no scintilla of resemblance to Rosemary. Clair is the reason I have my own business. And also why I don't launch myself at the next available woman. Gut-wrenching though it was to concede that she and I weren't for the long term, she's still my sanity, especially since she's been spending more time on Symi. Did I say nothing fazes her? Well, something did, once. That was my fault.

After an initial blip, Clair and Annie have become great friends – which has its good and its bad sides for me. I mean, obviously there's the Maggie thing that bonds them, with Clair being her niece and Annie looking after Maggie's croft and the dogs, but it's like they're more family than friends. That includes Jude. The bad side is that they have me in common, so God knows what conversations go on. I do know, though, there's that one thing about me – us – Clair hasn't shared, and bless her for that. Well, more than one, to be honest.

Now Jess, Clair's daughter, there's someone who seems to get fazed over almost everything whether she's here on Symi, back in Guildford, or across in Florida with her Godzilla grandma, who bales her out of most situations, with cash. Or Clair does, with a long talk. See, she's basically all right, Jess, but overburdened by money and astonishingly good looks. Great problems to have, no? Hardly surprisingly, she's Jude's ideal woman. She's dead cool with him, though, treats him like her wee brother, so it kind of works. He'll have grown up quite a bit since seeing her last year, so the testosterone may take a bit of reining in. Sounds as though it's already kicked off. Jess'll handle it, though. She can be canny when she chooses. She also stops me being a slob, clothing and home decor-wise.

Clair and Jess are two of the three grown-ups in my life. The third grown up is, no surprise, Annie. She's the Jiminy Cricket to my Pinocchio. Without her I'd have a whole flock of woodpeckers drilling away at my telegraph pole of a nose. Speaking of whom, I can't put it off any longer. Here goes. I'll just pour a sensible measure… and call up Skype, just to check everything's OK for tomorrow. Jude appears.

'Hi, Uncle Puke.' Uncle Puke. Long story involving Jess, for which I have yet to repay her.

'Jude, my man. You all packed?'

'Jeez, there's loads of it. You'd think we were going away for a whole year, no' a coupla weeks.'

'Is that what your mum said? A couple of weeks?' There *is* a plan, there's a relief. But Jude punctures that little balloon.

'Well, no. But that's what holidays are, aren't they? Two weeks?'

I've jumped to the conclusion I wanted, not the right one.

'Jude, is your mum there?'

'*Maaaam!!!!*'

I hear Annie sounding off in the background before she appears dripping and wrapped in a bath towel, hair a black patent skull cap. She speaks before her bum hits the chair. Confirms she has the name of the hotel, sorted which ferry and where to get tickets. Impatient with me for some reason.

'Was there anything else, Fraser?' This is hyper-Annie on speed, the dark side of the sparky sister I know and mostly love.

'Everything tickety-boo, Mighty?'

'What could possibly go wrong? And don't call me that.' I recognise when to drop it.

'Just to say we're all looking forward to seeing you and I'll be there tomorrow at Yialos to meet you.' She relaxes a bit, manages a tad of a smile.

'Yeah. We're looking forward to seeing you, too. Jude's as happy as Tatty in a jacuzzi.'

'Don't tell me the Scrymgeours have a jacuzzi?'

'Can you imagine Wally and –?'. I scream at her to stop, knowing an image of the elderly Wally and Nessie Scrymgeour, naked amidst the bubbles, will sear my imagination for weeks to come. Annie laughs.

'No worries, brother of mine, they prefer mud wrestling. Love to Clair and Jess.' And she clicks off before I do.

She's a coper, Annie. But even though she's dredged up some humour, I sense things are out of hand. She needs to be here and soon. Clair and Jess have till Thursday morning to work out a strategy. I'll handle the bags, they can handle the emotional baggage.

Did I finish my nightcap? Must have poured short. Just another drop. For luck – and getting my sums right.

FOUR

ANNIE – Mid 1990s to 2002. Glasgow, Scotland

When my big brother set off to discover the world, I wasn't totally alone. I had two schoolfriends, Carol-Anne and Shafiq. After the adoption news scrambled my brains they tried their best. Difficult for them to know what to say because they both came from large 'birth' families. They offered to help me find my real parents, as they put it. Ideas included putting an ad in the *Daily Record*, trying to get on the telly, or making a cinema commercial like the ones for the local curry house. Carol-Anne suggested making 'Orphan' posters. We photocopied a few at the local library and stuck up a dozen on lamp posts like I was a lost dog. I was afraid of annoying my parents, though so, after the initial impulse, I went round and took them all down again.

We three pals overcame a few odds, like my dad, George, was less than welcoming to Shafiq. When I complained, George told me to 'mind my wheesht' and Rosemary shook her head at me.

'But, Dad –'

'I've spoken!' said George. He'd never raised his voice to me before, so it was enough to silence me. What affection I had for him crumbled, knowing he was a racist.

Carol-Anne's parents were OK with Shafiq but it was difficult to shoe horn any more people into their house, so our wee gang ended up at the Youth Centre of a week night. Weekends we went into town, the cinema if we could afford it or just hung out at St Enoch's Centre. Shafiq didn't mind sorting through girlie clothes and accessories with Carol-Anne and me. We sort of knew he was gay and were fine with it. But at school, he was expected to hang out not just with the boys but with the Muslim boys, neither of which he wanted to do. Homophobia was a uniting force for the teuchter louts and a few fundamentalist Muslim lads who combined to beat the crap out of Shafiq. He ended up in the Royal Infirmary. Carol-Anne and I tried to talk to someone at school.

'And do you know, without doubt, who the perpetrators were?' said Mr MacDougall, Deputy Head Teacher.

'We know who's been bullying him. And it happened behind the school playing field.'

'Not on school grounds, though, and without indisputable evidence, there's very little I can do.'

'Indisputable, my arse', I thought. MacDougall was so straight he made a ruler look like a corkscrew.

Same story with the police, but they promised they'd keep an eye open for the bullies. After that, Shafiq's parents kept him in or at the mosque most of the time. We texted each other. Not the same as spending time together but it was contact. At least he knew we were with him in spirit. It was my first inkling that 'authorities' weren't necessarily there to protect people.

Another problem we had was Carol-Anne, the baby of five kids, having to go to church about twenty times a week. She loathed it. Her parents had photos of boys in suits with short pants and the two girls in knee-length sort of wedding dresses. Impressed, I told my mother that Carol-Anne was godmother to one of her cousins by the time she was ten.

George sniffed and said, 'They've branded her with the Crucifix, then.'

It couldn't be true, Carol-Anne would have told me. She swore she'd run away and become an atheist as soon as she could. Which, she did. More or less.

Navigating round racism and religious fervour meant I was at a loose end on a Sunday. I spent hours in my freezing bedroom on Fraser's second-best guitar, fingers numb, playing what he'd taught me, making up stuff of my own. My thirteen year-old experience of the world led to a lot of lyrical and musical howlers, some of it recorded on cassette tapes that I still daren't listen to. Back then, the logical progression was joining a band. Not a girlie line up. I wanted to be a rock chick, but the challenge was getting anyone to take me seriously. Shafiq encouraged me by text. Carol-Anne thought I was nuts.

I was fourteen when I met Niall through the Youth Centre at a musical evening. We were the only ones to bring guitars and, after hearing one another play, got chatting and our little duo began. Looking back, we were good beyond our years. Our first gig got booed off. It was at a working men's club. We didn't research their taste; Leonard Cohen and Alanis Morissette didn't go down too well. We learnt from it and the next, Niall's school's dance, was much better. These and other bookings started coming in. Rosemary and George would never have agreed, so everything was conducted well under the radar.

Niall and I weren't a couple but probably closer than most, creatively attuned and able to learn from one another. He was quiet and thoughtful, calmed me down a lot, and I gave him more confidence in himself. We learned about balancing our musical taste with what would earn us a bit of cash. We also discovered that bands are often at events to be ignored. Having reached such awareness, it was strange that we hadn't thought of a name for ourselves. Gruesome Twosome – or perhaps just Gruesome we thought. Until Niall's brother, Ainsley, fell about laughing and said people would think 'grew some'. While not entirely innocent of male anatomy, I didn't get it. Niall did. Eventually we settled on 'Stuck for a Name'.

Our most important gig was Ainsley's wedding at The Pollokshields

Burgh Hall. To my horror, Ainsley invited my parents. I wasn't keen because they'd realise how much time I'd spent rehearsing and playing, plus Niall's family could be pretty descriptive in their language. It would be an education for Rosemary and George.

The bride, Ruby, wanted us to include some Bob Marley and a few other reggae numbers we'd never heard of. Her grandparents were Jamaican and she had family coming from all over for the wedding. Reggae was a new discipline for us and a steep learning curve. We also played a specially composed song, 'Seeing It's You', after the ceremony, and Stuck for a Name went down like Appleton's Jamaica Rum. Shafiq and his 'date', Carol-Anne, were seated with my parents. George must have been under instructions to behave because he barely moved and certainly didn't make eye contact with anyone.

It wasn't until I joined their table that I saw the man. He must have been six foot two. Long, greying dreadlocks, almost to his waist. Old enough to be my grandpa, probably. Our eyes met and held. I excused myself and we moved towards one another. The first thing he said was – 'Stuck for a Name, that's good. So is Annie Buchanan.'

Jude, real name Judah, was over from Chicago for his favourite niece's wedding. Outside, in the Pollokshields drizzle, he wanted to know my story. And he told me about his life immersed in music. We were interrupted by Niall.

'Your Mum and Dad were wondering where you'd gone.'

He disappeared. Jude said,

'This happens only once. This.'

I knew what he meant. We were so out of kilter in time, and yet *this* was a profound connection. There was me, just fifteen. He was, perhaps, fifty plus? He didn't proposition me, nothing like. What I felt was pure – I could say 'love'. Whatever it was, I thought I'd never find its like again.

'Annie, I don't know what to tell you except I wish you a beautiful, fulfilled life. I watched you up there, so full of hope and promise, and I wanted to be part of it. But I can't. You have other people to meet, experiences to have. Just know that Jude will be wishing you well on your journey.' He moved to kiss my forehead, but I turned my lips to his and, for a moment, he allowed it to happen, then eased me back.

'Goodbye, Annie Buchanan.'

We'd formed an unforgettable relationship in twenty minutes. That September, I turned sixteen. Months after Judah flew back to America, he sent for Niall to join him, introduced him to some music contacts in Chicago and Los Angeles. I was heartbroken that he hadn't asked me. Years on, I understand why and respect him for it. Still annoys the hell out of me, though. Would I rather have been a successful musician and the subject of gossip in the American music industry, or a care worker cleaning up bodily fluids in a Scottish backwater? Hmmm. Difficult one. Later, at university, I formulated objective theories over his motives. Perhaps, even after all that time, I was trying to discredit him to ease my disappointment. One other thing I'll never forget him saying during that rainy interlude was, 'Finding out where we come from helps us know where we want to go'. It's stayed with me.

After that night, Rosemary and George, instead of applauding my musical talent, tried to curb it, fearing my education would suffer. I resisted fiercely until Niall went to America and Stuck for a Name evaporated into the Glasgow cumuli. First Fraser, then Niall; two people had left me behind. I was too depressed to catch up on neglected schoolwork and my end of term results crashed through the floor. I was grounded across the entire summer and had to have home tuition. I couldn't even take a summer job, so I had no money apart from my fiver a week allowance.

An infrequent phone call from Fraser might go thus:

Me: I'm going to die, or kill them, or run away.

Fraser: Make your mind up, hen. Do I go to your funeral, visit you in prison, or alert Interpol?

Me: It's not funny.

Fraser: I know. Why d'you think I left?

Me: Where are you, now?

Fraser: Portsmouth.

Me: You are *so* not.

Fraser: Portsmouth, Dominica. In the Caribbean.

Me: Do you know how much I hate you?

Fraser: You don't hate me, Mighty.

Me: I so do! And don't call me that!

During the creative time with Niall and then meeting Judah, I'd done a lot of growing up. And yet I was back to being my parents' possession, again. I chewed it over with Carol-Anne. Should I leave? Should I not leave? Fraser cottoned on to how serious I was and actually wrote a letter:

Dear Sister of Mine,

OK, it's dire. I get that. They're dire. Don't let them ruin your life, though. Live it despite them. And now I'm going to say something that will really piss you off. It would me. Sorry sorry sorry sorry sorry in advance. Here goes: Stay, at least up to you take your Standard exams, while you've got a roof over your head and food on your plate. If you want to bugger off after that, fair enough. They can't stop you. If you want to get your Highers later, you'll have a good start. If you want to be a rock chick, having your exams won't stop you. Just do it, Annie. Just take what you can. See you soon as. Tons of the emotional stuff, Mighty – Fraser

In the end, I took his advice and stuck it out to Standard Grades. On a wet morning, beginning of June (how unlike Glasgow…), the day after my last exam, I got the London bus from Buchanan Street Station. At the time,

I thought it was poetic, leaving not just Rosemary and George but the name Buchanan behind.

I left a note on my bed saying: ‘I’ve gone’.

FIVE

ANNIE – Blue Star Ferry, Aegean Sea, Greece

Second time we've been to Symi, Jude and me. Before that, we'd only been on a plane together the once and that was with my parents for a couple of weeks in Spain when Jude was three. He screamed all the way there and back. We were not popular. Kind of them but, thankfully, the offer didn't come again. Yesterday on the plane he went into a silent moody because I'd brought sandwiches instead of buying overpriced onboard gunk. The adolescent sulk was a pain for me, but much easier on the other passengers. He was starving by the time we got to the hotel on Rhodes and piled into the sandwiches anyway. Gave me time to zap off a few messages to tell my remaining friends where we were.

Now, in the warm breeze on the Blue Star ferry to Symi, my phone pings a message from Shona in reply to mine from last night – *'That was a sudden decision. You never mentioned you were going to Greece. Have a wonderful time – Shona x'*. I feel a teeny stab of guilt. Do I tell her only the negative stuff? Next to me on deck, Jude is in another strop because he's forgotten to charge the new Android phone his grandparents gave him for his birthday, so he doesn't have a screen to stare at.

We're just moving into the harbour. Like everyone says, it's a stunner. Almost a film or video game set – no, more a sort of 3D oil painting round the water. Not your average blue and white postcard stuff but houses in pinky-orange and rust colour and pale yellow, with light and dark borders round the tops of doors and windows and flowerpot orange roofs – Clair knows the right arty words. All down to the Italian occupation of the islands years ago, she told me. Jude's underwhelmed. Saw it all last year. Tech-bereft thirteen-year-olds and classy architecture aren't a natural mix.

That metal diarrhoea noise is the anchor dropping. The crew start throwing out ropes. And there on the harbourside is Fraser, looking like some actor in a holiday ad. Jude wakes up –

'Uncle Puke!'

– and jumps ship, ducking round the crew who are trying to hold back the holiday crowd and leaving dunderhead-moi to heft the luggage. Uncle and nephew start doing complicated, male hand-jive bonding on the dockside. I stagger about under Jude's backpack, the guitar, my shoulder bag and the wheelie suitcase until a guy offers to help. Blond, beard, and tall – I'd only recognise him again by looking up his nostrils. He speaks English with no particular accent but he looks more Scandinavian, or Dutch? For once I'm not so bloody independent and let him give me a hand. He delivers me to dry land, chatting the while; Do I know Symi? Where am I staying? Am I a professional musician? What are my musical tastes? Any other time, if I weren't looking like a luggage disposal point, I might join in the fun. But I need Fraser to stop the greeting rituals and notice I'm here so I can find a loo. He does it none too soon.

'Annie mou – kálos eeltháte stin Symi!'

'Yeah – I know I'm welcome, Puke. But I'm dying for a pee and a beer. In that order.' I turn to wave to my giant Galahad but he's already walking away. A shame. So I lead on to Nobby's Bar for essential relief.

Nobby must have been a strong personality; the place is still known as Nobby's even though he sold it and went back to Cannock a couple of years ago. Still strikes me as slightly weird, like the *Taggart* TV series keeping the name for years after Taggart died. Despite which, perched at the bar, we start sinking into Symi time. I have a beer, Fraser has a couple, and Jude, a Coke. Fraser's looking heavier than last time and, to put it kindly, his forehead's increasing, a change that Jude doesn't miss.

'You going bald, Uncle Puke?'

'You want your teeth rearranging, we'an?'

Family banter activated, we continue walking back up the harbour. Fraser points out the fire damage on the Customs House from a month ago. I'm more taken by the groups of people sitting on the dockside or trying to catch what shade there is in side streets – noticeably greater numbers than last year. Young men, families, women with tiny babies. Not tourists, refugees. They must have arrived this morning and already been processed. What sort of boats did they arrive in? Did all of them make it as far as the Symi coast, even? Will there be enough accommodation? Any accommodation? There are people moving amongst them, volunteers and aid workers by their interaction. Fraser notices my look.

'We *are* helping them. And we'll keep on helping help them. Just recharge your batteries a bit before piling in, eh?'

'I feel really bad about last year. I did nothing.'

'Annie, you helped as much as you could. You and Jude had just had the 'flu when you got here, you were knackered.'

Did I really help last year? OK, I gave to the food banks, made a few sandwiches, helped Clair sort the donated clothes. And I played with the various kids of refugees who stayed up at her place before they went on to Athens. But most of the time I just flaked out. And evenings I did some gigs with Fraser. So nothing really important. Which means now: Could Do Better.

'Fraser! Éla!' Literally, 'Come here!' It's Panos, a friend of my brother's we met last year. He's still relaxing on his boat, half-hidden in a sickly smog of vape. He remembers us, too.

'*Á*ni! Jude! Kálos eeltháte stin Symi!' Panos and his wife, Marina, were very hospitable to us last year with trips round the island on his boat, the

Giorgios, and a wonderful meal at their house above Harani, just round from Yialos harbour. The *Giorgios* is still fresh from its spring coat of blue and white. Panos insists that we climb aboard, giving me a huge smacker on the lips and a dose of his pungent moustache. He also presses a welcome round of retsina, including one for Jude. I decide to allow it this once; alcohol tasting of turps could put him off booze for life.

'How are you, Panos?'

'Ah, *Áni*, trouble, today – tomorrow, trouble. Marina make everyone detective me – I can do nothing!' He finds his wife's continued efforts to keep him alive annoying, despite his having cancer a couple of years back, meaning endless trips to Rhodes and Athens for oncology appointments and chemotherapy. Marina's spies really are everywhere, hence the vape instead of a permanent, smouldering roll-up. The salty old sea dog image is ruined by fumes of cafe crême – or, as today, mango and strawberry. His hair has grown back a luxuriant iron grey. That upsets him, too.

'Not good. Panos is old man. The ladies do not like me.' Fraser reminds him, unkindly I feel, that he never pulled the girls before his hair turned grey because Marina had had him watched from the day they met. His response is a hefty gob over the side into the green water where a school of weeny fish cluster gratefully. Jude is fascinated and adds a gob of his own.

'Enough, Jude! Thank you, Panos. We need to see Clair.'

'Yássas. See you tomorrow!' We leave him sucking mightily on his vape and expelling great nauseating clouds into the throng of newly arrived day trippers. Quaint, storybook Greek sketch, you might think, a smidge patronising, even. The other side to Panos is he's made the *Giorgios* available to the Hellenic Coastguard for refugee rescue missions. And Fraser is frequently on the crew.

Fraser and Jude between them lug our stuff all the way up the three hundred and odd Kali Strata steps to Harkin House, Clair's home in Horio. On the way, another message pings. Shona, again.

'Just googled Symi. Fabulous. You never mentioned your brother lives there. Lucky you.'

It seems unlikely I never said about Fraser living here, but obviously I didn't. Must catch up with her properly. She's been quite a support. But not now. Now I want to see Clair. And Jess.

SIX

ANNIE – June 2002. Arriving in London

An accident on the motorway meant I'd been on the road nine and a half hours when we pulled into Victoria Coach Station, but it was still daylight.

I felt pretty informed, having heard of Buckingham Palace, the Tower of London, Piccadilly Circus, Madame Tussaud's and a few other tourist haunts. Consequently, I had done no useful preparation – which meant no preparation at all. I believed all I had to do was ask someone the best place to stay for the night, after which I'd make a living out of busking; I'd brought one of George's old caps for the money. I see the same audacity supported by total ignorance in teenagers now and think, 'Oh boy, are you at the start of a bumpy road'. I should know, my arrogance and stupidity back then cost me a great deal, starting almost immediately. Hindsight was to became a weapon of self-abuse in a remarkably short space of time.

I queued at the information desk and asked where I could catch a bus into London.

'Which part?' Oxford Circus came into my head so I was directed to Victoria Bus Station, which confused me because I thought I was already there. In the short walk I must have passed several of the cheap hostels around Victoria. It is a bitter synchronicity that in my first ten minutes in London I must have missed at least half-dozen opportunities to avoid the same number of disastrous months there.

At Victoria Bus Station, I was overwhelmed by the number of stands. It took a while reading timetables until I found the 390 that went to Oxford Circus. One arrived in a couple of minutes, so I climbed on. The driver wouldn't take my Scottish five-pound note and I had to sort through my pockets for change. People started getting pissed off by the delay so I got off to go through my backpack, and the bus went without me. Welcome to England's capital city.

I found a kiosk and bought a packet of Polos to get some change. Luckily the guy didn't look twice, just took my foreign money. I got the next 390 and watched the passing street life. I was being transported, I imagined, to a wonderful future. Turns out the scenario for my next fourteen years was being scrawled unevenly on the back of a fag packet as the bus trundled along. Nice going, Annie Buchanan.

I had to sit with my backpack and guitar case on my lap because the woman next to me was pretty big. I almost had to fight her to get off when the rolling sign on the ceiling said, Oxford Circus. Jeez, the noise, the fumes, the lights, buses and black taxis, cars and people, thousands of them, everywhere. It was like a Pan Galactic street market. I stood there feeling like Granny's shubunkin when the cat dropped it on the hearth rug. No idea what to do or where to go, but I was still confident everything would work out, no problem. Putting on a cool but pally face I went up to two girls (safety in women) outside H&M having a smoke. They were a bit older than me, I reckoned.

'Hi, I've just hit town and I'm looking for a hotel -' Who did I think I was? Wyatt Earp? 'D'you know of one near here? Not too expensive.'

They sniggered and pretended not to understand my accent. So I repeated it slowly. The big one with the skin problem answered.

'No too ex-pain-suff? Ock aye the noo– I'll tell you what you what to doo.'

More snickering from the blonde with bad teeth.

'Turn left and walk all the way up to a great big white building next to a church. That's the BBC – you've heard of it, ock aye?'

'Yes.' Did I look like I'd lived in a hole all my life?

'And when you get there, turn left.' She was being dead patronising but I was in no position to bite back, so I nodded and said OK.

'And careful of the traffic crossing the roads on the way, it's very busy –' Seriously, how old did she think I was?

'– and you'll see this place called The Langham. It's all lit up to attract backpackers. Just go inside and up to the desk. Tell them I sent you.'

Suddenly, I felt stupid. Maybe I should know who she was?

'Who are you?'

She put on a big smile. 'Elizabeth Queen.' The other girl seemed to be having some kind of fit.

'Sorry, my friend's not well. Got to go. Ock aye the noo!' She linked arms with her shaking friend and they tanked into H&M – still open at seven o'clock? Maybe they had a first aid person there.

I knew I'd had the royal piss taken, but I had nothing else to go on, so off I set up Langham Place to the BBC building. It was massive. I went right up to the doors for a peep inside, but there was security, so I couldn't go in and do any celebrity spotting. Everyone coming out looked pretty ordinary, so after a few minutes, I crossed over the road to the hotel the girl had said. Looking through the glitzy windows I could tell it was posher than the BBC, even. No way was it a backpackers' hostel. In my slept-in shirt and jeans, if I put my foot on their swanky steps I'd end up back out on my arse. So there I stood on the pavement, the result of a tacky joke, lugging my backpack and guitar, and thinking this place was way too snotty for the likes of me.

The joke itself wasn't that important except that, because of it, I was in that particular location at that specific moment. A piece of my life where hindsight had no place.

An intense waft of perfume was enough to turn my head as a woman, or more an emerald green blur, passed me. She got as far as the kerb then dithered between getting into a waiting cab and looking back at the hotel. She must have felt my stare because she definitely took me in. Then I heard someone calling –

'Hey, stop!'

I was pushed to one side so hard that I staggered, imbalanced by the weight of my backpack, stumbled and ended up rolling on the paving. The man in evening dress headed for the greeny woman without stopping. She must have heard him because she turned round and scrabbled to get in the taxi. He grabbed her arm, they started arguing, she slapped him and started back to the hotel. It looked like she was crying. A bit like a normal evening round at Niall's house, apart from the dickie bow and the billion-dollar dress.

I was on my feet checking my guitar so, when she went over on her ankle as she passed me, I was able to catch her.

'Are you all right?' Why do people always ask that when things are obviously not all right?

'Yes, I –' She put her foot to the ground –

'Oh, hell! No!'

'Here –' The guy on the door swooped in to help as the James Bond clone in the suit reached us and sounded off.

'Thanks, everyone I'll take over, now.' She slapped him again. What a woman.

'No you won't! Get lost, Rupert!' Not what I would have said to him. Rupert didn't waste time arguing, he shrugged, buggered off and left in the taxi, leaving me and the hotel guy with the lady in the green dress. Between us we got her up the steps and into the hotel.

Another man and a woman in hotel uniforms rushed over and we got the invalid sat down. It wasn't till then I took a look at the place and – just – wow! All white marble and crystal chandeliers – like something out of a pantomime. With everyone helping, I started to leave, but green woman stopped me.

'No, no, don't go, I must thank you.' She tucked her hair behind her ear and started scrabbling in this wee green and gold evening bag like she was about to tip me.

'No, I don't want anything. Just glad you're – you're – I've got to go.'

'You're from Glasgow, aren't you?'

Fancy a southerner recognising my accent or was it a wild stab? Still, I gave her the benefit…

'Aye, Anniesland. Someone told me this was a hostel. Obviously thought it was funny.'

'Oh, my God, how very, very, very unkind of them. Look, please let me give you something for –'

'Absolutely not. I can pay my own way.' The hotel people were rushing about getting a stool for her foot and fetching bandages. She looked really concerned for me, though.

'What's your name?' I said it without thinking. She smiled slightly.

'Annie from Anniesland? Look, please don't be offended, Annie, but you're very young. If you get stuck or need – anything, give me a call.'

She put a card in my hand.

'I mean it Annie. Anything, anything, anything at all – give me a call.'

Anything at all. I got the message.

'OK, sure. Take care.' I'd never ring her, I thought, but I put the card in my shirt pocket. Outside, I decided to head back to Oxford Circus. Nowhere else to go.

SEVEN

ANNIE – Piccadilly Circus and Willesden, London

It was shortly after the incident at The Langham Hotel that I met Zeezoo. Well, before Zeezoo, I met Shelley, a friend of his, at Piccadilly Circus. I ended up there because once I got to Oxford Circus, I couldn't think what to do, so when I saw a bus with Piccadilly Circus on it, I headed in the same direction. At least it was another place I'd heard of. I was sitting on the steps round the statue of Eros, my spirits drooping round my Doc Martens, when Shelley sat next to me. She had spiky hair, a nose ring, and multiple studs in her ear.

'You look like you could do with company. What's your story?' She had an English accent but sounded sympathetic and was much more in my league than the woman at the hotel. So, I gave her a potted version.

'Nowhere to stay? Wanna come with me, Annie?' She was friendly and I needed a friend, and female which I thought, despite my recent experience, meant I could probably trust her. Shelley was short of cash, so I paid our tube fares. She promised she wasn't blagging, would pay it back. Honest. I didn't doubt she would because I was sixteen and ready to believe.

We changed after two stops, went on another six, then walked. I thought we must be nearly in Wales. After a while, she pushed past a piece of corrugated iron into an alley down the side of a house and went to the back door. By now, I felt slightly uneasy but didn't know what else to do. She rapped a tattoo of knocks. Someone let us in and Shelley said:

'Meet the latest. Minted.'

I didn't know what 'minted' meant but felt even more uneasy until the person who'd opened the door said, 'Hello, little pigeon.'

Shelley mimed two fingers down her throat – ''Kin 'ell bro– give it a rest!'– and pushed past. I was enveloped, guitar and all, in the arms of the second most awesome human being I'd ever met. The dreadlocks may have had something to do with it. With my vast experience of life I knew my character judgement was faultless. Looking back, I'd replace the word 'awesome' with 'sleazy, lazy, greedy, deceitful, treacherous, manipulative, abusive…' and so on. His name was –

'Zeezoo. Zeezoo from Zanzibar. And who are you little pigeon?'

'Annie from Anniesland.' Instantly, I regretted saying something so crass. But my vocabulary was limited by a determination to sound cool.

My new crush released me from the prematurely intimate embrace, took my hand and led me through to the front of the house. The smell of dope (I wasn't that naïve) was overpowering and prone bodies were strewn around the floor either on or in sleeping bags.

'Everyone, this is Annie – from Anniesland!' There was a straggly response, probably because most of them were so stoned one hand couldn't find the other to clap.

'Annie from Anniesland and Zeezoo from Zanzibar, eh?'– remarked one, less vacant than the others – 'Makes you the A to Z of Willesden in more than one way.'

I was to remember that, much later.

Several of them found the energy to laugh. Zeezoo responded by kicking a couple of the offenders playfully. He took my backpack and guitar off me and placed them in a corner.

'I'm going to put these here because they'll be safe. Know what I mean?' I nodded, having no idea what he meant.

'Then me an' you is gonna get a-quainted over a cheeseburger. That cool?' There were a few murmurs of amusement but not enough to provoke retaliation. I wondered how he was going to produce a cheeseburger amidst these conditions.

'Me an' you, Annie from Anniesland, is goin' out.'

'Out' was a McDonald's where he ordered a double cheeseburger. I asked for a chicken burger and we both went for thick shakes. When the server rang up the bill, Zeezoo turned to me and said,

'Thank you, Annie of Anniesland.'

'But –'

'Come on, my pigeon, you's not a mean girl, is it? So, I give you a bed for the night? So, how much you pay for that?'

Realising I was in a different world where I would always have to pay my way, I dug into my purse and, after standing him a second double cheeseburger to take away, followed him to a pub where I gave him the money to buy two double rum and cokes for himself and a shandy for me. He had to go to the bar because I looked about twelve; I remember being shocked at how expensive London prices were because I didn't get any change from a twenty pound note. We went back to the house after the pub called time. Despite all the warning bells, including the feeling that he was doing a bad impression of gangsta speak, I was smitten with Zeezoo from Zanzibar, his caramel skin and thin face, his deep brown eyes, mass of dreadlocks and beautiful lips. OK, for 'smitten' read 'in lust'. Was he a young substitute for Judah? In retrospect, transparently so.

By the time we got back, people had split into different rooms. The cannabis haze was laced with wood smoke coming from the fireplace. The top layer of body odour was soon confirmed when I learned there was no running water in the house. They were using the back garden as a toilet. The neighbours must have loved it, just as much as they adored living next to a house full of drug addicts, because that's what Zeezoo and the others were. I had a notion from TV documentaries about shooting up with needles. I wasn't prepared for the ceremonies around smoking crack. They heated and inhaled in so many ways. Some had bongs, glass tubes with a bulbous end, if they were flush. Over time I was to see people inhaling from beer cans, tin foil and even lightbulbs with the necks smashed off.

I noticed immediately that my backpack and guitar had been moved. Zeezoo scouted round the house and, after some raised voices, came back with them. Someone had opened the backpack. I searched through it and found two T-shirts, a pair of sandals and a sweater missing.

'Dontchoo worry, Annie from Anniesland. Won't let no one rob you. Zeezoo take care of you.'

I'd already been to the loo in the pub; in those pre-baby days, I had a strong bladder and knew I'd be all right for the night. I improvised a self-conscious wash with some baby wipes, Zeezoo watching all the time.

'You's clean, that's nice.' He took a used baby wipe, dabbed his armpits under his shirt and growled,

'Now come to Zeezoo.'

EIGHT

ANNIE – June 2016, Symi

Harkin House, high above Pedi Bay. Clair sweeps us into a group hug as we arrive. Jude signals reluctance over the tradition. It's a dilemma for him because he gets to kiss Jess but it also means kissing Uncle Puke. Tradition wins because he loves the whole alternative, bohemian atmosphere of the Harkins over that of buttoned-up Kilachlan, less tolerable now Maggie's gone.

There are three bedrooms. Jude and I are sharing one, Clair and Jess another and, tonight, there are two teenage girls from Iraq in the third. Fraser has space for a guest, but one who isn't too fussy about privacy, and I'm not that person. Jude's up for it, though. I tell him 'maybe', but he has to behave big-time for at least five days before he gets permission.

He is desperate to swim so, before doing anything else, we trek down to Pedi and flop into the water. We haven't even unpacked properly and just have time to shower off the salt back at the house when Clair summons us for an evening snifter. I drag on clothes pulled randomly from the case. It's G&T for us three women, shandy for Jude. Dinner is a gradual process of preparation, nibbling, and finally eating on the terrace where, come eight-ish, Fraser rolls up with work excuses which only Jude believes. The Iraqi girls are too shy to join us, choosing to eat in their room. At the table, Jude moans ungratefully about sharing accommodation with his mother. I am not having this.

My meaningful looks are wasted on Fraser, but all Clair has to do is give that sideways smile and he clicks.

'Oh, aye. See, Jude, if you want to stay with me – you have to earn your spurs first, pal.'

'Like, could you say that in English, Uncle Puke?'

'I agree with your mum. You have to stay cool for five days, first.' Major, negative reaction from picked-upon nephew/son who pushes away the delicious, flaky baklava (his favourite) and ice cream, slumps back, and flexes his legs (still in jeans despite the heat) under the dining table.

Fraser nudges him, winks, and motions to the door. There must be a bribe implicit in this because, after a face-saving pause, the put-upon youth takes his pudding to bed. He even manages a half-wave and what sounds like 'G'night'. Uncle Puke follows to supervise; the disappearing act will probably cost him around ten euros. Now to enjoy the remainder of a long, slow Symi evening.

The sky is deep and soft and warm, the air wraps itself around you and the jasmine makes you want to breathe in until you float away. Kids' laughter follows their pounding feet in the alley outside, the sounds disappearing into the quilt of heat as quickly as they emerged. Children out so late, alone and safe. I can't help but visualise others who are not so lucky, out on the sea. For them, the waves lap around a tiny dinghy, the salt water is deep and dark and cold, and if you float away it's because you have no more need of breath.

So much to love about the island. So much to make you sad. I try to give myself to the comforting sensations, but part of me resists anything approaching ease. The emptiness inside has come with me to Symi; it's made more profound by the tragedy of the refugees, but not caused by it. Nor is it the absence of birth parents because I am secure and loved by the people here and by other friends. And it isn't losing Maggie; I understand that aching loss in my life, in Jude's, in everyone's. Perhaps my feeling is the cumulative effect of it all? I can't tell. Being in this moment should make me very happy. But I can't be, because that emotional black hole destroys anything positive.

We've been talking about Maggie; sharing the loss of her makes it more bearable. Jess recalled Maggie making fun of her and Clair trying to milk Esmeralda the goat. Laughter all round followed by a moment of bittersweet silence.

'Hey, Annie.' Clair drapes her arms around my neck from behind, chin on my shoulder. 'You look done in, my lovely. There's loads of girlie stuff in the shower room and I've left a nightie on your bed. Leave the suitcase and sort it out in the morning, huh?'

I'm tempted. But I say what my brother would say, were he present…

'Now we've put the wee shite to bed, d'you think we could let his mammy sit up with the big people?'

Clair guffaws, battering my ear drum, 'You got it.'

Fraser swings in with thumbs up. Out comes the twelve year-old Metaxa – he won't sit in the same room with anything younger – and the evening turns liquid. Despite the long day and how tired I am, I'm wide awake, happy to keep on drinking and wise enough to match the Metaxa with multiples of iced water. Jess joins me on both counts. I wonder why she's spending all this time on Symi away from building her career. She finally managed to graduate in interior design from Bristol (from all the drama you'd've thought it was a theatre degree), so why isn't she capitalising on it? The answer's simple.

'I'm going to Granny's in August. There's loads of really rich people in Florida who don't know they need my individualistic approach to interiors – *yet*.'

'Have you got a work permit?' Me, ever the practical one.

'Granny's lawyer's on to that. Of course it would've helped if Mum had applied for dual citizenship when she could have.'

Clair makes a sad emoji face. 'I know, JJ, and I'm a rotten mother for making you come on holiday to Symi for – how many months?' They're a double act, these two. Sometimes you have to duck the barbed comments to avoid laceration.

Fraser splashes out another round of Metaxa.

'Now, now, kyries mou, this is a time of celebration.' 'Kyries mou'– 'my ladies'. I can't resist.

'Not at all paternalistic, oh Tyrannosaurus frater of mine?' He ignores this and raises a glass to me.

'Annie – kálos eeltháte sto i thési tou Clair.' Which welcomes me to Clair's I think, compounding his offence. As if she can't speak for herself. Anyway we all clink and 'yamáss'.

There's a slow silence which I sense I'm expected to fill. I'm not ready to dissect my son over the dining table. There is, however, another case to discuss.

'You can ask me. About the dogs, I mean.' I sense Clair has Fraser and Jess on a leash, because she asks, 'Have you found out who it was?'

'The police are too pressed and Wally didn't hear anything round the village. It's so lucky Jack and Tatty didn't get to the bait, but sad that the fox did. Normally they put down a poisoned carcass to kill birds of prey or other predators that go for the game birds. But it was butchered meat Wally found in the back field. He said it was probably rat poison. Who'd want to hurt the dogs, though?'

Unless it was to get at Jude, but I let that slide for now. Whoever it was meant business, but I don't want to go into details tonight.

Fraser frowns. 'There aren't any shoots near Kilachlan.' Said so low, he's thinking it rather than voicing it.

Jess is tearful. 'Shooting birds is cruel, too. Poor fox, though, how sad.'

It was. I shed a tear for it at the time. I try to lighten matters. 'Anyhow, Jack and Tatty are muzzled if they're off the lead, now. Not much fun for them.'

Clair sighs. 'Better than the alternative. But what a horrible feeling for you, love.'

'Well, events with Jude overtook things so… Wally and I are on the lookout and nothing's happened since – it was probably a mistake.'

Like the game meat thrown at my door eight years ago was a mistake? I'm trying to convince myself of that. Jude's best friends, Ben and Liam, taunting his ethnicity is evidence of racism; there's maybe a few people who'd like to see us go. But there's more good than bad feeling in Kilachlan and, on the whole, it's a healthier environment than Easterhouse. I've had enough of the conversation, though.

'I'm sort of trying to let it go. Could we move on?'

Everyone talks at once and we land on the latest series of residential art courses that are keeping Clair busy in the summer and free to paint in the off-season months. She has an agreement with a couple of hotels for her students. This is alongside her refugee work. I've not picked up a paintbrush since primary school and Jude's the same. Who knows, though? Clair might enthuse him. Like Fraser might inspire him to be an accountant – not. Jude's talent for maths is no better than his artwork.

The current artists are out at a Greek dance night at the Acropolis Hotel and won't be back at their own much before two, Clair says, if Theo the manager has anything to do with it. Everyone laughs. As usual, I don't know what the joke is.

She and Fraser, both, are heavily involved in refugee aid. He's been crewing rescues on the *Giorgios* but also looking at their options with money, changing it, moving it, retrieving it; given the nature of their situation, with varying success. And Clair puts up people as they're passing through, helps on food and clothing down in Yialos. Plus, if I know her, shares boundless sympathy and plenty of hugs. She and Fraser seem so relaxed with each other, you'd never know they'd ended the affair to rival Rhett and Scarlett. I don't know why they finished, just assume Fraser did something stupid. I certainly asked them both – got rejected like a flasher at a funeral.

Clair said, 'To everything there is a season,'– and refused to give me anything more.

Fraser was more direct: 'That's for me and Clair to know and you to mind your own, oh sister of mine.'

He's still in love with her, just have to watch his eyes follow her. But he's not going to get her back by drinking – or looking – the way he does. Besides, she's moved on, emotionally at least. Still, I'm only a psychologist, what do I know?

He's just as direct with me now. 'So what's the story with the bairn? Did he really break another kid's hooter?'

I'm glad we're finally there, I suppose. ''Fraid so.'

'Respect!'

Clair is sharp.

'It's nothing to laugh about Fraser. Annie's been having –'

'A desperate time, I know, I know. Sorry, hen.'

Jess touches my hand like a counsellor, voice soft. 'Jude's dealing with some heavy stuff, I mean with – you know –' She means Maggie. 'And going to big school. Then his balls about to drop.'

The rest of us erupt. Jess is bewildered.

'What? What?!'

I cut across the snorts of laughter. 'You're dead right, JJ. It's all three of them colliding. Or four, depending how you're counting.'

Another burst, including Jess this time.

I wait for it to subside. 'That's why we came here early. He's excluded anyway so I thought an extended stay with a male he looks up to– Gawd knows why –'

Fraser pings an olive off my forehead.

'– as the role model has just demonstrated – might take the pressure off. Only thing is, will he want to go back?'

Fraser's turn. 'And if he didn't, would that be such a bad thing? Living over here? It's an island, what can happen? Symi's a much more accepting place with so many overseas nationals. And there'd be no problem moving to Greece. I mean it's not as though we're going to crash out of Europe, even with this farce of a referendum today.'

It's a lot to take on board, but he has a point, even with the contrasting plight of the refugees. Certainly worth thinking about.

NINE

ANNIE – London

That first night in Willesden, Zeezoo and I settled onto my sleeping bag and got down to some serious snogging and heavy petting. But I stopped at actual intercourse. Not because it was my first time; despite being grounded, I'd managed to leave my virginity at a party in Drumchapel to celebrate being sixteen. It was just that, despite my horniness, it was all going a bit too fast. He was petulant.

'I look after you and you don't love me?'

'It's not that –' He rolled away from me, pulled up his cotton harem pants, plucked his burning roach from a saucer, stalked out – and didn't come back. I tried to sleep with my head on my backpack. From other parts of the house I heard noises that could only mean other people shagging. I wondered if Zeezoo was one of them and felt desperate. The availability of sexual partners was probably the reason he didn't force me. Too much effort. That long, sleepless night was like nothing I'd ever experienced. Nerve-wracking at the time. Pathetic, in retrospect. I toyed with the idea of going back to Glasgow and rejected it. I couldn't let them think they were right, not after only one night. Maybe I should send them a postcard to let them know I was OK?

I must have dozed off because I was aware of troubled waking dreams. I was still in yesterday's clothes, so I changed my shirt and knickers as rapidly as possible, listening out all the time for footsteps. As I rolled my shirt up, a business card fell out. Oh yes, that woman outside the hotel last night. I'd forgotten her; it seemed like a zillion years ago. It wasn't likely that I'd see her again, but I stuffed the card in my back pocket and forgot about her again. I hadn't even read it.

By then, I really needed a pee. Remembering how my stuff had disappeared last night, I took my backpack and guitar and hunted for a loo. When I found it, I shut the door again quickly. It had been used, but no longer functioned and smelt like the slaughterhouse from hell. Which is how I learned about the back garden. Back inside, I tried to clean up on baby wipes again. Then I sat and waited. No one was around. I took my guitar out and started strumming.

Zeezoo bounced in around eleven thirty and the sun came out again.

'Jambo, Annie from Anniesland.'

'Morning, Zeezoo.'

'No, jambo. Swahili for 'hello, good morning', innit. My muvva tongue.'

'Sorry. Jambo.'

''Habari' when we know each other better.'

A small Calor gas stove was the cooking facility for the food they'd managed to filch from local supermarkets along with a surprising collection of booze, which resulted in weird and wonderful, sometimes disgusting, cocktails, mixed in a jam jar and a Pyrex bowl, the only drinking vessels. There was no crockery or cutlery.

'Saves on the washing up, innit.' Breakfast was bread with butter smeared on by finger. How many dirty digits had dipped into the yellow mess in the carton was anyone's guess. Ignoring the high risk of disease, I helped myself but cleaned my fingers afterwards, again with baby wipes. But then everyone wanted some wipes, grabbing three or four sheets at a time until the pack was empty.

Later, Shelley took me out to show me how to shoplift while Zeezoo 'watched over' my guitar and backpack. The trick about nicking, Shelley said, was to look unobtrusive, wear your coat open ready to stuff things under your sweatshirt and spend longer looking at whatever it is that's *next to* what you want to lift. Fear made me a bit giggly for which I got a telling off outside a Tesco Express after the first fruitless foray of the morning. I didn't manage anything that day, but I put some of Shelley's 'wins' in my pockets: a cheapy watch, three packets of sliced ham, a disposable cigarette lighter – and some baby wipes to replace mine. She had a packet of mints, a pair of knee socks, a pack of sausages and some make-up. In supermarkets, you always had to take a basket and buy something. So I paid for two cartons of milk and a white sliced loaf. My cash was disappearing fast.

That night, Zeezoo and I progressed to greeting one another with the more familiar 'habari' by way of sex. He was uninhibited about making a noise or about anyone else being in the room while we were doing it. In the morning I bore the odd grin and snigger from the others until Zeezoo made it clear that their teasing displeased him. I was Zeezoo's woman and, poor wee eejit, I was that proud. And that worried. He wouldn't wear a condom. Against his religion, he said. So I kept a bottle of mineral water hidden outside and douched myself in the garden after sex. Not so romantic in the rain. As if it was any use, anyway. I may as well have stood barefoot on cold lino for half an hour.

Zeezoo was keen for me to go out busking; he'd be my PR man, he said. The first place we tried was Willesden Green tube. Early morning to catch the commuters would have been good, but he said he wasn't a morning person, so we arrived there near lunchtime. I was pleased and proud to play for Zeezoo and delighted when people started throwing coins in George's cap, but he got bored quickly, grabbed the takings, and wandered off. It wasn't long before the community police moved me on. I found Zeezoo in a pub a few streets away, the money gone. We set up at two other points with the similar results. Next day we tried Neasden but Zeezoo said he had business elsewhere so I carried on alone. I did well but always got moved on. I think the police were kinder to me because I was young and had a Scottish accent. Anyhow, I made twenty-three pounds seventy-two pence, enough to buy a few girlie necessities, food, and the odd drink at the pub. Fraser didn't know back in Glasgow that, by teaching me guitar, he was putting a living in my hands – literally.

Over the next few weeks, the squalor became familiar and I began to think of the house as home. There was constant coming and going, you never knew who or how many 'housemates' would be there from one night to the next. Zeezoo told his stories, one of growing up in Zanzibar, of his large family and their wonderful life by the ocean. I asked him why, if it was so wonderful, he'd want to come to a cold, rainy place like Britain?

'It's hot, Africa, sometimes too hot,'

And he'd laugh.

'Besides, I wanted to meet you, Annie from Anniesland.' His most consistent tale was that he'd got a place at a London college to take Business Studies and because of that he got a visa. It cost him a lot of money. But when he got to London, there was no one at the address and nowhere for him to stay. Then he got robbed, so he couldn't go home. But why hadn't he reported it to the police?

'Immigration.' His answer to every ill.

One morning I woke up to find Zeezoo bending over me, concern furrowing his face.

'There's bin a problem, little pigeon. I had to lend your guitar to a mate for some smack.'

My face must have registered my anger and dismay. 'But that's Fraser's –'

He was instantly suspicious. 'Who? You got another man?'

'No. Fraser's my brother. It's his guitar.'

'Don't worry, be happy, Annie from Anniesland. Trust Zeezoo. I'll get Freezer's guitar back. Come here.'

'Why can't you ask your friend to give it back, now?'

'That's a problem for me, 'cos I's too shy. But you can get it, Annie from Anniesland.'

'How?'

The 'how' involved Zeezoo introducing me to his mate. We walked to Gladstone Park and met him by the lake. He didn't have my guitar. Zeezoo made me wait a little way away while they talked then the mate looked at me and nodded to Zeezoo. The two guys moved off and I had to follow. We left the park and crossed a main road. I slipped my hand into Zeezoo's and he held it loosely, not giving me the reassurance I needed, as distant then as he is now, fourteen years – more like light years – away.

I never thought of ringing the number on the green lady's business card. Life had moved on so much, the whole incident outside The Langham wasn't even a vague memory.

TEN

FRASER – Symi

The EU referendum result's in. Clair and I are gutted; so's everyone else. 51.9% to leave against 48.1% to remain with 62% of Scots wanting to stay in. No great surprise there. And no guesses as to how far their decision will be respected. Where that leaves us ex-pats living on Symi, no one knows. Apparently there have been a few racist attacks in the UK already. And David Cameron has resigned. Knocked on the front door and ran away when the bogey man opened it.

I've hidden in my shoebox of an office in Yialos so I can turn the air blue until work time. As I step onto the open landing, the odour of souvlaki, drains, and exhaust fumes punch past and take up residence in Buchanan Accounting HQ, which is why I never entertain my clients there. One or two of them take the pain out of gainful employment, especially my next appointment, Tsampikos, who gives me the run of the menu at Restaurant Meandros. Plus he takes bookkeeping seriously, a practice usually incompatible with the Greek blood or psyche. When the taxman hits an island there's usually a sudden blizzard of receipts that bewilders customers for about a week until he goes back to Head Office. Then everything drifts back into the comfortable financial mist. One reason I love Greece.

I never took my final accountancy exams but I remember enough to make myself useful, so that's how I keep body and soul together, the income from that and perquisites from grateful clients, like today's meal (hence my few extra kilos). Plus a little guitar twanging. The Rockabilly Bookkeeper, me. I'm playing at Angelina's Music Bar tonight. Might coax Annie into joining me.

The sun slaps my head as I hit the harbour. My favourite client is sipping wine under an umbrella, following the lunchtime rush – 'midday bulge' would describe it better. God, I hate young Greeks. Most of them. Tsampikos is a couple of years younger than me, tall, lean, tanned, fluorescent-white smile, and eyes that can direct many a woman straight to bed. Except Jess, who has her pick of the Aegean.

'Fraizhe, yássou. A glass to take the edge off the hours ahead?' 'Fraizhe' as in 'beige'. He's the only person I've ever allowed to call me that. He also speaks perfect, idiomatic English. And he's so cool I don't even want to batter him.

'Thanks, Piko, but I want to keep a clear head. Maybe later?'

'Later, then. The books are in the wine cellar.' Truth to tell, my head's still a little thick this morning after polishing off the Metaxa last night. Woke up at my place this morning with the bottle by the bed.

At least it'll be cool in the cellar. Piko hasn't mentioned the Leave vote and nor have I. The Greeks probably applaud the UK; austerity has bitten hard here and Europe's failure to help with refugees has compounded their dislike of the EU. So I carry my gloom down into the depths below the bar where I know there'll be a bottle of chilled Sauvignon Blanc set by, despite my show of professionalism. My dejection can burrow into a hair of the dog.

An hour or so later, task completed, I take what's left of the bottle upstairs to the sunshine. Tsampikos has left for his apartment and a couple of staff keep the place ticking over until the evening, so it's OK to sit here and finish my wine. The day has certainly taken on a more relaxed feel. The referendum must have been wrong. There'll be a recount.

I'm distracted by seeing the remarkably tall guy who helped Annie at the ferry. Couldn't miss him, everyone else barely reaches his shoulder. I wave as he walks past.

'Hi there! Thanks for giving Annie a hand yesterday. You enjoying Symi?' He turns back.

'Oh, hi. Yes, it's a beautiful island.'

'You on holiday?'

'No. I'm with an NGO working with refugees. Just here for a few meetings. On to Leros in a day or so.'

I stand to join him. 'I'm Fraser, by the way.'

We shake hands.

'Alexis.'

'Been to Symi before?'

'Oh, yes. I know quite a few of the Dodecanese islands. You live here, Fraser?'

'Aye, near enough thirteen years. Seen some change. The crisis has really hit the eastern Aegean. How long have you been involved?'

'With the NGO, nearly five years, soon after the Syrian war started. With the islands, all my life. Look, I'd like to stay and chat, but I –'

'No, you've got your plate full, on you go. By the way, if you're at a loose end, Annie and I are playing up at Angelina's Music Bar in Horio tonight. Why don't you drop by?'

'Sure, if I can. Good to meet you, Fraser.'

'You, too. Maybe see you later.'

Is this me pimping for my sister? I'd know if there was someone in her life, Jude would have told me. She's been out with Donald Mudie, son of Archie from the big house in Kilachlan, a couple of times. He's part-time Scot and big-time London banker. But they're not an item, praise be. Not only is he a knob, he's a married knob. Annie's only interest will be collecting evidence against the arrogant rich. Alexis, though, he seems like a guy with principles, so I hope he makes it to Angelina's tonight. You can tell whether people are interested; seeing the two of them chatting yesterday, it certainly looked like they were. Shame he's off to Leros. But there are ferries. All I have to do now is get Annie and guitar to Angelina's.

She, Jude, and Jess are out today with Phanes – short for Aristophanes, no less – going round the island in his new boat, the *Xenia*. He's a wee waterfront rat with three boats the size of smart cars and aiming on becoming a shipping magnate. Power to him, though, he only had the one eight years ago when I first met Clair and Jess on Symi.

I heave up the Kali Strata to Horio. My apartment is about a hundred metres on from Clair's place, but I call in just in case she's back from teaching. She is. I open a bottle and sit at the table with her. She's looking like she's lost the will to drink. I wonder why for a moment, then remember the 'R' word. She manages to put glass to lip; we drink without talking. Most of her students are British and every one a Grecophile. Hence, they appreciate the ease of travelling in Europe. They were all as pissed off as her today and wanted to finish early to go and get drunk.

Annie, Jude, and Jess arrive around five thirty. Out on the boat all day they've missed the news, which must have taken some doing. When we break it to them they explode with disbelief. Jude has no idea what the fuss is about but he tests out a few 'stupid fucking bastards', under the cloak of their fury, and Annie lets him away with it. She is particularly incensed by what may happen to Scotland –

'We all know it'll be dragged down with the – the anencephalic xenophobes who fantasise about days of the bloody British Empire.'

Way wi' words, my wee sister.

ELEVEN

ANNIE – London

The mate who could get back my guitar, the one that Zeezoo sold for smack, had a place in a small block of flats. Zeezoo and I followed him up to an apartment with bare floors and a few bits of scratty furniture. Anything was an improvement on the squat so I asked if I could use the loo. When I found it I saw, to my disgust, it was barely better than the one at the squat, probably hadn't been cleaned since the last tenant. I returned to find Zeezoo gone and the mate stubbing out a joint.

'Annie, is it?'

'Where's Zeezoo?'

'Who? Ah –'And he laughed. 'Number twenty-six, eh? Like football, do you?'

'No. Where's my guitar?'

'Wooh – impatient. All right, I'll show you where your guitar is. C'mon.'

I followed him out of the room. He opened the bedroom door.

'It's in here.'

And, stupid lamb to the slaughter, in I went. As I did, I felt a huge thud in my back and fell face down onto the bed. He fell on top of me, pinning down my arms.

'Let's do this nicely, then you can have your guitar back.'

I couldn't breathe and yet somehow, I could smell the dank, dirty bed linen. As I started struggling he swore and turned me over. I screamed at him to stop, called for Zeezoo. Then his head moved towards me – must have been very fast – but it seemed like slow motion because I had time to think – 'You're not supposed to head butt a woman'.

I must have been out for a few seconds. If only I'd stayed unconscious for the whole episode. When he'd finished he left the room saying –

'Thanks, love. You know where the bathroom is.'

I found my pants and jeans, aware that my face was wet. It was blood from my nose and a cut across one eyebrow.

Shelley found me. I was sitting on the kerb near the dealer's flat, she told me later, holding a filthy towel against my face. I've no memory of her helping me back to the house. But I remember when we arrived Zeezoo was relating something to those crackheads who could concentrate. And Shelley yelled –

'You bastard, you sodding bastard!'– and then she punched him in the face.

I woke up in a bed and couldn't think where I was.

'Annie...Annie? Wake up, Annie.' A guy was leaning over me. Not Zeezoo. I didn't know what was happening.

'Annie, you're in hospital. I'm Michael, I'm a nurse.' He took my pulse and blood pressure, wrote them down and put a thermometer in my ear. He showed me a little card.

'We found this in your jeans pocket. Are these people your parents? Anyone you know well? Would you like us to contact them?'

I didn't know what he was talking about, so I told him 'no'.

A woman came and said she was from 'Rape – something' and asked me if there was anything I wanted to talk about. What like, I thought, politics? Religion? I shook my head, but she went on.

'I mean anything that may have happened to you?'

I still didn't know what she meant, must have blanked everything.

'Annie, we think that you may have been assaulted sexually as well as physically. Were you?'

All I could think of was Zeezoo. Him taking me to that place. And if I reported the man, Zeezoo might get into trouble. I had a question, though.

'Where's my guitar?'

I vaguely remember some fairly intimate examinations and having at least one injection and some pills, which I must have given permission for. When I was discharged – how much later?– I was wearing my old clothes and paper knickers from the hospital. A nurse passed me an address on a piece of toilet paper.

'Someone left this for you.' It was an address in Lisson Grove – at the bottom, it said 'Got thrown out. Come here – Shelley'.

The nurse handed me the card. 'And don't forget this.' I could make out the name 'Packham' on it. Printed in green. Packham? It meant nothing. I shoved it back in my jeans pocket. How long had it been there? Showed how often they'd been washed. Suddenly, the picture rose. Business card, green – the woman in green outside the hotel. Why hadn't I thought of her before? Walking through the hospital, I wondered about ringing her, but money for a phone was a problem. Perhaps I could reverse the charges? Yeah, right, and she'd accept a call from someone she'd probably forgotten. Or what if her husband answered? I abandoned the idea.

I queued at the reception desk for directions to Lisson Grove. Battered and completely alone in the world, I headed off with no money and no belongings except my dirty knickers and some paracetamol in a hospital plastic bag, a piece of toilet paper and an unusable business card in my jeans pocket. Still, at least I had my independence.

When I made it to Lisson Grove, I could tell by Shelley's face that I looked a mess.

'That wasn't on, what happened to you, Annie. We'll find him tomorrow.' I wasn't sure who she meant, Zeezoo or the man who'd… I couldn't even think it, let alone put it into words. We smoked a little dope and I took a couple of paracetamol. There was some cold pizza. Who knew how old it was? But I was hungry. I fell asleep before I could finish one slice.

Zeezoo was staying in Stoke Newington, I had no idea where that was. Next morning, Shelley said, she'd take me there. But it was well after two o'clock before I felt able to leave. We had to walk all the way. My progress was little more than a shuffle. Still in shock and pain, I kept feeling I was going to pass out and had to sit down. Shelley sat with me, told me her story, about coming down from Rotherham to escape a gang of rapists, older men.

'They stank.' And later.

'I know how you feel, Annie. Dirty. Disgusting, in't it?'

To make matters worse, my period started. I filched a wad of loo paper from the Ladies in a pub and got shouted at as I left for not being a customer. We could only have gone about three miles and Stoke Newington was a further three, but I couldn't walk any longer so we sat together in a shop doorway through the darkest hours. When we set off again, Shelley lifted some tampons from a Costcutter for me and a couple of sandwiches from the bins at the back.

It was mid-morning when we arrived. Zeezoo was still asleep. Shelley took charge.

'Look, Zeezoo– it's Annie. Isn't that nice? We need to look after Annie for a bit, don't we?' She spoke like a mother scolding a small child.

'Annie! Annie from Anniesland! My little pigeon. I bin so worried. Come to Zeezoo.'

One of his eye sockets was swollen and purple, probably the result of Shelley's handiwork. As he held out his arms, I was slow to respond, but he was all I had – apart from the clothes I was wearing. My backpack and everything in it had gone, Fraser's guitar too.

TWELVE

ANNIE – London

Life fell into a sort of pattern after that. Moving squats because we got news we were to be evicted or because Zeezoo took some whim. Sometimes, we slept rough in a park, or a doorway if it was raining. We lived on food filched from supermarkets and from hand-outs. There were no 'pay it forward' cafés then that we knew of. And there were drugs. I smoked dope when I could but refused stronger stuff. I'd seen what it did to you, sores, grey skin, sunken eyes, rotting teeth. My vanity protected me.

I decided to keep the hotel woman's business card safe, just in case. I put it between two pieces of cardboard, wrapped in plastic with some change for the phone, and tucked into my bra. If things got really bad, I had a safety net. God knows what my measure of 'really bad' was.

On my seventeenth birthday, we queued for food at the American Church. They gave me a packet of baby wipes; it was like the best birthday present I'd ever had. I had a 'wipe-bath' straight away in their loo.

I saw a lot of Shelley, she kept an eye out for me, especially with Zeezoo, who took criticism from her but no one else. She took me to the STI Clinic. I had a minor infection that I must have picked up from Zeezoo since being in hospital. It cleared up with antibiotics, a luckier outcome than I deserved. They gave me some condoms and femidoms and a tube of spermicide. After an amusing half-hour in a McDonald's toilet trying to work out the femidoms Shelley and I decided they were far too weird to use.

'Like having a jellyfish up your fan.' But she gave me some big sisterly advice. 'Blokes like Zeezoo think it makes them less masculine to wear a condom. You have to make sure he does and put it on him yourself. Make it a game. And don't expect him to be faithful.'

Evidence, I realise now, that Shelley had first-hand knowledge of Zeezoo – or whoever he was when they were an item.

I became more assertive with him. Clearly the wrong approach, or the right one considering that he started going missing. At first, it was two or three days at a time and he'd return with some gift, clothing, cheap jewellery, new or second-hand, nicked or traded for drugs. By this point I was more resilient and assumed he loved me because he always came back. Until he didn't. Shelley disappeared, too. I doubted they were together. Someone said she'd gone back up North. This made me sad because I'd thought of her as my friend, almost a protector. In truth, I missed her more than I did Zeezoo.

By November, the nights were long and unbelievably cold. I was in a Kilburn squat, but felt completely alone. That was when I reached my lowest. I actually had sex for money. Shelley had mentioned once that, if I was really stuck for cash, long distance lorry drivers were sometimes willing johns. It happened once, on an industrial park. I made him wear a condom, easy after my struggles with Zeezoo. A maggot in a corpse had more self respect than I did at that point. Why didn't I go back to Scotland, then? Because I wasn't going back defeated. I felt the lumpy plastic in my bra and made a decision.

The first time I rang, Lord Snooty came to the phone. I banged the receiver down. Stupid to ring in the evening when he was likely to be in. It didn't occur to me that she could be at work during the day so, when I rang one weekday morning, I was disappointed to get the answerphone. Did I think she'd been sitting next to the phone waiting for the call since last June? The number I'd rung both times had a London code, but there was a mobile number. Would it be hers or his? The card was crumpled and difficult to read. I was running out of change, but I gambled – tried three different numbers before it connected and a woman's voice answered. I gabbled with relief.

'Hello, my name's Annie. I don't know if you remember me? You hurt your ankle outside the Langham Hotel – last June.' There was a long pause – oh no, she's forgotten me – it's not her – then –

'Yes, yes, yes – Annie! How are you? Oh, dear, no– if you're ringing there must be a problem. Where are you?'

'I'm in London, Kilburn, but – it's just – I just –'

'Annie, what's your number?'

'I'm in a phone box.'

'Give me your number and I'll call you back.'

So I did – and she did. I offloaded my troubles like one of Carol-Anne's Catholic confessions. She was shocked, oozed sympathy, said she wasn't in London but would be, shortly, and promised to ring me next day at the same time. That morning, I stood inside the box with the phone to my ear and my finger holding down the cradle, pretending to talk to keep other callers out. Thankfully, she rang on time. She'd done some research on my behalf, gave me the name of a women's hostel in central London and said to tell them I was nineteen – otherwise I'd come under Social Services as a 'looked after' child. She would get in touch with me through them. OK, so I'd be nineteen. I went straight there. On the way, I realised I hadn't even called her by name – the lettering was distorted, but I could make out…was it Shona?

The hostel couldn't accommodate me immediately. The manager, Viviane, explained there were no rooms available, that I should be referred by a homeless organisation or prison or because of mental health issues.

And I had to have been homeless for six months. I told her about the squats, sleeping rough, and the rape. I wasn't sure which hospital they'd taken me to, but she worked out that it must have been the Central Middlesex. She put my name on the waiting list, let me have a shower, offered to wash my clothes and give me some clean ones. Light from the dull day outside caught the little gold cross swinging at Viviane's throat; I thought of George's remark about Carol-Anne's family branding her with the Crucifix. I had to admit, though, she was dead kind.

That afternoon, I trekked to the Central Middlesex in my charity clothes and explained. They found my file and referred me to the Rape Crisis Centre who counselled me, recorded my story and promised to contact Viviane. I left messages for Zeezoo everywhere I could think of. Back at the women's hostel, I collected my clean clothes. They'd had a phone call about me from a friend, a woman. It had to be the Langham Hotel woman. She'd be in touch, Viviane said.

They were still full but she gave me emergency funds to stay in a nearby hostel. It was almost worse than a squat. Packed together in bunk bed dormitories, it was more like a prison for the unwashed. During the next days, I sat on a pavement with a polystyrene cup, people walking past like I was invisible. A few were kind and dropped a coin in. Once, I got a five pound note. I recalled my first day in London, back when I was rich, trying to use a Scottish fiver on the bus. After a week, Viviane said they had space. Maybe she suspected I wasn't nineteen but she didn't challenge me.

The women's hostel nurse checked me out, said it wasn't unusual for my periods to have stopped given the life I'd been leading but that I should take a pregnancy test. I said maybe but not today. It was just heaven to have regular food and a real bed to sleep in, even if I had to share a bedroom with old Hazel, a long-term resident. I spent a lot of time in the activities room where you could take part in yoga, meditation, creative arts, and even study catering. One course leader said that writing about our experiences was a way of making sense of the world. I decided I'd write a story that Bill Paterson could read out on the radio, or a film he could act in. One day.

Best, there was a guitar. For the first time in ages I felt really homesick. The guitar meant Fraser, Niall, everyone at home and the music I loved.

THIRTEEN

ANNIE – London

I'd accepted the hostel nurse's reason for my periods stopping. But I did feel kind of rough and anxious. One evening, Hazel heaved herself round on the sofa in the day room, making everything creak, looked across at me and said 'You're up the duff, love'.

'I can't be.'

She inspected a scuffed boot toe.

'No "can't be" about it. Your tits are too big for the rest of you. I seen 'em when you get undressed. Get yourself down the 'ealth. They'll sort yer out. Probably get yer a flat. Shame I'm not stuffed, I'd get one meself.'

Hazel must have been in her seventies, or maybe living rough had aged her. Whichever, I ducked the mental image of her shagging and peered at the suspect bumps on my chest. They didn't look different to me, although my bra was feeling a bit tight. But I wasn't throwing up or anything, so I couldn't be pregnant? Could I? I wasn't going to lose face with the nurse at the hostel who'd offered me a pregnancy test, so I picked up a leaflet for the health centre and headed off. While I was walking I thought through the options for if I *was* pregnant:

1) Keep the baby and go to a mother and baby shelter in London
2) Keep the baby and go to a mother and baby shelter in Glasgow
3) Keep the baby and go back to my parents in Glasgow
4) Give the baby up for adoption – like me. No way.

I didn't consider the other 'A' word, just the idea of it freaked me out. Besides, if there was this wee fishy thing squirming inside me, it wasn't just mine, it was Zeezoo's, too, and it all came down to:

5) Find Zeezoo.

It was the middle of December by now, and raining on and off. I'd got this huge raincoat, a man's, that Zeezoo had given me. It was new, but it swamped me – even with rolling back the sleeves and knotting a couple of stretchy socks into a belt round the middle. Made me look like one of the wee forest creatures in *Star Wars*. I had to keep asking the way to Brick Lane. People either ignored me or said they didn't know. Probably a combination of Titanic ignorance and shock at being approached by something resembling an Ewok. Eventually, I picked on a traffic warden; I was sure she'd know the Brick Lane Health Centre. It was time for her break, she said, and took me to a café for a cup of tea and a hot sausage roll (in those days I was too poor and starving to have vegan principles). She asked me what part of Scotland I was from, said she hadn't been north of

Birmingham but it sounded lovely. I didn't say much. Too busy getting food down me. Debbie or Sue or whatever her name was drew me a map on a serviette of how to get to Brick Lane and put a cross where the health centre was. I knocked back the rest of my tea and left.

When I found it, I didn't want to admit I was in a hostel so said I was visiting for a week and staying in a hotel. The receptionist was obviously used to losers – or liars – coming in. His face didn't change. I had to wait for ninety minutes before a doctor could see me, which was handy for catching up on the Heather Mills/Paul McCartney wedding in an old *Hello!* They were married at St Salvator's church in the grounds of Ireland's seventeenth-century Castle Leslie. Hope they weren't offended I couldn't be there. They probably got my excuse note about shoplifting at a Tesco Express with Shelley that day.

The doctor asked me the relevant questions about unprotected sex, periods, morning sickness et cetera then gave me a paddle to pee on and told me to wait on a chair outside the loo until she called me back in. That's when I knew for sure about Jude – or the collection of cells that would end up being Jude. Could be into my second trimester, she said – I hadn't a clue what that meant. But probably about fifteen weeks or thereabouts, since I couldn't be too sure about my last period. I must have conceived soon after the rape. Fortunately, I remembered having a period then, so my baby wouldn't be the child of a rapist – although I had to admit that Zeezoo's moral boundaries were barely existent. I boo-hooed a bit and the doctor held my hand, dead kind. Said she'd make an appointment for a scan – or would I prefer to have it back home in Scotland? Very polite of her to carry on with the visitor fairy tale I'd told her. I said I'd sort it. The nurses gave me lots of leaflets with addresses for help and talked about whether I wanted to go ahead with the pregnancy – they were careful not to say 'baby'. How would I know what to do? I was still mindless with shock.

Hazel didn't say 'I told you so' in as many words, just, 'Best bugger off back to Scotland, love. Yer family'll look after you. Eventually.'

Yeah, right. It wasn't the prudish, judgmental sort of looking after I'd get from Rosemary and George that I wanted. I just wanted Zeezoo or, more realistically, the person I wanted Zeezoo to be. He'd be terrified, too, of course, but he'd be thrilled and proud. If he had a child he might be more responsible, and perhaps they'd let him stay. But was that a good enough reason to go ahead with the pregnancy? OK, my logic wasn't too sound. Maybe I had baby-brain even then. I hadn't seen him for three weeks. Had the Border Agency got to him? I knew one or two places he might be and tried a squat in Islington but didn't recognise anyone and no one there had seen him more recently than I had. I was dog tired by then so I went back to the centre and had me another bawl.

Hope, one of the staff at the hostel, knocked on my door.

'There's someone to see you, Annie.'

I mopped up quickly. Zeezoo? Shelley? Oh, god, if only it were Fraser. Or Carol-Anne. Or Shafiq… But I didn't recognise her, at all, this new volunteer at the hostel. Hope introduced us. But I didn't hear her name properly and wasn't really interested until the new person said –

'I'm sorry I couldn't get you into The Langham…' She saw I'd been crying and gave me a quick hug. Which, of course, set me off again. In my hormonal state, I told her about the baby and about Zeezoo and how I didn't know where he was. And she was just… lovely, said she'd help me any, any, any way she could.

FOURTEEN

FRASER – Symi

It's my turn to do dinner so I book a table. Having a slightly more predictable income these days is a definite plus. Even at mates' rates, though, Tsampikos' Restaurant is a liability beyond my assets. So it's lucky the pizza place is Jude's top choice. Annie doesn't care, so long as she can sort a vegan meal, and Clair and Jess are happy to chum along with us. Clair's showing a lot of trust allowing the two refugee girls, total strangers, the run of her house for a couple of hours, but she's really cool about it. The meal, too, will be laid back and we won't mention Jude's situation, unless he brings it up. I've been thirteen myself. He won't.

The pizzas are good, so is the red wine. To avoid friction, Annie allows Jude his phone at the table so the rest of us can chat. I ask Annie about the tall guy at the ferry. Flicker of interest from Jess. Just a helpful stranger, Annie says, then asks about the accountancy business. I have no news, either. So I mention my slot at Angelina's Music Bar tonight, how great it would be to have her on rhythm. She folds her arms, half smiles. At least it's not a no. Clair is knackered after teaching so I ask if she'd Jude-sit. The sound of his name drags him away from SnapChat.

'I *am* sitting here, you know, Uncle Puke.' I go for the usual bribery.

'Jude, my man, how's your financial situation?'

'I'm broke.'

'What about the fifteen euros I gave you last night? Never mind.'

Annie's eyes widen. 'How much?'

I waft a twenty euro note under his nose. 'Would all these euroonies help your cash flow?' He is eager. 'Then, oh nephew of mine, would they buy your Mum a night off?'

He knows he's been had. But what can a lad do in the face of hard cash? 'S'pose.'

I pretend-cuff his ear and we all make a shift for home. The major cash outlay may reap dividends towards my sister's potential happiness. That is, if Alexis the human skyscraper shows his face at Angelina's. En route, I twist Annie's arm – gently because she'll need it to play – and suggest a playlist. It works. Around nine thirty, we set off for Angelina's, she with her modest Epiphone acoustic guitar and me with my new Yamaha twelve-string. Jess will turn up later. Annie jammed with me last year and made a welcome change from my predictable solo, so Angelina welcomes her with a yell and a hug tonight.

It's about ten fifteen and no Alexis. Pity. I lead in with The Everly

Brothers' 'Bye Bye Love' in sad recognition of the referendum result, Annie joining in as and when she feels. On to 'Radio Ga Ga', 'Man in the Moon', and other well-known pleasers. We round off with a request, 'The White Rose of Athens'– it's inevitable. I remember Clair's reaction the first time she heard me play it. Her tears were emotion, not pain, you understand. Tonight, someone sends drinks across for us. Only right and just.

After the break, Annie thinks we're going into Floyd's 'Comfortably Numb'– but I play the intro to 'It's in His Kiss'. She gives me a 'You bastard!' look then takes the lead with me on backing vocals. She has a great voice, quite deep and bluesy, and she's flying although she'd never admit it. As I get the audience clapping along and '*duh-da-da-da-da-da-ing*' for the middle riff, Jess turns up with Phanes, our harbourside entrepreneur, and Alexis. Excellent. Except how does she know Alexis? He's not her type, surely? Or maybe she just met him here? I'm blethering like two wifies at a washing line, the result of too much time spent in platonic female company.

As the – ecstatic – applause dies, I solo on Radiohead's 'Creep'. I'm introducing the next number, the Beatles' 'Taxman' (to scare up more accountancy business, maybe?) when I notice Annie and her guitar have disappeared. I get through it myself, no bother, but announce a mini-break and find Angelina. Annie's gone back to the house, she says. Puzzling. Tired or a tummy bug?

I churn out another request and finish with 'Life on Mars' then join Jess and co. She is busy enthusing over luxuriating on the Florida money belt. Phanes doesn't relate to a word she says, is just happy to be bathed in her aura. Alexis is bored but trying to be polite. She pauses, briefly, to introduce me in her inimitably subtle way. Uses the Greek familiar construction talking to him. Why?

'Alexi, this is Fraser, my mother's ex-lover. Alexis works for an NOG on Leros. Sorry, I've forgotten, what is an NOG, Alexi?'

'An NGO. A non-governmental organisation called Nederland Redden en Helpen. I work with refugees. And we've met. Hello again, Fraser. You're a great musician, so is Annie. And I liked your choices.'

'Well, thanks, it's –'

Jess is bored already. She didn't notice Annie go and is too busy with her little audience to comment. 'Shall we have some more drinks, guys?'

I make my apologies and leave, disappointed that my plan's ganged awry. Sloping off like Annie did isn't her style.

The light's off in the Iraqi girls' room. It's well past Jude's bedtime and Clair must have put her head down, too, because Annie's alone on the terrace when I reach the house. Her guitar case lies skewed on the sofa and there's a whisky bottle on the kitchen table. I pour myself a vodka and take the whisky bottle outside – plus a roll of kitchen towel. I've been around women long enough to know.

'Annie?'

She sits with elbows on knees. There's a glimmer of wetness on her cheek and a string of mucus dangles from her nose. Like she was five again. I hand her a few leaves of towel. She sighs from the soles of her flip flops and blows hard.

'Thanks.'

We sit for a while, Annie hunched over, head lowered, me praying that neither Jude nor Jess will come crashing in. I take it gently.

'Sorry, I shouldn't have forced you to play tonight. You weren't ready.'

She rubs her forehead.

'It wasn't that.'

Mustn't push her. Change the subject.

'Jess recruited a professional saint, Alexis. Works with refugees on Leros. Think it was the guy who helped you at the ferry. Not many other people on Symi nine feet tall.' Nothing.

After a minute or so she speaks in a voice I can barely hear.

'Self pity. I thought it wasn't, but it is.'

'How d'you mean?'

'Seeing Jess, coming in with two guys, having fun. No responsibilities.'

There's nothing I can say. I'm so wrapped in my own life I've forgotten hers is going nowhere fast. Then Jess turns up at Angelina's with a guy I'm sure Annie liked. I put my arm round her, she leans against me and we stay like that until she wakes me up to go home.

Padding through Horio to my place, I'm having guilt pangs. I should have been more help, not just now but since she had Jude. When she said they were coming this week I thought she was joking me. The last time she did anything so impulsive was when she took off to London at sixteen and came back with the we'an on the way. This time may not be so dramatic, but to book their flights before clearing it with Jude's school is pushing it. In fact I'm wondering if she even did clear it – no, she's not that daft. Dumping the dogs on the Scrymgeours is strange, though. Annie may be a pain in the arse at times but she's a good mum. And she usually meets life head on, so I'm a bit – I don't know, puzzled – uncomfortable. Jude's recent troubles have obviously thrown her more than we thought.

Clair reckons it's not so surprising Jude's got problems at school, being mixed race and from a one-parent family in a small community like Kilachlan. Annie had a pretty rocky time growing up, and she broke out. Me too, I suppose, although I was a late leaver. Rosemary and George, never the cuddliest of parents, parachuted this wee bundle into the Anniesland semi with no warning. Having been the only kid for eleven years, I was pissed off. Wasn't I enough? And she was minute, like a mouse or something. But dead feisty, so I called her Mighty Mouse – which got shortened to Mighty. And, in the tradition of all big brothers, the more your wee sister hates something, the more you do it. So I shut out my new sister for six or seven years – until I realised she was an oddball, a cute one but definitely odd, and we became pals. She'd follow me around when I let her, even when I called her Mighty – mostly. She had this weird crush on Bill Paterson, an actor old enough to be her dad. Grandpa, maybe. So I might say:

'Someone rang for you, Mighty,'

'Who was it?'

'Oh – no-one I know. Said his name was Bill Paterson.'

Her eyes would light up, then I might say –

'Told him you were on your honeymoon.'

And the demon midget would fly at me.

'You did not. You're a bloody liar!'

'Woo!' So I'd boogie off – rapidly – in Michael Jackson mode:

'Billie P is not your lover, he's just the boy who says you've got a big bum, so he hides way up his lum...'

Lum – an old Scots word for chimney – and Annie would steam after me.

High points: teaching her to play guitar, the lyrics to some rock standards and favourites of mine and how to harmonise. Instead of mooning over Boyzone and trying to look like Posh Spice, like most weeny-boppers, she was into Bowie and the Kinks, Pink Floyd, Queen and the Beatles. I was a great Radiohead fan, too, but they were a little beyond her pre-teen tastes. She belts out a mean riff these days. If I'm honest, she's probably better than me.

When I moved out to share a flat in Yorkhill with a couple of pals, I'd pick her up in my rusty old Fiat, occasionally, and take her back to the flat for a jam session, or I'd go for Sunday lunch in Anniesland and we'd spend the afternoon playing guitar in my old bedroom, Annie on my spare acoustic. How many big brothers would give up part of their weekend for their kid sister?

In the end it wasn't just accountancy did my head in, I had quite a bust-up with Rosemary and George. Well, with George. My 'chaotic approach to work' upset him, but also, in his opinion, I was a bad influence on Annie. A bell in my head called 'Time!'. I'd had enough of George's influence on *me*. I mean, *accountancy* for god's sake. I should have been a rock star. What was I thinking? Looking back, I can't understand how I stayed so long. Was it my wee sister or cowardice?

I promised Annie I'd keep in touch, that I'd come back for her, but it was more of a sailor's farewell than a big brother's. The moment I arrived in Spain I was having way too good a time to think about anyone else. Sure, I sent her the odd postcard, rang a few times. But if Rosemary or

George picked up I'd cut off. Why Rosemary chose to have 'the adoption talk' just as I left defeats me. Annie must have been poison gas around the house after being nuked like that. And they're surprised she ran off at sixteen? By the time her prodigal brother returned, she'd got herself into a major situation called Jude. I sometimes wonder if I'd stayed… Ach, who knows?

Inside, the vodka bottle sits on the bedside table leering at me. Think I'll have a small one, wash down my conscience.

Next Morning

We took the Iraqi girls down to the Piraeus ferry, early. They left the room like a new pin. We waved them off then turned back to offer accommodation to whoever needed it most – which is usually all the new arrivals. What can you do? With help from an interpreter, a refugee who'd been helping volunteers, we invited a recently arrived Syrian couple with a baby. Clair hung around to help them register while I did a bit of shopping and climbed back. Even after they arrived, the mum and dad couldn't stop thanking Clair, me (who did nothing) and the very walls of the house. Dry land must have seemed like Paradise after what they'd been through. They're in the guest room now and we're hoping they'll peep out for something to eat soon. The baby has a slight fever, so Clair's given her some Calpol but is ready to summon help should it intensify.

This week's painting group goes home today, so she's in the little utility room cleaning spare paintbrushes and palettes for any forgetful students next week. I sit on a barstool on the terrace catching some rays, communing through the open window. Annie and Jess have gone down to Yialos, so I've a chance to talk it through.

'Annie needs a real break but I don't see how.'

Silence apart from the scraping and washing sounds. Then she says,

'Perhaps we could do that, give her a break.'

'Go on.'

'Well, I suspect Jude would behave better for us than he does for her. So why don't we encourage her to take off on her own for a while? Island hop, perhaps. Just do as she pleases, have some thinking time.'

'Wouldn't she be lonely?'

Clair peers over her glasses at me, her shorthand for 'don't be stupid, Fraser'. Right as usual. Still, I'm feeling tenderly for my wee sister and find it even affects my wallet.

'Maybe we could get Carol-Anne out here. I could whistle up the fare.'

Good job she and Jude don't visit that often. Clair melts.

'Oh, how lovely of you, darling. Wish I'd had a big brother like you.'

We have one of our few uncomfortable silences as unintended associations swarm back and forth through the casement between us. I swat them with a blokeish clearing of the throat and blunder on.

'I'll ask Jude if he's got Carol-Anne's number.'

'Um – well, I don't know if…but you *could.*'

We both know it's unlikely that Jude would have her number and likely that I'd have to fend off a lot of irritating questions as to why I wanted it – plus fork out another sizeable bribe to keep his trap shut. On the other hand, we don't know whether Annie and Carol-Anne are on or off at the moment. But it helps us through a sticky moment. Another throat clearance from me.

'Jude's off with the lads. Catch him later.'

Then twenty minutes of near silence until my phone blasts out the guitar riff from Another Brick in the Wall. It's my speaking of the devil-ish sister and she wants to know if I was thinking of playing a set at Angelina's tonight. She's changed her tune.

'Could, I suppose. Any particular reason?' Clair will definitely want to go out tonight so Jude-sitting could be a problem. But she's already countered that one.

'Great. I'll ask Andy's Mum if Jude can stay there overnight.' Andy is Andreas.

'Look's like we're on, then. There's just one thing, though…' I'm on twenty-four hour call for the *Giorgios* should it need to go out.

FIFTEEN

ANNIE – London

The day after my Langham lady turned up, I went to the squat in Notting Hill. With one shoe flapping and a marquee tent of a coat, it felt like a million miles trek. When I got there it was boarded up. Joos, one of the squatters, was coming along the road.

'D'you know where Zeezoo is?'

He laughed.

'What's the big joke, Joos?'

'Nothing, nothing. You are, like, not into football, eh? Only the music?'

I'd heard jokes about Zeezoo and football before that I'd never understood but I still thought Joos was being pretty weird. 'What's the deal about football?'

He thought this was even funnier.

'Look, it's really, really important that I find him!' I wasn't telling this creepy guy why. He stopped laughing enough to tell me the police or someone had raided the squat and everyone was gone. He couldn't remember if Zeezoo had been there and didn't know where he was. Then jokey Joos tooled off, miming kicking a football as he went.

If he had been there and it was the police who had broken up the squat, they would have handed Zeezoo over to the UK Border Agency. It could even have been the Border Agency who raided the place. Either way, my baby's father could be in trouble. My insides hit the floor.

Back in Marylebone my hotel lady had come in again to see how I was. She was dressed all in green, and expensive as a Harrods shop window. I said I was sorry I hadn't known her name, but it looked like Shona on the card. She paused for a beat, then said,

'No, you're right. It's Shona. Please call me Shona.' It sounded a bit odd, like she'd decided it on the spot. Then she said, 'I've been thinking over what you said about your boyfriend and wondered whether you'd like to check the Immigration Return Centres? Just to put your mind at rest.'

I didn't know whether it would be worse to find him in one, or know he was still free, but missing. We sat at a computer; there were about half a dozen centres around London, the nearest two near London Airport. How would I get to any of if I didn't have money? And even if I did, I had to have ID like a passport, a driving licence, or a utilities bill to get in. Me? Driving licence? Utilities bill? Ha ha.

Shona rang Colnbrook and they said they'd need his name and date of birth. I knew his name and I thought his birthday was in April but wasn't sure. How come I didn't know something as personal as that? I thought he'd said once his second name was something like...Sedan?...and it was followed by hoots of laughter from the other squatters. I told her 'Sedan'. She looked surprised.

'Sedan, like the chair?'

'Yes – I don't know. Zeezoo Sedan. Birthday's in April – but I don't know when. Tell them he's got dreadlocks!' She told the operator, then spelled 'Zeezoo' and 'Sedan'. It sounded like more laughter from the other end. Shona thanked them and drew a little sad face on the pad. Not there.

Next was Harmondsworth; the conversation went the same way with the same result. Another sad face. I suggested maybe he hadn't been caught. Shona wiped a tear from my face with her thumb. I liked that, it was like a mum. Like mine used to be when I was little. Except she didn't have glossy red nails.

'Look, Annie, you're an adult and you know your own mind. I don't know Zeezoo's story. Are you convinced by what he told you?'

I went through his most popular story, ending with, '... and he didn't have a visa so he was an illegal immigrant.'

Shona ran her hands through her hair, tucked a strand behind her ear again.

'But he would have needed a visa to get into the UK.'

'Oh, yes, I remember, he said he *did* have a visa but it was a fake one from the college...'

I started reinventing the story to make it more plausible, ending with, 'He's not a liar!'

She backed off and continued as though the last exchange hadn't happened. 'What was the name of this college? Do you know?'

'No. Why?'

'If we knew the name they gave we could find out whether –'

'Whether it was a scam? Of course it was.'

'OK, OK, OK. You've had a long, upsetting day. Why not go for a lie down, hmm?'

'Because I want to find Zeezoo.'

Shona nodded and stood up, replacing the strand of hair behind her ear once more.

'Cup of tea?'

Next morning, she came to my room and told me to get washed and dressed quickly. We were going to visit a couple of centres north of London. Her car was outside. She went downstairs to wait. I was surprised to see her so early, I hadn't even had time to refuse breakfast. I hadn't felt sick until I found out I was pregnant. It must have been psychosomatic because I never actually barfed. When I managed to drag myself downstairs, I heard an argument going on in the office. Shona came out looking annoyed and Viviane was behind her.

'Mrs Packham, it's a kind impulse but it maybe you're getting a little too–'

They both saw me. Shona turned to her.

'So what do you want me to do? Disappoint her?'

'Well, you'd better go ahead for today. But these things are for discussion in future if you want to continue volunteering here.'

Shona was quiet for a few minutes in the car then suddenly got very chatty. Asked me about Glasgow, about my interests, did I have any dreams? There was me, sitting in my mega-mac. Dreams?

'At the moment, all I want is to find Zeezoo.'

'Yes, yes, yes. Totally understood.'

I didn't feel much like talking. She filled the silence by telling me about when she grew up. Her father had been in the Diplomatic Service. I didn't know what that was and didn't ask in case it was boring. She'd lived in South America, Hong Kong, and Thailand before she was seven when she was sent to boarding school in England. It sounded amazing but Shona spoke as though she didn't enjoy her childhood much.

'My brother and I got flown to wherever they were in the world for Christmas and sometimes the summer holidays. Otherwise, we spent our school holidays at my grandmother's in Scotland, Lochgilphead. D'you know it?'

I knew the name. We'd probably passed through it on one of our long, aimless family outings when we got lost and Mum and Dad would have one of their silences because she hadn't read the map properly and he refused to ask anyone the way.

We drove up the motorway, taking over an hour with all the traffic getting out of London. The first Immigration Return Centre was more like a prison, with wire fences round it. I couldn't bear the thought that Zeezoo might be in there. We went to the front office where a woman in uniform told us it wasn't visiting time and to go away – well, not in so many words. Shona said why we were there (without going into the pregnant bit), passed across card and explained that she had brought identification as I had problems accessing mine. Eventually, the woman rang someone in an office and went through it all. There was that laugh, again, from the other end of the phone. Perhaps I wasn't the only one looking for him. But no, there was no one of Zeezoo's name or description. Shona told her to hang on to the card.

'Our contact details in case he's brought in.'

'Our contact details' like we were family.

Then another long drive. We stopped at a posh pub for lunch and Shona took a travel bag out of the boot.

'I thought these things might be about your size. It'll cheer you up to have some new clothes. You can change in the Ladies.'

We found the loos and she said to meet her the dining room. I couldn't believe what was in the bag. I mean, really nice gear. Sweaters, T-shirts, underwear, socks, and a pair of Ugg boots – phenomenally expensive. And a pair of maternity jeans. When I saw them, it hit me. I hadn't properly decided about the baby, yet. It sort of brought it all home. I didn't know what to do, I didn't know what to say. I went back out to dining room with the bag.

'Thank you, Shona, it's very kind of you but I can't accept these.'

She hardly even looked at me. 'Annie, I come from a very wealthy family. What looks expensive to you is like throwing away small change for them. You've got yourself into a pickle. You have some hard choices to make. The first is whether you truly want this baby. The second, and all the others, depend on what you decide. If you decide to keep it, you owe it to the baby to keep it as warm and comfortable as possible.'

I dropped into the chair opposite her, sack of spuds-like. Didn't know what to do, what to say. She did.

'If you don't want to stay pregnant, by all means, hand the clothes back. If you decide to stay pregnant, you can accept the clothes and say "thank you", or you can give them back to me and say "sorry" to your baby. D'you want a look at the menu? I'm going to have the salmon.'

People talking, cutlery on plates, glasses chinking, the kitchen door opening and shutting – it all got louder and fuzzier until I shrunk into a shell of quietness, hearing only her words 'whether you truly want this baby'. This had nothing to do with the baby's father, nor Rosemary and George. It was everything to do with me. This baby would be my real family. The isolation faded, the room returned.

'Thank you for the clothes, Shona.'

After lunch, which Shona paid for, of course, we went on to a centre near Oxford. If anything, it was worse, with barbed wire, bare brick walls and dark green paint. There was a small airport opposite. I wondered if it was purpose built to get unwanted people out quicker. Shona switched off the engine. It was getting dark.

'All right?'

At the gate we weren't even allowed to speak to anyone. We would have to ring to make an appointment.

'I'm so sorry, Annie.'

It was at that moment I gave in and admitted it to myself; all the time in London I'd been making excuses for Zeezoo, for my life with him. I would call it denial these days. But then, it felt like I'd stuffed every suspect or unpleasant aspect of him in the back of a drawer and shut it quickly. There was his name, for one thing. Why had I gone along with it when I knew inside he was fake? There was the rape. It was a set up to pay off some kind of drug debt. That's why my guitar and all my other belongings had gone. And I'd thought I was being so tough and streetwise putting up with it and him. Every single sordid, unwashed item of my life suddenly came tumbling out of that overladen drawer. I stuffed them back in and locked it.

Shona was waiting for me to speak. Surprising what a relief it was to say, 'No, it's OK. I don't think Zeezoo would really want this baby, after all.'

In the same way I knew I wanted it, I knew he definitely wouldn't.

'Are you sure?'

I nodded. We went back to the car and returned to London.

That drawer stayed locked until I met Clair. I told her one morning on the strand at Kilachlan before Jude and I moved in with Maggie. It was a while before Maggie was well enough to hear it, but it was only fair she should know just who she had in her house. After her, I kicked the drawer shut for a few more years.

SIXTEEN

ANNIE – London

Shona dropped me back at the hostel. Passing Christmas lights and decorations on the way back into London had got me thinking about Glasgow. Even made me smile. Then I thought 'How would Mum and Dad feel about an illegitimate grandchild? An illegitimate, *brown* grandchild?'. Apart from one postcard from the hostel to say I was fine, I hadn't been in touch with them since I sneaked out that early morning. They must have been calling me all sorts and grinding each other to mince. Maybe they wouldn't even want me back? And Fraser? Who knew where he was? Last time I heard, he was crewing on a yacht around the Caribbean. I doubted his hair had turned grey with worry – then felt bad, because I knew he cared about me.

That night I rang. My father answered. I said I was coming home.

'That's good. Good. Aye, that's very good, indeed.' He sounded like someone hearing their dry cleaning was ready. But for George it was like jumping and clicking his heels for joy. When I went to the hostel day room, Hazel wasn't there, so I borrowed the guitar and tried to work out the chords of Madonna's 'Papa Don't Preach' (because I *was* keeping my baby) but very low so no one would complain.

Next morning, I went downstairs with two carrier bags packed – that was how much I owned by then. I went to see Viviane in the office, to tell her.

'I wish you the very best, Annie. It's been lovely getting to know you. If you have time, let us hear how you're getting on.' She gave me a card with their contact details. From the way she spoke, I got the feeling that she hoped I'd get in touch but didn't expect me to.

'Sure I will. Could you tell Shona?'

'Of course. Is there anything you need? How are you getting back to Scotland?'

'Hitching.'

She looked concerned. 'I'm not sure that's a good idea, Annie.'

'I'll be all right.' I was seventeen, not a child. Why wouldn't I be all right? I still hadn't learned.

'There's the emergency fund. We could make you a loan.'

I refused the loan and picked up my carrier bags. Didn't want anything hanging over my head. Despite my ungrateful behaviour, she still asked, 'Have you had breakfast?'

I couldn't wait to be gone.

'Not the way my gut's feeling. I'd throw it up by the end of the road.' I flashed a smile. And that was the last I saw of the women's hostel. One thing I knew for sure from my time in London was the best way to get back to Glasgow. Marylebone Road became Westway and after about a million miles, connected up with the M40 and motorways up to the M74. I'd made a 'Glasgow' sign to hold up at traffic lights on the south side, westbound, and hoped for a lorry heading my way. Not at the first set of lights – too near the hostel. I headed for Marylebone Road, crossed over, and walked in the direction of the traffic. The hunger pangs were starting. Why did I have to put on such a show of bravado? I was debating finding a sandwich bar that could sell me something for 50p when I heard someone calling. Several people turned round but it was for me. Shona.

She offered to drive me to Scotland. I mean, mental! I said absolutely not. So she insisted on paying my fare. Given the choice, I would have preferred going by train, but she took me to Victoria Coach Station and bought me a ticket for Glasgow; I ended up heading North the same way I'd arrived. In my coat pocket was a note with just 'Shona', her mobile number and email address. She wasn't supposed to get personally involved with clients, she said, but I was special. Looking back, I realise how difficult I made it for people to help me, only letting them by making out I was doing them a favour. Also, I'm surprised at how brief a time I knew Shona in London in relation to the long-distance friendship that developed.

SEVENTEEN

ANNIE – Symi

It's gone breakfast time and I'm still in the bedroom festering with shame after last night, both for running away and for the indulgent tears. Not used to Fraser being so – well – 'nice'. I mean, I know he's got my interests at heart, but his sympathy is usually on the edge of taking the piss. Was he ever that prickly with Clair? Was that why relationship ended? Who knows? I'm not going to find out from them. At the moment, I'm too busy feeling mortified.

'Kalimera, Annie mou!' Jess breezes in without knocking, dressed to slay and obviously about to make my day happen. Way too bright for my draggy self.

''Morning, JJ. How're you doing?'

She plonks herself next to me on the unmade bed and gives me a hug. 'Bit better than you, mou. What's the matter?'

Like I'm going to say seeing her with Alexis made me feel jealous?

'Nothing – I'm fine.'

She mimics a frown. 'You don't look it. What happened at Angelina's last night? Lady problems? Symi squits?'

Discreet as a rutting warthog.

'Nothing like that.'

'Oh, Annie mou-mou. Want me to bugger off? By the way, I shall be incredibly hurt if you say yes.'

Gets a laugh out of me. 'That's better. Now slap on your very best face and gear. You're coming out.'

Where? Rhodes for a spot of clothes shopping, perhaps? An afternoon at a spa then cocktails with her pals somewhere before a nightclub and a boutique hotel in the old city? As if I could keep up with her at that level; one, there's Jude, two, there's the price tag, and three – see one and two. Besides, I can't remember the last time I was actually interested in even looking at clothes. I've a uniform for work, and for the rest of the time jogging pants and a hoodie do me. Shorts and T-shirts are my notion of extreme sophistication, eclipsed only by the sarong Clair gave me last year. In my negative internalisation I miss part of Jess's reply.

'... to Yialos. Got some stuff for the clothes bank. Then we'll go for a coffee, yes?'

That's Jess, either buying them or disposing of them. Still, if that's really all she's doing, why not tag along?

'OK, then. Thanks.'

'Cool. Jude out?'

'Off with Andy and Erik. Wouldn't shift him from his pit this early at home.'

I like Jess – JJ to friends. She is what she is: pretty and self-focused but actually with her heart in the right place, outrageously inappropriate one moment and extraordinarily generous the next. Maybe a touch of Attention Deficit Disorder? Being Clair's daughter and Maggie's great niece she must have a few of their humanitarian genes knocking about in her. She doesn't look like either of them, though. Well, maybe something of Clair's bone structure, but instead of her mum's explosion of brown watch-springs, she has the most gorgeous, shiny, Cleopatra hair, almost perfectly kink-free without torturing it with straighteners, which she does, anyway. And her eyes are astonishing, like the Afghan girl's in that 1980s portrait, only bluer. And she has impossibly large pupils, as if she's permanently high. Except she's not. We've shared a joint back in Kilachlan (wouldn't risk it here), so I know how ridiculously dark her eyes can get. And, to make matters far, far worse, she has the perfect figure, model-slim but with sizeable boobs. So, you get the picture. Jess is one hunk magnet. Which is what gutted me seeing her with Alexis last night. How could he resist? Whether or not she responded would be irrelevant.

On the way down the Kali Strata, we revisit conversations censored by Jude's presence yesterday; first, that there is no particular man in her life; second, that she hasn't set an exact date in August for going to Florida, yet. Says she wants to get a bit more inspiration from the Greek Islands before launching herself on her grandmother's community in Naples. I never knew there was a Naples in the States until I heard of Granny Connie, Clair's mother. No relation to Maggie, they were sisters-in-law – reluctantly it seems. Naples must be a wealthy area if Yankee Doodle Granny lives there, so a good place for a fledgling interior designer.

'They must have interior design companies there, already, JJ. Have you not thought of hooking up with one of them to start with?'

She gives a little laugh that sums up my ignorance of the interior design business in Florida and what she thinks of it. 'No, Annie. I prefer to work with personal contacts. Granny is queen of the Yacht Club *and* the Country Club.'

There you go, if your granny's a royal sailor *and* a royal yokel, you've clearly no need of an employer – or the advice of a care worker from Kilachlan. I can forgive Jess a lot; she didn't have that easy a childhood, according to Clair. Apparently, Granny Connie released the dollars fairly late on and she's still revelling in it.

It's already stove hot as we descend the Kali Strata into the town. In a ridiculously big, floppy sunhat, her cotton voile shirt flapping open to reveal a micro-bustier, Jess's style turns heads as much as her looks. Despite the black hair, her skin is very fair, so she can't tolerate too much sun, always wears a supra-high factor lotion she bought in the States. I doubt it's vegan, but then Jess is a 'relaxed' vegetarian. My skin tolerates the Greek sun much better – a clue to my uncertain heritage? Nonetheless, I don't take risks and am equally strict with Jude, having no idea of his inherited melanin level, either. I'm in regulation T-shirt and shorts that have seen a good few summers and a baseball cap Jude discarded as being uncool. Heads will not swivel as I pass, I'm usually mistaken for an undersized twelve-year-old lad.

We pass between the upmarket gift and clothing shops at the bottom of the steps and head for the clothing collection point at the old Post Office. There are still as many refugees sheltering in the shade, backs against plaster walls, legs stretched on concrete or cobbles, eyes dull with resignation, adults and children, alike. Jess stops by one or two on the way, letting them look through her bag of clothes. One woman shakes her head and pats Jess's hand in thanks. The garments are unsuitable for her age or, more likely, her religion. Another rakes through, grabbing, grabbing, no doubt thinking that if not for personal use they may be worth a few euros. By the time Jess reaches the old Post Office, there'll be very little to hand in. It doesn't matter, so long as they help.

As we leave the collection point, a tall figure blocks the sunlight from the doorway. Instead of keeping moving, the figure stops.

'Annie? Jess?' It is my outsize bellhop from the ferry – Jess's companion at Angelina's, last night. She greets him warmly.

'Alexi! Are you NOG-ing here?'

He bends to accept her continental kisses, laughing. 'No, I'm NGO-ing. Nice to see you.' His eyes find me. 'And nice to see you, Annie. I was very impressed by the little I heard at Angelina's Bar last night. You have a great voice. But you'd gone before I could tell you.'

No kisses for me but he knows my name. *Alexi*, I think, the Greek construction for Alexis? Nerves drain from my mouth and I can't reply. Jess glances at me and fills in.

'We're just going for a coffee. Want to join us when you have time between your – GNOs?' Is she really that ditsy or just conditioned to flirting? He seems relaxed about whatever it is.

'Sure. Where will you be?'

'The kafeneion next to Giannis's. Know it?'

'I'll be fifteen minutes.'

Jess strides out ahead of me between the swanky yachts and pricey tourist shops. I begin to wonder whether I – we, *Alexis?* and I, have been set up. And d'you know what? I wouldn't mind at all, apart from feeling a bit goofy. The difference between him and my only – dalliance – in the last eight years or so, is… Well, they're just that, *different*. I permit a pleasurable wriggling inside that can only mean trouble.

Jess and I reach the kafeneion and find a table with an umbrella. She is too bright.

'Fancy meeting Alexis! We were talking about you, last night.' Ah, a clue. *Alexis/Alexi.* And I'm right, she *is* scheming.

'Don't worry, Annie mou, I didn't give away any family secrets. Just bigged you up!'

'Did I reach five foot two?'

'Eh?'

She orders an Americano and I ask for a Cappuccino.

'Chocolate sprinkle?' the waiter asks. In my pubescently anxious state I forget 'yes' and 'no' and nod stupidly.

The coffees and Alexis arrive together. Jess, subtle as a neon Cupid, shifts along to ensure that Alexis and I are sitting together. He catches my embarrassment, grins and gives me a tiny nudge, making the nerves around my elbow and solar plexus blossom. Being his co-dupe makes the encounter easier. It surprises neither of us when she spots an unnamed, unseen person, excuses herself on an urgent, implausible pretext, slaps twenty euros on the table and gambols off. All we can do is laugh.

'If this is a blind date, I'm glad I have twenty-twenty vision –' he says, then, 'Oh, Christ, I'm appalled at myself for that – that – what would you call it?'

'Cheesy remark?'

'Exactly, "cheesy remark".'

Definitely exciting that communication is on more than one level. And excellent English for a – *what are you, Alexi?* There are laughter crinkles around his eyes. He's older than me. Fraser's age? Since it's nearly twelve and I feel more comfortable, I say, 'Would you feel like going for a beer?' And he says,

'I have a meeting at one, but – yes, ne, ja – affirmative enough?'

Oh dear, here I go…

Yialos is packed with day trippers. Waiting staff serve diners in a performance choreographed by familiarity, holding laden plates aloft and slewing brimming glasses around tightly packed tables. Laughter, chinking of cutlery, and hubbub of chat vacillate in the heat. I'm feeling dorky, now, in the baseball cap but, as we are outside, I need its layer of protection. I could say Alexis is bare-headed but his blond hair is so thick it would take a very determined ray to reach his scalp.

Sitting at the top of the harbour, we knock back a couple of draught Mythos. He packs a small clay pipe with tobacco and lights up. Flailing the match out, he offers me a puff.

'It's called a Cutty.' I shake my head disapprovingly and he shrugs. I'm a little disappointed by the smoking but, on the plus side, it takes the edge off him being perfect.

'So, Annie – Annie what?'

'Annie Buchanan.'

'Music in the name, even. Tell me the story of your life.'

'In twenty minutes?'

'Fifteen. It's a five-minute walk to the meeting – unless you join me on the way.'

'Maybe five minutes for your legs, Alexi. You must have noticed I'm vertically challenged.'

'OK, Annie Buchanan, so you're a joker, a musician and, at some point, you were born. What else?'

'On holiday here.'

'With your brother, Fraser. Seeing him on the harbour crossed our wires a little, so–'

'You checked us out? That was cheeky of you. Alexis what?'

'Giannopoulos.'

Even with my curiosity aroused, this is unexpected. How could he have a Greek name? Ah, adopted. Something we have in common?

'Say again?'

'Alexis Giannopoulos. OK, too much information – from both of us. We should be flirting our pants off by now, given the time constraint.'

'You're very direct, Kírios Giannopoulos.' I'm proud of dredging up the Greek 'Mr'. As he raises his glass I'm drawn to his eyes again, how kind they are. And the colour of his tobacco smoke. I notice eyes a lot, making contact being useful in psychology. Which we do, now. Whatever this is, it's mutual.

He's director of a Dutch aid organisation, Nederland Redden en Helpen, and he's on his way to stand in as Area Director on Leros until the new appointee can take up the post. Leros. That name takes me straight back to uni, holds a mixed fascination. It's a few islands north of here. Hearing of his connection to the place is tantalising. I want to know what he knows – and more about him. As I trot beside him to his meeting, he explains why Giannopoulos. No wonder he's keen to be back on Leros.

Phone numbers swapped but only a vague 'getting in touch' agreed. Fair enough, he's working. And so should I be.

At the supermarket, I buy soap, toothpaste, deodorant, chocolate – and put them in the collecting basket for refugees. Three needs and a needed luxury. *It's called a Cutty.* I bag some kids' sweeties and wander through the lanes, handing them to refugee children in the street. Who knows better than me that a small luxury can make life a whole lot better when you've no home? Some of the adults are fluent in English, others have a word or two, but most have none. *Seeing him on the harbour crossed our wires a little.* When it's appropriate, I hunker down with them, share what I can. There's an old saying, *'Kind words butter no parsnips'* but there's also the value of counselling. Some old sayings really are crap. But kind eyes are the colour of pipe smoke? I do a high five with a few kids and take part in a football kick around until we're stopped by a shopkeeper for getting in the way. *We should be flirting our pants off by now.* And then – *yes ne ja – affirmative enough?* How and when can I see him again? It hits me – an almost guaranteed way to reconnect with my friendly giant. I call Fraser.

On Symi, I wear my bikini instead of underwear just in case the opportunity for a swim arises, also I have invested in a waterproof container for my phone. Nos beach is a short walk away. Even if the water is rather crowded, I swoosh gloriously to celebrate my cunning. Is this what it's like to have no responsibilities? *OK, Annie Buchanan, so you're a joker, a musician and...*I let the sun dry me. *We should be flirting our pants off by now.* Can't let that go. As I walk, I am led by kind eyes, the colour of tobacco smoke. Chunk of ripe old Edam, that's me.

I take out my, fortunately, still-functioning phone and start a message to Carol-Anne. I'll copy it to Shona.

EIGHTEEN

ANNIE – 2002 London to Glasgow

On the way home in the coach I felt a thread between Zeezoo and me stretching, stretching, stretching till it almost snapped. Whatever he'd done, he was still my baby's father. We would always have that connection. I worried about how George would react to a mixed race baby and whether Rosemary would lay off the booze a bit once she had a grandchild? Could I go back to college and take my Highers? And how much would it hurt pushing a baby out?

I left from Buchanan Bus Station in June and, thanks to Shona's cash injection, arrived back there in December. Catching the bus to Anniesland was like rewinding a movie. The great homecoming was an anti-climax. George opened the door and scolded me for taking the bus instead of ringing then put the kettle on while Rosemary eyed up my new clothes. They behaved as though I'd been on a school field trip, not away in London for five months. I went for a bath and wondered, while I was soaking, if my mother would take a closer look and see the maternity label on my jeans. She must have done because I found my clothes hanging in the wardrobe; she hadn't cleared up after me since I was ten. Later, sitting in my old dressing gown and slippers at the table watching a plate of eggs, chips, and beans congeal, it was like I'd never been away. I had a sneaky feel of my breast. There it was, ripening. London was all true.

The pregnancy announcement came and went as if nothing about me surprised them. George just nodded as though he'd always known it would happen, Rosemary sighed and clamped her face in her hands, pure drama because she already knew. Inevitably the question about the father came but all I would own up to was 'of course I knew who he was'. I held their stare until they understood I wasn't going to say any more.

I couldn't let anyone else know I was coming back because my phone had been nicked at the squat, too. I actually had to ask my parents if I could use theirs. It felt like being five again. I went to use the kitchen extension then couldn't remember either Carol-Anne's or Shafiq's numbers, having had them programmed on speed dial for so long. That was when I let it all go. The door opened a crack and George came in, gave me a piece of kitchen towel. Poor sod, he didn't know how to hug, but patted my arm, murmuring 'There, there, lass'.

Carol-Anne squealed when I called round, the first Saturday morning. We hugged and jumped up and down for a bit.

'Come in, come in!' But my news was definitely not something I wanted her entire family to hear. I gave her the headline on the way to the

Byres Road.

'You are so not!'

'I so am. Due in May.'

She expressed her reaction in creative dance, which attracted a few comments from passing Christmas shoppers. I'd had to borrow my mum's coat and pulled the hood over my face to hide the embarrassment of both the coat and my exhibitionist friend. A vision of myself impersonating an Ewok at the Health Centre in London flashed up. Was that only five days ago?

The enormity of it all meant Carol-Anne actually *phoned* Shafiq. Phone calls were only for urgent news, everything else was text.

'Shafiq – you'll never guess what!'

The three of us settled into large cappuccinos and I went into my story. I stopped myself short of mentioning Zeezoo's name. It always made people laugh, for whatever reason, but I'd have laid money it wasn't a good one. Even though she was my friend, I wasn't living with Carol-Anne's sarcasm for the rest of my life. Shafiq was too kind to torment anyone.

'Z-Zak.' And I swore them to secrecy. The only person who knew his real name was Shona – and even she didn't know the full contents of my locked drawer. There was no one else close enough to tell. Niall was in America and wouldn't have been that interested in my reproductive system's functions, anyway. Besides, I wouldn't want Judah to know.

The school made an appointment for me to see the Pastoral Care teacher at six o'clock one evening. Probably didn't want the other students to see someone who'd gone to the bad. The teacher suggested I come back for the autumn term after having the baby but, in the meantime, I could catch up with reading and have homework set for me.

Christmas Day was heftily dull at home, even though Rosemary and George wore party hats. Over breakfast, Rosemary said 'Fat chance of a virgin birth around here' and George actually dared to say 'Hold your wheesht' to her but so quietly she didn't hear. Fraser rang from somewhere else in the Caribbean and blew a party hooter in celebration of my pregnancy. I told him he was celebrating prematurely because I was carrying Jesus 2 and in future we'd be having Christmas in May. He laughed so much that I did, too. At my own joke.

'You coming back at all, oh brother of mine?'

'Soon, hen. Is the bump too big for the guitar?'

I didn't want to admit his old acoustic had been stolen. 'I'm only four months, Fraser.'

'You could write all I know about baby stuff on a pin head. So, are you playing?'

'Sure.'

Apart from the hostel, I hadn't played since busking in London. It was impossible to confide in him about anything because I was being overheard – or listened to. When he rang off I had a wobbly moment, but slapped on a smile and tore into the mince pies. A whisky would have been more to the point. Being seventeen and pregnant scuppered that one.

I couldn't even look forward to having Carol-Anne around, I thought, with the million times she had to go to church over Christmas – until she turned up with her overnight bag during *Bargain Hunt*.

'I've had a mammoth row with the Holy Family. Told them they were Catholics of convenience.'

'What's that?'

'Something your dad said once. All right if I stay?' The festive season looked up.

NINETEEN

ANNIE – Glasgow

One of the more memorable fights I had with Rosemary and George was about going on the Iraq anti-war march in Glasgow. In the end I rang Fraser's mobile, wherever he was in the world – Mexico, I think, it must have cost a bomb on the landline. He said he'd speak to them. He did, so did Carol-Anne. She promised to look after me. I was six months pregnant by then. Apart from everyone being so angry it was a brilliant day, eighty thousand people in Glasgow, but the police said only thirty thousand. There were over a million in London, they reckoned, but the government played that down, too, and the war went ahead. When we got back from town, Rosemary surprised me by sending out for fish and chips to warm us up.

Carol-Anne went back to school to take her Highers. I spent my time reading, eating, doing homework, eating, going to antenatal classes/the doctor/the midwife, swimming, and eating. I almost put on the required weight and still fitted the size eight maternity jeans. Rosemary wanted to throw out the raincoat Zeezoo gave me, already had it in a bag for the charity shop. I snatched it back.

'Oh well, if it means that much. Here, I found this in the pocket.' She handed me a piece of paper. It had 'Shona', a mobile number and an email address on it. Made me feel a bit embarrassed that I'd lost touch with her. I shoved the coat into the bottom of my wardrobe and flicked the note into my top drawer. I'd email her or something. Soon. As it was, I didn't get in touch with her for another few years when I responded to her friend request on Facebook.

For a while I wondered whether the baby had just disappeared, like its father. But the baby bump, the enormous boobs and the constant need to pee convinced me that I probably was pregnant and that there would be an outcome. Jude was born on Tuesday, 20 May 2003. He decided to take his time, though, nearly two weeks late (that could've been vagueness about my last period). As it happened, I was just leaving McColl's on the Great Western Road when my waters broke. Splat down the pavement. They rang me an ambulance from the shop and I ended up in the labour ward, swearing my head off. I refused to let them call anyone, despite which, they found my notes. Rosemary sort of swam in and out of vision. She would have been on the hooch by that time of day, so I probably swam in and out of hers, too.

It was very quick for a first baby, they said. If that was quick, what possesses women to ever have another one? It was the nearest thing to medieval torture I could've imagined – like 'You will push this roast boar out of your vagina'. I'd opted for a natural birth but when it came to it I was screaming to get something for the pain. I was too dilated for pethidine and there wasn't time to get the anaesthetist so they gave me gas and air.

He wasn't the bonniest of babies. The doctor and midwife had always been on at me for being underweight, even though I was eating for the Glasgow Hawks. Anyhow, he was a wee scrawny thing. After I had my first cuddle I passed him to Rosemary, keeping a hand underneath him for safety's sake. She didn't even flicker at Jude's dark golden skin, cuddled him, welcomed him to the world with her booze breath, told him she was his grandma then, thankfully, passed him to the nurse who took him to an incubator for observation. I was left wondering what it had all been about. I was worried for his health, yes, but it was all so unreal I couldn't quite believe what had just happened and that I was now officially responsible for another human being. A male human being.

Stupidly, I kept wondering if Zeezoo would turn up. Baby brain again, I suppose. Carol-Anne came to see us after her exam. Shafiq turned up later and they both goo-gooed at him through the glass. But no George. Perhaps Rosemary had warned him about the colour scheme. He was out, too, when Rosemary brought us home in a taxi. How was he going to avoid us in a three-bedroom semi? The answer was, he didn't. He was absent when we arrived because he'd been out to buy a baby buggy – straight out of *Top Gear*. Honest to God, it was massive, virtually had tractor tyres. He didn't actually want to hold Jude, who was still the size of a Chihuahua puppy, but he gave him his finger to clutch and called him a 'braw laddie', which he definitely wasn't then.

George was a born grandpa; put a birth announcement in the *Glasgow Herald* and the *Scotsman*, helped with night feeds, volunteered for babysitting at all times outside office hours, witnessed Jude's first step, and heard his first word – 'Ood'. Surprised it wasn't 'bugger', given my mothering style. He used to sit fiddling with his cameras, Jude on his lap, and never a peep when the demon baby grabbed a tiny precious component or swept a valuable widget off the desk. He balked at changing nappies, though. So did Rosemary, who went through the motions of being a grandma when she was sitting down – seldom when she was upright, fortunately. She was fond of Jude and bought him cutesy baby stuff, but it seemed like she wasn't keen on babies in general. Which made me wonder why she'd ever wanted me.

Then something scary happened. August sometime it was, a Saturday, hot, Jude would have been about three months old. I walked him to the shops to buy some ice cream. I was just nipping in for a moment so, rather than wake him, I shot in on my own to grab a tub. I had to queue to pay and kept glancing out at the buggy, conscious that I shouldn't have left him but fairly sure he'd be safe in 'guid auld Glasgae' and got talking to one of our neighbours. Next glance, it had gone. I hurtled out of the shop, scanning every direction. No buggy. Then, five missed heartbeats later, trucking round the corner came George, pushing it. I tanked down the pavement hollering at him for being so stupid. All he could say was, 'No, no Annie. No!' Jude was screaming. The shopkeeper came out demanding payment for the ice cream, thinking I'd scored it – even though I was a regular customer – and everyone else in the queue came out to look.

After the excitement died down, it turned out my dad had seen some woman lean over the buggy, then push it away. Naturally, he went after her and as soon as he caught up she legged it. Couldn't describe her except she had a headscarf on and was about medium height. The relevant CCTV camera hadn't been functioning, so it was impossible for the police to tell where she'd come from or gone to. What puzzled me was…

'Why were you there, Dad? I'd only gone out for ice cream.'

'Och, I just fancied stretching my legs.'

We made the news on Radio Scotland, interviewed over the phone and all. I hadn't noticed it before but soon realised that he didn't like Jude and me out of his sight. Ever. Which made it difficult when I decided to move out.

TWENTY

ANNIE – Glasgow

My teachers said I had the potential for university. Being the single parent of a feisty two year-old would not be an obstacle. It was all up to me. Lacking musical tuition, I believed I wouldn't stand a chance with the Royal Conservatoire of Scotland or Liverpool Institute for Performing Arts. So I decided on Psychology.

Why Psychology? Would you believe it was Bill Paterson? With the assistance of Dennis Potter. I watched it with Rosemary the month before Jude was born. This guy with horrible skin lay in a hospital bed and went off into fantasies. With songs. Bill was his psychiatrist. I was all set to be a psychiatrist until I found out how long I'd have to study, like get to be a doctor first. No way. So I went for Psychology instead. It was only after I got the offer that I found out you had to study almost as long to get anywhere serious. Stupid or what? So, I was the undergraduate who went to lectures and didn't drink in the Union bar – much. Studying Psychology.

I fell in love with the whole learning thing. I couldn't have been luckier, getting Peter as my tutor. Nearest thing to Bill, the imagined friend of my childhood. The whole time I was there I wanted to make Peter proud of me, as if I needed extra motivation. And there was a nursery on campus; being with so many other kids really brought Jude on. Then came Eloise.

My first sight of her was in the Humanities Faculty, walking along a corridor with several other students, all yammering at once; she was carrying a pile of books, laughing and looking at the person to her right. The sun from the end window lit her from behind, her long hair was flying out in all directions. She turned her head slightly as she passed me. I'll never forget that image of her.

A couple of days later in the refectory there was a tap on my shoulder. I looked up from the extract on the difference between caregivers' and non-caregivers' psychological health – strange detail to remember.

'Hi! I'm Eloise. Are you waiting for someone?' The accent added to her appeal.

'Er – no. I have a tutorial in half an hour but I'm not…' I gabbled on for a while hoping some cowboy from hell would brand my mouth shut. Her eyes smiled at me over her horn-rimmed specs.

'Would you like a coffee?'

That was the first time I was ever late meeting Peter.

Eloise was an Erasmus student, French, in Glasgow for six months, studying Philology. I thought it was stamp collecting but looked it up anyway. Turned out it was dead intellectual stuff about language. Why would she be interested in a no-brain like me? Our friendship developed swiftly and we decided to rent a flat together. My parents couldn't understand me wanting to abandon the financial and physical comfort of home and were concerned by how Jude would react to being uprooted. I told them that it was about independence, that Eloise and I had done our sums and that they'd still see Jude. They had to accept my decision.

Eloise, Jude and I set up home in the tiny flat in Easterhouse, all we could afford, for the rest of her six months studying in Glasgow – and then some if she could manage. But she had a fiancé in Toulouse who would eventually reclaim her. Keeping jealousy at bay, I didn't want to know any more but wondered 'Why me? What do I have that she needs – Jude?' It was a mystery the whole time we were together. We cuddled but never stepped across the boundary into sex. Lesbians afraid to commit?

The only flaw was catering. Eloise was a dedicated carnivore, being French may have had something to do with it, and I was vegetarian at the time. I didn't want Jude influenced into wanting meat. She believed he wasn't getting enough protein and I pointed out that meat was only processed plant protein. That aside, she was fabulous with Jude, taught him French, sang songs, did finger-painting. George came to the flat whenever possible to help out with anything that needed fixing. It never occurred to him or my mum that Eloise and I were anything but flatmates, even though we slept in the same bed. Must have thought we were like their favourite comedians, Morecambe and Wise, who shared a bed but were definitely not gay.

Carol-Anne was in Nottingham studying art and Shafiq was working in a family business in London. I seldom mentioned Eloise to them. After all, she was just sharing the flat, wasn't she? When either of them was in Glasgow, we'd meet at a pub or a coffee bar. Was I ashamed? No. Guarded, yes, like I was about Zeezoo.

I had someone other than Jude to rush home for. We went everywhere together, cinema, theatre, meals out, and paid fellow students to babysit Jude. How could I afford it? I couldn't. I got more and more into credit card debt. Between the fun with Eloise, the responsibility of Jude, and the money worries, studies took a back seat. Did my work suffer? It did. Peter called me in to talk about my falling grades, wanted to know if there was a problem he could help with. I told him it was just a phase; I'd get over it.

And yet it was all so brief. After about four months together, I came back with Jude one late afternoon expecting to find her home, but the place was empty. I didn't think anything of it. She'd be in the library or have an unscheduled tutorial. I gave Jude his tea, bathed him and put him to bed. When she wasn't home by seven I texted, but no response. I rang and got voicemail. My head thumped with anxiety. I took a couple of paracetamol, went to lie down in the bedroom… and saw the note addressed to me.

'Annie – I learn that your friendship is untruthful. I cannot live with you any more. I am sorry for all of us. My love to le Petit Prince (her name for Jude)– Eloise.'

Her cosmetics had gone from the dressing table. I checked the wardrobe and chest of drawers. Everything gone. What was untruthful about our friendship? Had she wanted more? For us to have a sexual relationship? Had she 'decided her fiancé was more important? Was she fed up with playing 'Mummy and Mummy'? Or did she simply not love me? She wrote 'I learn'. Had someone said something or was it just her choice of English?

Soon after came the dread – 'How am I going to manage?'. Going back to Anniesland was unthinkable. I had to cope. And the way I did it was by just cutting her out of my mind and my emotions, denying the missing parts. Like I did with Zeezoo. And borrowing.

I barely saw her at university. If we passed in a corridor she would ignore me. She wouldn't return my calls or texts and returned a letter I sent her care of the Faculty. After a month, she was gone completely. I told Jude, Rosemary, and George that she was in Toulouse caring for her sick mother. But Eloise surprised me again. Before going, she paid six months' rent in advance; the agency wouldn't say, but who else could it have been? My parents certainly had no interest in funding the Easterhouse flat. Somehow, that made her desertion even worse. I felt bought.

Then things looked up slightly. Fraser came home from Greece at the end of the season and took a bar job in Glasgow for a few months. It was a tight squeeze in the flat, and even tighter when a Greek friend of his, Nikos, joined us for Christmas, but we managed. His share of the rent was a great help, too.

TWENTY ONE

ANNIE – Symi

Angelina's quite pleased that we've offered to play tonight – I think. She already has Sammy and Sam, a male duo, who sing songs from the shows. But it's far enough into the season for people to have discovered Angelina's and for the bar to stay open until the very early hours. If Fraser and I are prepared to take the twelve thirty to two a.m. slot, she'd like us to do a few sets. He's on call for crewing tonight, so warns me I may be solo if the boats go out. A risk worth taking.

Throughout the remainder of the day, I rehearse on the terrace as insurance against having to play solo. The Syrian couple take it in turns to sit in the shade of the canopy, sipping lemonade. Their baby, Lilah, is sleeping in the air conditioning of the bedroom. With the door shut, she shouldn't be disturbed, but I keep the noise down to make sure. There are several messages of good wishes for this evening at Angelina's, including Shafiq and Shona whom I've promised a short video. No Alexis, although I can see from the two ticks that he's received my WhatsApp, making my heart drop two ticks. Clair's coming and will bring any of last week's students who've stayed on, perhaps some friends from the Symi community. Everyone works so bloody hard here in the summer, only the teenagers have the stamina for frivolities like music bars and Angelina's is at least a generation out of touch for them. Sensible Symiots use any spare time to sleep.

It happens. An alert from the coastguard: *three* boats have been sighted coming from Turkey and they need the *Giorgios* to cover at least one, probably two of them, as it can take on some fifty people at a pinch. Fraser must go. I can do this on my own. Having said which, my stomach tries to escape through every orifice. But I talk myself through it. I have busked, I have faced of all manner of people in a different life, I am solo tonight and there's the chance of Kirios Giannopoulos walking in. What it's all about, if I'm honest. *We should be flirting our pants off by now* has become an earworm. 'The refugees are more important, Annie', says one of my multiple personality conscience prompts. How could I forget it? Those tragic, desperate people out there. I remember the sailors' hymn, 'For those in peril on the sea'– if anyone is it's those poor souls.

This rescue call involves Clair, too. She'll be at the port when they arrive back, whatever time that might be. Mobile signals will be sketchy but between them, the services estimate that pickup could be anytime between half past midnight and two in the morning, so arrivals will be long after that. Clair is stern.

'Don't even think about cancelling, Annie. The refugees will keep on coming. You are allowed this.'

Jess gives enthusiastic support and agrees to do the backing for 'It's In His Kiss' which she heard last night. Clair volunteers to join in, so I take them through it. At least I'm solid on that.

Eleven o'clock and off the three of us yomp up to Angelina's, sitting punter-side while Sammy and Sam belt out numbers from the new Broadway hit *Hamilton*, *La Cage aux Folles*, and a few from *Cabaret*.

Too soon, it's my turn and I wonder how appropriate my choice is. I start with 'Skyfall', a popular opener because of the Bond connection and for Adele fans. It also sets the tone for 'Make You Feel My Love' because it unites Adele who's recorded it with people who remember Dylan, who wrote it, plus it suits my voice. Most of her tracks do. What I lacked was a tum-ti-tum singalong. I thought hard about it this afternoon and tried to engage Clair in ideas – God knows where Fraser was when I needed him – and could only think of the Kaiser Chiefs' 'Ruby'. So I introduce it tonight and try, more or less successfully, to get the audience to sing the refrain. Happily, Jess and a few others of them know the song well enough to carry it. 'It's In His Kiss' goes down fairly well with Clair and Jess *shoop-shooping* for all they're worth. For the remainder of the two sets I stretch from Queen to Joan Armatrading. But half my consciousness is on the alert for Alexis. Who doesn't appear.

The mood at Angelina's didn't hit a high. With my mind elsewhere, I may as well have been a compilation tape. Unprofessional. Clair and Jess do what they can to soothe, but their manner gives them away. I was lousy. As they help me pack up, Fraser gets through. It's been a difficult night. The Coastguard should arrive at the north end of the harbour in about an hour with the *Giorgios* and another two boats following. It will mean a walk into Yialos for the refugees but the main harbour has too many private vessels moored at night.

The cobbles are damp with condensation. We take care returning to Harkin House where we dump my stuff then head for the harbour bearing what blankets, water, and food we can plus torches to prevent twisted ankles and falls on the uneven route. Several others join us on the way down.

The people we have come to meet will have experienced uncertainty and fear, rough seas, soaking by salt water, hypothermia and, in some cases, loss – human loss. All of them will have lost financially. Clair tells me they usually have no idea where they're going when they put to sea, the smugglers just point in the direction they should head in the laden dinghy. Often, the fuel runs out or the inadequate little outboard motor is swamped by seawater and they're left to drift. It is chilling, unforgivable, that the world clucks its tongue and turns its back, thinks of these people as a nuisance when they are completely innocent of the cause of their distress.

At the waterfront we turn right for the quay, caressed by the gentle night airs. Black water slaps the stone wall, pinpoints of light across the harbour shimmer in the shifting atmosphere. In this calm, a crisis hardly seems real.

The port police have arrived ahead of us; two vehicles are already parked by the moorings. Our eyes focus towards Turkey, from where the inadequate boats were shoved westward. Excepting the police, for whom this is part of a very long day's work, the mood is quiet, exchanges brief, all our concentration on the void from which the boats will emerge. Jess seems to project her whole being towards the incoming refugees. Simultaneously, she and Clair reach out, hold hands, and I envy their instinctive connection. As if sensing my thoughts, Clair nods me to join them and the three of us huddle. Three thirty, three forty-five pass and still we are rooted. The police chat and smoke. I quell my irritation. This is their daily life. Soon, I'll go home to the relative peace of Scotland. They have a Syrian interpreter with them. He chain-smokes, too, standing apart from both groups. I wonder at his story; his manner signifies neither hope nor dread. Does his detachment come from the regularity of stress, shock, loss? PTSD? But in this moment such an assessment is too clinical. He could be profiting from the situation. I dismiss the thought instantly, not wanting to admit even the possibility.

A shout from a policeman with night binoculars. They've been spotted. From the depth of darkness, a blue light grows unsteadily – the Coastguard patrol boat. I strain to hear its engine and imagine as much as register the granular hum. It will be much faster than the *Giorgios* or the other boats. Time stretches its passage as we watch. Now, the battery of lights on the boat pick out black shapes and the odd flash of orange lifejackets. Its outline sharpens, and now we see the foredeck is laden with people, as many as the captain dares. The motor's hum is a grumble then a roar. The grey vessel slows, a huge glittering wash ahead of it as it pulls toward the mooring, the anchor chain grating rapidly.

There is a procedure. We step aside as one of the police stands ready to catch a rope, secures it around a bollard while the boat manoeuvres sideways to align with the quay, another rope flying out and attached. The passengers are lit from above but we can see their dark soaking clothes, their trauma. Once the gangplank is down, the crew help women and children first and we go forward to connect in any way we can. The *Giorgios* is almost forgotten in the immediacy of this moment. But someone yells sight of it and my insides jump. Is Fraser OK? In such moments of distress, we all look out for our own, selfishly, naturally. Survival of the genes, the tribe.

Shaking away the sensation, I hold out my arms to a couple, the woman howling, loss clear in her anguish, her body language, the man encased in pain, holding her but unable to help. I wrap blankets around them, try to convey sympathy. There are about twenty refugees and slightly fewer of us. We don't have enough volunteers or provisions for the numbers who are, undoubtedly, arriving. The newly arrived shuck their now useless lifejackets into an untidy heap.

Another engine. It is the *Giorgios*. Before I can turn to look, the interpreter joins us, speaking rapid Arabic. I wait. Only the man replies. His wife has subsided to exhausted sobs. I hold her hand, brush the hair from her eyes beneath her black hijab. The interpreter turns to me.

'Their child, a boy, was sick. When they got in the boat, they saw he had died. The smuggler threw his body in the water. I have told them they will be taken into Yialos for processing.' Questions fill my mouth but the interpreter moves on. The facts are cold, the truth harsh. Nothing more to be done. Jess calls me and I have to leave the couple, wrapped in their blankets and in their grief.

She is with a young boy and girl who seem to be alone. The interpreter said the boy, Sayid, is nine and the girl, Maya, five. They are from Aleppo, their parents are in Germany, and they were travelling with their aunt but have become separated. Jess and I exchange looks that decide who'll take whom. We keep both children within reach of one another. I crouch to see Maya's lowered face. She is tiny, probably as small as I was at her age. She still has her lifejacket on and won't let go of the sodden toy rabbit she clutches against her chest long enough for me to take it off. I whisper to the bunny then put my ear to its head and manage through our conversation, bunny and I, to persuade Maya to let me remove the orange jacket. As I mop her face and wet hair with a tissue, I kiss her forehead and feel a little arm creeping round my neck. I hug her tight, pick her up and she wraps her legs around my waist, limpet-tight. At this moment, I would adopt her in a heartbeat. Barely has the thought gelled than I see, just beyond her black curls, a tall figure, the light behind him turning his blond hair into a halo. He, too, carries a child, followed by its mother who carries another. As he passes there's a shared moment that's more than kind eyes for both of us.

I realise Maya has peed on me.

'Annie!' Fraser follows Alexis, leading a group of young men, all stripping off life jackets. He directs them to the orange heap, then asks me, 'Where's Clair?' His first thought. I glance to where she is engaged with parents and three children.

'You all right, Fraser?'

'Aye. See you back home.'

Four of us sit on the terrace, drinking tea as the dawn grows to sunrise over Turkey. We are too drained to talk. Sayid and Maya are in Clair's room, asleep at last. She, Jess and I will, somehow, fit in my room with Jude.

As the first strong rays strike my face, there is an incoming text from Alexis: We must meet today – lunch? AG'.

I text back 'Yes, ne, ja – when, where? AB'.
It is my fourth day on Symi.

TWENTY TWO

FRASER – Christmas 2008. Glasgow

I travelled back to Glasgow in November to spend some time with Annie and the we'an. Christmas Day 2008 at Villa Buchanan in Anniesland was a small affair, even with the addition of my friend Nikos from Symi. Rosemary and George made him welcome in their way. But Nikos was used to more effusive displays of greeting and was concerned that he was unwelcome. I did my best to reassure him.

'It's not you, pal. We're a miserable race of buggers. Blame it on the English.'

'Why?'

''Cos we wouldn't have an excuse otherwise.' For which I got a cushion thrown at me by Annie.

I was on a kind of a high, despite spending Christmas with the folks. Clair had just invited Nikos and me up to the West Coast for Hogmanay. I felt like I was thirteen, not the wrong side of thirty-four. As it happened, that invitation was to change all, well almost all, our lives for the better.

Jude was five, cheeky as they come and thoroughly spoilt by his grandparents, regardless of my input. Rosemary and George had given him a small-boy-sized bike with training wheels for Christmas which he wanted to ride round the living room immediately. Other gifts were a minor distraction, apart from the Spiderman outfit, which he could use straight away. But once it was on, the biking demands started again. Annie clearly knew if she didn't do something soon, she'd be relegated to the kitchen doing womanly things while we guys took him to the Temple Park playground. She posed a question for which there was only one answer, an implicit one.

'How about I take Jude to the park with his grandpa and you two guys stay and help Mum with the lunch?' She eyeballed Rosemary. 'And easy on the beverages.' No argument allowed.

George and Annie took off with the boy racer while Nikos and I were on sprout peeling duties with Rosemary. To be fair, even if she was stocious, she'd know her way round the kitchen better than my father. The orange juice she wielded was highly suspicious. A small sip while she delved into a cupboard confirmed it was practically 40% proof. She staggered back to the kitchen table brandishing a jar of cranberry sauce.

'D'ye know, it makes an awfy pleasan' change to have my darlin' son'n and – andanan – another attractive young man in the house!'

'C'mon, now, Mum, that's enough.' But Rosemary was on a roll. Infused with alcohol, she was priceless and horribly indiscreet.

'I was a flower child, y'know, Nik-olos. But I went to seed through carelessus – cresslessens – ach – bad luck!' And she began again the story of Reading Festival, at which she saw Genesis, Aerosmith, and Georgie Fame, and people dived off Caversham Bridge into the Thames. I nodded along with it, acknowledging as I did how much of an effect she'd had on my musical taste, and positive to be fair. Before the sprouts were done, however, Rosemary was sauced and I forgot her influence for a while.

The biking party arrived back to raucous laughter from the kitchen and the table still not laid. Spiderman, thinly disguised as a small person in a padded coat and jester hat, burst in on we three tipplers, mittens flailing from the elastic down his sleeves.

'I only fell off four times! Why are you all red, Grandma?' Why, indeed? Rosemary pissed? Who'd've thought?

The meal was disastrous by culinary standards and right off the catastrophe scale by any others. Jude was too excited to eat and demanded absolute attention. Rosemary fell asleep mid-sentence, head propped on one hand, hiccupping gently between snores. I hauled her upstairs while Annie shouldered Jude and transported him, writhing and roaring, from the room and, much against her usual judgement, sat him in front of a video with a glass of pop.

Nikos and George were left alone in the dining room with the part-burnt, part-glutinous mess that was their dinner. When Annie and I returned, George, in purple party hat, had partitioned every charred scrap to the edge of his plate and Nikos was contemplating his wine thoughtfully. Seeing us, George remembered his manners and broke the silence through his pepper-and-salt moustache.

'Olympiakos. Gai guid team.'

On the way back to Easterhouse in the car, Nikos brushed off any apologies.

'In Greece a good celebration requires at least one broken nose and a divorce. Often the same people.'

Back at the flat, once Jude was clamped into bed, Annie made Horlicks for three and plopped a shot of Nikos's twelve-star Metaxa into each mug. We toasted 'Almost over for another year'. There was a thud at the front door. I got it and discovered a poacher's feast, by the look of it – rough cuts of meat, bits of bird and rabbit – spilling out of a sodden paper package. The stench was gut-churning and the doormat was soaked in blood. I went back in for a bin bag and a cloth, told Annie not to go out there, was very firm. She went, anyway.

'What the f –?'

'Annie, I said… Look, it was meant for someone else. Need to wash my hands.' I took the bag and mat down to the bins at the back and dumped them while Nikos washed down the door.

It must have been a misdirected sick joke on a neighbour; why would anyone do that to Annie? Nikos wished us goodnight and headed for the cupboard-sized space that was normally Jude's room. She and I sat in silence in the orange glow from the gas fire, passing the 'festivities' through emotional sieves. Finally, Annie gave into tiredness.

'Well, that's me for my bed. Wonder has Rosemary sobered up yet? She'll have a cracking headache tomorrow.'

I cleared the throw from the futon sofa. 'Och, George knows the routine.'

She helped me pull the frame out and make the bed. 'And that's a good thing?'

'OK, how serious is it, Annie? Mum? Alcoholics Anonymous in the frame?'

'Doubt it. She has a new drinking friend.'

'You're not saying it's an affair?'

'It's a woman, Blanche – Blanche McSomething. Anything's possible, I suppose. She's not from Glasgow. Don't know where.'

It was a peculiar setup. Mum had met this woman in the checkout queue at Morrisons. They'd struck up a conversation, gone for a coffee, and had been meeting occasionally ever since. Annie had no idea how long, said she hadn't paid that much attention to how often Mum'd said 'Blanche, this' and 'Blanche, that'. It was the sort of constant remark you end up blanking out. But she did suspect that first time they met was probably the only one where coffee was the favoured tipple.

It defeated me, Rosemary and George's set-up.

'What's the matter with our parents? They've never been close since I can remember. And they're getting worse.'

Annie knocked back her spiked Horlicks, sat on the futon and patted it for me to sit next to her.

'Fraser, this is going to be difficult for you to hear and for me to say. But given the Christmas Day it's been, it can't get much worse.'

'Gawd, that sounds ominous, oh sister of mine.'

'You must have done biology at school at some point?'

Major mental readjustment.

'Ye what?!'

'Being serious. Do you remember any of it, Fraser?'

'We did birds and bees, if that's what you mean? What's that got to do with anything?'

She headed for the Metaxa and sloshed us another couple of measures. Definitely worrying.

'It was something about male preferences that came up at uni, a theory about breeding selection. According to a lot of studies, it was accepted that – that two blue-eyed people wouldn't have a hazel-eyed child. Consequently –'

'George can't be my father.'

I made the statement with no surprise; momentous though it was, the news wasn't startling.

'Don't look so worried, Annie. Do I look gutted? All that puzzles me is – surely, he must have been suspicious? Even dull old George?'

'Maybe he knew. Or maybe Rosemary was sleeping with him and the – your – father, too. Sorry for that image.'

I remember leaning back, feeling something like relief.

'It explains a lot about my upbringing.'

Why she chose that moment to tell me, I don't know. She asked a couple of times after that if I wanted to take it further and I said I'd let her know if I did. I suppose Rosemary was the one I should really have talked to but I haven't – so far. Maybe I'm afraid she doesn't know who my father was. I wonder how much Annie's told Jude about his, that is if she can, or whether she'll ever want to find out about her own. Odd kind of three way bonding we have. All of us with a question mark for a father. And for a mother, too, in Annie's case.

TWENTY THREE

ANNIE – Glasgow, Oban, and Kilachlan

Maggie understood without questioning, cared without smothering and, when I needed it, she was my escape. I was the child Rosemary chose but Maggie was the mother I would have chosen.

She lived in Kilachlan, about ten miles from Oban. Harkin Croft was more like the witch's house in *Hansel and Gretel*, pretty enough to be made from sweeties. Maggie wasn't a witch, though, she was a fairy godmother with a sense of humour. The way I got to know her was through Fraser who'd not long got together with Clair.

One weekend, just after New Year, I borrowed Mum's car and took Jude up to Oban to meet my pal Rory from uni. He'd dropped out before the second year to 'live on the land' on Mull but came to the mainland occasionally to visit his folks, get his washing done and fill his belly, so he'd never stopped being a student, really. Fraser asked to tag along with me so he could go on up to visit Maggie. She invited the three of us to lunch the next day.

While we were eating Jude began scratching like a maniac. Chickenpox. Just like that. No spots in his bath the night before, next day, scarlet and pus polka dots. Maggie insisted we both stay with her until he was better. She was brilliant at distracting him from the itching. Games with the dogs, drawing, telling stories, singing daft songs. We stayed for two weeks. Neither of us wanted to go home. Clair rang every day. I hadn't met her then. When I answered the phone a couple of times, she was friendly enough. Maybe it was me, but I thought she sounded a bit forced.

When I was back in Easterhouse, Maggie and I rang each other several times and talked for hours – or, I talked and she listened while I unburdened. Fraser had decided to move in with Clair in Guildford and I was feeling pretty stretched renting the flat now neither he nor Eloise were around. Out of the blue, Maggie suggested Jude and I might be happier in Kilachlan with him at the local school and me doing distance learning. The words were barely out before I wanted to pack our bags and go. But what I said was that I'd consider it and speak to my tutor. Peter thought it was, given all the circumstances (that he knew of), a positive move, so I decided I'd do it.

But before I'd had a chance to ring her with the news, Maggie had a stroke. Clair was in Florida because her stepfather had died so Fraser took the call in Guildford. I dumped Jude on his grandparents, borrowed Mum's car, met Fraser off the train at Glasgow Central and we raced up to the hospital in Oban. Clair made it from Florida in two days. The three of us stayed in Harkin Croft, taking turns to sit with Maggie in the hospital. Now Maggie needed help, I had another good reason to move up to Kilachlan. Unfortunately, I was trying so hard to appear practical about it, I upset Clair. It seemed to her I was muscling in on her family. Fraser was furious with me. One morning I joined Clair on the beach and tried to smooth things over, told her about London and Jude's father. Apart from Maggie – and Shona – she's the only person who knows it all. She softened at once. My staying with Maggie would solve a lot of problems for us all.

It sounds as though it was a straightforward process moving in with Maggie. Far from it. Negotiating with uni was the easiest part. Peter still backed me, so long as caring for Maggie wasn't a burden too far. But she had daily carers to help her physically, so Jude and I would be, simply, company and there for emergencies. Lectures were on webcam, now, and I could email essays. So long as I could guarantee to get in for a tutorial once a month it would be easy to make the switch.

Rosemary and George were my biggest problem. They'd be heartbroken not to see Jude so often and royally pissed off with me for being the cause. Also, I thought they'd be jealous of Maggie and resent me looking after her instead of them. I called Carol-Anne, who said:

'Taking Jude from them? Christ on a bike! You're a dead woman.'

'Cazzie, you're about as much use as a blowtorch on an Arctic Roll.'
We decided the problem needed alcohol and pasta to arrive at a solution. She came up from Nottingham that weekend.

'You've one heap of shit to shift, Annie. How's Jude about it?'

'Already packed his Spiderman suit.'
Two bottles in, she came up with the gem, 'You could always tell them you've got TB and you need the sea air.'

'Oh great, Cazzie. And what do I say when I don't turn green and expire waving a camellia?'

She sat there and drained almost an entire glass. I remember sensing the seismic waves like she was about to erupt. I wasn't wrong. I can't remember it word for word but it went something like…

'What do you want? Christ's sake, Annie! You're my best friend and I love you. But God help me, you get right on my tits, sometimes!'

'What? Where's all this come from?'

'"Me, me, me, me –" your mantra's never changed. From when Fraser went travelling and we all had to feel heartbroken for poor wee abandoned Annie.'

'Come on, that was –'

'Then the adoption drama. How old were we? Eleven, twelve? Shafiq and me did everything we could think of to help you through it, didn't focus on anything else for months. But d'you know what? I don't think you were that bothered.'

'How can you say that? It was colossal!'

'No – no – because you'd seen what an also ran I was in my family and you were Princess Annie Buchanan of Anniesland as far as your mum and dad were concerned.'

'Oh, now you're just –'

'Is it not true? Ten times the pocket money of everyone else, new clothes, new shoes – no hand me downs for Annie –'

'That's just envy, you don't –'

'What was next – oh yes, the misunderstood rock star, knocking around with that Niall weirdo and, suddenly, I had no bezzie mate, well, no female bezzie mate, any more – until you were grounded, then you wanted me back.'

'You weren't interested in music!'

'But I was still your mate! You just dropped me until I was useful again – then you buggered off to London. But you didn't want me there, either, did you? Because it was *your* drama. I was just the numpty who stayed at home being interrogated by your parents, my parents, the school, the police – oh – till the dramatic homecoming of the prodigal daughter, *pregnant*. You really did have the spotlight and the star treatment then, didn't you? Special lessons and attention from teachers, fast-tracked into uni because of what you'd been through. Jesus, it made me squirm with pissed-offedness!'

'You make it sound as though I planned it all.'

'Not the minute details, but the big picture, that was definitely you. The whole giving birth thing – Holy Martyr Annie for her bloody suffering. You may have been adopted and incredibly precious, but you'd had enough contact with my family to know that some women lob out a kid every year or so, nothing special –'

'It's not my fault if people are sexually incontinent at the say so of the bloody Pope!'

'Oh – that's your Daddy George talking there, isn't it? How did racist George cope with you having a brown baby, eh? It was like you'd won the jackpot. You almost whooped for joy – because of the racism he'd suffer. Or you might. Right. More attention points.'

'How bloody dare you! Me? Exploit racism?'

'Yes, you. So, you must have been bloody disappointed when it didn't happen. Not with George, or your friends, or at uni.'

'You honestly believe that?'

'Well, weren't you? Now you've got your tutor panting to get into your knickers and some rich besom way up the coast ready to solve all your money problems. And it's *still* not enough. You're *still* turning it into a drama. You know what, Annie? You're the centre of your own universe, of Jude's and your parents'. Not mine. Settle for it.'

Inevitably we drank a lot more wine, in silence probably because I don't remember much else. I think the outburst is something we've both put in another of those locked drawers. It was too big, would destroy our friendship if we ever admitted it happened. We've had a few tiffs since then but nothing we couldn't get over. Sometimes, though, just sometimes, I hear her words knocking to get out.

By Monday morning we'd achieved two atomic hangovers and not a lot else. Jude was late for school and I still had to face my parents. When Rosemary made the usual phone call about Sunday lunch I astonished her by saying yes.

There were tears from her and a heavy outward breath from George. I guessed it wouldn't be tactful to ask for help with the move. One of Carol-Anne's brothers lent me his Transit van and she came up again to drive Jude, me, and our gear to Kilachlan the following weekend. A fateful one for her, as it happened, because that's when she met my mate Rory again (on one of his home comfort trips), saw him as an escape from Graphic Design, and moved into his steadings on Mull.

TWENTY FOUR

ANNIE – Symi

We meet at Giannis's fish restaurant. Long legs poking out beyond the shade of the umbrella, crossed in the sunlight. A spiralling pattern of smoke. Sunglasses. Hair still wet – from the shower? Swimming?

'Hallo, Annie. Hoe gaat het?' Dutch. I assume it's a 'how are you?' and answer in Greek. At least that's another language.

'Kála, efháristoh. Essí?'

'Kála, kála.' He reaches out to me instead of standing, as though we're already familiar. I like that. I hardly have to bend to hug. But we don't hug. We kiss. On the lips. His moustache and beard are surprisingly soft. The tobacco is intense, but I sort of like it. He keeps hold of my hands.

'It was wonderful to see you there, last night. Even in the middle of all the trauma.'

Lava bubbles inside me.

'Me, too, you – I mean me, you, too–'

Anyone would think English was my second language. He twinkles at my clumsy tongue then runs his fingers across his scalp.

'Sorry about the hair. I went swimming by the hotel.' People swim at Harani near Hotel Nireus, just off the harbour. My mouth gallops off without me –

'I slipped down the metal steps there, last year. Took the skin off my back.'

'Ouch. Sorry I wasn't there to rub antiseptic cream on it.'

We share a moment of 'Who made the crassest remark?' and dissolve with laughter. Relief. He asks then orders me a beer, hands me a menu. Doesn't know I'm vegan. I don't want it to be an obstacle. There is almost nothing I can eat – perhaps fava bean dip? Gigantes beans? I look across. The sunglasses are tipped back. Those eyes. I'm lost.

'Annie, I have to go to Leros. Today.' Oh. No small talk, then. Oh oh oh.

'Will you be back?'

'Not for a few weeks, I would think. Until we have someone in post. Leros is our Operations Centre.'

'Ah.'

'So I wanted to ask you – do you think you might join me there? Even for a small while?'

Yes, ne, ja!

'I don't know. There's Jude.'

'I understand. He's welcome, too.'

No! Ochi! Nee! 'Thank you. I need to speak to–'

'Of course, Annie. There's a lot for you to consider.' Like hell. Clair and Fraser can handle Jude for a week or so.

'I've considered it. I'm coming to Leros. By the way, I'm vegan.'

He laughs. 'You would be.'

Yes, he's definitely some years older than me, I've decided. I'm curious as to what he's done with them – and with whom. There'll be baggage. It's our second date, so it's reasonable to find out. I decide to prompt.

'Tell me about your happiest memory.'

'Ah, you're using some psychological technique on me. Are you Freudian or Jungian?'

'Neither, trying to get to know you.'

'OK. Happiest memory… I suppose it was the first time I snorkelled. In Blefouti with my parents. I was about four, I think.'

'You're a water baby, then.'

'If we're talking astrology, no, I'm an air sign. Libra. What are you, Ms Buchanan?'

'Ach, I don't believe in all that.'

'Are you telling me you don't know?'

''Course I do. But you're not to laugh…Virgo.'

He laughs. Obviously not a gentleman because he goes on to ask,

'And is giving birth your happiest memory, Ms Virgo?'

The cheek of him!

'No. It was a wet night in Paisley. My happiest memory, I mean!'

I don't give him time to ask me to expand.

'My turn. What were you before you became – Fraser's words, not mine – a professional saint?'

'Ouch. I deserved that. I was an architect.'

That's a massive change of direction, I'm thinking.

'So why –?'

'Why did I change career? Because I realised how serious the Syrian crisis was. I was in a position to do something really useful and I knew enough wealthy people to ask for funding. So we set up NRH.'

'We?'

'Several of us,' he says, smiling. I've been caught out fishing so move on rapidly.

'I was going to ask you for your saddest moment, but there must have been so many.'

'I know exactly what it was. Remember the toddler who drowned on the Turkish coast and became a photo opportunity? A celebrity in death. How many people knew his name? It was Aylan Shenu. How soon was he forgotten? Along with all the others? Only nine months ago. And yet, if a Western child goes missing… Recognising that was my saddest moment. One of my angriest, too. Hey, that's a conversation for another time,

Annie, not as I'm just about to leave.'

This time, I walk him to the Rhodes ferry, carry his camera for him; not that he couldn't manage it, but I thought it was nice symmetry, me carrying his stuff. We say a long, smoochy goodbye, which promises more and better things to come, and he leaves me, floundering on dry land. I don't wave him off. Not my style.

He'll need a time to settle in to work on Leros. Much as I'd like to jump into his backpack and go with him, I must spend time with Jude, with Fraser, Clair, and Jess and get stuck into more volunteering here. Besides, the more experience I get, the more help I'll be on Leros. And absence makes…

I'm confident that Clair and Fraser can handle Jude for a week or ten days, I should let them know as soon as possible. Can't go back to the house yet, though, my head and body are buzzing with Alexis, so I head for Nobby's and sit with a large Mythos, thinking about him and about Leros.

As a first-year at uni I was in Peter's tutorial group; he asked us to watch a Cutting Edge documentary, *Island of Outcasts*, on YouTube. We couldn't quite take in what we were seeing; it was about a psychiatric hospital where patients had been transported en masse, sometimes without even notifying families. They took psychopaths, people with learning disabilities, patients with depression and other conditions – and treated them all alike. Some were even mentally well and physically disabled. Apart from two qualified professionals, the staff were mainly local people, untrained and with little or no knowledge of mental health care. Unbelievably, many of the patients were chained naked, washed down with hoses and left in the sun all day with hardly any shade. This wasn't in the nineteenth century, though, it was the 1980s on a Greek island called Leros. After the hospital's practices were exposed, the authorities closed it down. The scandal wasn't the fault of anyone from Leros but of central government outsourcing irresponsibly. Peter asked us to make notes on cause and effect of the situation.

You can imagine our responses: causes centring on ethics, mindset, underfunding, geography – a mainland plus two hundred and seventy-seven inhabited islands (we were all proud of our homework on that). The list of effects on the incarcerated patients ran on endlessly and extended to third parties including family breakdown, guilt, post-traumatic stress disorder in relatives and staff… on and on we went, high on our insightful – hindsightful – analyses. Peter waited until we faltered to a stop.

'You've all formed reasonable hypotheses, but overlooked an important omission. The interplay between knowledge and compassion, which was a major flaw in the implementation of the project and in its outcomes. The job of clinical psychologist is to practise knowledge tempered by compassion and compassion tempered by knowledge.' Then he laughed. 'Compassion does not give you permission to become emotionally involved with your patients, by the way'.

I think about that project with a lot of irony these days. We have bucketsful of knowledge and boundless compassion at grassroots, but a lot less of it at management level. And practically none of either, politically. Especially when it comes to funding.

Even though I saw that documentary, I can still hardly believe it. It had the sordid fascination of a horror movie. Going to Leros and seeing the hospital building first-hand may give it more credibility.

I sit there in Nobby's, keeping a wary eye out for Fraser, mind all over the place, and I text, text, text away until my phone rings. It's Shona getting back to a message of a few minutes ago – that quick! Asks about Jude and Fraser. I describe the rescue last night. We have a long talk, mainly about what's going down on Symi but I mention Alexis's organisation and that I'm going to help out on Leros for a bit. She, it seems, is at a loose end and I hear myself suggesting she might do some volunteering in the islands. What the…? She says it would be good to meet in Greece, she'll think about it.

More immediately, I should spend some time with Maya and Sayid who've been with Clair and Jude for a few hours. I wander back via the supermarket up near Harkin House. It's my turn to do dinner.

Unbelievable. By the time I arrive at Clair's there's an email from Shona waiting, saying she'd actually been thinking about volunteering with refugees for a while and our conversation's given her the nudge she needed. She'll be over in a couple of weeks and perhaps we could meet somewhere? Wow! Wonder where she means – Symi or Leros? It would be amazing to see her again in person after all these years of emails, Facebook, WhatsApp messaging – and the occasional phone call. But Leros? How will that work with me and Alexis? I'll reply to the email later, maybe suggest Symi would be better. But when?

Clair has Sayid and Maya busily creating at the table on the terrace. Jude lost interest a while ago, Clair says, and wandered off to find Andy and Erik who are helping Erik's dad paint his boat. She sees my look of alarm.

'Don't worry, he's wearing his swim shorts and an old T-shirt nearly down to his knees that can be thrown away.'

The children have paper, pencils, crayons, paint, glue, cardboard, all sorts of bits and pieces, an episode of *Blue Peter* in the making. They seem very absorbed. Sayid is a little domineering. Whether it's his age, his culture, or his nature is difficult to tell. But it doesn't seem to bother Maya, who generally takes his advice. He is in loco parentis, in a sense. I may be no artist but I'm interested in art therapy; I wonder what kind of images they will produce.

The Syrian couple's baby, something over a year old, I'd guess, has recovered from her fever and sits in the shade on a blanket, carefully shredding a hole in it under the loving gaze of her parents.

I fiddle a bit with the arty stuff to no great effect and manage, in dribs and drabs, to give a sanitised version of the Leros project to Clair. She, God love her, is immediately enthusiastic, even says she and Fraser had been wondering how I could get some time out and yes, they'll take on Jude. So that's it, settled. I am going to Leros. Only question is, when? As for Shona, Clair would be delighted to meet her if she's thinking of coming to Symi. Clair, alone, knows the origin of the friendship; it can be handled, she says, so long as Shona remains as discreet as we are.

I've been interested in Leros since uni. Come to think of it, I'm sure I told Shona all about the island back then. It's an unfortunate collision, her coming to volunteer now that Alexis has loomed over my horizon but I can't put her off. I compose a careful email suggesting Symi as a better destination than Leros, that Clair and Fraser can help her with volunteering work, and that I'll meet her here when I get back, whenever that may be. Let her decide. Suppose I'll have to play it by ear after that, only thing I can do.

Sayid produces a painting of men with guns by a raging sea with sharks in it. Maya portrays what must be her family group. The tiny, distant figures are, I suspect, her parents.

TWENTY FIVE

ANNIE – Kilachlan

Two days in Kilachlan were enough to acclimatise Jude to the wonder of sea, forest, hills, and mountains. He loved it, especially playing with Maggie's West Highland Terriers, Jack and Tatty, on the strand. The beach had everything for a small boy, surf to splash in – even in March – white sand to build castles, rock pools for terrorising crabs and the occasional scattering of Highland cattle, about which he was astonishingly cool for a townie. For me, the air, space and light were bliss after Easterhouse.

We took longer to adjust to life with Maggie. The stroke hadn't affected her mental acuity, but her poor right hand was a tight claw and her right leg dragged. Worse was her speech problem. I saw the real Maggie in there amidst all the malfunctions that upset her so much. I knew to give her time to get the words out, to massage her right hand, to help her with physiotherapy exercises. I took out some books on speech therapy from university library; it was interesting and useful to know the best ways to help her. Through it all, apart from the odd outburst of frustration, Maggie never lost her warmth or her sense of humour.

'What a poser.' My first reaction to Donald Mudie. We were on Kirk Street. I'd driven Maggie into the village so she could manage a short walk round, me supporting her. She didn't want to be seen in a wheelchair. This dude in a thousand-pound flying jacket, designer chinos, and green wellies stoats up, completely out of place in Kilachlan and not sounding or behaving like he belongs – like David Cameron in a Benefits Office. Despite which, Maggie told me later, he'd grown up there – when he wasn't at boarding school.

'Miss Harkin, marvellous to see you up and about!' He took her hand, but he was looking at me. 'And who is your friend?'

I shook hands with him.

'I'm Annie. Staying for a while.' I'd already been there a month.

'Well, ceud mìle fàilte, Annie. I'm Donald Mudie. If there's anything I can do to help, anything at all, do call Mudie House. They can always get me.'

'OK. Thanks.'

'Lovely to see you, Miss Harkin. Annie.'

Annoying thing one: he was an arrogant tosser. Annoying thing two: he was fit. Maggie gave me a look that said, 'Watch it, Annie'.

She filled me in on Donald; one of twins with a sister as plain as he was handsome, he took after his father, Archie, in brains, and his mother, Isobel, in looks so got the best of both worlds. Isobel worshipped him, danced round him like a puppy – except now she didn't always recognise him. He was a 'something in the city', meaning London. Forty-ish, married to a gorgeous airhead. History repeating itself, Maggie said, because even before the onset of dementia Isobel, while beautiful, was not 'intellectually driven'. Archie and Maggie were friends of many years; he'd supported her through the death of her great love, Julia. He was, she said, a rogue, but a generous one.

I knew first about Maggie's partner, Julia, from Clair. A love story that had ended amidst the tragedy of bigotry even worse than the racism Jude had encountered. Having been together some twenty years, they were separated by Julia's outraged parents as their daughter lay dying. Maggie wasn't allowed to visit the hospital or attend the funeral. There were pictures of Julia around the croft. Jude said I looked a bit like her.

For such a little roustabout, Jude was an instinctive carer. I wondered whether he might have a future in healthcare as a nurse or physiotherapist, doctor even? I found his first day at school in Kilachlan as nerve-wracking as his first in Glasgow. He was bright, gregarious, excitable, and sometimes rougher than he meant to be. ADHD was not diagnosed, though. I hoped the teachers would recognise his essential goodness. In those first days, I needn't have worried, he settled in happily and started making friends. After six weeks or so, it was another story.

Racism is comparatively rare in the Highlands and Islands. In the cities there have been incidents with EU immigrants and some Asians who were, absurdly, accused of taking jobs. It never crossed my mind that, in this small community, my little son might be a victim. His best friends at school, Ben and Liam, began picking on him and were overheard telling him to go back to where he came from. They were cautioned by the headteacher, made to apologise, and their parents were summoned. Therein lay the root cause, parents instilling prejudice at home. The problem with hauling the families into the school was that it seemed to fan their prejudice.

That spring, there was a daffodil display worthy of Wordsworth in front of the croft. It lasted well into April. One morning Jude and I stepped out the front door and were stunned to see the head of every single flower cut and fallen in the dew. It was so shocking I could hardly breathe. Instantly, I identified the culprits in my head and felt guilty that I'd brought this trouble to Maggie's door. Then I felt angry with myself for taking on their guilt. How could they involve our darling Maggie in this disgusting behaviour? Wally Scrymgeour, Maggie's gardener and neighbour, lived a few doors away. I knocked on his door and asked him if he could get to the croft discreetly and fast. As we walked to school, I concocted some story for Jude about preparing the garden for the summer, hoping all the while that Maggie wouldn't wake up and see it before Wally could get there.

When I got back, Wally had started clearing the scene of 'deflowering'.

'I'm awfy sorry, Annie. I'll get it all away before Miss Harkin's about.' Fortunately, Maggie was only just waking. I took her a cup of tea and told her to have a little lie-in. Then I used the time look up the local police number, walk to the top of the field where the signal was better, and report the vandalism. Same old same old. Without evidence they could do nothing.

Maggie noticed that the glorious display had finished but Wally colluded with my story about readying the garden with the slight elaboration that the trumpets had all withered. Being so uncertain of herself, she accepted it.

I texted Carol-Anne, who agreed that the racist parents must have had something to do with it. They already avoided me at the school and in the village. It was a horrible feeling.

A week later a postcard of some daffodils came addressed to me with the message in capitals: 'That will teach you not to take things for granted!' I snatched it from the doormat to keep it from Maggie and Jude. The postmark was unclear and, again, the police could do nothing. Wally and his wife, Nessie, popped round more often than usual which was something of a comfort. Life calmed down in Kilachlan and there were no more outside problems for a while.

Despite the damage the stroke had done, Maggie progressed well with her speech and, after some months, was able to walk down to the beach, holding on to me while Jude careered around with the dogs. I like to think the stimulation of having us with her played a large part in her recovery.

Of course, she had a lot of help from therapists, physio and speech, and also from Clair and Jess who were up every three or four weeks. I always worried, then, that Clair was never totally happy about Maggie's arrangement with me.

About a month after my brief encounter with the Mudie heir, the landline rang and I heard this whole pound-of-plums-in-the-mouth voice.

'Annie, Donald Mudie here. I'm in Glasgow on business and wondered if you'd care for a bite to eat?'

'In Glasgow?'

'Not unless I'm the devil and you want to sup with a very long spoon. I was thinking more of Oban.'

'I can't.'

'Can't what, Miss Buchanan?'

'Have dinner with you.'

'I haven't said when, yet.'

'Ever. I can't get a babysitter. So I can't ever have dinner with you, Mr Mudie.'

'Leave it with me. And work up an appetite.'

Next day, when Nessie Scrymgeour came in for the washing, she took me aside.

'Mr Mudie says you're in want of a night off and he's asked me to sit with Jude and Miss Harkin this evening.'

I was instantly suspicious. 'Donald Mudie?'

'No, his father. Archie. Said he'd pick you up at six thirty.' When I told Maggie she said that with Isobel sinking into Alzheimer's, Archie would probably be glad of some company.

'But why me? Why not you?'

'Perhaps he wants to ask you about giving a hand now and again.'

'But I could walk across. Why's he picking me up?'

'Because he's old school – and the Range Rover doesn't get many outings these days.'

Quite a coincidence, I thought, son then father calling. Dinner up at the House would be an experience, though. And if helping out with Isobel meant earning a bit more cash…

I dressed as smartly as was possible, given my student wardrobe. Archibald Mudie turned up at six thirty and parped on the horn like Mr Toad, but instead of heading back home he turned south.

'Mr Mudie, we're going the wrong way.'

'I think you'll find, my dear, that we are heading exactly the right way.'

'Mr Mudie, are you kidnapping me for your son?'

'Oh, I like that, 'kidnapping'! Not as such, just connecting with a little of the old spirit. Now be a good girl and –'

'Mr Mudie, don't patronise me. Take me back to Harkin Croft, please.'

'Sorry, no can do. Just make a young man very happy and have dinner with him. How can that hurt?'

So I was delivered, like warm meat on a plate, to Donald Mudie at one of the classier restaurants in Oban. Much as I objected to the subterfuge and the upper-class arrogance as I saw it, I enjoyed the great – vegetarian – food. Donald started by apologising, admitted to being married, and asked if we could be friends. He seemed a hundred years older than me in worldliness although he wasn't much beyond Fraser's age. I tried being po-faced to start with and let him do the talking but, being me, after a couple of glasses of wine I forgot and spilled tales of my musical youth, my psychology course, and the funnier dialogue between Jude and Maggie. He said very little about his life in London and nothing about his wife.

I still didn't like the voice or the air of entitlement, but I had to admit I was having a good time. Suddenly it was ten and I felt pumpkin mode coming on.

'Don't worry, I'll get you straight home. I'm staying up with the ancestors tonight.' He paid the bill, which would have been astronomical so I didn't make an eejit of myself by offering to split it. Then he dropped me back at the croft. In his Porsche. Actually came round to the passenger side to open the door. That was the nearest to anything physical.

'Thank you, Annie. It's been fun. Perhaps we could do it again

sometime?'
Then Nessie came out the front door, putting on her headscarf, said all was well and struggled into the Porsche for a lift home. Was she in on it, too? When I told Maggie about it, she waggled a warning finger. I was adamant.

'It's definitely not likely to happen again.'

'Not likely, eh?'

It did happen again, though, in Oban, Glasgow and a few other places besides. He never touched me, apart from a peck on the cheek which I never returned. Talk about 'treat 'em mean, keep 'em keen'– he loved it. And it gave me a taste of a different life. Why not?

TWENTY SIX

ANNIE – Symi

My contact with refugees, here, has made me understand the disengagement many of them present. Hundreds have been separated from close family. Many are young men whose relatives helped them escape from being recruited or killed by IS. There are families with children, grannies and grandpas, so desperate they'd risk floating across in a plastic paddling pool if that was the only option. Some have a sad, small collection of belongings with them. Few have any money left over from what they've paid to unscrupulous smugglers. One boy had been clubbed round the head by them and there are rumours of murder. I've started a diary. Basis of a thesis?

Wednesday. 8 a.m. Families arrived soaking wet from crossing. Kids in shock. Some with parents, some alone – most won't eat. A couple of refugees interpreted & helped with them. Assisted aid workers, sourcing towels, dry clothes, food & toys. Took all day.

Thursday. Kids who arrived yesterday running about & playing. Amazing resilience, but what's being suppressed? German doctor on holiday came to centre 11 a.m. to offer help. She was still there 1 a.m. when I left.

Friday. Psychology student from Aleppo. We discussed dialectical & cognitive behavioural therapies!!! English way better than mine. There's been trouble with Golden Dawn (fascist movement) who don't want refugees in Greece. Like 1930s Germany, one vulnerable group of people identified as enemy & cause of problems.

Saturday. 100 plus arrived. Met artist, 2 builders, 3 engineers, a baker, and 5 unaccompanied kids. Tourists sitting at bars watching. My Greek improving daily. Panos's wife Marina's a regular and Ali Mavrakakou, a local GP.

And so it goes on, day by day. Turkey's doing a roaring trade in flogging lifejackets. Profiteering. Where there's a war there's money to be made. Fair makes you want to get the bastard traders in a headlock and pump the cash back out of them – then throw them into the middle of the Aegean in one of their own lifejackets. Without even a leaking boat. The wake-up part is: plenty of Syrians are making a fortune from their own people's grief, too. I mentioned to Fraser what Alexis said about the media's different reactions to Western children and Middle Eastern refugee children. All he said was: 'Had you not worked that out yourself?'

Then there are the 'voluntourists'. People who help out with one hand and take selfies of themselves for Facebook with the other. I'm treading a fine line here because I am on holiday and getting involved. With some integrity, I hope. I can do more on Symi because I'm supported, it won't be so straightforward on Leros. But the experience I'm getting must make me useful to Alexis as something more than a flirtation?

Fraser and Clair have a Jude rota and he seems happy knocking around with the pals he made last year. Racism does not rear its ugly head in his little circle. It's a bit different down in the port sometimes, though. I'm torn, feel I should be spending more time with my boy.

Ali Mavrakakou doesn't react when I say I'm Fraser's sister. Well, there's some reaction, but so little it seems odd. Fraser's a regular good guy who most people like. Why is she so reserved?

I don't have to wait long. Jess and I have a 'relief' girlie night in the bars around Yialos.

'This is going to sound strange coming from me, Annie mou, being so much younger than you.' All of six years.

'Thanks for the warning, JJ.'

She slaps the air. 'Sorry, that came out wrong. This is me, your not much younger – *caring* – friend. How did you leave things with Alexis? The Towering Libido?'

I am not prepared for this.

'Why do you ask, not-much-younger-caring-friend?'

'Because he's a great bloke and he's totally stuck on you.'

Whoa – I don't know how to respond. She jumps into the space.

'Just wanted to say, you've got the chance of a really choice bloke there. You have to grab these opportunities. Fraser did with Mum but then he managed to nuke everything when he shagged Dr Maccaracca –'

'Ali Mavrakakou?'

'Yeah, her.'

I *knew* there was unfinished business there. Oh Fraser! You absolute dildo!

'It was *after* he met Mum but he thought Mum and him were finished – you know, like on *Friends* – Ross sleeps with some girl when him and Rachel are on a break –'

I vaguely remember.

'Anyway, Phanes told me about Fraser and Dr – Mavericko?– so I warned Fraser he had to be honest about it with Mum, but he didn't listen, so Mum heard it from Nobby –'

I'm beginning to feel confused – but Jess is on a roll.

'– and then I totally blew it with Nikos over me and this guy in Florida – anyway, you don't want to hear that. Nikos has another lady, now, and well…' She trails off. Oh dear, I hadn't realised she still had feelings for her ex-boyfriend. Could her 'don't care' attitude be an attempt to compensate? Her voice is a little uneven as she continues.

'Alexis is an astonishing guy, I mean his whole life is so – worth living. I'm glad you're going to catch up with him on Leros. We can handle Jude. Oh – and you won't say anything about Dr Mammarou, will you? To Mum or Fraser?'

I promise not to. At least that's one puzzle sorted. How much I'd love to slap Fraser. Perhaps Jude gets his violent streak from me.

There's been no news from Shona since I emailed back, even though I've texted a couple of times. Hope she's not taken umbrage.

TWENTY SEVEN

ANNIE – Summer 2009 onward. Kilachlan

Soon as I'd told Carol-Anne about the daffodils she suggested that we all went to live with her and Rory on Mull. Ridiculous, of course, but I was touched by her enthusiasm. That summer, Clair came up to Kilachlan to look after Maggie and the dogs for three weeks while I took Jude off for a holiday on Mull. I fed the chickens and the sheep, learned to pull wool from their fleeces (Carol-Anne's responsibility that she'd left a bit late) and how to dye wool and work a loom. Jude learned to ride their poor old nag, Gertie. Carol-Anne and I spent a lot of time roaming the island with or without Jude. The first time she and I had to ourselves, she confided to being bored out of her skull. No wonder she wanted Maggie and us to go to live there.

'You don't have to stay, Cazzie.'

'Got any other ideas?' None that didn't involve being single and taking up graphic design again.

Back in Kilachlan, distance learning was a stretch. The days I had to attend uni for tutorials were hard work, going in by train, lugging books and sometimes staying over, either with the folks in Anniesland or with a pal. I couldn't take Jude into Glasgow with me because it meant him missing school so I had to find a way of him seeing his grandparents. Rosemary and George licked their wounds for a long time after we moved. But when they visited Kilachlan and saw how much we loved living there, they sort of understood.

Next thing, they wanted to move to the Oban area and came up several weekends to look at property. I suppose I should have seen it coming; George had hit retirement age the year before. Inside a month of their first visit they'd put in an offer on a bungalow in Dunstaffnage – not exactly next door but just a spit across Connel Bridge. I felt a bit encroached upon. All Maggie did was hum 'You don't know what you've got till it's gone' and I accepted that I should value them while they were around. Maggie always knew what she had in Julia. Maybe that made losing her so much more difficult. Rosemary and George were amazing when you think about it. They'd adopted me and Jude was the son of me and someone they'd never met and were never likely to. Yet they definitely cared about us, even if they weren't that expressive. Well, George did, certainly. To Rosemary I was more of a rescued kitten who grew up to be a wildcat. Jude, for all his faults, was cute – still is when he's in a good mood. Anyhow, they moved up and it turned out it wasn't too bad having them closer.

Something that bothered me, though, was cutting another tie with Glasgow. Carol-Anne was oxter-deep in agricultural trauma with Rory on Mull. Shafiq was in London and Niall, the lucky bugger, was in California by then. There were pals from uni and old school friends, no one that close, but certainly no one I might consider an enemy. I say that because another weird thing happened.

When I went down to collect my Finals results, everyone was clustered round the board to see the printout. I traced down the names and grades. Where mine should have been was a rough black line of felt tip. Everyone else was too excited or depressed by their own results to get involved. I headed for the faculty office. The walk down that corridor was like the journey to the guillotine. So many possibilities went through my mind – I'd failed disgracefully, I'd been accused of cheating, they'd made a mistake over the grade or I'd broken some kind of rule – I hadn't noticed anyone else's name deleted.

Marion, the Faculty Administrator, was there.

'Annie, whatever's the matter?' When I told her, she went straight to her computer.

'Annie, you did very well. You've got a 2:1. Aw, love…'
She came across and took my hands.

'Look, I'm going to print the list out again and put it on the board. Whoever's done this must be sick or very jealous of you.'

She retraced the walk of shame with me, ripped down the old list and put up the new one and locked it inside a display board. It caused a lot of murmuring, some arm rubbing for me, a couple of hugs and a few odd looks. No one had seen the culprit. But they must've wondered who I'd offended enough to have done such a thing.

I rang Maggie to tell her the good news, then the folks, and asked them to call Fraser, who was back on Symi, because my top-up was running out. But that unpleasant feeling at having my name deleted destroyed the pleasure of success and, after a couple of drinks at the Students' Union, I hurried to Queen Street Station. From the train home, I rang Peter, who'd hidden in his office, no doubt to avoid student euphoria or angst. I didn't mention the crossing-out incident. He sounded disappointed that I hadn't come to see him.

Maggie had champagne waiting for me and Jude had made a congratulations card. An extravagant bouquet from Donald arrived at the croft next day. How did he know? Maggie explained:

'Nessie to Archie to Donald.'

After my degree result, Peter suggested I should do an MSc. I had my doubts. I'd cleared my overdraft and credit card mess, thanks to my rent-free accommodation with Maggie. I'd also borrowed from the refunded rent for the flat, when I eventually got it (minus eye-watering administration fees). It was firmly in my mind to pay it back to Eloise, my 'ex-flatmate' as and when we… what? Got in touch?

But an MSc.? Would I ever stop being a student and earn some money? Maggie said the only person preventing that was me, so when Jude – who hadn't a clue what an MSc was – said 'Go for it, Mum!', I did. I studied Psychology and Health and thought I might specialise in geriatric psychology later, given my time working with Maggie. I completed the MSc in a couple of years but decided I needed a breather before looking at a doctorate. That's when I started doing shifts at the local care home. I could get back to Maggie in five minutes if need be and I was there for Jude. Maggie said I didn't need to, but I wasn't prepared to live off her.

She was stoical about her own situation, seldom if ever complained. I knew what she had to bear and it became clear that older people who didn't have her strength and/or similar support would have an even harder time. Jude had played a large part in elevating her spirits. They'd bonded at first meeting, despite the chickenpox, and he'd become as devoted to her as the two Westies, Jack and Tatty. And I… well, I've already said what role I'd have liked for her in my life.

Maggie died on a Sunday in late April. Clair, Jess, Fraser, and I were there. I can hardly bear to talk about it. Jude and I had the privilege of sharing five and a half years with her. For the effect she had on us, she might have been with us all our lives. I will carry her gently in my heart forever.

That sad year went further downhill. As if losing our darling friend weren't enough, some ghouls decided Jude and I deserved more grief. A few weeks after Fraser went back to Symi, Jude got an envelope from there, addressed in block capitals. His Uncle Puke wasn't known for written communication but it was possible after the sad time we'd all had. Inside was a postcard with a view of the beautiful harbour. Then Jude turned it over and saw:

*YOU KILLED MAGGIE, YOU BLACK BASTARD. SHE WAS ASHAMED OF YOU AND YOUR F***ING WHORE MOTHER. THAT'S WHY SHE DIED.*

He tore it up with curses he shouldn't have known, ran out, up the field. I followed so far then let him go, went back and collected the pieces. Clair was still with us and found me with the bits in my hands. She rang Fraser immediately and left an urgent message on his voicemail. We put the torn card and envelope in a plastic bag then took the dogs and searched for Jude. Clair found him on the beach. It had appeared to him, just for a moment, that it was his uncle's card. They sat and talked for a while. Jude seemed calm but wouldn't eat dinner. Fraser rang later, spoke to Jude, then to me and Clair. Said he'd let the police in Symi know. Clair was really keen that we should go to Symi with her but we'd already planned to visit Mull. She stayed on an extra week and made sure the Scrymgeours were aware of our vulnerability.

For the next year, apart from the occasional meal out with Donald Mudie, I lived a life of retreat. There were no more incidents and nothing to report from Symi. Next time the Buchanan/Harkin clan tempted us to visit, I took them up on it and we went for the last week in July, first in August. Blisteringly hot, but apart from that it was fine. Jude made some good mates; I was on the lookout for him, though. I'd assumed the racists in Kilachlan weren't enterprising enough to have organised anything to be sent from Symi. But as Clair pointed out, malevolence does not rule out intelligence.

TWENTY EIGHT

ANNIE – Symi

Clair is gently morphing into Maggie. I arrive back near midnight. She's there on the terrace, feet up on the lounger, book on her lap, head bowed in sleep. Since I told her about London, that freezing morning on the beach at Kilachlan, she has respected my vulnerability. Like Maggie, she gets me. Could have told me not to volunteer here, to take a break from caring for other people. But she hasn't because she knows I can't *not* get involved.

The family with their young daughter left a week ago. Sayid and Maya have been escorted to Athens. Tonight, the Menaged family from Homs, mother, father, and two children, are staying; I recognise a new baby whimper that stops as suddenly as they do with feeding.

The whisky bottle on the table winks at me in the light from the porch. It's not a hot weather drink but it's what I need. I fetch a glass and some ice from the kitchen, unscrew the cap silently – or so I think.

'Hello, my lovely, when did you get in?'

This woman is a true Scot. Sleeps through a baby crying but wakes at the sound of a whisky bottle being opened.

'Just now. Whisky?'

'Parakalo. Grandma's just resting her eyes.'

'Grandma – as if.' Clair a grandma! Even with her wise head, no way. A few corkscrews of silver have peeped through her mad hair, but apart from that, you'd put her at Fraser's age. No, younger. Fraser's not looking his best these days. I speak as I pour. 'How's the family?'

'Sort of all right, considering. The little girl managed some scrambled egg. I wasn't sure what they'd eat so I made them your aubergine and chickpea casserole. There's plenty left. Fatima's a seamstress and Sami's a plumber – fixed that knocking pipe for me, bless him. They're going on Tuesday.'

'You are such an Earth Mother, Clair. If only they could all sink into your arms.'

'Oh, that's most attractive, Earth Mother.'

'OK, Superstar.

She nods approval. I should ask…

'Jude all right today?'

'As good as – brass.'

'Oh dear, what did he do?'

'Oh, he just got a little over-extended. Playing football with Andy and Erik and the lads till way beyond supper deadline. Fraser sorted it.'

I know there's more to it but I'm too pooped to ask. She swings her legs off the lounger and joins me at the table, feeling about for the specs propped on her head, touches my glass with hers, gives the Gaelic toast.

'Slàinte.'

'Slàinte.'

She says nothing, waits for me.

'I don't know how they do it, Clair, the aid workers, I mean. I understand professional distance, but this is something else.'

Her smile wraps around me.

'Tell me about one person you met. A refugee. Tell me about a woman.'

There are so many, but one in particular springs to mind, so I settle into her story.

'OK. From Baghdad travelling with three kids trying to get to her husband in Munich. He went ahead to find a job and accommodation for them, then arrange safe passage. But the bombing got so bad she had to leave. They've been travelling three weeks already. She's an English Literature professor – *English Literature*. And here she is with her children and they've almost nothing but the clothes they stand up in. He – her husband – may not even know they've left or where they are because communication's so hit and miss. I don't feel sorrier for her than another person because she's educated – ach, it's just… how a whole life can get turned over. And when you think about who's doing the bombing and the low-lives smuggling them for huge amounts of cash – you get really…'

Clair touches the table with her fingertips and leans towards me.

'You were telling me about one woman. Not the war itself, not the political situation, one woman and her life. You can only address one person or one situation at a time. Don't take on the world because you'll lose – unless you become a political agitator or a politician, and that brings its own grief. You can't do it all. Even you, Annie Buchanan.' She traces my cheek then sits back. 'So, how were you able to help her?'

'I took her to the old Post Office building for some bottled water, toothpaste, sanitary towels; helped her sort through boxes of shoes and T-shirts for the kids. I'm putting her in touch with Fraser about finance. But, mainly, I just listened. She was ridiculously grateful. I felt like a fraud, I mean, I'd done nothing. Nothing.'

'Darling, you more than most people, know how important listening is. Not just because of your training but because of your life experience. You made a connection with that woman in a world where she thinks no one cares, where she's been treated as a statistic. That makes a big difference.'

The phrase 'compassion tempered by knowledge' comes to mind. Perhaps this is it. Clair hasn't finished.

'One of our aid volunteers was interviewed on a daytime chat show. They asked him whether helping refugees meant more of them would come and did that worry him or was he happy to keep on doing it? And he said "I can't walk to my house and step over a ten-day-old baby who's sleeping on the street". It certainly made them think. But how many people *do*? Not literally step over, maybe, but cross the road so they don't have to look? Andrew can't, nor can you nor many others like you. The fact that you can't – and don't – is important to all the mothers and all the babies, your woman from Baghdad. Oh, that reminds me, I pinched a few of your tampons for Fatima. Jess had run out. You don't mind?'

'Course not. Dr Mavrakakou and I were talking about sourcing sanitary stuff coming up the steps when we bumped into Fraser, then – oh –' As I'm saying this stupid thing I see Clair's reaction, which is to remain so completely impassive that it confirms what Jess said about my brother and the doctor.

'Sorry, me and my bucket mouth.'

'Nothing to be sorry for, Annie, it doesn't matter. It was a while ago, before Fraser and I really got together.'

She's not telling the whole truth, but I have to accept. We finish our whiskies and have a hug before we go to bed. If Maggie was the mum I would have chosen, Clair is the big sister I never had.

When Fraser took off from Glasgow, it felt like my best friend had deserted me; I was afraid I'd never see him again, despite his promises. Worse, he left me with Rosemary and George, who were about as warm as my granny's front room. While I'm away, my son will be among affectionate, funny people who will listen to him. Better off than with me.

When I tell Jude I'll be going to Leros for a week or so, he thinks I want to take him with me and initiates a strop, doesn't want to go because he likes it here. Andy – Andreas – and Erik are his best friends and he's learning Greek from them (swear words, I'm pretty certain), he's been good and wants to stay with Uncle Puke (he's been nothing like angelic, which is why he's only recently transferred to Fraser's cave). When I can get a word in, I tell him I'm going alone and he'll answer to Clair and Uncle Puke. Plus there's Jess – need I say more? Instant mood reversal. He punches the air.

'Result!'

'You won't miss me, then?'

'Ach, stop being so needy, Mum.'

'Wow! You been reading my mind-y books?'

'No, I've been watching Jeremy Kyle with Nessie.'

'Oh, for –'

'What's wrong with that?' Life is too short to enumerate.

'You have to promise you won't give Fraser or Clair any grief.'

I leave out Jess, who is immune to Jude's misbehaviour.

'I won't break their noses, if that's what you mean.'

Not the response I need. He has to actually be civilised for a week or so *at least.* He agrees – 'You got it.' – and treats me to a high five and a knuckle bump, normally reserved for his mates. But there is an agenda: extra pocket money for 'contingencies'. I'm surprised he knows the word.

'"Contingencies" is a word accountants use. That what you want to do, Jude?'

'I'd rather jump on the school piano and tap dance in the nude.'

I love having a kid who can make me laugh, even when he's being diabolical. And he knows exactly when to turn it on, the cheeky bugger. I tell him, seriously, that I'm going to Leros to do some volunteering there with a friend. He's still on a roll, though, and sighs dramatically.

'And there's me hoping you were off to get yourself a sex life with Hagrid.'

An allusion to Alexis, obviously. 'Jude!'

'Well, it's about time, Mum. You're dead old, now. And Donald Mudie's too posh to do that kind of stuff.'

How does he even know about Donald? Or Alexis? Maybe I should get real. Donald and I will be the talk of Kilachlan, even though we've only had dinner a few times. First time Jude's mentioned it, though. And Alexis, well, he's hard to miss. I give him my Miss Trunchbull face:

'OK, Sherlock. One, Donald is a friend. Two, thirty is not geriatric. And three, my sex life is none of your business.'

'It is when you take out your frustration on me. Your PMT's bad enough.'

I know who's inspired these gems.

'OK, Jude, too personal. Tell Jess she just helped you talk yourself out of a pay rise.'

He beats a knee – thankfully bare since Andy and Erik have convinced him shorts are cool – and lampoons Donald's plummy accent:

'Hell and damnation – and thrice drat!'

At least he's lightened up. I'm glad to see a happier Jude emerging. But will he turn out to be a butterfly or a vampire bat?

END OF PART ONE

PART TWO

TWENTY NINE

ANNIE – Leros, Dodecanese Islands, Greece.

Greek ferries: you can hang out in the breeze on deck amidst the diesel fumes, smokers and backpackers or sit indoors with people lounging around tables arguing and watching Greek soaps on ceiling height screens. To get to Leros from Rhodes takes about five and a half hours at night. So no sunbathing on deck, but you can sit on a hard plastic seat and listen to the slosh of the sea. That's where I am.

We arrive at Leros in about twenty minutes. Alexis has recommended a place to stay and they'll meet me at the port. How jammy is that? Shame he couldn't be there. So much the better when we meet. But life is good. More or less. On the 'less' side, Shona didn't take my hint. If I was going to Leros, so would she. To echo my son, 'Hell and damnation – and thrice drat!'. She must have googled Alexis and 'NGO Leros' because she got in touch with Nederland Redden en Helpen, offered her services as a volunteer, and gave my name as a referee. Quite a reversal of status. When Alexis asked me about her, what could I say? Couldn't diss her, she's a friend; no reason to, anyway. So, there it is. Glorious vistas opened by Alexis have Shona shadows cast all over them. He's had to go to Samos, will be tied up till Saturday, and she's busy, some sort of induction, probably. I concentrate on the positives. That's cool, gives me a chance to settle in, adjust, prepare to help. I've indulged in the mobile roaming fee to keep in touch with Symi, so Alexis and I can speak. We haven't exactly had phone sex, but a certain amount of flirting the pants off has gone on. How literally in either case I'm not prepared to speculate or admit.

Passengers for Leros pile off, half past midnight. I'm looking for a sign with my name on it – and there it is, I think – 'ANI BUKANA', held high by a big daddy of a guy.

'Mi léne Annie.'

'*Ání* Bukana, kalispéra! Welcome to Leros.'

'Efharistóh.'

'You speak good Greek, *Ání* Bukana.'

'Annie.'

'*Ání* – good! I am Státhis. Alexis is my friend and your *good friend.*' He gives a throaty, insinuating laugh. A bit premature but I hope to…bear it out?

Státhis has a car waiting and we speed off into the soft night as he chats away in a mixture of English and Greek.

'You have kithára? Plinky, plinky! Elvis Presley, no? Jimi Hendrix?' Alarmingly, he takes both hands off the wheel to mime, from which I deduce kithara means guitar. Anxiety doesn't help my persistent confusion over 'neh' meaning yes and 'ochí' meaning no. So I mumble both.

Ten minutes of mystifying chat later we swing downhill to some apartments. I unclench my fists and relax my terrified buttocks. He insists on carrying my luggage up the outside flight of stairs, wheezing mightily, and shows me into a studio where he demonstrates a fridge with bottled water, light switches and other features. All I want is the loo and bed. He takes my hand in a huge warm grasp.

'Kaliníchta, *Áni* Bukana.'

'Kaliníchta, Stathi. Efharistóh polí.'

'Parakaló.'

And he's gone. I'm in Pandeli. I've no idea where that is but it feels good and I sleep most of the night.

The morning sun slices between orange curtains, piercing my eyelids. I have to get up to see what's behind. Oh wow, look at Pandeli! Denim blue sea, white harbour, little island in the bay, tavernas along a beach – where has this place been all my life? And I'm off, before showering even, down the steps and the hundred yards to the beach, hobbling down a patch of shingle and crashing into the transparent water. This is holiday. Shona may not have had time to do this.

'Kaliméra, *Áni* Burkana!' Státhis's friendly voice booms out 'good morning' as I return to the apartments – followed by a hoarse greeting from someone I can't see –

'Kali-*méra*!' Státhis sits at a table on his terrace, shaded by a roof of thick grape vine.

'Kali-*méra,* kali-*méra,* kali-*méra*!' comes the strange voice again. A Mynah bird flaps up and down in its cage. I hate birds being caged. Sadly, it seems to be popular in Greece. In addition to the Mynah, Státhis has five or six tiny cages containing finches and canaries. He does a front crawl stroke motion

'*Áni*? You sea swim?'

'Ochí– neh – yes.' Státhis doesn't seem to mind me mangling his language.

'Kála! This – this here – Chaos!' Not the state of the terrace but the name of the Mynah bird. Chaos – it fits. Státhis waggles his ear between a finger and thumb indicating I should listen then speaks to Chaos.

'Chao! Angela Merkel!' Chaos comes back on cue:

'*Thánados stin Angela Merkel – Thánados stin Angela Merkel – Thánados stin…!*'

Státhis laughs extravagantly and pronounces, 'Death to Angela Merkel!'

Right. I knew almost all older Greeks weren't too keen on Germans even before the EU business. This is proof positive that Státhis is a paid-up member.

A beautiful, angry Greek woman comes out of the house, gives Státhis a slap round the head with a fly swat and a verbal ear bashing, accompanied by gestures to Chaos.

'*Yássou, Yia yia – Yássou, Yia yia*!'– 'Hello, Grandma'– chirrups Chaos in a child's voice.

Státhis rubs his scalp as the woman comes down the three steps with her arms open, hugs and kisses me.

'Kaliméra, *Áni* Burkana, welcome to Pandeli! I am Neféli.' Mrs Státhis, I presume. I manage to ask in her Greek how she is but forget to put it in the polite form. She clearly doesn't mind and turns to Státhis with surprise, as if to say 'She speaks Greek!' then, in English, invites me up to the terrace. She pours me a tiny cup of coffee and, still in my bikini and towel, I drink the alarmingly strong, sweet coffee and iced water. We make some sort of conversation with comments from Chaos, until eventually my hosts let me go to get showered and dressed. As I climb the stairs, my phone pings. Alexis.

'Welcome to Leros. Leaving Samos. Lipsi overnight then home. See you Saturday lunchtime. Missing you. A x'

A little plop of disappointment it didn't say he'd be back sooner, but the inner tingle is definitely active. I text back instantly. Have to admit, though, much as I can't wait to see him, I'm enjoying this utter freedom, if only for a couple of days.

Back in the studio I notice a little welcome pack with information about shops, buses, scooter and car hire, and a small map of the island. A day of sheer freedom lays ahead of me, making me feel light-headed at the range of choices I could make – laze on the beach, spend an afternoon on the booze, explore the island on foot/by bus/hire a scooter, or… go to the old psychiatric hospital. Hmmm. Much as the video of that dark institution has loomed over me for the past seven or eight years, I feel somehow that today isn't the day. Leros is too new, I don't have the feel of it yet. Maybe tomorrow.

Thanks to my civilised quarters on Symi, I have a selection of clean clothes. Normally I'd fling on anything and get Jude up and out, but today it's only me and I have the luxury of deliberating between three pairs of shorts and half a dozen t-shirts.

Wandering up the hill, I stop to sniff the glorious jasmine spilling out of a garden then take it slowly until I come to a sort of square with a few shops and kafenéions and a small roundabout – or is it just a tree in raised bed? Traffic and people treat it variably. According to my little map, this place is Platanos. At the bottom of the road opposite, the sea smiles back at me, a fish out of water, that can only head towards it. As I do, though, I pass a building on my left and make out the Greek lettering way above the door as 'bibliothiki'. Library?

Only a nerd like me would go to the library on their first day on a Greek island. Jude would have something strong to say about it. Since being a student I've been addicted to the places. I haven't heard from Shona yet, and, when I link up with Alexis and her, I may end up too busy to do this. I decide on the spot that the freedom to be a nerd can be part of my Leros project, and I go in. Immediately, I'm greeted by the librarian who, of course, speaks fluent English. He is charming, elicits questions that I didn't even know I wanted to ask, and brings up Google Earth on his computer to show me exactly where the old psychiatric hospital is. Every Greek person I speak to reinforces how lazy most British are at learning languages. At school, prior to legging it to London, I picked up some French and a smattering of German. But most of it ist gegangen aus la fenêtre maintenant – even though Eloise revived an interest in the Gallic connection for a while. Still, fortunately for me, all these clever Symiots and Lerians have allowed me to get about knowing the barest minimum of Greek.

My librarian friend directs me to some English books about Leros upstairs in a reading room where he thoughtfully switches on the air conditioning. After an hour's browsing, I read something that makes me forget the chill air on my bare arms and legs. *'Can you make a fly? Then learn that you should not destroy what you cannot create.'* Little Avrilia, who'd just swatted a wee beastie, was getting a lecture from her big sister. I remember Neféli swatting Státhis and laugh, destroying a potential light bulb moment.

Little Avrilia became *G*avrilia in her later years just to make life awkward for everyone and as Mother Gavrilia became a Lerian legend in her own lifetime. The sister's telling-off influenced her profoundly, pretty much in line with the Buddhist precept: 'refrain from harming living things'. I wonder how she felt about eating meat after that, or any life form she'd ingested before she became Mother Gavrilia? I have a global guilt trip over the time I used to eat dead animal and wear leather shoes. But how many insects did I mash before that? I make a mental note to craft Avrilia/Gavrilia's fly for Jude's consumption – eeucchh, wrong word...

Anyways, sitting upstairs in the library in Platanos, I have one of my spectacularly prescient moments. Why do we – from art critics to butchers, kids to warlords – destroy anything we can't create? Freud's death instinct competing with a life instinct? For power, satisfaction, expediency? Is it anger, impotence, envy – or a combination? I recognise this as a gut reaction, not my professional one. Peter would remind me that destruction can also be a form of expression or self-harm.

I'm racing mentally but try to let it go before I swat myself like Avrilia's fly. I've been let out to play on a Greek island. I should be soaring up with socking great orgasmic skyrockets of bliss, not going back to school. I close the book and step out onto the balcony, straight into a

Taser belt of heat. Like I don't love it. There's a view of that ridiculous sea and Aghia Kiriaki island. You don't get views like that from the Westerhouse Road library in Glasgow. I feel an instant need to be down on the beach, plunging into the water then dripping out for a cold beer.

Downstairs, I say 'efharistóh polí' to the librarian and emerge, blinking, into the oven outside. Sensible Annie, mother of one, picks up a few litres of water from the mini-market and camel-plods down to Pandeli beach under their weight. Before Jude, I'd have grabbed a sports bottle and legged it. Even so, I feel myself gradually regressing now the constant pressure of responsibility is four islands away.

By the time I make it to the studio, the sweat's lashing out of me. I swap into my bikini and make for the vodka-clear water. It's almost cold enough to put you off an instant body flop – but I do it and, yessss! Magic. After twenty minutes, hunger cuts my aquatic frolic short. As I reach the studio, Státhis waves to me from his garden.

'Yassou, Áni Burkana!'

'Yassou, Stathi!' I like it here.

THIRTY

ANNIE – Friday. Leros

I've waited long enough for this. Now, *today*, I'll go to the old hospital. Alexis hasn't texted, so I don't know whether he'll be back today or tomorrow. I'm squirming with frustration, anticipation and at least one far more basic sensation. What to do about Shona, though? I grab a packet of crisps and an apple from the tiny supermarket and eat them on the bus. It's a single-decker and the twenty-minute journey passes a spectacular sea cliff to the left. We arrive at a promenade where the driver announces 'Lakki'. Across the water, there's a majestic villa set back from the shore, in the trees. It must be a hotel or some millionaire-type summer home. If there's time, I'll check it out.

Státhis has told me to ask the driver for Lepida. From Lakki, we follow the harbour to the right, going on as it disappears and reappears and end up where the road divides. The driver motions for me to get off. I'm now on the far side from Lakki town. The librarian said that I have to walk through the new hospital grounds until I reach the water again, so I pass between the concrete pillars and guess my way through the single storey buildings set amongst pine trees. And suddenly it leers at me. The old psychiatric hospital.

In front of it is a collection of prefabricated houses surrounded by a chain-link fence topped by barbed wire. The compound mimics a zoo, but is filled with men, women, and children of all ages. This must be the hotspot where refugees must wait thirty days before being released to move on. It's packed. Is this what Greek Prime Minster Tsipras meant by a 'warehouse of souls'? Several women dressed in black, wearing hijabs, glance round at me, one has a baby in her arms; in this metallic heat, they are just standing. What are they thinking? I remember my Iraqi professor, place my right hand on my heart. One responds. I become aware of my skimpy clothing, my freedom to roam the island. We really are in two different worlds. There is nothing I can do for them at the moment.

Two men in uniform, chatting by the entrance, light cigarettes. Both wear reflective sunglasses. I can't tell whether they're police or military. Can't imagine such casual wear or behaviour in Britain.

And then I stop myself. We have Immigration Return Centres. I've seen their grim exteriors. What are they like now Britain has been declared a 'hostile environment'? And we don't even face this intensity of human need.

While I've been off on my flight of humanitarian outrage, the women have moved. Guiltily, I feel relief and walk on round the perimeter, towards my original destination.

The three storeys of white decay induce a contraction of fear in me making me pause a few moments to steady my heartbeat. It is an archetypal ruin of Gothic horror proportions. Above the central block are five squat gables, almost too ugly for a haunted castle. Large, worn capital letters are barely legible, above the huge, peeling front doors. This is the setting of the obscenity we witnessed in the documentary. The irony of two such inhumane enclosures, this and the hotspot, being metres, albeit years, apart is striking.

The main doors are too daunting to tackle. There is a wide space to the side of the building, so I head round and find an open door that leads through a dark hallway, its floor littered with rotting paper, plastic waste, and goat droppings, into a courtyard. As I step into the light, I recognise this as the place where patients were left naked in the sun. For a moment, revulsion halts my breath as waves of emotion threaten to swamp me. I hadn't anticipated such visceral reactions.

This, too, is filled with garbage; old lever arch files, polystyrene, plastic, paper, and the ubiquitous goat droppings. The door to a small side room hangs wide open and I step in, reluctant but fascinated. It is ankle deep in notebook-sized paper. Not patient records, surely? I pick up a few, ready to be further inflamed, and recognise they're old lottery grids. Who dumped them here and why come this far to do it? The banality of the fly-tipping seems like desecration. Is this what people think of this place, just somewhere to tip rubbish? Even the ones who worked here? Or just a few wasters? It created a lot of employment so there must be quite a number of ex-employees around. Are younger people sheltered from its history? In reality, most people, particularly staff in the tavernas, bars, and shops must be too preoccupied with making a living to let it concern them. True, the scandal came to light well over twenty years ago. And, yet, even that seems shockingly close. I'd have been three or four.

I look around a couple more spaces, all clogged with litter, and decide I've seen enough. I'm tired, hot, and depressed; my spirit is no longer up to entering the building proper, so I leave the hospital and go back down the side of the hotspot. To my left is another, more modern but equally decaying concrete building. I wander inside and find a couple of filthy mattresses and some abandoned shoes. Someone has been sleeping here but not recently. Refugees?

Down at the bay's edge again, I decide to continue along the shoreline towards the large villa I noticed on from the far side. It is set back from road, almost hidden by trees but not as gracious as it appeared. Marbled steps, thick with, yes, goat droppings, lead up to double doors. Curiosity leads me up the once elegant flight and I reach a large veranda with a view of the hills across the water. Someone wealthy must have led a life of privilege here once. What happened?

Crashes and bangs echo from inside as shutters flap in the slight sea breeze. The front doors are open. After the spookiness of the hospital, this is a stroll through fairyland – although bird droppings mingled with those of goats ensure the place doesn't smell fairylike. There are several small square rooms with ornately tiled floors either side of a high-ceilinged corridor. One or two have been swept clean and, again, there are mattresses. This has been a more recent bedroom for someone. I venture upstairs to the second storey, where it's pretty much the same. As I leave one of the square rooms, a panicked pigeon clatters up past me. At the end of the corridor, I pull one of the jammed wooden shutters back far enough to reveal the open window space behind it. There is wiring across it, but the square gaps are large enough for the pigeon to get through. Back by the staircase I watch the pigeon perch on a wire then fly out. Shame I can't do the same for everyone imprisoned at the hotspot. Or waiting to leave Symi. Or Greece.

I want to know the history of this place. It doesn't look like a regular home. Perhaps Státhis will be able to tell me, or the librarian.

Outside, I carry on along the waterside past some aged, rusting hoists and what look like old rail tracks. A sign written in Greek, English, French, and German forbids me from taking photographs, a fairly comprehensive warning. Ahead of me are two old prison-like blocks and, way beyond, a group of buildings with a battleship moored alongside. A naval base? Shortly, there's a sign saying it's a prohibited area. Not a good idea to get banged up on my holiday. Time to head back.

After a hundred metres or so, I gamble I'm far enough away from the forbidding signs to take a photo of the grand old villa. I'm fascinated to know what the place is and who it belonged to. But even at the water's edge, under the tamarisk trees, I can't get far enough back for a wide shot of the whole building. I take a partial shot and send it to Alexis. He might know. It really is very picturesque, so I'll take another from the other side of the harbour. It is seriously hot, now, I'm low on water. I don't know when the bus is due at Lepida and it's a long walk back to Lakki. I hurry, head down, past the hotspot, not because I can't bear to look so much as through respect. I wouldn't want to be gawped at. There's a queue of parked cars along the roadside which must belong to staff, people who can come and go, like me.

I try to make sense of what I've seen. Within metres of one another, the three environments are diverse. But there are links; between the hotspot and the old hospital in terms of incarceration and between the hospital and the villa through decay. But neglect applies to all three; to the fabric of the two old buildings and to the people in the hotspot – people whose desperation is so badly neglected by the majority of the world. It's a damning correlation.

When I arrive, exhausted, back in Pandeli, Státhis asks me how my outing was. My Greek doesn't stretch to asking him about the villa. There's been no response from Alexis. He'll be on the ferry from Samos to Lipsi. Maybe he hasn't had my message yet.

THIRTY ONE

ANNIE – Pandeli, Leros

I'm working hard at filling in time until seeing Alexis, which is and isn't hard. Currently, I'm at the other end of the experience scale to my morning trip. A distant memory tells me, *'Do not put your fins on and try to walk forwards into the sea'*. So I'm trying to back in without making an exhibition of myself.

I learned how clowns got the idea big feet are funny last year. Fraser, the bastard, laughed while, be-flippered, I entertained the entire beach at Nimborio by trying to walk into the sea forwards. Now I know you either go backwards or carry them in and slosh about like a drunken Orca while you try to yank them on underwater. If you have a handy boat or jetty, you can heft off doing the 'Giant Step', arms and legs all at right angles, looking like a flying swastika. It'll take time and a guaranteed absence of Fraser, Jude or Jess for me to work up to that one. At least Clair would wait till I was out of earshot before falling about laughing.

Seaborne, I propel myself up and down from the hotel at one side of the little bay to the harbour on the other. Dinghies ferrying rich Americans, Germans, and Turks from their yachts to the beach tavernas can be a hazard. Luckily, I have a fluorescent snorkel tube and my flippers leave a Titanic wake, so I'm hard to miss. Every so often, I poke my head up like a seal with an exhaust pipe to get my bearings. Up on the hill behind the tavernas are some short, round windmills. Doesn't look as though they're working, though. At harbour level I can just make out the late night bar. The welcome pack said it opens late evening and closes when the last customer goes. Definitely one to check out with Alexis. And Shona, I suppose. Splashing back the other way, I notice that there are houses on the headland behind the hotel. Must have a great view.

What a day of contrasts. I'd really like to go back to the hospital with someone who knows more about it. Perhaps Alexis will have contacts? But for today, I'm tired, happy and getting hungry. I faff about again trying to get my fins off and exit the water more like a pregnant turtle than Venus rising.

Leros, unlike Symi, has its own water supply, so I stay greedily in a cool shower for a straight five minutes then dry and dress slowly. It's forever since I've had the time, even the inclination to debate over what I'm going to wear, although I've only the contents of a half-full backpack to choose from. My phone rings. It won't be Jude. Probably Fraser or Clair, ringing with his latest misdemeanour. But the screen tells me it's –

'Shona! Hello.'

'Hi Annie, how are you and Jude enjoying Leros?'

'Jude's staying with friends on Symi. I'm here on my own.'

'Oh?'

'Just having a bit of "me" time. Loving it. The place and the freedom.'

'Look, I'm sorry I haven't been able to see you, yet. Been having a few issues with… well, are you free tonight?'

'Sure am.'

'Marvellous! D'you know Aghia Marina? The tables by the water at the internet cafe? Seven?'

'I'll find it. See you then.'

I make a tomato sandwich and open a beer, sitting on the terrace looking past the small isle, Aghia Kiriaki, to Turkey. Me, Annie Buchanan, international traveller with friends on remote Greek islands. I am becoming so sophisticated I won't be able to talk to myself soon. It'll be good to see my old friend. But. Big but. A shame about the Alexis complication.

Old friend? Well, hardly ancient – she must be a dozen or so years older than me. Same as Alexis. We've known each other about twelve years, too. No, Jude's thirteen, so nearer fourteen years. Means she was only slightly older than I am now when we met in London. Has she moved on since? I should do better with my life, I know, use my qualifications. Can't hide behind being a single mum for ever.

Later in the afternoon, I sit at a beach bar for the Wi-Fi and find a message from the Adoption Counselling Service, offering me an appointment in August. I'll wait before replying. Leros is partly about finding out who I am without the responsibility of another person's life. I haven't seen *that* Annie since she was seventeen.

Six fifty. My T-shirt's already clammy when I arrive at Aghia Marina and scout around the waterfront seating. Shona doesn't have any photos up on Facebook and may have changed a lot. I'm curious to see if she fits the picture memory I have of her. But I'm early and pretty sure she's not here, so I order a beer and sit, trying to shake off my irritation that she's here on Leros. At another table, a group of people chat and laugh. I feel just a sliver of envy. Apart from Symi, the last time I was in a group like that was – how long ago? They're speaking what sounds like English but I can't pick up anything, so I shift my attention. Light on water casts hectic golden nets along the sides of the boats, a fisherman with a brownish roll-up stuck to his lower lip coils a greasy rope snake and a small ginger dog sniffs a mooring post then anoints it in the way dogs do. Tied up at the dog's favourite post is the tourist boat *Barbarossa* that runs trips hither and yon with drinks and snorkelling thrown in. Looks fun but out of my financial league. A few tables away, three young guys in training to be Greek gods pose behind their reflective lenses, denimed legs extravagantly splayed to give the genital bulge maximum effect. Lads, I could tell you so much about yourselves you'd all crawl under your beds and refuse to emerge until you're thirty-five. If I could speak Greek.

As I look away, I realise a tower block has moved between me and the sea view.

'Kalispéra! No luggage or guitar with you tonight?'

Alexis! He drops his backpack and opens his arms. I propel myself up into them.

'Oh, Alexi, is it really you? I thought you weren't – When did you get back?'

'Just now. Didn't want to stay over on Lipsi, so I hitched a lift on a local boat. Oh, Annie! Sorry I wasn't here to meet you.' He buries his head in my neck. He is glad to see me, no doubt. We have a long tobacco-ey kiss. There are a few whistles and jeers from the noisy table. Alexis sets me down and makes a rude gesture to them, greeted by an escalation in catcalls.

'My team. Just a minute… are you here on your own tonight?'

'No – I'm meeting Shona.'

'Ah. I didn't notice her.'

'No. I expect she should be along in a minute.'

The noise from the table continues. He shrugs an apology.

'Afraid we have to meet the gang.'

I'm picking up a strange signal, here. Shona and I are friends, but he's acting coolly.

'Hey everyone, this is Annie. Come from Symi for a break. Great musician, by the way.'

From the names and various 'Hi's' and 'Kalispéra's', I deduce that this group is international, largely Greek professionals plus foreign aid workers. Everyone wiggles their chair round and I squeeze in next to Alexis, who folds into his like an Ikea flat pack deconstructing. The friendly welcome doesn't mask that everyone's in some stage of exhaustion, so I'm surprised when Alexis tells me they have to return to work in fifteen minutes or so. Which means him, too. I could cry with disappointment.

Some of them call him 'Alexi' when they speak to him, others just call him 'Dutch'. One of them, Yiannis, I think, fires a quip in Greek and there is an explosion of laughter. Alexis points at him beadily and says, 'If you can't say it in English, don't say it at all,' greeted by a chorus of 'wooh!'– from which I suspect I'm the subject of speculation. I find this encouraging. Alexis retorts in Greek, so I don't understand – what Jude must feel, surrounded by adults. He apologises to me and tells the gang –

'She's here to meet a friend who's volunteering. Shona. Shona Packham.' By the firm way he says it, I sense a subtext. Also, I notice some uncomfortable looks, the odd whisper behind a hand.

One of the women, Fenne, asks brightly if this is my first time on Leros, and normal service is resumed. I tell her yes, mention Pandeli, the hotspot, and the old psychiatric hospital. Work stories surface. The hotspot is one of five in the islands; it opened last March with no warning to the NGOs and there's still some sore feeling about it. The organisations and volunteers are having to provide most of the services because the military does nothing more than the very basic. No wonder everyone looks knackered.

Yiannis changes the subject to beer and, despite the fifteen-minute work curfew, they order another round of drinks. We're on Leros time. The topic's moved from Shona, but it still unsettles me. According to her, she's been inducted into NRH, but it sounds like she hasn't. Maybe they think she's a 'voluntourist'. Better to say nothing until I hear her side.

The waitress, a gorgeous young Greek woman with cafe latte skin, like Jude's, and a tiny black eye patch of a dress, takes our order. Alexis's eyes don't slide after her like Fraser's would have. Didn't he notice her?

I'm just giving my order when I spot Shona sitting a few tables away – but do a double take because she's barely recognisable: a lot heavier, longer hair, and looking older than I'd imagined. I wonder about calling to her then decide, given the negative reaction earlier, it would be better to join her. I whisper to Alexis then excuse myself from the group. He doesn't stop me, just mutters,

'I'll call later,'– kisses my hand and blesses me with those smoky-kind eyes.

THIRTY TWO

ANNIE – Aghia Marina, Leros

'Shona!' She stands as I speak.

'Annie, Annie, Annie! It *was* you over there. I wondered but… well, I didn't like to… Really, really, really sorry!'

Oh yes! She still speaks in threes. She lets me hug her but doesn't engage, barely pauses as she sits and waves me to a chair.

'Are you all right? The internet went down, so I had that to deal with that and then the –'

It's Alexis. He passes me my beer.

'Hi, Shona. Annie left her drink behind.'

'Alexis. How surprising to see you here.' I notice Shona doesn't use the familiar 'Alexi' like the others and is almost offhand, with him. It's a small waterfront bar but she behaves as though he's crashed a cocktail party at Balmoral. She looks the part of an aristocrat, though, in her long lime green linen dress and impressive pearl studs; definitely not standard refugee-volunteering gear.

Alexis shrugs. 'Hitched a ride back from Lipsi. And look who I found.' His hand is on my shoulder. Is it just for my benefit or is he indicating something to her? It seems a little possessive but I don't mind it. She bristles as though he's intruded on an intense relationship and ignores him to speak to me.

'Well, Annie, what say we have a drink here then go along to Milos for a meal? The seafood is to die for and it's a fabulous setting, right on the water.' It is embarrassing. I am also aghast at the seafood bias. She continues, brittly.

'I'd invite Alexis to join us, but he is absolutely obsessed with work.' He just gives one of his gorgeous grins and speaks directly to me.

'Annie, my apartment is just up behind the waterfront hotel in Pandeli, near the Vromolithos road. Just so you know.' It is code for so much. Must be in the houses I noticed while I was swimming; is that why he recommended the studio? He touches my hair, making my very follicles rejoice.

'I'll text you later. Goodnight, ladies.'

'Alexis?' Shona's voice is crisp. 'What time should I arrive tomorrow?'

'Not necessary. Spend the day with Annie, you have a lot to talk about. I'll call you.'

'But –'

'No, really, Shona. Have a good day tomorrow.'

She smiles tightly and beckons the foxy waitress as he shoulders his backpack, climbs pillion on a scooter, and takes off along the coast road. Most of his team have left the table and a couple of them wave to me. Odd that Shona's not in their company or required for work tonight, quite apart from not being needed tomorrow. I'm also somewhat deflated at being consigned to her for the day instead of being with him.

'So, Annie, how come you're on Leros and Jude's still on Symi? What a shame, I'd have loved to have met him. What's he up to? Apart from pugilism?' She's too posh to say 'hitting other kids'. It's obvious Alexis has riled her, but she relaxes after a while and we make our way to Milos Restaurant. It is a beautiful setting, as she said. The feeling evaporates, however, when they say they're fully booked. She's annoyed and argues with the patron, who is charming but adamant. I persuade her to try a smaller place we passed on the way. They're pleased to have us. She orders stifado and I opt for the wonderful gigantes beans and a Greek salad. Without feta.

Alexis is right, Shona and I do have a lot to talk about. Throughout the evening I fill in the full story on Jude, on Fraser, Clair, and Jess, playing at Angelina's music bar, and helping out with Symi Solidarity. She, though, tells me little news from before her arrival on Leros. Her frustration over Alexis limiting her contact with the refugees is almost palpable and she changes the subject abruptly by raising her glass.

'Enough, enough, enough! We all have to live in this world. We can try to make it a better place for others, but not by making it worse for ourselves.' The way she trots it out, I wonder whether it's original; it sounds like something a dodgy life guru might say.

She insists on covering the bill. No argument. Turns her thoughts to tomorrow.

'Well, darling, since I'm unexpectedly free, what do you fancy doing? The *Barbarossa* is running trips to the White Islands.'

'Oh, I don't know, Shona, it's –'

'I know what you're thinking. Too expensive?'

'Well, maybe. I wouldn't mind going to Xerocampos. You can see way across to Kalymnos from there. My welcome pack said there's a great taverna behind the beach – with sun loungers. And we can go by bus.'

She doesn't look impressed. 'Is the bus part meant to persuade me?' But she agrees.

We take a taxi up to her Platanos hotel, after which I walk down to Pandeli. Fifteen minutes later, I'm watching the bay's nightlife from my terrace. Night mellows the bursts of laughter from beach tavernas and softens tiny wave plashes on the pebbles. Cars and motorbikes growl and buzz in and out of the weft of darkness. I refresh my insect repellent, open the penultimate bottle of Mythos, and loll on a lounger, counting stars, squinting at headlights a few kilometres away on the Turkish mainland. It is warm, it is still and I am distant from my problems.

The bottle slips from my hand onto the tiles, waking me. The atmosphere's no cooler but quieter. One last breath across the bay and I'll away to my bed. As I turn from the rail I catch a tall figure heading for the sea front from Castelo Bar. A goblin grabs my tongue and lungs.

'Hey, Alexi! Ale-e-exi!'

He scans upward.

'It's me, Annie!'

'Annie – hi! Thought you'd be asleep. Want to join me for a drink?' We head for the late opening bar where we drink a lot, talk about nothing and everything and make each other laugh. Shona is not mentioned which leaves a kind of question mark hanging between us. The craic doesn't stop, though, till he says he has to be at work by seven a.m. to help with breakfast, and I realise that's in four hours. We saunter back along the shingle, holding hands, and kiss then kiss some more before he climbs the steps up to his apartment and I the ones to my room. I sort of hoped that tonight might be the night, but he's completely knackered. Perhaps we're meant for greater things. I hope so.

THIRTY THREE

ANNIE – Leros

Despite drinking until three this morning, I challenge myself to a morning swim, then duck it in favour of a long shower – in which I stand trying to work out whether I feel insulted that he didn't make a move or I'm simply hungover. It was late, though, and he had to get to work. Besides, I still woke up with a smile on my face.

As arranged, Shona and I meet for coffee at the kafeneion in Platanos. She looks exhausted.

'You OK, Shona?'

'Of course, why wouldn't I be?'

I try to dilute her acidic tone by complimenting her.

'Your dress is gorgeous. You look really stunning in it.' It is pale green with three large embroidered hearts on it, one at the neck, two at the waist.

'Oh this? Thank you. Stella McCartney or Christopher Kane. Can't remember which.' Stella McCartney I've heard of. I incline my head as though I know the guy's name, too. In the same league, no doubt. She smoothes down the fabric, fluffs her hair out then tucks it behind one ear again. Almost preening.

As we wait at the bus stop opposite the shoe shop, I tell her about Mother Gavrilia and not destroying anything that you can't create. It doesn't interest her. The bus takes us through Lakki and past Lepida where I point out the big villa which earns a 'hmm'. The Xerocampos terminus is a dusty circle on the sea front where the driver stops for a chat. The taverna is ahead of us, tables laid out on a terrace divided from the beach by tamarisk trees and a little wall. It appears to cheer Shona after the indignity of travelling on a bus.

We find a couple of sunbeds shaded by a large blue umbrella and, while Shona arranges herself and her designer beach towel, I go into the taverna. She's adamant that we shouldn't drink before noon. A blurred-at-the-edges Fraser tilts into my mind. Strange how an issue surfaces when you encounter it in a different context. I make a mental note to speak to him – or Clair – or Jess, even, about his drinking. When I return with our soft drinks Shona's taken off the dress, revealing an amazing swimsuit. I'll bet she never gets it wet, not with those puffball pearl studs still in.

Xerocampos Bay is more of a long, wide inlet, its horizon filled by Kalymnos and a couple of smaller islands in front. Smudged by the heat haze, they appear mysterious, mystical. I spot a small ferryboat departing from the stone dock far to the right of us and watch, lazily, as it vanishes into the sea vapours. Perhaps, if Shona can't work with the refugees tomorrow, we could take a trip on it? Maybe we'd just disappear for ever into the Greek mist (myths)? Bad pun. I am definitely Fraser's kin. What there is to see on Kalymnos, I've no clue beyond lot of rock climbing and hiking. Definitely not for Shona.

Five ducks appear from behind the jetty, paddling their way down its length and turning sharp right in convoy along the beach, having a ducky chat on the way. I draw Shona's attention to their cuteness and snap them on my phone. She's not that taken – 'Sweet.'– and settles back to her Kindle. She doesn't seem interested in what she's reading, either, keeps putting it down and gazing down the bay. Nor does she want to chat, even though so much must have happened in her life since we last met. Deflated by her attitude, I reach for my snorkel gear and go for a flip-flap until my stomach tells me it's lunchtime. At twelve thirty, we shift to a shaded table. Shona perks up at the range of food and orders a good lunch, encouraging me to do the same. After all, we have until five when the last bus leaves. Longer if she's enjoying herself – and she's starting to because a fair amount of wine is going down. Taxis and restaurants are her spiritual homes, I think – when she's not in Harvey Nichols or Harrods, presumably. I'm sure I've read a paper on life choices dictated by finance; as if anyone needed to explain it… Wait, no – I'm thinking of Boarding School Syndrome: repressed emotions, inability to empathise, a need to control and so on. Problems I don't have and Jude's never likely to. Is Shona affected, though? It's usually people who are sent young; she said she was something like seven, I think. But who knows?

The tables are filling with diners in couples or family groups. Momentarily, I miss my family and am surprised that the sentiment includes Rosemary and George. Once they'd got over the foreign-ness of the place, they'd love it here. I speculate anew on how they will feel about me researching my birth parents. Must reassure them it's mostly for Jude's sake – well, isn't it? My longing for the Symi family is greater, though. What are they all up to at the moment?

Shona and I haven't exchanged a word for ten minutes; do we really have so little in common? Did I get it wrong, thinking she came to the islands because of me? Feeling more and more ill at ease, I try enlivening lunch by asking her about ex-partners; Shona isn't exactly beautiful but she has a lot of assurance and some men find that intriguing – or a challenge. She considers my request momentarily then launches in. She was married to Rupert when she and I first met but 'deleted the miserable sod', her words, and made a new life. She whizzes through her affairs: a naval officer, a minor royal (whom she won't name), a wine producer, and a theatre impresario (whom she won't name), none of them long term, but always parting as friends. She's now vaguely involved with the CEO of a charity, also nameless, who researched and approved NRH before she offered her services. It sounds too glamorous to be true. But why would she lie? Given her obvious wealth, she clearly lives in that sort of world.

Afterwards, she insists it's my turn. Zeezoo she knows about. There was no real boyfriend before I left home and Jude arriving when I was seventeen eclipsed my romantic and sexual development until Carol-Anne lost patience and set me up with a series of goofballs. Shona is amused and slightly shocked by my outrageous descriptions. I omit my brief encounter in Pollokshields; Judah was a waking dream, a glimpse of what might have been. Jude is the reality. And I edit out Eloise, her warmth and her tactile affection. Was she part-mother, sister, friend? I still don't understand what we had or why it ended. Shona interrupts my rambling.

'What about Alexis? I thought you came here to see him. You two seemed *a deux* at Aghia Marina last night.' Something prompts me to be evasive.

'Ach, he's sweet, but I'd get short of oxygen way up there. No, we're just friends. I'm here to help out, like you.' To throw her off the scent, I invent a brief fling with a Philosophy lecturer whom I'm considering dumping 'because he prefers thought to action'. She doesn't get the joke, so I go on to the sexual desert that is Kilachlan and the absurd attentions of the self-appointed laird's son.

Shona bangs her glass down and refills it. 'Why absurd?' She's several class and finance levels above me, she must find it baffling.

'Because fit though Donald Mudie may be –' I stop as her wine goes down the wrong way. She waves away my assistance, gulps some water and recovers.

'You were saying? About this – Donal?'

'Donald – yes, he's an arrogant, adulterous pain in the arse, despite which, I quite like him. But he can't understand why I wouldn't fuck him, even if he paid me his entire bloody hedge fund.'

Shona sits silently for a moment then bangs the table with her fist. 'If there's one word I can't stand it's the 'f' word. It's quite, quite, quite disgusting. I can't bear to hear it. I'm surprised at you, Annie! And shocked.'

I'm almost breathless with surprise but, being nearly a bottle of retsina in, I go for it. 'Really? You can't stand the "f" word? But I've heard you say "sod" and "bugger" and those words don't bother you?'

'No. Why should they?'

'No reason. Except they're all about anal sex – and the "f" word's about vaginal sex.' I wink knowledgeably. 'That mean you prefer it up the bum, then, Shona?'

Incisive analysis is a dubious benefit of a university education, plus I'm in my cups and I think it's funny. Not so Shona, who pushes herself unsteadily to her feet.

'I cannot believe you're speaking to me like this!'

I've obviously gone too far. Me and my mouth.

'Shona, I'm sorry, I really am.' She wavers.

'I didn't mean to offend you. Please sit down.'

Thankfully, she does, mainly because she can't stay upright. I do some more big-time apologising and we get the bill. Which she pays. We link arms down to the beach, spend a quiet afternoon dozing and catch the five o'clock bus. It's a golden evening, the sort where you never know who you might bump into. After leaving Shona, I take it slowly down the hill to Pandeli, thinking about the conflicts of this place. It's such a beautiful island, rugged scenery, an impressive castle, Lakki's fabulous natural harbour, welcoming bays at Pandeli, Vromolithos, Alinda, Gourna, safe sea, friendly people, food to get fat on, good beer.

But there's another Leros, one that went through occupation by the Ottomans and the Italians, the terrible experiences of World War Two and occupation by the Nazis. And then civil war, rule by the Colonels, the shame of the old psychiatric hospital, and now the awfulness of austerity – and the tragedy of the refugee crisis. (Did I leave out the leper colony? That was an Ottoman institution.) How come this island has such a powerful pull? That so many foreigners want to live here? Is it the beauty of the place (I've seen its equal), the spirit of the people – or something else? Are Lerians different to most other Greeks? I don't know what it is, but there's something.

As if warning me from further speculation the sky has darkened, clouds are building from the west and moving quickly. Rain? On my holiday in Greece? It's still as hot but everything looks different in this uncanny light, the gold trapped and filtered by the grey. Near the bottom of the hill I hear Chaos the Mynah bird rattling out strings of unintelligible noises in response to the coming storm. Státhis yells, 'Stase, Chao!'– 'Shut up', presumably. I am learning all the time.

He and Neféli are at the table under the vine roof with two gorgeous little girls of about nine and seven.

'Kalispéra sas, Neféli, Státhi.' I've used the correct form of their names and the plural. Very proud.

'Áni Burkana – Ela! My grandkids.' He gestures for me to join them.

'Efharistóh.'

'Hi, Annie. My name is Neféli and my sister's Iréne.' This is the older one who has the eyes of a doe and molasses hair to her shoulders, named Neféli after her Yia yia, her grandma. Iréne must be named after an aunt – or her grandma's middle name. If anything, she has bigger brown eyes, a slightly rounder face and curling ebony hair.

'Hi. Pleased to meet you, Neféli, Iréne.'

'Pleased to meet you, *Áni*,' they chorus.

Suddenly there is a brilliant purple-white flash followed by a thunderbolt that makes the furniture bounce. Chaos goes bananas until Yia yia Neféli plops a cover over his cage. Rain strikes the ground like artillery fire. The vine roof is thick enough to keep us dry – apart from the odd rebel drip.

'Full water,' remarks Státhis, gesturing a downward motion.

'*Á*ni – sit,' says Yia yia Neféli, then disappears into the house followed by the girls. Hands resting comfortably on his generous stomach, Státhis does his little tippling mime.

'Drinky drinky?' He chuckles at my enthusiastic 'parakoló' and pours sweetish, very cold white wine. I can certainly handle this. Then little Neféli and Iréne appear, followed by their grandma, laden with dishes of feta, olives, crisps, and sweet tomatoes. We dig in, the adults chatting through the little girls who translate for us. Oh, shame on me.

I show them some photos of Jude on my phone. They must find it incomprehensible that I'm here without him. 'Polí omórfo,' they say, 'very handsome'. Little Neféli wants to have another look and Státhis teases her until she runs and hides indoors. Yia yia metes out further punishment with the fly swat on naughty Pappous, Grandpa – and coaxes her granddaughter out again. The rain stops, but we carry on drinking and eating. Around ten, I thank them profusely, we all hug each other and say 'Kaliníchta'. After all the worry and bad feeling in Kilachlan, this is the tonic I need. Leros could get to me like Symi has to my brother and Clair. I decide, as I climb somewhat unsteadily to the studio, that if I were to put down roots anywhere other than Scotland, it might well be here. Easy to say after only three days.

I stay on the damp terrace for a few minutes, just in case anyone should pass by. But no one of interest does.

THIRTY FOUR

ANNIE – Leros

From the balcony where I'm towelling my hair dry, I hear sounds of an argument. It can only be Státhis and Neféli. I look down and see Neféli come down the steps with a large stockpot wrapped in a towel, which she plonks on the foot well of her scooter. A couple of full shopping bags are lashed to the back. The argument rises to a crescendo as Neféli mounts the scooter and wheels around with the stockpot, astonishingly, remaining upright, and shoots off, making one final obscene gesture in the direction of Státhis. Can't imagine what all that's about.

Shona and I meet again at the kafeneion on the square for coffee and croissants. She doesn't argue when I want to pay. I hadn't noticed the taxi waiting, but it's for us. In Shona's world, taxis wait for you instead of you waiting for taxis and you pick up the bill because you can, not because it's your turn. On the way in the cab, we seem to have run out of conversation so I try Jude's number, but get voicemail, then Fraser – same. Clair will be teaching, so I call Jess and get a drowsy 'Wha'?'– and give up.

The bay at Lakki is huge with the dock on one side and a large marina on the other. The open sea isn't even visible from a lot of the town. Across the water, the two large grey ruins are rotten teeth in the green grey mouth of the hillside. The taxi turns left before we reach the seafront, heads up through Temenia village then joins the road I walked on Saturday, dropping us outside the hotspot. Several people are gathered outside. From the way they're grouped and their interaction, they look like aid workers. Inside the fence, no one's visible other than armed policemen – or soldiers, I can't tell, wearing the mandatory reflective sunglasses. Something is wrong. Alexis is with his colleague, Fenne, whom I recognise from the other night. He excuses himself and comes across to us.

'Sorry, a situation developed yesterday and there are still repercussions. It's not a good day for you to be here.' Shona wants to know what's happened, is keen to be involved, but he deflects her.

'Thank you, but it's delicate, we've been at the hospital and we're about to have a meeting with some of the other NGOs. Sorry to put you off but it could be volatile here. I'll call you both later.' Shona glances at me involuntarily as if she's thinking, 'What's it got to do with her?'

'Alexis, I'd really like to know what's –' Fenne joins in.

'Shona, it's very difficult. A lot of NGO workers have to leave, including me. I'm on my way to Kalymnos but I hope to be back in a few days. Come – why don't you keep me company as far as the bus stop?'

Shona eyes her coolly.

'Thank you, Fenne, but I don't answer to you.'

Alexis is abrupt. 'Shona, would you please go, now. I will call you later. You may have to leave the island, too. Annie, I'm sorry. I'll be in touch.' He kisses Fenne on both cheeks then turns his back on us. I try to calm matters and speak to her as she picks up her backpack

'Thanks, Fenne. We'd like to join you.' I take Shona's arm to guide her away but she shakes it off, clearly furious. The three of us climb into a people carrier with several of the other aid workers. The driver, Babis, is from Leros and works for another NGO. Fenne tries again, she is friendly and warm.

'I know you want to help, Shona, but the situation is unstable. Spend the day with your friend, get to know Leros. The war museum at Merikia's interesting. It's just around the bay. Too far to walk, though, and it will be hotter today. Babis will take you as far as Lakki and you could take a taxi.' Shona doesn't reply. Her arch behaviour is unwarranted and embarrassing.

I am concerned to know what's happened that's so serious. Fenne makes a judgement and answers me.

'OK. There was a confrontation between refugees and right-wing supporters yesterday. It got nasty, with some injuries and a car damaged. And after the disruption inside the camp about ten days ago…So, until the situation is calmer, aid workers have been asked to leave in case we become targets.'

'What about Alexis?'

'He's Acting Area Director. And being Greek helps. He's staying on to keep communication open, but he's withdrawing from a lot of his open contact.' I nod in question towards Shona. Fenne lowers her voice to a mutter.

'She's not established as a volunteer, yet, could be a holidaymaker so no perceived risk.'

I'm assuming Fenne wants to catch one of the smaller ferries or a hydrofoil from Aghia Marina. But we turn right at the road junction; I ask if she's going to Xerocampos.

'Yes, there's a small tourist boat that goes from there to Myrties on Kalymnos. Much quicker. And cheaper.'

'We were there, yesterday. I saw it.' We're soon in Xerocampos, where all the aid workers get off and I'm sorry to see Fenne go, but have to say goodbye. Babis chats to us on the way back, apologises that he can't take us all the way to Merikia as the transport is needed, but drops us next to the taxi office in Lakki.

There are three worlds here: the refugees and NGOs, tourists, and the people who live here. Shona, though, seems to be in a world of her own. She hasn't said a word since being so rude to Fenne. I suggest that as it's way too early for lunch and since we're halfway to the museum, why not go there? Wouldn't it be interesting? She shrugs.

'If you want.'

The museum is in one of the old hillside tunnels, dug out during the war. On the approach are wartime vehicles, including a plane. Lakki harbour, we learn, is the deepest in the Eastern Mediterranean and saw a lot of action in WWII. I am intrigued, not so much by the exhibits as by the photographs. When you see war films of the time, they seem just that, films, not real. It says in the guide that *The Guns of Navarone,* based on a fictitious island but featuring the battle of Leros, was filmed around here. There are photos of the Greek gun emplacements. Other photos, though, show the proud German victors posing by aircraft and tanks contrasting with the numbed acceptance of captured Greek and English men, standing together or piled into open trucks. They communicate across the years. I shudder a little more in the dank air. It's obvious to me there's one very big reason we need the EU; we don't want this to happen again. I think of Chaos croaking 'Thánados stin Angela Merkel'. Sadly, Státhis and I don't have enough common language to argue the point.

Shona glances briefly at the weaponry, uniforms, and other accessories of war but is obviously bored and excuses herself to get some air. I'm torn between being polite and learning more. Wartime Leros wins.

About thirty tourists squeeze onto benches to watch a video about the real Battle of Leros. I hunch against the rock wall as the grainy black and white film starts. The island was bombed extensively by the Germans. Lerians lost family members, homes. My Granny, Rosemary's mother, would have been alive then. Maybe she knew a British airman or soldier who fought the Germans in the skies over Leros or on the ground? From the sea? I make a note to ask Rosemary when I get back home. Would it interest Jude? He surprises me sometimes, well, pretty often.

My conscience pricks about Shona outside on her own, so I slip out as the documentary finishes. On the way, another photograph catches my eye. It's the big old villa I visited. Turns out it was built for Mussolini. No wonder it looks grand – but the Germans invaded Leros before he could set foot in it. He must have used some choice Italian swear words knowing his luxury holiday home had become a Third Reich guest house.

Shona stands rigidly in the midday sun, clutching an elbow, inhaling deeply on a cigarette. She holds it to her side almost guiltily.

'I don't really – well, not often, I hate these vape things. Been trying to give up for years.' Her fingers are nicotine-stained. Odd I hadn't noticed before. The expensive nails are a good camouflage.

'I don't remember you smoking in London.'

'No, I didn't so much, then. I'll ring for a cab, shall I?' She already has a taxi flyer out and dials.

'Kalimera. Do you speak English? Er – …' Her Greek is worse than mine. I let her struggle on. Just as well most Greeks reply in English.

Shona finishes.

'I *think* someone's coming. Hope he won't be long.'

The air is amber-hot and it's not even midday yet. I take out my factor fifty and offer her some. She regards my bunny logo vegan spray as though it might be contaminated.

'Thanks, I have some. Want to try it?'

It's French, looks expensive, and is no doubt tested on animals because they want to sell it to America and China.

'You're all right, thanks.' We each reapply our own sunscreen. She has on her straw sunhat; sensibly, I pull on my baseball cap. We decide to wait in the shade of the trees. Shona has a low patience threshold.

'Where's this taxi? I could do with a cold drink.' I offer her my water but she has her own. The gods are with us, a taxi driver has deciphered Shona's garble. Ten minutes later we're back in Lakki. I hope we can go our separate ways soon. Spending time with Shona is testing my tolerance.

THIRTY FIVE

ANNIE – Leros

We go straight to a waterfront table and order a beer and a white wine. They come with olives, cubes of feta, and bread. I love this boozer's perk in Greece. Even more reason to think about ending up on Leros. How superficial can I be? Shona takes off her hat, tucks her hair behind an ear and restarts our conversation.

'So, how's Jude getting on while you're away?'

'Fine. He adores staying at Fraser's place. It's such a cowp – I mean –'

'It's a mess?' Of course, she'd have learnt some Scots slang, staying with her granny in Lochgilphead in the school holidays – although I doubt her granny was anything like mine.

'Sorry. Yes, it's fine for a thirteen year-old boy but not me. Clair's keeping –'

'Clair, Fraser's ex-girlfriend? Daughter called Jess?' It's more of a statement than a question. I'm a little taken aback by the amount I have, apparently, told her and by how much she's retained.

'That's right. She's busy with her artists' holiday retreat at the moment but she and Fraser are both keeping an eye on him. And Jess is there at the moment, so between the three of them they'll keep him in line.'

My turn to ask about her life. What, though?

'Are you still living in London, Shona?'

'On and off, between going away to – various places, helping out.'

'Are you with any particular organisations?'

'No, not especially…' She trails off. It's strange, after all these years of sharing my posts and photos that I know so little of *her*. I don't like to intrude, but I'm curious, so I probe.

'Tell me about your CEO friend.' This is the one who advised her on Alexis's organisation.

'It's as I told you. When you said you were in Greece, my – friend – who is involved with charities, assured me that NRH was a reputable organisation. So I contacted them.'

'Ah. It all happened very quickly. Won't you miss him? Or is he not that special?' She gives me a sideways glance.

'I hardly think that's relevant.'

'Sorry.' I have a talent for wrong-footing her. There's something that doesn't quite fit, though. It's not beyond my imagination that Shona has friends who have friends, especially in the circles she moves in. But with her volunteering experience, it's odd that Alexis is keeping her at arm's length from the refugees. It didn't take long for me to have full contact on Symi. To be fair, though, Clair and Fraser gave me credibility.

She sips her wine and, for a few minutes, just as at Xerocampos, we're both struggling to find a topic of conversation. I don't want to fall into the same hole I dug there so think carefully about a suitable opener. Fortunately, Shona speaks first.

'How long are you planning to stay on Leros? I'm assuming you won't want to be away from Jude for too long?' My relief makes me chatty, flippant, even.

'Well, no. But Fraser and Clair are pretty competent gaolers – and Jess is on standby to corrupt him.'

I laugh but Shona doesn't, so I blunder on.

'Joking! He's made friends with some local kids so he can be at one or the other's place or on a dad's boat, it's very laid-back. Sometimes we don't know where he is all day. And he's a good swimmer, so I don't have any fears that way. Symi's a very safe island. I just wish it could be such a safe haven for the hundreds of refugees arriving every day.'

'Yes. Shame I couldn't have gone there. How lucky that you have such supportive family and friends on Symi. And your parents live nearby in Argyll, now, don't they? Even so, it must be hard being on your own at times.' She has turned the conversation. This is the Shona I remember; interested in people. Wrong of me to be pissed off with her for coming to Leros. She seems genuinely concerned about me.

'Well, it's frustrating more than anything, being tied to Jude's rollercoaster.'

'Rollercoaster?'

'Such as nose-breaking and other stuff.' I'm relieved that we're back on track and go into detail about the exclusion and the probable causes.

'I mean, I love him to bits, don't get me wrong. But having a kid at seventeen means you miss out on a whole chunk of freedom while you're growing up. By the time he's independent of me – which it seems kids never are now – I might be too old to just take off and have fun.' She listens, but her face seems a little – set.

'Well, against all the odds, you're obviously doing a sterling job of bringing him up. When I look back to that frightened little soul at the hostel –'

'Don't! I can't believe how naïve I was.'

'We're all naïve at seventeen, Annie.'

'If we're lucky.'

'How do you mean lucky?'

It seems obvious to me. 'Well, imagine being a refugee child, or a girl being raped by soldiers or a young boy forced to go into the army, nine year-olds working in factories in Bangladesh, sleeping in railway stations. We're only a kilometre from the hotspot. What have the children there seen?' She cuts across me as though I've gone too far again but I'm not sure how.

'You *will* have fun, Annie, I have no doubt. Just be thankful for your friends and family and what they've done for you. And what they're still doing for you. Someday you may have the opportunity to repay them, every one.'

I'm being lectured, now. She's one of the most confusing people I've ever met. To distract myself, I squint at the mouldering grey buildings on the other side of the bay; I can't see the psychiatric hospital from here, it's obscured by a small headland. I can see Mussolini's villa, though, and point it out to Shona, then ask if I ever mentioned the old psychiatric hospital.

'I don't recall. Shall we order lunch?' She's obviously reached compassion overload. After an hour or so we agree on splitting the cost of lunch again. As I need the loo, I offer to pay at the counter across the road but before I leave, I remember to take a photo of Mussolini's villa on my phone. Having once been through the disaster of dropping a phone from my back pocket down the pan, I wisely leave it on the table and take just the cash with me.

The heat is bearable in the shade, but crossing to the taverna means stepping into a kiln. In the loo, I wash my hands and splash cold water over my face then remember my brush is in my bag on the table with my mobile, so run wet fingers through my hair. It's pretty short so it sticks up, turning my head into a stubby sea urchin. As I queue to pay at the till, I turn and wave at Shona but she has her back to me. By the time I'm back at the table my hair's practically dry.

We walk up to the big supermarket for some odd bits of shopping and arrive sweating and parched. Lugging the all-precious water and a few other basics we ring for yet another cab. As I get out at Platanos, I see a mobile on the seat. Thinking it's mine, I pick it up to look at the screen –

'Mine, thanks.' Shona hurries around the car and whips it from my hand.

Both too exhausted to do anything but collapse in the cool of our respective rooms, we agree to text about dinner. In Pandeli, I send Alexis a text saying I hope his day has improved.

After a rest, my mood rises. It's a brilliant evening on a beautiful Greek island and I'm going out for a meal with… Shona.

I'm getting into a lather at the studio, attempting to knot my sarong into stylish eveningwear. I try to channel Gok Wan and what he would do. The sarong still ends up looking like a bag my Granny used for boiling clooty dumplings. In Kilachlan, summer means a lightweight sweatshirt and jeans. Jude's kitted out for Greece, so why not me? That old sense of incompleteness. Shut it!

Giving up any ideas of beach chic, I wrestle on a clean T-shirt and shorts, fiddle with a bit of makeup, and squirt on a lot of insect repellent. Done. On the way down to the taverna, I phone Clair, then chat to Fraser. Both say Jude's fine and behaving well. Wish I could either a) believe them or b) bottle whatever they've got and take it back to Kilachlan. Jude picks up briefly but is monosyllabic, so I tell him I love him and let him end the call.

We meet at a fish restaurant. I've already checked out they'll do a vegan meal. Shona hasn't heard from Alexis and spent the afternoon watching Sky TV at the hotel. On a Greek island. In summer. She's more animated than earlier, though. She's had a few 'aperitifs' before strolling down from Platanos, maybe? No matter, we manage to get through a couple of bottles of retsina, which is beginning to grow on me. Less of a tooth-peeler on successive glasses.

'Strange,' says Shona, slurring ever so slightly, 'I thought you'd prefer a French wine.'

'Not me, anything over ten per cent proof will do.' I check it – it's twelve point five. Shona sniggers, undermining her usual upper class air then speaks rapidly –

'Excuse-moi, j'ai fait une erreur; je pensais que tu aimais tous ce qui est français, y compris les garçons ainsi que les filles…' And she purses her lips in a kissing motion. Impressive, coming out with a sentence like that when she's pissed. I catch some of the words but not the sense. Something about liking everything French and then boys and girls. Must be the drink, but I remember it and, decide to piece it together sometime. We take photos of one another on our phones and Shona asks the waiter to take one of us together. We laugh and wave tipsily. Soon after, we call it a night. I need to stretch my legs and she needs help to remain upright, so I walk her to her hotel. Thought she could hold her booze better than this.

THIRTY SIX

ANNIE – Leros

When I get back to Pandeli it's about half eleven but I'm not ready for bed. There's still plenty of activity in the bars and tavernas. I collect my guitar from the room and sit on a rock below the hotel, strumming, singing under my breath. Hoping that Alexis will pass by? The castle up on the mountain is lit in green, looking like a giant Technicolor caterpillar. My phone rings. I assume immediately that there's a problem on Symi and pick up without looking at the number but –

'Annie – it's Alexis. Sorry, did I wake you?'

'No. I'm down on the beach.'

'Alone?'

'Shona's not with me, if that's what you mean.'

'Mind if I join you?'

'No, ochí, nee.' He must have been walking down the steps as he rang because he's with me in a couple of minutes.

'Hey – glad you brought your guitar with you.'

'I do very limited requests. Anything you'd like to hear?'

He sits on the pebbles.

'Whatever you like playing. I love your voice.' Is he flirting the pants off me? I try the Buchanan acid test, give a chord rich intro then go into Jude's favourite – even now. Part traditional, part my lyrics…

'Aunty Mary had a canary
Up the leg of her drawers
When she farted it departed
With a round of applause.

Umpty lairy, Tatty falairy
She's a naughty wee dog
Jack's a wee shit, I'm an eejit
'Cos I bury his logs'

It works, he laughs. But then he kneels up on the stones, which must hurt like hell, pulls my face to his across the guitar and kisses me so softly I just want to breathe him in, tobacco and all. He stops, suddenly.

'Sorry – sorry.'

'Why are you sorry? Suddenly decide I was a minger, eh, Alexi?'

'A minger?'

'Forget it. Why did you stop? I was just getting into that –'

'Annie – it's been a bloody awful day. At the end of it I knew the only person I wanted to see was you. But it's unfair of me. I shouldn't involve you in –'

He's the reason I'm here – and he's said the right words. I slip off the guitar strap and step off the rock as he stands up. Jesus, he's tall!

'C'mon. I've a few beers in the fridge that need drinking.'

I'm not lying about the beer. It's in the fridge but it's not necking beer that's on my mind. It doesn't matter whether I really feel something for this guy or I'm just high on having the freedom – it's good and at this moment it's what I want. Luckily, my room is three minutes away. The old London corner of my brain niggles, 'Does he have a condom?' I elbow it away, set down the guitar and gesture to the bed.

'Sorry, it's the only place to sit. Beer, then?' He stays standing, shakes his head. I take a step to him.

'D'you want to talk about today?' Another negative.

'How can I make it better?' He's strong for a skinny bloke. Catches me and lifts me to his lips. His mouth is warm and soft, however strong his impulse. He's holding me tight but kissing me tenderly and I respond. When he sets me down, he holds my face in his hands.

'Sorry, another cheesy remark coming up, but – I want to drown in you.'

I remember a line from English Highers that went like 'shipwrecking in your thighs', *Under Milk Wood* was it? And that's what I want him to do. We fall across the bed, struggling out of clothes. He swears, kicks off his trainers to free himself of his jeans. We are both naked. The scent of him excites me. I feel his erection, already wet. This man wants me. Wants someone. And I match him, ready in seconds, manoeuvring my body below his, impatient for him. Once inside me he gives a groan to scare a dinosaur, raises on

his elbows briefly to look at me. I pull him back, bringing my knees up against his body, my hands gripping his shoulders. And we're away like our lives depend on it. Now we're both making primeval noises until he grunts like he's been stabbed and all motion stops. But he knows I'm not there yet. He kisses me as he slides out, sucks my nipples, runs his fingers along my body and inside me until I

almost want him to stop. Then his face heads south. This man has a clever tongue. I wonder happily if my pubes will tangle with his face hair. The tingle's building, I flex my legs, teeter on the edge forever then topple into the pleasure star-bursting through me. And

I laugh. I laugh because I've done it. Because I have abandoned everthing to the moment. Because my Rampant Rabbit was never this much fun. Or this messy. Alexis laughs too, and I know he's sharing my joke… whatever it is.

We lie, collapsed and smug awhile.

'You know, Annie, we're very good at this.'

'I'm better at it than you are.' He frowns into my eyes. 'Is that a challenge?'

'Might be.'

'OK – give me a few minutes. I'm older than you, you know.'

The next time is longer, slower, chatty even. I peer down the bed at the length of his legs against mine. We're absurd together. Eventually we sleep, tangled, not waking until the sun makes its Turkish battle cry through the orange curtains.

Morning

He sits up suddenly, looks at his watch.

'Shit! It's late. Could I shower?'

'Sure, go ahead.' I tie on my neglected sarong and make coffee. He emerges, strafing himself with the towel. He has golden chest and pubic hair and on his arms it's white against his tan. His eyes are pale in the strong morning light. I'm trying to resist what I'm feeling but already it's too late. It would be sensible to start preparing for disappointment. He said '…I knew the only person I wanted to see was you'. But was that just 'cos he needed a shag?

'There's no milk.'

'Black is fine.'

'What time do you have to be at work?' He looks at his watch and shrugs.

'Half an hour ago?' He pours some cold water into his coffee and drinks it down, standing. We both feel that slight unease of the morning after the first night.

'Look, Annie –'

'It's OK, you don't have to–'

'You don't know what I'm going to say. What I want to say is don't worry, I know I'm – er – clean.'

'Me, too.' That's that out of the way. So is this it? He puts the mug down.

'I don't know what work will be like today but I hope we can – may I call you?' So polite. Can't have that.

'You better had. No, don't kiss me. I haven't brushed my teeth.'

I feel uncertain about the rest of the day. Should I ring Shona? No, she'll call me if she wants. Should I bother Alexis at work? Or wait submissively for him to contact me? The answer comes with my call alert, Joss Stone singing 'This is a man's world'. I flob out of the shower and pick up, eyes too full of water to see who's calling.

'Ah, you're up. Do they do coffee at these beach tavernas?' Shona.

'Uh – yes and yes. Where are you?'

'Bottom of the road. I'll go to the beach café.'

'I'll meet you there, Shona. Give me five – ten.'

I dry and dress at Super Woman speed. She's immaculate again, bottle green tie-front shirt, matching sun visor, and expensive cream jeans, a smidge too tight for her curves. Mean of me but satisfying to notice. Coffee and croissants are on the table.

'Thanks, Shona. Sorry to keep you.'

'Morning swim as usual?' I decide to lie but don't know why.

'Uh, yes. Round the headland to Vromolithos and back. What's on the agenda for you today? Have you heard from Alexis?' I know she hasn't. She tucks her hair behind her ear and I notice she's not wearing the pearl studs but small diamond ones.

'I'm not needed, apparently. I thought we could go to Patmos for a couple of days? There's a ferry in a couple of hours. I want to see the Cave of St John. It sounds awe-inspiring.' Oh no, not a girlie jaunt away from Leros.

'Yes, it must be.'

'You don't sound that enthusiastic, Annie?'

So many ways of answering this. If last night hadn't happened I might've said 'great'. Instead, I go for – 'Thanks, Shona, it's just… I'm here to help NRH, too. If I can't, I'd like to have a look round Leros, hire a scooter, take in the Temple of Artemis and see the cartoons in the place on the hill above Xerocampos.'

'Yes, I thought you might have other plans.'

What? It's the way she says it – did she see Alexis leaving my place? She couldn't have. That was nearly half an hour before she called. To deflect the uncomfortable note, I show interest in her trip.

'I hear Patmos is really worth seeing, especially the Cave. What time's the ferry?'

'Oh – lunchtime-ish.'

We finish breakfast, she allows me to split the meal again and I wish her an enjoyable few days, promising to stay in touch. As she walks up to her hotel, I feel a weight shifting. I am free to see Alexis. Should I be comfortable with my choice? She's been a supportive friend for many years. I decide my libido's an old friend, too, and it's time I got back in touch.

THIRTY SEVEN

ANNIE – Leros

I go to the rental place at the back of Pandeli beach. Hiring a scooter began to sound interesting as I was saying it to Shona. But the Temple of Artemis? The cartoons above Xerocampos? How did they pop into my head? I start off towards Lakki but have an adolescent rush of insecurity about bumping into Alexis, double back and head to Alinda then left towards Partheni and the airport, following my little tourist map. Wearing a helmet is decidedly uncool on Leros. Grannies down to kids flout possible head injury all the time, sometimes overpopulating the scooter like a circus act. But while the road surfaces are good, the tarmac at the sides unravels treacherously, so feartie-cat Buchanan is sporting Darth Vader headgear.

A track leaves the road just before the airport. It takes me about forty minutes to find the temple and even then, having rattled up an even smaller, evil dirt track, I'm not sure it's the right place. All I can see is a collection of knee-high stones approximating walls and a little chapel with a white and blue door, like an evil eye. I wander about taking random snapshots thinking, 'This is significant – not' and 'Was it wise to wear sandals and shorts and wander about in long grass?'. Leros has nine kinds of snakes and poisonous or not, I don't want to encounter one. Besides, I'm only doing this to justify not going with Shona. Enough. I stalk gingerly back to the scooter and wheel it down the track to the road.

Now where? I reach the main road, continue along past the airport and see a sign to Aghia Kioura beach. It's another death defying road. But I manage to skitter down it to be rewarded by a beautiful little area of sand, with a few shady tamarisk trees and heart-breaking turquoise water.

'This'll do me.' And here I stay, indulging in that 'first flush' of thinking about Alexis. Also, feeling – I'm not sure what – about Shona, and hoping that Jude really is behaving. As the beach starts clearing, I realise I could eat for Scotland.

I take it gently back to Pandeli and arrive near six. Two voicemails and a text pop up on my phone. Both voicemails are silent. Bound to be Jude, I don't bother checking. But the text is Alexis. 'Kalispéra. Te kanís? Dinner?' I feel my cheek muscles contract into a soppy smirk as I text back 'Kalispéra. Kála – essí? Yes neh ja!' My Greek runs out and I add 'Where? When?'

Then I try ringing Jude. It goes straight through to voicemail. I ask what he's been doing with Andy and Erik, tell him I love him.

We meet in Platanos, kiss on the mouth. He's trimmed his beard and moustache – for me? We're easy together, a relief, strolling hand in hand to Aghia Marina and on towards Krithoni. I must look like his four-year-old daughter – well, maybe eight-year-old. He pats my hand.

'By the way, I hope Státhis and Neféli didn't mind having an extra tenant last night?'

'I doubt they noticed. You know them?'

'I know Neféli more than him. She helps out at Pikpa – that's a centre where refugees can go for a meal, let the kids play, get some new clothes, do their washing, you know, run by volunteers. She's a great cook, brings a little feast all on her own every Sunday morning.'

'Ah – so that's where she was going with all that stuff yesterday. She and Státhis were having a hell of a row, then she got on her scooter and shot off.'

'Yeah. He's not so keen on her helping but fortunately she goes ahead and does it anyway. Strong woman.'

'Why's he against it?'

'There are quite polarised opinions about the refugees, even within families. It's always the same, this split between empathy and resentment. The ex-pats living here are all pro refugee and do a huge amount of good work. Look, here we are.'

He's booked Milos, the place Shona and I couldn't get into that first night. His friend, Babis, is on duty for another NGO tonight and will call him if need be. We have a table on the terrace outside, right on the water with a view of the stubby white windmill along the little causeway. It's an idyll and we're part of it. I excuse myself to make another call to Jude. Voicemail again. I leave a similar message and go back to the table.

'How's Jude?'

'Ignoring his mother.'

'He's thirteen. That's what you do. He'll be fine.'

'I know.'

Alexis orders in Greek, has quite a chat with the patron and introduces me. He's explained, he says, that I'm vegan and has ordered a special selection of mezes. A long slow evening stretches ahead. And at last we talk, really talk. More accurately, I talk. I just open my mouth and my log jam of a life comes piling out. He has an unnerving ability to make me offload, as though he's paralysed my frontal lobe and I have no inhibitions.

My stream of consciousness covers my adoption to Jude's birth. But not in neat chronological order. He prompts me to backtrack. So, I talk about university but edit out Eloise as I did with Shona. Why? He's not going to be homophobic;

A) he's pretty well acquainted with the human condition and

B) he's half Dutch – they're cool about everything.

I don't tell him about my blanks, either, my 'missingness'. That's for someone more devious than a therapist, let alone a potential – potential what?

I elaborate on Maggie, how much I adored her, grieve for her, that she spoke another language, German perhaps – or Dutch, in her last few days. Hoping Alexis may be able to identify it, I try to recreate a few words that I'd noted on my phone. He says it could have been Dutch but sounded a little more like Flemish, thinks it approximates 'I want to go home, Mummy'. Says what we thought was 'Michelin', as in Michelin-starred restaurants, could be 'Mechelen' with a phlegmy 'ch', a town in Flanders. He's intrigued and in forensic mode. If I hadn't already taken a dive for him…

'It got even stranger when Clair went through the legal stuff. The important documents were in a tin box at the croft. Maggie's parents' marriage certificate came out first. Clair always thought her grandmother, Maggie's mother, was just Jessica Jacobs. But she had a middle name, Magdalena. Then came Maggie's birth certificate. Her name wasn't Margaret but Magdalena.'

I go on to the will. Maggie left Harkin Croft to Clair and Jess, but gave Jude and me the right to live in it for our lifetimes, plus some cash to look after the dogs and the goat, way more than necessary. The rest of her money was to start a charity in Julia's name for educating the kids of one-parent families. I explain.

'See, Clair, Jess, and Jude were – are – all children of one-parent families.'

Alexis picks up on Julia. 'Who was she?'

'Julia was Maggie's lesbian partner.' Then I feel bad for mentioning Maggie's relationship so easily, but concealing mine with Eloise. To Alexis, however, Maggie's sexual orientation is irrelevant.

'Didn't Clair mind that her aunt left her nothing else?'

'Clair has a terrifying, disgustingly mega-rich mother, Connie, in Florida. She and Jess are OK. Maggie was her father's sister. He was an artist, like Clair.' I round off the Maggie story with a Harkin puzzle.

'What was even stranger on Maggie's birth certificate, was that her birthday wasn't 1930 like Clair thought, it was 1923. We couldn't think why she would lie about her age, that she was seven years older than she'd said.'

It's over an hour, I think, before my conscience prompts me to shut up. I look at my watch. It's after midnight. I have, in fact, been talking for more than two hours. Jess pops into my head: *'Give it all up and you have nothing left to excite a guy'*.

Even so, Alexis says, 'That's fascinating. Look, my mother's visiting Antwerp at the moment, about half an hour away from Mechelen. Shall I ask her to take a look around? Parish records, graveyards? Any local knowledge? You never know.'

'That would be amazing – if she wouldn't mind.'

The waiter is hovering, so we pay and start the walk back. Wee Skinny Malinky and the BFG. It wouldn't seem that odd if he hiked me up onto his shoulders.

'Look, Alexi, you don't have to walk me back to Pandeli. I'll be absolutely fine.'

'Are you saying you don't want to stay with me tonight?'

I don't know how to play this. 'No, I just wasn't assuming – I mean, we've only well, you don't –' After talking for hours I've suddenly run out of words. I feel myself being jostled sideways. He's taking the piss. I shunt him back. He pushes me back again and I'm going for him when he ducks, grabs me round my waist and tucks me under his arm.

'Put me down!' I struggle but he proves again how strong he is for a lanky guy.

'Do you give in?'

'No!'

'OK.' Instead of walking on, he bends down and puts me on the floor – in fact on the road – leaves me there and strides ahead.

'Hey!' I scramble up, run after him and whack the backs of his knees – something I learned in London. He goes down. I push him forwards and straddle his back.

'Now who gives in?' It seems we both do because suddenly there's a car horn and headlights. We're up, grab hands and run, both destroyed by laughter, swing right on the corner and on up the road until we stop, gasping, by the classy gift shop. He leans against the wall.

'Are you staying with me or not? I can't breathe enough to persuade you.'

'OK.'

His place is typically Greek with white walls and wooden furniture. There's a sleeping platform and double doors leading out onto a small balcony. He opens the fridge.

'Beer or wine?'

'Wine before beer, queer… I'll stay on the wine.'

'I have no idea what you've just said except you'd like wine.' High on each other we sit outside.

'Tell me about you, Alexi. How long since you started NRH?'

'About five years.' I'd assumed longer.

'So have you completely given up being an architect?'

'I don't know that I have given it up. NRH was something I had to do at the time. So, now tell me about London. You skirted round that.'

'Alexi, no, you let me go on – So, tell me about your father. Is he here on Leros, now?'

'Yes. I'll take you to meet him.'

'Really? I'd like that.' He laughs.

'I'd better warn you, he's in his late seventies and he's with another blonde. Australian, this time. Fortunately, she's beyond childbearing age or there'd be even more little Philanders running around the Eastern Aegean.'

It's my turn to laugh. 'Philander as in philanderer?'

'Afraid so. It means lover of mankind. Pappa confined it to womankind from Northern Europe, though, and exclusively blonde. So that makes you safe. It seems this one, Gretchen, has German ancestors. And now, I prefer to hear about someone else. Tell me about London, Annie.'

'But what about you? I don't know anything –'

'Another time. Let's continue with your theme.'

'It's an awful lot for one night.'

'Start with Jude's father. Did you meet him there? What was his name?'

I hesitate. The few people I've told think it's funny. But I say it anyway.

'Yes. His name's Zeezoo.' Alexis chuckles. There it is, that reaction –

'Not you, too, Alexi!'

'Zeezoo? Not *Zizou* by any chance?'

'What d'you mean, '*Zizou* by any chance'?'

THIRTY EIGHT

ANNIE – Leros

We're on the balcony of the apartment way up on the hill overlooking Pandeli Bay. I am in shock. Of all people, I didn't think Alexis would make fun of me. He explains gently.

'Zinedine Zidane. The footballer. That's his nickname. Zizou. Z-I-Z-O-U.'

I can't quite take it in. My head's a piggy bank of pennies dropping. So it wasn't just 'Zeezoo' sounding funny that made everyone laugh, it was because it was a super-famous footballer – whose nickname I didn't know and couldn't spell. How come I didn't catch on before? I know the answer as I ask it: Because everyone in London was in on the joke, and because I didn't tell anyone but Shona, Clair, and Maggie and they knew bugger all about football*'*. So 'Zeezoo' wasn't even his name. I'd had my doubts. But I never wanted to admit I didn't know the real name of my son's father. And what made it worse was remembering what the rapist said: 'Number twenty-six, eh? Like football, do you?' 'Z', last letter of the alphabet, number twenty-six. He must have used a name beginning with a different letter for all his *'little pigeons'*. How far along the list was Shelley – Beckham? Rooney?

Alexis touches my arm.

'Hey, what's the matter?'

'I've just realised what a socking great self-deceiving numpty I am. Was. Am.'

He waits then stands, holds out his hand – 'Come, Annie… come.'– leads me into the room, pulls a t-shirt out of a drawer and takes my glass from my hand. 'There's the bathroom, get undressed and put this on. You can use my toothbrush if you don't mind.' I do as I'm told. And I use his toothbrush, probably the most personal thing you can share, apart from sex. More, in fact.

When I come out, he's descending from the sleeping platform. 'The bed's ready and there's some water up there for you.'

I go up the little wooden steps and crawl across the floor-level mattress, gulp down half the glass of iced water he's left there. The bathroom is really just a shower, sink, and loo behind a plasterboard wall, I can hear his every action. I don't mind. It's good that he feels so uninhibited. Another pragmatic Dutch thing, or being magnificently Greek? Either way, it's a kind of comfort.

He re-emerges wearing boxer shorts, joins me in bed, and opens his arms. I snuggle across, head on his chest as he pulls the sheet over us and snaps off the light. The touch of a kiss on my hair. His breathing becomes regular. He manages to whisper,

'Goodnight, Annie,' before sleep engulfs him.

I reply, 'Goodnight, Alexi.' And despite my foolishness and this world of uncertainty and conflict, I feel secure enough to fall asleep.

THIRTY NINE

FRASER – Angelina's Bar, Symi

Maybe it's his mum being away or, more likely, discovering that my place is not blessed with the same home comforts as Clair's, but Jude was a bit down, yesterday. We got to talking about Maggie. Desperately unfair for him to have the perfect adult flown into his young life, only to have her snatched away before he had any idea how to deal with loss. Not that any one of us does, if we're honest. But he was just coming up twelve then, a time when your whole world takes a sideways slant and keeps whipping the feet from under you until you're – how old? I don't know how to finish that thought. I'd just started feeling sure footed in my thirties when I tripped over into the worst place in my life. That's how losing a Harkin woman affects you.

I was booked to play at Angelina's this evening and I'd normally have had Jude stay at Clair's, anyway. So, when he asked if he could sleep over with one of his pals, it sounded like a good idea. Late night football around Horio, a few computer games and a gut-bursting Greek supper would be great medicine for him. Of course I said yes.

But it got me to thinking about that time when Maggie melted out of all our lives. Clair and I weren't together as a couple, hadn't been for about a year, but we'd kept it from Maggie. It was easy with the double lives we led between Britain and Symi.

Maggie had another stroke. Then she caught a cold. Annie was watchful, said that with older people, particularly when they're static, it could turn to pneumonia. It did. Soon as I heard how close the end was, I got a ferry to Athens and a plane home.

Maggie was dipping in and out of consciousness. She started talking something like German – or Dutch – not as a foreigner would speak it, in fragments, but gunfire rapid. The rare times she was conscious she'd sometimes look straight into your eyes and through you. No recognition. It was the loneliest thing in the world, thinking Maggie didn't know you.

I was with her on my own when she died. Annie was at the croft with Jude, Clair was sleeping in a chair outside, Jess had nipped out for – something. A minute or so after she left I just felt that Maggie's soul had fluttered out. If they can, people wait for their loved ones to go before they die. I know Maggie loved me for loving Clair. But she loved Clair and Jess more, and she couldn't have let go while one of them was in the room; the pull to stay would have been too strong. That's what I told them. I don't know if it helped.

With all these memories seeping back, I wasn't in prime entertainment mode. Found myself winding up the evening with three older birds on a package holiday who'd stumbled on Angelina's and tried to rediscover their long lost – I dunno– fanciability?

So, here we are, after my set, standing each other a few rounds. I'm getting maudlin, talking about Maggie. Two of the birds decide they've had enough, pay Angelina and whiffle off. Saga Nora of the unconvincing blonde hair's up for more, though.

'It must have been a difficult time for you. Especially the funeral. I know when my –'

'Oh, aye. It was a green burial – in her own back garden – typical of Maggie. Woven willow coffin with a magnolia tree planted over it. Magnolia for Maggie, I suppose. Should've been buried with Julia, but we didn't know where Julia was, it was so long ago. Thirty plus years. Jewish cemetery somewhere.'

'Julia? Her mother?'

'No. Her – partner. Maggie and Julia were a couple. Julia's parents kept Maggie away when Julia died. Would have in life, if they'd have known.'

'So she was a –?'

'Aye. It was a really sunny day –'

'Look, Fraser –' Saga Nora is losing interest. I can tell by the way she finishes her drink and places the glass neatly on the bar.

'I'm sorry, but I'm really tired. Do you think you could call me a taxi?'

Difficult to get a taxi way up here so I offer to take her to the nearest pick-up point. If I can walk, that is. Angelina's dealt with my bleeding heart before. She has the door shut and bolted before we're a couple of paces outside. So, blootered though I am, I make sure I put the lady in a taxi. Not that I had any inclinations towards her, I just need a witness to see I'm doing the right thing. I am super-careful these days, and with good reason after what happened two years back. Long story and not for now.

After dropping off Saga Nora, I'm in the mood for another drink, so I'm sitting on my balcony with a top-up when I get a call from an unknown number. He's using my name so either he's trying to sell me something or he knows me, but I don't know him.

'Sorry – who's this?'

'The name's Mudie. I don't believe we've met. I'm a friend of Annie's, from Kilachlan. I need to get in touch with her.' Mudie… a tiny distant bell tinkles through the vodka and tonic. Mudie… Maggie's neighbour who nearly killed me with his lethal moonshine, way back?

'Archie?'

'Archie's my pa. I'm Donald. Look, I need to get in touch with Annie.' Kerr-ist! The big banker who's been trying to date her. My hackles rise at his posh-boy voice.

'So if she's your friend, why are you calling me and not her? How did you get my number anyway?'

'From your parents, and quite rightly, they were as cautious as you are, Fraser. They gave me your number but not hers. I used to have her number but I can't get through on it. I must speak to her. Is she there?'

'No. She's off for a few days on her own. And it's a bit late to be bothering her. I can give her a message.'

'Gosh, yes – it's midnight here, it must be –'

'Aye, two in the morning, here.'

'Fraser, I wouldn't bother anyone this late if it weren't important. Please will you give me her number and I'll call her first thing in the morning?' I've heard of scams like this before. I'm not giving him anyone's number.

'Look, Mudie, you give me yours. I'll pass it on, then, if she wants to call you, she can.' I can't see Annie using her precious minutes calling this poser in the UK. What sounds like a bad word comes from the other end of the phone.

'Hey, mind your language, pal.'

'OK, I apologise.' He's still banging on.

'Please text her straight away. I have to speak to her about Shoonagh. She may know her as Shoonagh Packham – or McCandless.'

'I'll think about it.' I cut him off and finish my drink. After my wee sister, eh? He's dripping with offshore funds, no doubt, and trying to ooze into her knickers. And he's married. It can wait. Then my conscience niggles. Not my decision to make. I text her: 'Donald la di dah Mudie wants to speak to you about Sheena somebody. Want his number?'

Five hours later my phone rings frighteningly early for the vodka I sank and the time I got to bed. It's Annie. She gives me a two minute ear-bashing. Apparently, I sent a text saying: 'Done old lady dad muddy wants to speak to you about she end somebody. Want his number?'. I check and so I did.

Annie's stratospheric – not so much as a 'please could you?' or 'thanks for letting me know'.

FORTY

ANNIE – Leros

I must have slept because I open my eyes to bright daylight, alone in the bed. The room glares at me, the intruder.

I find the loo, then call Jude. Guess what? Voicemail. I leave him another message asking him to call me, back it up with a text, then have a shower. As I'm drying, I check my phone and notice I've missed a message. It makes my insides contract, my first thought being Alexis. Shame on me, I should be hoping it's Jude. I'm disappointed to see it's a text from Fraser. And it's bollocks.

I ring him.

'What's this pile of shite you texted? Only just got it. Were you at Nobby's?'

I read it back to him. He explains the gist of the conversation with Donald.

'Sheena?'

'It could have been Siobhan. Or Shula.'

'That's the bloody Archers. I've got Donald's number, I'll call him.' Which I attempt to do straight away. But his number isn't there. I can't understand, I have it saved and he has mine. Come to think of it, why didn't he call me? I ring Fraser.

'Fraser, can you give me Donald's number? It'll be recorded on your phone.'

He does. Then I ask about Jude, tell him I'm going straight through to voicemail. Fraser says he's sure Jude stayed with –

'Erik – he stayed over with Erik last night.' It's usually Andy he stops over with.

'Erik? Not Andy?' My brother hedges.

'Aye, maybe it was Andy.'

'Yeah, the names sound so similar, Fraser. Find him and get him to call me.'

I do all the polite, girlie things one does when leaving a bloke's place in the morning. Want to leave a good impression with Alexis. As I open the front door, something catches my eye on the small table next to it. A single pearl stud. A large pearl. Like Shona's. Can't be many of those about on Leros. It's missing the sleeper. Strikes me that she wasn't wearing the pearl studs yesterday morning at breakfast. I leave it on the table. There'll be a good reason – won't there? Even though it's Alexis and Shona we're talking about and they're pretty awkward with each another. Since Zeezoo, however, infidelity's been an insecurity of mine. Maybe there's another reason they're being scratchy?

Alexis's place is, indeed, in one of the many little apartment houses on the hill that I've noticed on my swims in the bay. Many have Nordic sounding names on plaques by the front doors. All I have to do is follow down the steps to reach Pandeli.

I want to think about Alexis and why he wants to hear my stuff and not share his. It's either because he's dealing with such traumas with the refugees that my ordinary experiences are a distraction or there's something he doesn't want to revisit? The ex? Something else? Over-thinking? Moi? No, analytical.

I'm annoyed with Fraser for splitting my mind between my wants and my responsibilities. Just once, once in forever, I wake up with something other than parenting or work on my mind, and he shatters it with garbage about Donald Mudie and Jude's whereabouts. Jude will be with a mate on Symi, but that's not the point. Yeah, as his mum, I should know *which* mate and *where* on Symi.

Donald's message isn't such an issue. Probably his ego can't admit his looks and cash won't buy him a grapple with my private parts. Quel saddo. Devastating to confess, however, there have been times when I wouldn't have minded being grappled by Donald. But I'm no working class hero. An affair with a married moneybags, fit though he may be, would be a complication too far.

I'm impatient for Fraser to tell me where Jude is and why neither of them have rung. Another part of my mind is telling me I don't have to wait for Alexis to contact me. That kind of confidence, at least, is excellent progress. So I text him, then Jude, again, and Fraser, send belt-and-braces email to both Alexis and Fraser, send Jude a Facebook message knowing he won't read it, email and message Clair and Jess with instructions/requests re. Fraser and Jude. Then wait for replies.

While I wait, I look up Shona's Facebook; she's been on it six years. Her profile doesn't say anything. There are quite a few large blanks in her posts, too. She's never specific about what she's doing, just volunteering with the homeless or with refugees, domestic abuse victims et cetera, not where. A security thing? Even a direct message to me over six months ago, the first in a year, doesn't mention anything personal, just wishes us Happy New Year and asks for news. My reply, probably written late at night after half a bottle or more of Chardonnay, rambles on about Jude's problems at school, mine with the other parents, my boredom and frustration. I joke about 'a city-type', not named, obsessing over my body. Reading it back, I'm surprised there's nothing about the price of cheese. Her reply is supportive. Next message is from her, asking me how things are going. I don't reply until the long snarl while I was waiting for Jude at the therapist's, a month later. There's a definite one-sidedness to the communications. The most I know is that she's well off, largely from the car she was driving in London, the clothes she bought me there and the ones she wears now, also from the way she's always volunteering and never doing paid work. Oh yes, and being able to drop everything and fly to the Aegean.

After all that soul-baring on Facebook Messenger, I forgot to let her know when we were leaving for Symi, just included her on the group message when Jude and I arrived on Rhodes. Is it really her current squeeze who helped her link up with NRH on Leros? And why's she so antsy that Alexis has given my sex life a jump start? She's made it clear she's not a lesbian.

Speaking of the provocateur, Alexis rings.

'Hey, korítsi mou. Are you OK? Sorry I left early this morning, but you were sleeping so peacefully, I didn't want to wake you.'

Korítsi mou? What's he just called me?

'No, that's cool. How's your day so far?' A silence then – 'Ah – I don't know how long I'll be. Want to meet later?'

'Yes. Can't I do anything to help, though? I mean with Fenne and Shona gone?'

'Sorry, have to go–'

What's going on, now? He sounds very stressed. It's lunchtime and I've no food in, so hike up to the little supermarket at Platanos, ringing Jude and Fraser on the way. Both go through to voicemail. I try Clair who, mercifully, picks up. She's in Yialos.

'No, I haven't seen either of them today. I think Fraser's over in Nimborio so I expect Jude's with him.'

'I spoke to Fraser this morning, he said Jude stayed over with Erik or Andy, he can't remember which.'

There's a noise like she's muffling the phone. 'Annie, can I get back to you? Won't be long. Bye.'

I wander round the supermarket and head back down the hill, still waiting for Clair. At the room, I open a beer and go out to the terrace. I remember Donald Mudie's message. Should I try him? Or leave the line open for Clair? My phone rings, saving the decision. It's a London number.

'Annie – thank god I've got you. It's Donald Mudie.'

'Why aren't you ringing on your mobile?'

'I can't get you from my mobile for some reason, Nessie gave me your number. I'm on the office landline. Listen – do you know a woman called Shoonagh?'

'Um, no– there's a Shona doing volunteering here on Leros, except she's –'

'Have you ever met her before?'

'Yes.'

'Listen, Annie, this may be something and nothing but an old school pal of mine, Jim McCandless, has a sister, Shoonagh. They were both at boarding school in the UK while their parents were working abroad –'

'And this involves me, how?'

'They used to stay with their grandmother in Lochgilphead for some of the school holidays, not a million miles from Kilachlan. I was at school with Jim and he invited me there a few times. We went sailing on Loch Fyne. Anyhow, the sister had a few problems, shall we say, some of her behaviour was a bit irrational. Part of which was having a crush on me, silly child. But no matter. She became more disturbed, I gather, as she got older, ended up in psychiatric care quite a few times. She'd be forty-five, now.'

Lochgilphead? No, it can't be the same person, surely not?

'Shona's name isn't McCandless. I think you've got the wrong –'

'Married name, Packham.'

A chill strains through me. Donald continues.

'I haven't seen Jim for three or four years, but I bumped into him the other night and it jogged my memory. One time at her grandmother's house she had a fit of temper and cut the heads off all the flowers. I thought of your daffodils at Harkin Croft. This Shoonagh still goes to the Lochgilphead house, so she could have –'

It's feeling very uncomfortable. Even so, I argue.

'It doesn't mean that she –'

'He said the family tries to keep tabs on her but as soon as she's discharged she disappears. There's a pattern. She volunteers for things then overreacts if she feels undervalued. Sees herself as a Mother Teresa figure. She can be obsessive, even threatening sometimes. She's also pretty bright, manipulative, and very plausible. They found out she'd gone to Greece this time, just a few days ago. And, yes – I'm getting Greek myth – er – I think he said she's got a form of – erm – can't remember the term.'

'Narcissism?' We looked at narcissism in third year at uni. 'What's she done, Donald?'

'Stalked people, vandalised property, that kind of thing. She's got court orders not to approach the HQs of a few charities. They think she tried to kidnap someone, once, but –'

'Are you sure about this?'

'It's what her brother says. Have you seen her recently?'

I have a very bad feeling.

'I'm not sure it's the same person but, if it is, yes she's been with me here on Leros – and now she's gone to Patmos for a couple of days.'

'Well… just take care when she comes back. Oh, by the way, she has quite distinctive dark red hair. At least, she did then.'

Shona has dark red hair.

FORTY ONE

FRASER – Symi

It's early afternoon. We've tried all the kids and parents that Jude might have been with this morning and drawn a blank. Clair and Jess both are insanely pissed off with me.

'You actually OK'd him staying overnight with someone without ringing first?'

'Forgive me for not being a paranoid parent!'

'You're supposed to be looking after him, Fraser. That means you have the same responsibility!'

After a bit more Fraser-bashing, we split and search the island. It's nearly three so we have to be fast to catch the beaches. Clair takes the car to Harani, Nos, Nimborio and back, then Marathounda and Panormitis. Jess takes her scooter to search Pedi, leaves it there and catches taxi boats to Aghia Giorgios, Nanou, and back. I pound Horio and Yialos.

Panos is vaping outside the kafeneion opposite the *Giorgios*' mooring, ready for a chat but I don't have time.

'I'm looking for Jude. Don't suppose you've seen him?' It's heaving with tourists in a last minute shopping frenzy before the late ferry returns to Rhodes, so I'd have trouble spotting him, let alone Panos, who's only seen him a few times this year. He's obliging, though.

'No but I will look.' Which means he'll stay rooted to his chair.

I scout round the streets behind both sides of the harbour, asking at a few shops, but the answer's consistently negative. Thing is, Jude could be mistaken for a Greek lad. He wouldn't stand out except for his hair, perhaps, which he wears impossibly short and sort of geometric. God knows where he gets that done in Kilachlan.

I've run out of ideas. Passing the ferry agent I give it a try, on a very slim off-chance. Dimitris and Poppi won't know Jude but might recognise a description. No, they haven't seen him. There was a boy of about that age in today, but he was with a woman, and he was wearing a baseball cap so they couldn't really see his face.

'What about the woman? What was she like?' I'm clutching at straws. And no, they couldn't describe her, either. They have a brief conversation in Greek from which I gather she took her sunhat off to enter her PIN number. She was in her forties, probably, and she had red hair tied back, dark red hair, says Poppi. Oh, and the boy's cap was a football club one, maybe, says Dimitris. Blue, he thinks, with a white badge and a red lion on it. *Oh, for – that's Jude's Rangers cap.*

'Where were they going?'

'Rhodes. The three o'clock ferry.' The worst news. They could get anywhere from Rhodes. Then I remember Donald's phone call. He wanted to talk to Annie about some woman – pretty urgently. I am in profound shit.

My next stop is the police station. From there I ring Clair. Her first thought is, 'D'you know where Jude's passport is?'

She and Jess hunt everywhere they can think of at her place and mine. We can only hope that Annie's got it. An hour later Clair joins me at the police station.

Something's going through my head, something about the woman. Dark red hair's unusual enough to remark on, here in Greece. The woman with the boy had dark red hair. It reminds me of another woman, two years ago, and another trip to the police station. Surely not? I dismiss it. Way too tenuous a connection.

They've been seen! Panos's wife Marina was on the 15:00 ferry today to visit her sister on Rhodes. She rings me, says she saw Jude and said 'hello'. He was with a woman. When Marina asked where they were going, Jude got as far as: 'We're going to see Mum in Le –' when the woman cut in, said they didn't want to spoil the surprise and would appreciate it if Marina didn't give them away. Then she hurried Jude off. He was wearing his blue Rangers cap.

I relay this information to the police. They get onto Police HQ in Athens who will alert all ports and airports, and inform the British Embassy. They also contact the Rhodes police. Jude's picture will be uploaded to Amber Alert Hellas, the service that broadcasts images of missing kids. He'll soon be on TV throughout Greece.

The 15:00 from Symi would have arrived in Rhodes Port at 16:00. Could they have caught another ferry after that? If not, they must still be on Rhodes. I look up the timetables. Fortunately, there weren't any from Rhodes to Turkey after that, which would have brought a whole new bag of complications. But there's a 19:00 to
Piraeus Athens, calling at Kos 01:20, Kalymnos 02:50 and arriving at the mainland 13:10 on Thursday. Just hope word has got to the ferry operators. At least the airport check-ins will ask for identity as usual practice. The odd thing is what Jude said: 'We're going to see Mum in Le –'. If he meant Leros, why were they travelling to Rhodes – the opposite way?

FORTY TWO

ANNIE – Leros

I ring Clair. She's apologetic.

'I'm sorry, Annie, Fraser's out and he's not picking up.'

'What about Jude? Where is he? Have you seen Erik or Andy?' Just too much of a pause, then –

'He was with Andy overnight but he left after breakfast. Look, I'm sure he's fine. Fraser's just disorganised, you know what he's like.'

'No kidding.' I imagine the head-banging Clair's going to give him. She tries to reassure me.

'Symi's a very safe island. We'll find him.' If anyone else tells me how safe Symi is… I tell her about Donald's call.

'Annie, if this woman's gone off to Patmos – even if she *is* the person Donald's talking about – there's nothing to worry about, for the time being. But you might feel better if you came back to Symi.'

'For the time being' resonates. My wise head says, *'Go to Symi. It's what any parent would do'*. Back to Symi it is. But there's Alexis, I'm not going to just text him, I have to actually *see* him before I go.

Packing takes all of five minutes, then I visit Státhis and Neféli and try to explain in English, a smattering of Greek, and a lot of mime that I have to get back to my son on Symi. My mime isn't exactly Marcel Marceau standard, but somehow my meaning gets across. Greeks will do anything for their kids, especially sons, so they don't mind me going at short notice. Besides, another tourist needing a room will arrive on the next boat. I pay them what I owe and leave my morning's shopping for which they say 'efháristoh' many times. Státhis mimes tears and Yia yia Neféli kisses me goodbye.

The sun's high but I suffer the hike up to Platanos and down to the travel agent at Aghia Marina, texting, texting, texting all the way. Once there, I learn that I can't get to Symi today. Have I burnt my bridges by checking out from Státhis and Neféli? I have a sneaking feeling that I will find accommodation elsewhere. I buy a ticket for tomorrow, cross the road and dump the backpack and guitar under a sun shade, ready for a beer. Alexis calls.

'Annie, I just got your text – what's the problem?'

'Tell you when I see you.'

'That may be some while. Where are you?'

'Aghia Marina.'

'Go and wait where we sat on Friday night –'

I can hear loud voices.

'Where are you, Alexi?'

'At the hotspot – sorry, I – 'He ends the call. I sit obediently where he told me and order a beer from another scantily clad Greek goddess. Why Alexis's dad goes for blondes defeats me when there are all these luscious beauties on his doorstep. Must be a case of the grass is always greener, or Anglo-Saxon-centric propaganda. Where did I get to be so cynical?

It's mid-afternoon and the sun sears the harbourside to glaring white. I realise that everything inside me is contracting with tension and drink the first beer way too fast. My phone pings an incoming text. It is Shona, with a picture of a building on a hilltop and the text: *The Cave of the Apocalypse, Patmos. You don't know what you're missing! S*

Oh well, she's doing something she'll enjoy a little more than hanging about on Leros. I text back: *Looks fabulous. Glad you're having a good time. On way back to Symi – Jude gone AWOL wee bugger. Annie x*

At least she won't mind the '*bugger*', we've established that.

It takes a moment or two for me to realise that someone, a couple in fact, have joined me at my table, an elderly man with a waist-length beard and a middle-aged woman, blonde, wearing a baseball cap. She speaks first.

'Hi – I'm Gretchen. You must be Annie.' The tumblers in my brain are slow to release the memory. These two must be Alexis's dad, Philander, and his girlfriend – can't be too many Gretchens on Leros. At the same time, I am aware of Philander eyeing me up and down, cheeky old sod. I ignore the impropriety and speak to Gretchen.

'Hi. Alexis told me about you.'

'What? The blonde floozie from Oz?'

'No, I mean Philander and you.'

'Ah. The old Greek paedo and his adolescent victim?' She laughs and lights a cigarette, her gravelly voice a testament to a long addiction. Philander mutters to her in Greek.

'Shut up, Philo, you know I only understand you when I want to. Annie, Alexis sent us to rescue you. Dunno what's going on but whatever it is he seems to have a soft spot. Wanna come back to ours? Sure you do.' She snaps her fingers and yells, 'Signómi! To logoriásmo, parakoló!'

Asking for the bill in Greek. Impressive. Before I can interject, the transaction is done. Gretchen shoulders my guitar, Philander offers me his arm.

'Let's go home.' It's the first time he's spoken to me. Must be the strong, silent type.

We head out of town along the sea front and stop at one of the villas facing the opposite shore of the bay. Gretchen pushes the creaking metal gate into a small yard.

'Welcome to our humble abode.' We pass through a heavy, carved door into a lobby then on to an exquisite interior of small, tall rooms, painted white and furnished simply but beautifully with antique sofas, armchairs and woven rugs, ornaments in recesses, Turkish lamps on tables and hanging from the ceiling. The air is scented with musky herbs. All I can think is it's a fairy palace and I would love to live here forever.

'Gretchen – Philo– this is so beautiful.'

Gretchen sets down my guitar and Philo relieves me of my backpack then leads me up into a courtyard at the back of the house, shaded by trees growing out of marble paving, covered in just enough verdigris to make the area comfortable and real. I am home. Gretchen seats Philander and me.

'Just chill, Annie. Alexis knows you're here.' She disappears, leaving me with the old guy. No matter his age or the Gandalf beard, he is still handsome. More than anything, his eyes are youthful, and the way he looks at me produces a tad of the effect that Alexis has on me. This is one sexy geriatric. I sense he is phrasing a question, so put my head on one side, looking directly at him, inviting him to speak. Instead, he laughs and shakes a finger at me.

'No, no, not yet, Annie.'

'Not yet what, Philo?'

'I think you know.' He's right, I do. He wants to know why Alexis, why Leros and why I'm leaving suddenly.

'Whatever the question, Philo, I should probably tell Alexis the answer first.'

'That *is* the right answer. It tells me a lot about you. How much do you know about Alexis?'

I relate those facts I know while Philander works his worry beads – kombolói – swinging them around and between his fingers in a perpetual series of rapid loops and swirls. His concentration on me emphasises how little I know about his son, making me tail off. Gretchen saves us by returning with a tray of iced mint tea. It is sweet and piquant and Gretchen is an easy companion.

'So what do you think of Leros, Annie?'

'I think I'm in love –' Where did that come from? Gretchen jumps in.

'I know what you mean, Annie, very easy to fall in love with this place, especially with some of the islanders.' She and Philo share a look that near brings the blood to my cheeks. I try to move the conversation on. Philander opens a pack of Marlboros and proffers it. I shake my head. He takes out two cigarettes, lighting them and passing one to Gretchen. I'm sure I've seen that done in a film, there is a familiarity to it that I find quite sweet, despite my views on smoking. She blows out a long plume of smoke, careful to avoid me.

'So, what's your story, Annie?' she asks, not out of interest I sense, but because it's the way these conversations go.

So I tell them about Jude and why I'm going back to Symi. They're quiet for a few moments, then Philander asks –

'Does Alexis know this? No, I thought not, he would have said when he rang. On Symi, as with Leros, the only real danger comes from outside and, even then, children are not at risk.'

'I just can't help thinking…' I trail off, not even wanting to voice what I'm thinking. Has Jude fallen into a ravine? (In Horio? Come on!) Drowned? (He wouldn't have gone swimming on his own.) Has he had an accident? (So many people around, he's bound to have been seen or heard.) Philander said, the only real danger comes from the outside. But Jude *is* a child, despite his height. Anyone can tell that.

Philander's phone rings. He has a conversation in Greek then passes the phone to me. It's Alexis to say he's coming home in about an hour and that I should take a taxi up to his place. I agree but know I won't. The walk will give me some thinking time, despite hiking the guitar and backpack. Plus it'll save a few euros.

I thank Philander and Gretchen for rescuing and entertaining me. They are full of sympathy over what I face on Symi. Philander takes me by the shoulders and, for a moment, I fear a Panos-style nauseating kiss. But he wishes only to sympathise and embraces me, his feathery beard touching my cheek. He's taller than me, of course, but it's hard to believe that he's father to the lofty Alexis.

'I am sorry for your fear. We will think of you on your journey and hope that your son waits for you. I said nothing to Alexis of him being missing, it is for you to tell.'

'Efháristoh polí, Philo.'

'You speak good Greek.'

Gretchen gives me a long hug.

'Hope to see you again soon, sweetheart. When you get your kid back and all this fuss is over, bring the little bastard here.' 'Bastard' meant as a term of affection, I know. Over her shoulder, I see a table filled with photographs of children, some blond, some dark-haired, all smiling. Would it be from a happy childhood on Leros if, indeed, they are all Philander's offspring? None of their mothers are apparent. Maybe Gretchen has taken care of that. There is a newer photo at the front, a couple in evening dress. I know, instantly, even without the beard, that the man is Alexis. They are both blond and she is nearly his height. Who is she? I say nothing, but continue the farewells and assure them no, I don't want a taxi. And off I go.

FORTY THREE

ANNIE – Leros

I have underestimated the walk and rather wish I'd booked a ride while I could. It is approaching dusk. Darkness will drop quickly. The door of the apartment is open. He's on the phone, speaking Greek. His body language is closed, head bowed. I put my stuff down quietly. He sees me, holds my look for a moment. Something very bad has happened. I wander out to the balcony, anxiety over Jude clouding my mind. It goes quiet inside. Alexis joins me, passes me a beer.

'What's happened, Alexi?' His fingers touch his brow, damming back thought. His stillness disturbs me.

'Tell me?'

The words, when they come, are quiet, almost whispered.

'Another boat sank today. People drowned. There isn't enough mortuary space for them all.'

I reach for his hand.

'But they found room for the children. They found room for the children in ice cream freezers. Ice cream.' His body is in a vice, this man who's seen it all. The photo of him with the woman – what if?

'Oh God, Alexi, you didn't say, but – you've got a kid, too, haven't you?'

His mood spins from anguish to rage.

'What the fuck kind of question is that? Would that make it any worse?' It's like he's slapped my face. 'People with children think they're special – no one can feel anything like they do. Well, they're wrong. Having children is a biological process. Millions of people do it every second. In most cases all it needs is the female to open her legs and the male to ejaculate. Whether I have or haven't impregnated some female, doesn't change the pain or the grief or – or – the loss when a child – when children die!'

'Alexi, being a mother is –'

'Is what? Sanctified? You planned your son? You and his fake father? At least your child has a mother, a safe place to live. But these have been bombed out of their homes. And who cares? The people who manufacture the bombs? Russia? The UK? Europe? No. So they escape to Greece, but there's no place for them here, even when they die. Lucky for the children they're small. They must think they're in heaven, lying in an ice cream freezer. Oh no, I forgot, they're dead and there is no heaven.'

His words are wounding, the image devastating. My mother's remark zings back across the years – 'You were a baby of the Ice Cream Wars'. And that film, '*Comfort and Joy*'. None of that here, not for anyone. 'Ice Cream Wars' has taken on a new meaning.

There's another memory, about ice cream and children, reaching for me. Ice cream and Jude.

Alexis's phone rings, he goes inside to speak. Sounds like Dutch. I put the beer down, follow him in. But his back is to me and I feel it's deliberate. Am I welcome any more? I shoulder my stuff and make for the door, careful to make no sound but wanting him to see me, hoping he'll stop me, say he's sorry for taking it out on me. I need him to know Jude's missing. I wonder should tell him, too, what Donald Mudie said about Shona – Shoonagh – whatever her name is? Another fake identity that I fell for? As I leave, I notice the pearl stud is still on the table. Outside in the alleyway, I remember there's no point in going down to Pandeli because I've given up the room. No doubt I could go back there but, instead, I climb up to the road and head for Vromolithos. The night air is no longer soft but cloying. I am aware of being alone and feel spooked. I can go to the taverna up the road for a while. They have Wi-Fi. Alexis will be able to get in touch with me by phone, text, email or message. All the way there, I hope for the sound of his voice and fear the footsteps of a stranger, but hear neither. As I turn down the slope to the taverna, I dial Jude again. *'This person's phone is not responding'* says the hateful female voice.

Once on the covered terrace, I text, then wait. Ice cream and Jude – what was it? I WhatsApp and message him, almost hopelessly. With the other part of my brain, I want to ask Clair for advice about Alexis. But I'm afraid to ring her and find out that Jude's still missing. He must be or she would have called me to say he's safe. Ice cream and Jude…I'm seeing Glasgow.

It's time for some objective thought. And what I think, in the midst of my concern for Jude, is this: Alexis is right, people do assume being a parent gives them exclusive access to compassion. I told him my problems as a mother but didn't expect him to fully appreciate them unless he was a father. Didn't even find out if he was. My double standards. No wonder he's angry. I have to apologise if there is to be any relationship with him. And I want there to be. But it's all been about me this far. Christ, imagine me not knowing whether he has kids or not. I still don't know; the picture means nothing and I know almost nothing about Alexis the person.

I pick up my backpack and guitar. A group of people at the next table ask me cheerily if I won't stay and give them a song?

'Sorry, I've got nothing to sing about.' Not that they'd want to hear, anyway.

I knock. He opens the door.

'Alexi, I'm so sorry. I really am.' He looks down but doesn't move aside to let me in. This isn't going to be easy, but I try.

'I've behaved like I'm the only one who's got problems – or feelings. I call myself a mother but I behave like a child. And this – what happened today – it's desperate. Of course you're devastated.'

He reaches out and turns me around. Is he sending me away? No. He takes the guitar, eases my backpack off and carries them inside. Speaks on the way.

'You're a really terrible person, Annie Buchanan, I don't know what I see in you.'

'I can come in, then?'

'Unless you want to stand on the doorstep all night.'

We're all right.

FORTY FOUR

ANNIE – Leros

It's late. The phone keeps ringing for Alexis. I prepare a salad and we eat on the balcony. We're at peace, quiet, allowing wounds to heal. Between his phone calls, there is no opportunity to tell him about Jude so I ring Clair to let her know I'm on the first ferry back tomorrow. She talks about a sighting; Jude really is missing. She and Fraser have been at the police station for some hours. And she asks:

'Annie – do you have Jude's passport with you?'

'No– why would I –? Oh, God – it was in my room, in the drawer by the bed. Have you looked there?'

'Yes, but I'll get Jess to check again.' My whole body cramps. Alexis is still on the phone. I don't call my parents, unprepared for the level of alarm they'll express. Carol-Anne's phone gives a '*not available*' message.

Grasping at straws, I ring Donald Mudie. He's relieved to hear me and shocked by the news of Jude. Says it's possible that Shona is involved, that it might help to know more about my friendship with her.

'You really think it's Shona? But she sent me a text from Patmos. With a photo.'

'Was she in it?'

'No. Just the Cave of the Apocalypse.'

'She could have photographed that from a postcard or the internet… Annie, are you there?'

How stupid of me. Is she responsible for Jude disappearing? If she is, the text was meant to throw me off the scent. No, the photo threw me off, but the words gain disturbing substance *'You don't know what you're missing'*. Missing. Jude is missing. It *is* her. Shona has Jude. And now I've told her I'm going to Symi… I tell Donald.

'I can't believe I fell for it, Donald. I just don't know what to do next, apart from go to Symi.'

'The best thing you can do at the moment, Annie, is be practical. Try to work out whether she has been playing a part in your life secretly since London. Maybe jot down some dates of contact with her, any negative incidents?'

'Donald, I've got more things to–'

'Like when the daffodils were chopped.'

'But I'm sure that was to do with the kids at –'

'Really? Has anything else happened? Anything else that's upset you?' Oh, Donald Mudie, if only you knew. But I say I'll think about it and maybe make a list while I'm on the ferry back. He'll call this McCandless guy, the brother.

'I can't imagine how you must be feeling, Annie. I'll do everything I can to help.' It's the first time I've heard anything in his voice that sounds genuine.

I twitch the salad around, nibble a few olives, try to fend off hearing Alexis's angry words again: *'Lucky for the children they're small. They must think they're in heaven, lying in an ice cream freezer'*. The thick air chills as my imagination flashes up a frame of Jude, dead under sliding glass. The shock prompts the memory I was grasping for – ice cream and Jude – the baby snatch attempt in Glasgow – I'd gone to fetch ice cream – left Jude outside in the buggy…

I jump at the hand on my shoulder.

'I'm sorry – I've let the salad get warm –'

Alexis's attempt at lightening the situation has the opposite effect. Suddenly it's all too much. I start trembling, my voice shreds but I'm beyond crying. I struggle up as my breath rasps faster, faster and I can't get any air into my lungs. He disappears and comes back with a paper bag, holds it over my nose and mouth, even though I struggle to push it away. Gradually, gradually the panic recedes. I start to droop and he lowers me onto a chair where I slump, exhausted, but he makes me sit upright.

'Keep your airway free.' His professional voice. He brings me a glass of water. This balcony has suffered a hell of a lot of high emotion from me.

'Is this about earlier? Or something else?' he asks.

I tell him about Jude, Shona and the text. He leans back, hands on head, breathes out, straightens.

'Oh, Annie, you held that inside all evening? And then I threw all that at you. No wonder you had a panic attack.'

He rings the Leros police to pass on the development of Shona's text, makes a note of a number, then fills me in.

'Forward Shona's number and the Patmos text to this mobile. They will contact Symi. They understand that you'll be on the ferry tomorrow.'

Then he holds my hands, asks me carefully about any knowledge or memories I have of Shona. The only times we actually met before Leros were in London all those years ago. The hostel might still have details. We look up their number. It's way too late in London to ring now, even though Greece is two hours ahead. But it's something I can do on the ferry tomorrow.

Later, joining me in bed, he says:

'Shona said she had a British DBS certificate but that it was out of date. Her passport said Shoonagh but I thought maybe it was just the weird British spelling of her name. I was waiting for a check on her other credentials. But something about her felt – I don't know – uncomfortable. Her sense of importance, as if I was subordinate and she was doing me a personal favour. And the way she dressed didn't tally with the sort of work she was expecting to do. I decided not to let her near the refugees as an NRH volunteer until I received some kind of reference. I should have moved faster.'

'You had so much else to do. You wouldn't expect a volunteer to–'

'Disaster tourism isn't uncommon, I've met some pretty weird people in that way and they waste everyone's time and patience. Look, tomorrow I'll contact other NGOs in the islands and ask them to pass on Shona's description.'

Neither of us sleeps well, if at all. His long body tangles the single sheet as he agonises through dreams. I can only watch, my mind split roughly 80/20 on Jude and him. Where's my son? Will I ever see Alexis again? Then I feel guilty that it's not 100% Jude.

FORTY FIVE

ANNIE – Leros

Morning. As we are leaving, Alexis stops at the door.

'By the way – this pearl earring. I trod on it on it going down your steps on Monday morning. I should have mentioned it to you. It didn't look like something you'd wear, though.' I feel relief and alarm simultaneously.

'No. I think it's Shona's.'

'Ah. That's why it looked familiar. Has she ever been up to your studio?'

'Not by invitation. Alexi, do you think she spied on us on Sunday night? Actually came up to the room?' He's cautious, puffs out his lips.

'Who knows? She's a sad individual if she did.'

I definitely suspect it, remembering how distant she was with me next morning.

We manage to load my backpack and guitar on his scooter and putter to Lakki. He drops me by the harbour café and returns to the hotspot via his office. But he's back in time for the ferry, holds me like a father, kisses me chastely on the forehead. This relationship has been on a long journey in four days.

'Good luck with the hostel, Annie. They may be able to tell you something.'

I'll worry about the credit card bill another time. How can I even think about it? When will I see Alexis again? Will it be with Jude? Weird priorities. I'm sitting inside the ferry at a table with two elderly Greek couples. Likely their English won't be that fluent so they won't pick up on what I'm saying. It's early in the UK but someone answers at the hostel. Three sentences in my signal goes. I try again as we dock at Kalymnos. This time, I get the new manager, Kate. Viviane left a couple of years ago, she says, but she will check their records. While I'm waiting we leave port and the signal drops again. It's stronger as we approach Kos but I get the answerphone at the hostel, it'll be lunchtime there by now, I reckon. I call Fraser. He has no news, he says. I don't know whether to trust him or not. He won't tell me it's bad news while I'm stuck on a ferry. We leave Kos. While I can get a signal from the Turkish coast I check on the times I was in touch with Shona and all my 'unfortunate' incidents as Donald asked. There are hundreds in anyone's life, no doubt. I can't get a handle on how big or small the incidents should be that I'm looking for.

OK. The baby snatch attempt. Summer 2003 is freshest in my mind because of last night with Alexis. The Donald connection reminds me of the daffodils; that was a big one. I was convinced at the time it happened because of the trouble at Jude's school and that the postcard I received afterwards was part of it. *'That will teach you!'*, it said. I'd connected *'teach'* with *'school'* and the problems there. But maybe it wasn't. That was Spring 2009.

We need a chronological record, but my mind isn't working that way. Past disasters hit me randomly. My God! The dogs! Wally said the poisoned meat looked like diced steak, that it didn't make sense. It wasn't too long ago, comparatively – when, though? I check through my messages and there's one at the time from Clair saying how awful and did the police know? That was February of this year, 2016. Right, *think* Buchanan.

I'm writing all this down, checking for mobile signals, trying to remember. What else? Oh – the rotten game meat thrown at my door that Christmas. I couldn't bear to think Eloise might have been behind it. Besides, she wasn't even in Glasgow by then. She left me on Wednesday 22 October 2008, the only really precise date I remember. She was around university for a while after that, but I'd assumed she would be home in Toulouse by Christmas. Maybe she wasn't? Or did she pay someone to do it? But she'd covered the rent for me, why would she be so hurtful? Then I made a connection. That note: *'I learn that your friendship is untruthful…' 'I learn…'*. Someone *told* her something, someone who knew me well enough to construct a story about me. Someone else who knew I was vegetarian then and that meat would upset me. I write October and December 2008 on the list.

'Teach', 'learn', both require action by another; is there any significance? What else, what else? The second postcard, the one sent to Jude from Symi after Maggie died – June 2014. *'YOU KILLED MAGGIE, YOU BLACK BASTARD. SHE WAS ASHAMED OF YOU AND YOUR F***ING WHORE MOTHER. THAT'S WHY SHE DIED'*. It was definitely sent from Greece, had a Greek stamp and postmark on it and sealed in an envelope, designed to get to Jude without me seeing it first. Clever. It struck me then as prudish of whoever sent it to put asterisks in 'fucking'. Definitely not like the racist parents of Kilachlan. I flicker forward to the taverna at Xerocampos and Shona's reaction to the 'f' word, as she called it.

There are television screens attached to several bulkheads. As I look up Jude's face appears on the screen, rippling anguish through me. It is the Amber Alert Hellas bulletin for missing children. My heart rate doubles as I see the text scrolling across the bottom of the screen, with his name and age, Symi and yesterday's date on it. Someone's been busy on my behalf, which is amazing – but it makes it much more real. As the next child appears, I try to return to making the list, stave off the panic with no Alexis to calm me. Thankfully, we are just arriving at Symi. My mobile rings. Fraser.

'Fraser! Jude's on Amber Alert, I've just seen it on telly.'

'I know, the police on Symi activated it. Listen, Annie, don't get off the ferry at Symi, stay on till Rhodes.'

'What for? I'm coming to Symi.'

'Because Jude isn't on Symi. Rhodes is likely. I got here an hour or two back. The police here are up to speed about everything. Just do me a favour and don't argue, eh?' He doesn't give me the option of answering back.

If I felt foreboding before, it's worse now. He's been kidnapped from Symi. I am so numb with shock, I can't think, can't move. My heart is thundering. I concentrate on stillness, shutting out the noise of the ferry and the babble of passengers, until I feel calm enough to take a sip from my water bottle.

After a break of hundreds of years, disembarkation for Rhodes comes over the speakers. As I rise to leave, one of the couple stops me.

'I hope you find your son,' says the man.

'God bless you, my dear,' says the woman, hugs me and kisses me on both cheeks. So they did understand English. I concentrate on the mantra, 'Don't be nice to me, don't be nice to me, don't be nice to me!' while I manage to say:

'Efháristoh polí.'

In the queue below deck, possibilities cartwheel across my brain. At least someone might be there to help me with my backpack and guitar, this time, maybe even grab a taxi. Fortunately, in Greece they only check tickets on embarkation but even so, I worry that this will be a first time. Then, shuffling down the metal ramp, I see a big sign with 'ANNIE BUCHANAN' that makes me feel a little bit better. It's Fraser. The great numpty.

FORTY SIX

FRASER – Rhodes

Back on Symi, the text arrived around ten a.m.; Jess tried to respond but with no luck. She and I went straight to the police with it. We were there when Annie called from the Leros ferry; I didn't let on what had happened, just took the next ferry. I searched; Rhodes Old Town, the shopping area, the sea front. At the height of the tourist season it was a game of needles in haystacks, but I had to try. While I did, I rang Annie and told her, pretty firmly, not to get off at Symi but to meet me here.

Now I watch her ferry come in. My wee sister looks like a child again, walking down the gangway, holds it in but I can see it's an effort. Glad I made the big sign for her; it raises a smidgen of a smile. In the taxi I bring her up to speed.

'OK. The reason I got you to stay on the ferry is because Jess received this. It was sent from an unknown number.'

I pass her my phone. On it is the picture of Jude astride a cannon that Jess forwarded to me. He is outside the ramparts of the castle by Rhodes Old Town. The text reads *'In Rhodes and gunning for you Jess! Heh heh'*

'It arrived after you'd got on the ferry. That's why you had to stay on until Rhodes, Annie. He's here – or he's been here. And someone he knows must have taken that picture.'

'Christ! D'you *think* he's still here?'

'I don't know, Annie. That could have been taken yesterday.'

She goes quiet, more worrying than throwing a wobbly in my opinion. There's some deep breathing going on. I hold her hand. After a long exhale she takes out her own phone and calls the hostel she was at in London. She's still speaking to them when we arrive at the police station.

While we're waiting to be seen, Annie shows me her list of 'Shona incidents'. I look at the note about the postcard Jude got from Symi, blaming him for Maggie's death. Poor wee lad, having that laid on him. And devastating for me to realise he might have thought, even for a second, that I'd sent it. From the date, I just know there must be a link between that card and what happened to me two years ago.

'Annie, there's something you don't know and it's about time I told you.'

'As if I need to be more frightened.'

'Sorry, hen, I must tell you because I think it involves Shona. The Symi police know already. When I went back there after Maggie's funeral, Panos asked me to host the round island trips on The *Giorgios*. He still enjoyed going out on the boat but his cancer treatment was making him too tired to do much. So I said OK. This particular day, we stopped for snorkelling and I stayed on the boat with him, keeping an eye on everyone in the water. It was time to move on for lunch when one of the swimmers looked to be in difficulties, so I dived in with a lifebelt and swam across to help her, calmed her down, got her to hold onto the lifebelt and hauled her back in. Once onboard, though, she wouldn't have me anywhere near her. Said I'd 'probed' her under her swimsuit. Got hysterical. The other passengers didn't know how to react. We went straight back to Yialos and I took myself off to the police. Panos, bless him, chummed me along. The woman disappeared, then put in a complaint the next day and left the island.'

Annie speaks quietly. 'What did she look like, Fraser?' I describe the woman and see the recognition hit her.

'That was Shona.' The words drop like a lead weight from her mouth to my guts. She presses her knuckles into my arm.

'Why did you never tell me before?'

'Ach, it was a "need to know" thing. I sure as hell didn't need it and there was no reason for you to know it.'

'Fraser, will you stop being flippant? I'm your sister, you should have told me. Were you afraid I'd think there was any truth in it? For God's sake, you're about as predatory as Postman Pat.'

'Now who's being flippant?'

'OK, OK. Sorry. Look, I'm just really, really sorry I've dragged this woman into yours and Jude's lives.' She means it, actually believes it's her fault. I give her a brief reassurance but turn the focus onto the connection between this Shona female and the disgusting postcard Jude got. Annie rubs her forehead, gestures as she speaks.

'It's obvious, then, she sent the postcard to Jude from Symi. Christ! How could she do it? I wondered when I was writing out the list on the ferry. She made a big scene about me saying 'fuck' the other day. Whoever wrote the postcard had used the word with asterisks. I mean, why would you bother when you're sending something that offensive anyway? But I thought it was too much of a coincidence. It was definitely Shona who accused you, though, and it's obvious she knew where Jude and I lived. So there's no question, she sent that card. She pretended she didn' t know you
lived on Symi when I said I was coming to see you. No wonder she wanted to go to Leros instead; you'd have known her straight away.'

Our eyes connect, recognising we're in a lot of trouble. There's no doubt, now, it was Shona at the travel agency and on the ferry with Jude. This woman clearly has mental problems. I try to think rationally –

'Annie, we have no indication that she's physically threatening. Just that she has some issues.' Stupid me, I always forget Annie's a psychologist and not a normal person.

'Fraser, it's obvious she has issues with me. I don't know why or what they are. She may have some form of psychopathy or a personality disorder – like narcissism, but there's no point in me guessing. The only certainty is she's got Jude.'

Rhodes is busy and the police have plenty to occupy them. Knowing they're paid diddly squat, I could understand if they didn't jump to just because we have a problem, but they have all the information from Symi and so do the Athens police. They're sympathetic and efficient, which gives us a lot of reassurance. Annie forwards photos of Jude from her phone. In two of them he's wearing his Rangers cap. That got him recognised on Symi. I just hope he's still wearing it. The ones I gave the Symi police were on Amber Alert Hellas. Clair and Jess have sent any pictures they have in case one may be the optimum image of him. Annie doesn't have a photo of Shona, even on Facebook, and the police don't suggest photofit, so she texts Donald Mudie, just in case Shona's brother can send one.

We wait, but there's no news. So we go to the hotel, where I've booked mates' rates, naturally. Annie is in no mood for eating or drinking, but I persuade her to the taverna up the road and, while we – I – eat, we go through her list again. There's one missing incident that she can't quite recall. Then it hits her.

'Graduation!' she says, and writes it down in her notebook. At university, her name was crossed off the degree results list. They had to reprint it. June 2010.

Even at special rates the hotel is a bit of a stretch. Annie and I share a twin room. We call Clair to update her; she and Annie speak for half an hour. Clair's letting Annie do the talking, listening to her guilt and incomprehension for bringing this on Jude. What none of us can make out is how this woman contacted Jude or got him to go with her. Jess chips in. She's fairly sure that Shona – I find it hard to even say the name – must have 'groomed' him. Jude is on Snapchat and Instagram with his mates, they're pretty easy apps to join. The
thing about Snapchat is that photos disappear after a certain time, so they'd be hard to trace. Planning a meeting and a journey with all the arrangements necessary would be difficult without Shona having Jude's mobile number. Annie says there's no way she could have it. He could have sent it to her on Instagram, says Jess.

'But I've warned him about social media,' says Annie, 'and the police did a talk on it at his school. He knows not to "friend" strangers.'

We talk in circles until bills are high and batteries low. After we sign off with Clair and Jess, Annie's still stressing about how Shona got hold of Jude. We disappear down the same ratholes so many times that we start sniping at one another until I put a stop to it. There won't be much sleep tonight. The same questions will keep churning round. Annie texts while I doze.

About three o'clock, she sits up. I'm still awake if drowsy.

'Lakki! The taverna. That's how she got it!'

'What?'

'Jude's number. I went in to pay, then I went to the loo. I left her outside and my phone was on the table.'

'Don't you have a lock on it? You know, a PIN?'

'Oh, yeah…NO! No– I took a photo of the Mussolini villa before I left, it wouldn't have had time to do the automatic lock, so she was able to get his number from my contacts. Jeez, she must have been quick! And when I went to pick up her mobile from the seat in the taxi, she nearly bit my arm off. Then in Pandeli she asked the waiter to take a photograph of us at the taverna. Jude will think we're friends… I thought we *were* friends. Had she already planned taking him? She must have been pretty sure I wouldn't go to Patmos. Christ, she's sharp!'

My sister flops back, despairing, still can't come up with a motive other than Shona's mental health issues and we have no real idea what those are. All Annie knows is that she blew hot and cold, friendly and distant on Leros.

Early next morning, we visit the police again with the new information. They are very hospitable. One of them recognises me from my days as a tour rep in Lindos on the south of the island and I remember his improbable name of Dennis – thus Denni to his friends. Dennis is a sergeant, now, and our case officer. He shows us to a small interview room set aside for tourists in trouble, and instructs a junior to bring us the inevitable coffee and cakes. They are tracking for Shona's and Jude's phones but have no results. Must be switched off. Annie is adamant.

'No way! Jude never switches his phone off.' She's right. It's worrying. As I'm thinking this, we get a call from Clair. She's had a text from Jude with a photograph of him at a ferry rail waving at the camera with Kos town in the background. The long wall and walkway are distinctive, she says. The text itself says *'Hi Clair. Why Kos? B-Kos! Heh heh!'*. It is from a number she doesn't recognise. She will forward it to us, obviously.

With Dennis, we re-sift through everything we know, analysing it to shreds. Shona has Jess's number and Clair's. It seems as though she's letting Annie know that she has control over several areas of her life. I remind her of Marina's sighting on the ferry. Annie's already been there.

'He said "We're going to see Mum in Le –". He was going to say 'Leros', must have been because that's the hook she would've used. Is that where they were going or just where she *told* him they were going? And how did she explain why they were travelling south from Symi, in the wrong direction? Would Jude even have realised? And now they're on Kos.'

How can anyone know? They do, however, seem to be travelling north, now, so Leros may well be a possibility.

Then three things happen. One is a text from the hostel manager in London, for Annie to call her at the office after nine a.m.. It's nine fifty here, so with the time difference we have to wait over an hour before ringing. The next is a call from Donald Mudie, that winner of a lucky sperm race in a small gene pool. But Annie's glad to hear from him. Seems she texted him her 'Shona list'. He has a rough framework from the brother that seems to correspond but will 'firm it up'.

Last, we hear from Jess who's spoken to Jude's pal Andy – Andreas – on Symi, who says that Jude connected with a young Greek girl on social media after he arrived on Symi but was secretive about it. It had gone on for a while, Andy was vague, but Annie had been away for a day or so when Jude first said about the girl and then, later, that he was going to meet the girl's mother who was friends with his mum on Leros; he'd seen a photo of both mums together on Snapchat.

Annie nods. 'Remember what I said about the waiter taking a photo of us at the taverna on Leros?'

Wow, the woman's devious! The girl's 'mother' had arranged to meet Jude on Symi and take him across to Leros to surprise his mum – where, *coincidentally*, her daughter was staying. It was a big secret and Jude made Andy swear not to tell. Fortunately, Jess can be very persuasive. We share it with Dennis, who speaks better English than I do Greek, which is lucky because my language skills are getting a pounding.

Annie and I retire to a seafront bar. I grab a bite and try to persuade her. She hears from the hostel and spends some time on the phone. Then there's a call that sounds private and of the lovey-dovey nature and she wanders off. I hope it's Alexis, she could do with that particular comfort right now. So could I, come to that. But I nuked that possibility a while back.

FORTY SEVEN

ANNIE – Rhodes

Despite his workload on Leros, Alexis has called three times. There hasn't been any response on Shona – or Shoonagh – from the other NGO's, so far. Most checks relate to charity funding, potential links to terrorism, and the safety of employees and volunteers. He's amazingly supportive, but a lot of me wonders whether a new relationship like ours can survive all this drama.

Clair is running another course and can't leave Symi but the amount of concern and warmth she's sending my way make her presence almost palpable. And I have my brother with me, providing surprising strength.

We are in a café bar on Rhodes seafront. It's eleven, Greek time, so I ring Kate at the women's hostel.

'Hi, Annie. Got some information but don't know how much use it'll be. Viviane's living in France, now but we've spoken and she remembers the volunteer you described very clearly. She felt that this woman was getting too close to the clients. I've looked up the notes. It was a Shoonagh Packham and your name is mentioned. She took you around some Immigration Return Centres to find the father of your unborn baby, yes?'

'That's her.'

'Did she ever display any signs of anger with you?'

'Not really. She was a bit cross at one point, but she was very generous. Well, a bit too generous.'

'Mmm. Viviane had doubts when Mrs Packham was befriending you. She wasn't supposed to have unsupervised contact with clients because her Criminal Records Bureau check hadn't come through – that's a DBS now. It reached a head with another client after you left. We had to take out a court order for her to stay away from the hostel.'

Kate wishes me good luck and we end the conversation – about the woman who has my child.

Donald mentioned narcissism when he rang on Tuesday. Some thoughts on her condition are forming but without consulting someone with more experience, I can't draw any conclusions. Peter may be able to help. I get onto my iPad and rattle off an email then sit back, mind swooping and looping like Philander's worry beads.

Where is my boy? Is he on Leros? Kos? Somewhere else? Why doesn't he reply to my texts? Her, of course. She's irrational and vindictive, punishing me for something I've done and using my son as the weapon.

Her behaviour will have been as plausible to Jude as it was to me. How could a thirteen-year-old boy see through it if I couldn't? But he might be feeling a little uncertain by now. I want to do something, be somewhere, searching for him. The airport is easier for police to monitor now the alert's out, asking for documentation even on internal flights. I hope. Ferries are more difficult with hundreds of people embarking and disembarking all the time. All we can do is wait. And it's soul-destroying.

There's a party of French tourists chatting away, smoking Gauloises or something equally disgusting. Hearing the language reminds me of Shona's comment at the taverna in Pandeli – something about liking everything French, including boys *and* girls. *'compris les garçons ainsi que les filles...'* My mind is a tangle of connections that latches onto Eloise's note – *'I learn that your friendship is untruthful'*. What I suspected isn't so unreasonable – 'Eloise! She got to Eloise!' What could Shona have said or done to make her hate me? The anger rises in me in a way it hasn't before. And I can't look at it objectively as a professional because it affects me, personally. That perfect time in my life ruined by a bitter, jealous woman. And I can't tell anyone because no one knows quite how I felt about Eloise or about the truth, whatever that was, of our relationship.

The game meat hitting the front door. Shona? Who else? She must have been watching me in Glasgow and in Kilachlan. She cut the heads off the daffodils. And, of course, put poison down for Jack and Tatty. If she was prepared to kill them, what else might she be capable of? I can't even go there.

Alexis rings. His colleague Fenne, bless her, has been working on our behalf on Kalymnos. There was a direct ferry from Rhodes to Leros today, stopping at Kalymnos. She went up to the port just in case, by the slimmest chance, she might spot them on the 11:35 Dodekanisos Express, but there were so many passengers she was unable to report any success. It didn't mean, though, that they weren't on it. It's due in Leros at Aghia Marina, 12:25 and the police will be there to meet it. Alexis promises he will be there, too. If anyone can spot Shona, he can. But when the ferry arrives at Leros, there's no Jude or Shona. Maybe they went to Athens? Was she able to smuggle him onto a plane somehow? All we've got to go on is Marina's report of Jude saying: 'We're going to see Mum in Le –', on a ferry heading south, away from Symi and Leros.

Why would she take him to Leros, though? People have seen her on Leros, might recognise her. But, if she *has* taken him there, we can't get across because there are no more ferries from Rhodes today.

My iPad pings an incoming email. It's my old tutor, Peter. Concerned for me, obviously, but maintaining a detached, professional viewpoint:

'Analyse the issues this woman may have with you, Annie. She has known you since before Jude was born. Did she have maternal feelings for

you or sublimated feelings for the unborn child? Did she see your return to Scotland as you leaving her OR taking the child from her? And has she at any time thought you were actively against her? Remember that narcissism, if that's what her condition is, is related to paranoia. Let me know your thoughts. Stay calm. On balance, it is unlikely that she will do anything to harm Jude.' He gives me plenty of input, maybe too much. *'On balance'*– what comfort is that when Shona is completely *un*balanced?

My phone rings again. I've never been in so much demand. Donald Mudie.

'Annie, hello. Jim McCandless and I have just landed at Rhodes. Jim has a pilot's licence, he can hire a plane and get you almost anywhere you want. Where are you?'

FORTY EIGHT

ANNIE – Thursday. Rhodes

'Jim McCandless and I have just landed at Rhodes'. The cavalry's arrived! I tell Fraser, who is less than impressed. His problem. I ask him to book rooms for Jim and Donald and he obliges moodily. Doubt he'll pull any matey strings. We all meet in Reception; I am ridiculously pleased to see Donald. Jim McCandless has similar-coloured hair to Shona's, if thinning and fading a little, and is way taller and slimmer than his sister. He doesn't exactly put Donald in the shade, but he has such a sense of style – dressed in a pale linen suit and open-necked shirt, he's several digits above the usual dress code for here, probably never stayed anywhere so downmarket. He's also extremely charming, but not in a smarmy way. Firm handshake and eye contact. Instantly, I try to correlate what I see of him with what I know of his sister.

We ask the hotel for a private space and are shown to a small conference room usually used for sales pitches on coach tours and boat trips. Summer sounds of chat, laughter and the occasional plosh come from the pool just beyond the window, ripples reflect busily on the ceiling. The last time I noticed water reflections was Aghia Marina. Unbelievably, that was only six days ago, Friday, pre-disappearance of Jude and revelations about Shona. And before Alexis and I – what?

We sit round an oblong table. Jim is a quiet man. He refers to his sister as Sh*oo*nagh and begins by apologising for my distress. Knowing I'm a psychologist, he confirms her condition as Narcissistic Personality Disorder which, in addition to paranoia, is linked to depression and, in some people, bi-polarism. I pass my notebook to him. He studies it sitting with his back to the light, so it's hard to read his features. After a few minutes, he nods, clears his throat and begins.

'Just as background, our parents worked for the Foreign and Commonwealth Office and their careers were spent overseas. Shoonagh was sent to boarding school fairly young, we both were. I was academic and sporty, just what they expected of a son, whereas she didn't excel at school and, frankly, had a weight problem. It is possible that she had Attention Deficit Disorder, although it wasn't diagnosed. She sought attention and could be quite volatile when she didn't receive it, which was most of the time. I believe Donald mentioned to you, Annie, her de-heading all the flowers in our grandmother's garden? It was a reaction, we believe, to my father taking me on a sailing trip around the Med and sending her to our grandmother at Lochgilphead. There were other, similar manifestations of her mental and emotional state. When psychological intervention was agreed, my parents assumed that she would reach a level of self-awareness. They never accepted that their own behaviour towards her had been a major cause of her problems.'

Donald glances at me, lips compressed in a look of reassurance. Fraser sits a little away from the table, arms folded, staring down. From outside a peal of laughter followed by a yell and a loud splash punctures the tension. Jim pauses for a sip of water, runs fingers through his hair and continues.

'While she was undoubtedly bright she never did well in exams, so missed out on university and wound up in employment well below her ability or potential. The resultant frustration didn't help, as you would imagine. She took refuge in – well – glamour. Any salary plus her allowance from the family went on clothes, beauty treatments, spas and the like, to create an image of success. Then Rupert, a friend from schooldays along with Donald, turned up through business and we got together to reminisce over shared holidays. Rupe was on the rebound from a long-term relationship. Maybe Shoonagh was a reminder of happier times, I don't know. I'm certain Shoonagh saw him as an escape. So, as they say, she and Rupert married in haste.'

I notice Donald raising his eyebrows almost comically. Is he implying his own situation to me? Inappropriate. Jim continues.

'It didn't last long and certainly didn't end well. He left her in late 2002.' That jerks my memory. The first time I rang Shona, a man answered, the one I'd met, I supposed, and I ducked out. A picture of myself, bedraggled and desperate in the phone booth accompanies the thought. The split with Rupert must have happened after Shona and I met at the Langham Hotel and before she came to the hostel.

Jim is still talking.

'She was distraught at Rupert's departure and couldn't be contacted for several days around mid-December. Naturally, we were extremely concerned. I traced the women's hostel from a note on her phone pad. When she was teaching adult literacy, she'd intruded on the lives of the students. It didn't take a great leap of the imagination. The hostel staff were chary about confidentiality, but confirmed she'd been warned over contact with a young woman who had since returned home. I'm assuming that was you, Annie?'

Of that, I am fairly sure. Interesting that Jim had access to her flat; obviously he kept a careful watch. Did her intrusion into my life start so early on?

'Jim, are you saying she tracked me down in Scotland?'

'Her absence around that time points to it. She may have followed your coach to Glasgow by car and stalked you from the bus station to your home. That's how she would have known where you lived.' Now I see why she didn't want me to take the train. Despite the sunny day outside, I shudder. Jim goes on.

'I found her alone in Lochgilphead; she must have intended to monitor you from there. I persuaded her to come back to London. But this is how clever she was – is. After a few more months of therapy, she appeared to have "levelled" and was volunteering and organising fundraising functions as before, or so we thought. Then she went missing for a day from a charity event at the Edinburgh Tattoo, left them in a shambles. August 2003.'

He glances at the list again. 'Looks like that's when your baby was snatched. Once more, she'd lulled us into thinking she had recovered. Instead of which, she was waiting for an opportunity to continue…' Jim falters, but we get his meaning. Poor man, he's apologising for events beyond his control. For all his quiet pragmatism, he's an amazing brother. Whatever her problems, Shona's lucky to have him. I want to encourage him, thank him.

'Go on, Jim. This is making so much sense.' Here's me telling a top businessman he's good at presenting. But he manages a brief smile.

The company had my number as next of kin, so I became involved straight away. We didn't know exactly what she'd done, but she returned to Edinburgh in a heightened state, was unwilling to give a reason for her absence. So, another admission into psychiatric healthcare and some relief for us all until she disappeared again and turned up in Hawaii where Rupert and his girlfriend were on holiday. We thought we'd stopped her credit cards and still can't work out how she got her hands on her passport. I flew over and brought her back again. More therapy. Then, when Rupert and Tamara had a child, she arrived at the christening, caused a major disruption. Again, inexplicably, she had discovered the date and location. That time it was serious. The police were involved; she was sectioned under the Mental Health Act and spent a month in a medium secure psychiatric hospital. After which, we had her transferred.'

To another private hospital, no doubt. An image of patients in the Leros hospital documentary flashes through my mind and I feel a flicker of anger at the privilege money can buy. If you have enough of it you can bypass most things. Jim confirms it with his next sentence:

'My parents had retired to their property in Barbados. Shoonagh was treated there for nigh on four years. That's why there's a large gap in the – er – 'incidents'.'

So, not only does she get exclusive mental healthcare, but when the shit hits the fan, she gets a first class flight to Barbados to stay with Mummy and Daddy. I imagine Fraser's thinking the same. Then I pull myself up. I am a psychologist; boundaries have been blurred by personal involvement and I'm reacting unprofessionally, which won't help Jude or me. It's not in my nature to be so judgmental – or is it?

What Jim says next delivers a wake-up slap.

'When our mother died in a scuba diving accident, Shoonagh and Dad left Barbados and came back to the UK, mid-2008. He wasn't up to watching over her any more. Losing Mum was probably what caused his heart attack soon after.'

'I'm so sorry to hear that, Jim.' He flickers acknowledgment.

'Surprisingly, Shoonagh seemed stable; I hoped that these life experiences had put things into perspective for her.' Little point in saying, *'No, Jim, it doesn't work like that'*. Shona's proved it doesn't. As it happens, he echoes me.

'Of course, she was still as volatile. But by then, I had other matters to deal with and couldn't be as vigilant.' I notice that Jim waivers between 'we' and 'I'. Who, along with him, comprises the 'we'? Just the family?

He and I go through the remainder of the list. The convenience of the house in Lochgilphead meant that she could make forays down to Glasgow and, latterly, to Kilachlan, which explains the daffodils and the following note. I have included, by this point, the crossing out of my exam result, Fraser's assault accusation, Jude's postcard from Symi and, lastly, the attempted poisoning of the dogs. Shona is certainly intelligent and clever enough to leave space between her
intrusions into my life and determined and vindictive enough to involve my son and brother. And probably my lovely, Eloise – whom I still have not mentioned. Perhaps I should. After all, maybe Shona was jealous of the friendship and saw Eloise as a rival? But I can't. I just can't do it. So I turn the conversation.

'Jim, do you think Shona – Shoonagh – is envious of my having a child where she was denied one? My tutor suggested that she might have seen my return to Glasgow when I was pregnant either as my leaving her, or taking an unborn child from her.'

'It's very difficult to draw any conclusion about my sister. This may illustrate why.' He slides his laptop across to me. On it is a Facebook profile. It belongs to Shoonagh McCandless, but it is the woman I know as Shona Packham, the name I mis-read off her business card. So, she'd created a Shona Packham profile just for my benefit? I find this even more unsettling.

The Shona I know never posts a photograph of herself. But Shoonagh McCandless changes her profile picture every few days, showing off a new dress or hairstyle, beautifully manicured new nails, a pose against a sunset, on a cruise liner or in a hotel foyer. There she is in Barbados, London, Paris, Edinburgh – and Hawaii, where she was on yet another mission of destruction – plus Symi and, more recently, Rhodes. I even recognise one or two outfits. The vanity of it is astonishing, as is the sycophancy of her admirers – mainly other women who have nothing between their ears but a credit card. She would have been totally at home in the luxury of the Langham Hotel.

The dual accounts show another aspect of her: her duplicity and how she has kept two worlds separate. Fraser comes to look over my shoulder. Knowing him, he'll be pretty angry about the casual acceptance of the wealth gap.

I come to a decision: it's time to be open about my contact with Shona, not just on Leros but in London. I start with a brief description of my journey south and encountering Shona and then Zeezoo/Zizou; it seems incredible that it all happened on the same day. For once, no one laughs over my gullibility over his phony identity. I condense the period of intense squalor, skipping to the hostel and my pregnancy.

Jim listens intently, Donald concentrates on the table. Fraser is granite. He's hearing a lot of things he didn't know. They all are. I relate the phone call to Shona and her rôle both in placing me at the hostel and in the search for Zeezoo. As I do, even I see more clearly Shona's proprietorial attitude towards my unborn child. There's a silence when I finish. Jim splays his hands.

'So she has connections with you in London, Scotland, Symi, and Leros. She may choose any of those to play out her – shall we say 'conclusion'?'

Fraser agrees –

'Quite. We still haven't addressed the fact that she took a ferry going in the opposite direction to Leros, so maybe she has no intention of going there at all.'

Another possibility strikes me.

'Well, we know she's been to Kos. Perhaps she just had to get Jude away from Symi as quickly as possible. So she had to catch the next available ferry.'

'But they'd have to go back through Symi again travelling north. Wouldn't Jude have thought that was odd?' asks Fraser.

That's logical, Jude can be annoyingly forthright. I think it through aloud.

'For sure, my son would be sharp enough to notice – unless she'd convinced him that it was all part of the game. Yesterday's photo and text from Kos shows they're travelling north again.'

Donald speaks for the first time.

'Presumably there was surveillance at Kos?'

'Aye,' says Fraser, 'with it being a major holiday island, there'd have been plenty of port police around. Although if your sister is that sharp, Jim, there's every chance that she got past them.'

I agree.

'We have no idea whether they got off at Kos. Fenne watched people leaving the ferry at Kalymnos today, so no-one thinks they're there. Unless she just missed them. And Alexis and the police met the only ferry they could have caught arriving at Leros, so…'

Fraser's phone signals a notification and we all look expectantly. He flicks it on then sits up.

'It's Jude! It says *'Hi Uncle Fraser! Having a FERRY nice time here. Heh heh.'* And a photo of him – god, I know this place – it's… Jeez – yes! It's Telendos Island. In the background. They're on Kalymnos. Telendos Island is opposite Myrties.'

Something in my brain explodes. The little boat at Xerocampos goes back and forth from Leros to Myrties.

'They *are* going to Leros! I saw the local ferry when we spent the day on the beach at Xerocampos, even suggested to Shona we go to Kalymnos for a day. So she's remembered. And going that way, she'd avoid anyone seeing them arrive on Leros. She's keeping us a step behind. We have to go back to Leros. I just know they'll be there.'

Donald turns to his friend. 'Jim, how long would it take you to hire a plane?' Jim clicks through some numbers. 'Onto it.'

Fraser passes his phone around. And there's my boy. I notice he's wearing a red baseball cap. His Rangers one is blue.

'It's the Olympiakos strip,' says Fraser, 'And he sure as hell didn't send that text. His name didn't come up. And he didn't call me Uncle Puke.'

Within the hour Jim's located a six-seater plane and fielded the admin for hiring it. We'll take off for Leros at six thirty. I go straight to the police station and share what Jim and I have compared. Fraser texts Clair.

Jess is on her way from Symi and will join us at Rhodes airport *'come hell or high water'*, her words.

FORTY NINE

FRASER – Arriving Leros

Jim's piloting. Annie and I sit behind him and Donald. Jess is at the back, having made it from the ferry by a hair – and a bewitched taxi driver. She's in her element and I wonder, ungenerously, just how much Jude figures in her motivation. I have known her for eight years. Skipping a generation, her drive springs from ego, just like her grandmother, Connie. She wasn't above trying to split Clair and me before we'd even really begun. On the other hand, she's come up with some useful information re. Snapchat etc. And she involves herself with the refugees on Symi. But is that just so she can talk about it?

As we approach the island, Jim says, 'It looks like a jigsaw piece. See?'

We all look down and Annie says –

'That's just what Clair said.'

Clair's the comfort we need in this situation. The comfort I need, maybe.

The airport on Leros is a strip of concrete and a glorified shed in the north of the island. Alexis is waiting. Now I see them together I realise how much older than her he is. But it looks like Annie and Vertigo Joe have chipped a couple of notches on the bedpost by the way they say hello. Sometimes I feel I'm just the ghillie trotting after the three females in my – pack, herd…coven?– while they go hunting. Still, this bloke works at the sharp edge of a charity, unlike others who hide behind a desk being paid executive shedloads *'because they could earn it in the private sector'*. He must be OK.

Alexis tells us there have been another hundred or so refugees shipped from Farmakonisi Island to Leros by the coastguard, so the police and NGOs will be overstretched tonight. It's late. There are now five of us, three guys and two women needing somewhere to stay. OK, Annie will be with Alexis, so three guys and one gal. Alexis calls Annie's recent landlord who fixes accommodation for us. He has only one room left, can put up two of us and find two more rooms in a hotel. I saw the way the walking wallets reacted to Jess and, as her mother's ex-lover, feel bound to intervene. They can have the hotel rooms, Jess and I the one at Státhis's apartments. Not the best outcome for me as Jess gets the double bed and I'm on a sun lounger.

Státhis says he will scramble a *'find Jude'* alert across the island.

Before we arrive at Jim and Donald's hotel the manager has printed off about fifty copies of Jude's photo from Amber Alert Hellas. Annie and I borrow his scooter and take off with half the photos, Jess and the two toffs take a cab.

We meet again after midnight, too wired to sleep. Annie takes us to a late-night cocktail bar where the owner lets us pin up Jude's photo. We all have a nightcap and try to engage the other drinkers in the *'find Jude'* project. They're of varied nationalities and with differing levels of interest. A Turkish guy who's moored his yacht in the bay asks us why we haven't checked boat hire?

'Lord, yes!' says the brother, 'She can handle a boat. Why didn't I think of that?' It's too late, now, to do any research but the Turkish guy says he'll pass on details around the yachting community and takes my number. I stand him, so to speak, a *Sex on the Beach* for his enterprise.

I'm returning from the gents when there's a breakthrough. Annie gets a simple text, presumably from Jude, no photo this time – it says *'How's Leros, Mum? Heh heh!'* and a sunglasses emoji, again from a withheld number. Immediately, Annie tries calling Jude but he's unavailable. It will be her, McCandless's sister. The Rhodes police have Jude's and her mobile numbers so should be able to pinpoint roughly where they are. But only when the phones are switched on and I suspect the woman is canny enough to know it.

FIFTY

ANNIE – Leros

Alexis takes me to the Leros police and explains the situation. They are coordinating with police in Rhodes, their administrative centre, and have all the necessary details from Symi already. There is nothing else for us to do, so we return to Alexis's place where he drops me off before going on to his office in Lakki. He thinks it may be a long night.

Sleep comes nowhere near me. I keep calling Jude, even though I know it to be useless. That text *'How's Leros, Mum? Heh heh!'* is meant either to lure or deflect me. But I'm on Leros now, so I'll go with the 'lure' option.

Along with Jim's account of his sister, Peter's email revolves in my brain – I left Shona behind when I returned to Scotland, I took the unborn child with me. And now, when she invited me to Patmos, I declined in favour of Alexis. Demonstrated that she less important to me. Maybe if I'd said yes to Patmos, none of this would be happening – and if I'd called her, even when she was on the way to Symi, she may not have taken Jude. She wanted my attention and she got it but only when Jude went missing. Is it too late to call her now? Apologise. Attempt to befriend her, share my thoughts with her. She'd see straight through it. Or would she? If it doesn't work, I'll beg to get him back…at least then she'll feel she's in control.

She doesn't answer my call, so I text her, using some amateur Neurolinguistic Programming to impress how much I value her.

'Hi Shona – here on Leros, still. That photo of the Cave of the Apocalypse is beautiful. How I wish I'd been with you. Thank you for your kindness in inviting me to Patmos. I've missed you since you left on Tuesday. I should have come with you because you keep returning to my thoughts. Hope you come back soon. It's too hot to sleep and I'm thinking of you now. Did you enjoy St John's cave? How is Patmos? Let me know when you are returning to Leros. I understand your frustration at not being allowed to carry out your kind offer to volunteer on Leros and appreciate your knowledge and compassion. They have been my cause to be thankful to you for many years. Jude is still away, which worries me. Even so, he deserves to have kindness. He's a great kid. I look forward to your return to Leros. Missing your company here. Please come back soon. Thank you again for all your kindness and generosity. Lots of love – Annie xxx'

I've used lots of *'you'*, lots of *'your'* and *'come back '/'return'/'returning'* and *'kindness'* deliberately. Then I go back and edit because I notice almost every sentence started with *'I'*. The *'knowledge and compassion'* was involuntary, though, it's a guiding premise of mine, now, sparked off by Peter's seminar about Leros and the psychiatric hospital. Did I ever mention that to Shona? But I send the text.

Now I worry that I've overdone it, been clumsy, and she'll know what I'm trying to do. Oh God, she'll see it as disrespect. Have I made matters worse?

An incoming text strikes lightning through me. My fingers turn to logs. It's a withheld number again, but I know it's Shona. When I manage to open it, there's no message, just a photograph of some buildings I can't quite make out – then I stop breathing. It's the psychiatric hospital and the hotspot.

Alexis is still out working. As I'm flinging on clothes, I ring Fraser, bawl at him to get up and meet me in Platanos Square. Within seconds I flee the apartment and hit the road full pelt in the near dark, trying to find the taxi number. Suddenly I go flying, stumble down the steep tarmac edge and crash full length down the narrow gully at the side. Don't know what hurts, yet – standing brings electric prongs of pain. Must have twisted my ankle. I grasp around for my phone, see it glint in the streetlight a couple of metres ahead and hobble to it – the screen is smashed. It's the most I can do to stagger to the hotel where Jim and Donald are staying. The young receptionist is goggle-eyed, I look down and see my bare legs are covered in blood. He runs round the desk, tries to make me sit down, but I won't and yell at him –

'Ochí– ochí! Donald Mudie – Jim McCandless – parákalo!' Poor lad grabs a phone and calls them, then disappears and comes back with a first aid kit and stands frozen, inadequate to the gory task that's me. Pain encases my ankle. I manage to say, 'Néro, parákalo? Zésto néro?' Hot water. Even in this state I feel a chirrup of pride at finding the words. The receptionist nods furiously –

'Neh – neh!' And he's off again.

Donald appears in thrown on T-shirt and shorts.

'My God, Annie! What's happened?' He catches the lad carrying a bowl of water. 'Thanks, mate, I'll do this.'

I fight through the shock and pain to tell them – 'Shona's texted me a photo of the old psychiatric hospital. We have to get a cab there. I'm meeting Fraser in Platanos Square.'

Why do I choose now to notice that Donald's quiffy hair is thinning? Jim appears, collars the put-upon receptionist – does the English thing of raising his voice – 'Taxi, please! Much important!'– and is instantly put in his place.

'Yes, sir, of course. Where would you like it to go?'

A taxi careers up in a heartbeat, Donald's barely had time to wipe my blood away. He grabs a handful of swabs, sticking plasters and a bandage from the first aid box and we go. Fraser and Jess are hopping up and down in Platanos Square and manage to squeeze in. Our driver doesn't mind the overcrowding at all, especially at the sight of Jess. She starts to explain the reason for our haste but he's already there. Státhis's *'Jude virus'* has worked.

'You're looking for the crazy lady with the boy? No worries. Let's go.'

He puts his foot down. Every swerve raises our tension by a factor of ten – 'My name's Kostas.' – and he takes his hand off the wheel to shake hands with everyone in reach. I wish they wouldn't do that…

Light gradually lifts the sky as we speed along the main road to Lakki. Fraser wants to know what I've done to myself and gets dirty look for his trouble. He inspects my phone and decides it's only the screen broken, it still works. He and Jess have Jude's number and Jim has Shona's. I try to find Alexis's number, but can't make it out through the cracks. Donald's still trying to mop the persistent blood off my hands and knees enough to stick plasters on. Jim is speaking to Shona's voicemail. Good luck with that! We're there in under ten minutes and pull up at the side of the hotspot. Kostas is out of the car first, urging us on.

'You, my dear, stay in the car!' He's talking to me. I have no intention of staying in the car. Don't know what the elderly *'my dear'* is about, he can't be thirty yet. Donald helps me out.

'Hup you come, Annie!' He's in a sort of cowboy pose, inviting me to jump up for a piggyback. Get real, Mudie.

Kostas is dialling.

'The crazy lady and the boy – their names? I'll call the other drivers.' We've got nothing to lose.

'Shoonagh and Jude. Thanks, Kostas. Would you call the police, too?'

'Of course, my dear.'

Donald insists on supporting me in some way and I lurch along with his arm around my ribcage. Jim and Kostas sprint to the zombie white monster of a hospital, Jess and Fraser after them. Then a text comes in – I don't know who it's from can't read it because the screen is a starburst – is it Shona?

FIFTY ONE

FRASER – Leros

The ruined hospital has a scary presence. As we run towards it, we're all shouting – Shona! Jude! The names echo from the deserted buildings to the right. We'll need to search those, too. Lights flip on in the flimsy houses inside the hotspot to our left and a baby starts crying, then another and another. Poor kids, as if they haven't enough problems without us waking them. We stop at the old building in total darkness. All I have with me is the light from my phone, Jim too. Kostas has a torch – naturally – and takes charge –

'You – Mr Scotland –' (good spot of accent!) '–come with me. Jess, my dear, you too, I would like.'

Even in this moment of crisis, Kostas is on the pull. Mr Scotland takes control.

'Thanks, Kosta, but Jess is better out here with Jim –'

'Hey –!'

'Jess, this is not the time to get feminist. C'mon, Kosta. I'm Fraser, by the way.'

Kostas leads us up the side of the building into a shambles of a courtyard and we force one of the doors open. The place is manky inside, too. Rubbish everywhere on the tiled floors, dust and must fill our lungs. A few mattresses, some discarded shoes, and clothes in three rooms – no doubt pre-hotspot refugees. What must it have been like sleeping in a dank old horror of a place like this after a terrifying crossing from Turkey? We go on calling and waiting, calling and waiting. But not a sound comes back apart from the cries of Jess and Jim outside. I don't even know if calling is the right thing to do. Lights stab through the front windows casting jagged shadows as two cars approach. The police come around the side and into the building, yelling. Kostas turns back and they all shout. No animosity, it's just the Greek way. The four officers split and take the top floors.

We've covered the ground floor so Kostas and I go outside. Jim and Jess have drawn a blank. Annie and Donald have caught up and wait for the police to come out. Jess, Jim, Kostas and I go back to the deserted buildings on the approach to the hospital. It occurs to me that we haven't been very scientific about this. I stop the others.

'If Shona had Jude in one of these buildings she could have kept him quiet while we passed on the way up to the hospital then bundled him off somewhere.'

Kostas comes up with reassuring if slightly illogical information.

'The police spoke to the hotspot guards. They didn't see anyone go past this evening and they've been on duty since ten o'clock.'

'So why are the police –?'

'They look in the building to be sure. So we must look here.' I can't help feeling we're wasting time and opportunity. It's my nephew that's at risk here.

As if he's reading my mind, Jim says, 'So sorry, everyone, for all this business. I'm sure Shoonagh wouldn't cause him any harm. Just wants to– make us aware of her, well, her place in life…' He tails off but I can't resist it.

'She can afford a full-page spread in the bloody *Times* if that's all she wants!'

He says nothing, moves into the building. Jess gives me a *'Did you really have to?'* look.

Tactfully, Kostas joins Jim while Jess and I scout through the one-storey buildings. They're quicker to cover. Jess and I have only the searchlight apps on our phones which could give out at any minute. I bark my shin on a stray solid object and swear mightily. A relief of sorts but a painful one. Same picture here as the hospital. Filthy, smelly, garbage everywhere and pathetic belongings scattered in small rooms. There is no way they'd be in here. Lady Shona wouldn't put up with it. We meet Kostas and Jim outside. Kostas motions back down the road to the water.

'My friends called to say they're going down to the old school buildings, we must search also in the Mussolini Villa.' And he's off, so all we can do is follow. I look back briefly but there's no sign of Annie and Donald. Must still be up at the hospital.

The air is almost cool. It's getting bright at the top end of the harbour. We see white fingers of headlights before we hear the cars. Taxi cabs with the *'Jude virus'*, no doubt. Four of them whip past the end of the road so we turn and pant after them while sensible Kostas goes back to the hospital for his car. When he catches us up, he has Donald and Annie in the back. One police car returns to the hotspot main gate, the other veers round us and zooms on.

Annie says she's been to the Mussolini villa but it's not on the photograph that Shona sent. Kostas chips in.

'The police are going to the Naval Base at the end. It has security cameras that cover the road. If a car went as far as the school buildings without authorisation they would stop it. My friends are going to the villa. It is more possible that the lady and the boy are in there.'

We reach the villa. Pretty impressive place – well, it must have been sometime. The other drivers are already there. We can hear their voices and feet, doors banging, see lights flashing. Jess, Jim and I follow Kostas. My feet stick to something I don't want to know about.

By now our phone lights are on the way out so we stay tight behind Kostas who leads us to the first floor. His torch shows goats have been everywhere and we're walking on the evidence. We go into room after room, each a small square with tiled floors. A closed door gives and we enter another spooky box. But the floor's been cleared in this one. Jess is as driven as anyone but stays by my side. She gives a shock of breath. Emotion grates her voice.

'Fraser…' Kostas directs his torch. Caught in the intense beam we see a huddle of four people. They are frozen with fright, dazzled by our searchlights. Not who we're looking for, but –

'Sirs, lady please!' A man stands, hands splayed in a gesture of surrender. 'Please. We good – no bad. Please, please? No hotspot.' Crouched at his feet in a muddle of blankets and clothes are a woman and two children – and she's holding a baby. The children whimper and she tries to quiet them.

'Oh no,' moans Jess, then, 'OK, it's OK. We won't hurt you.' She takes Kostas's torch. I put an arm out to hold him back, don't want to move. Jess goes forward slowly, holding out her hand. What's she doing? She's giving them money!

'For you. For your wife and babies.'

The man sinks to his knees and kisses her hand.

'Efharistóh. Teshekoor ederim. Shukraan lakum. Thank you.' I recognise the Greek, Turkish and Arabic before the English. Poor sod – how many languages does he have to know *'thank you'* in? And Jess – well, giving money may be all she can do at the moment but I'm touched. She isn't happy at the hand-kissing, is mortified.

'Goodbye,' she says, 'good luck to you and your family.' Kostas seems at one with Jess, takes back his torch and gives her a hug. Maybe it's genuine and maybe he hopes his luck's in. We leave the room and close the door, move on calling Jude. But our hope is fading. Soon, we've covered the top floor. Kostas calls the others downstairs and directs them through the front door, away from the refugees. We all make our way down the fouled steps. Now what?

'Jess – where's Jim?'

'Staying out of your way, I imagine, Fraser.' Fair point, well made. We find him with Annie and Donald by Kostas's car. Annie's spitting feathers because she can't access the text that came in. The likelihood is that it's from Shona. It could be another 'clue'. Then she has an epiphany –

'That photo Shona sent me – it was the hospital from the distance. And there were trees in front. The only trees are at the edge of the water. It must have been from the shore opposite – is that what she was telling me in the text?'

Jim follows her thought. 'From the shore opposite – or from a boat?'

'God – yes! You said she could handle a boat?'

'Certainly. Experienced sailor.' Oh boy, we're near to something –

'They're in a bloody boat!' Annie spins round and yells to Kostas,

'Can you take us back to the hotspot, please? Parakaló?'

He's in the moment, hardly waits till the doors slam before he's spinning round, back the way we came, leaving Jess and me behind. We see them skid to a halt in the distance and the four of them make it to the water's edge. It's light enough to see a small launch in the middle of the inlet. Annie screeches at a pitch I didn't think a human could reach –

'The white boat! Jude!' It's possible to make out not only the boat but two figures in it, both in orange life jackets like the refugees wear. It has to be them. Alerted by Annie's scream, others come pelting up the road. We all direct our eyes to the water. Then – I can't believe what happens – one figure knocks the other overboard – and powers up the motor. She's pushed Jude in! She's leaving him there to drown! Then the boat turns and heads up the gulf towards the open sea.

A policeman bellows into his phone – everyone shouts – at Shona, at the boat, at each other, to Jude. I am propelled by fear and fury, reach Annie with my lungs on fire, Jess behind me.

'Annie – Annie – listen! He's in a lifejacket, he's a strong swimmer –' Donald holds Annie back, everyone yelling and swearing. Nothing else to be done. My heart is out there as I make it to the edge, Jess behind me. I pull off my shoes and dive in, striking out towards Jude.

All I can think is he's alone in the sea and I have to get to him. The cold water is broken glass as I hit the surface, surge under and force up – adrenaline pumps me forward – every breath tears through the length of my body – Jude's face lifts and sinks below black waves – fear grips me each time his head dips from sight – I swallow lungsful trying to yell to him. I'm just near enough for him to hear me when the blue mast lights of the Coastguard boat catch my sight – three white searchlights, one from the bridge, two from the deck, sweep the water and home in on us – I pound on towards Jude – salt in my eyes, chest closing – a megaphone tells me to rest…

The swell from the boat lifts us as the divers plunge in. They secure lifebelts around us, haul us to the side and up onboard, baby aliens to the mothership. Jude clings to me, whimpering, as we're whizzed back to the far side of the bay – how long? For ever and no time. Swathed in blankets, I cradle the shocked boy and watch the Greek flag ripple and snap in the slipstream at the stern.

As if I need a reminder of how much I owe this country.

FIFTY TWO

ANNIE – Next morning. Leros

I ring Alexis from the new hospital this morning to update him while they're checking Jude. He says he's thinking of me, that Philander and Gretchen send love. But he doesn't offer to join me. It feels a bit lukewarm, to be honest. I want him around, but I suppose it's a bit soon to introduce Jude to the new man in my life – or Alexis to him, especially under these circumstances.

We're at the Port Police HQ in Lakki. It's around nine. Jude's been given an outsize T-shirt and shorts to be going on with as the clothes he was wearing are not only soaking but also evidence. I've been promised this will be a brief, preliminary interview and then I can take him for a rest. Everyone's very friendly and we're offered breakfast, coffee and cakes. The Coastguard caught up with Shona shortly after landing Jude and Fraser last night and she's somewhere else in the building. Jim has been allowed to see her under supervision. He won't have had time to tell them her history. I hope he's able to delay questioning until they're aware. There has to be a better attitude towards mental health in Greece, these days, and that should mitigate her behaviour.

The officer interviewing Jude is young and friendly, appropriately gentle with him so soon after the trauma. Jude reacts positively but, as the story unfolds, he apologises frequently for being stupid; he would say gullible if he knew the word. We both reassure him, constantly, that he's done nothing wrong and that it's most important he tells us all he can remember. The officer suggests, quietly, that maybe Jude does the talking without any assistance. She's right. *'Shut up, Annie, switch off the mind-y woman.'* It's soon clear that Jude needs a break to rest. Jess has arranged for him and me to stay at the same hotel as Donald and Jim. Once in the room, he's asleep before he can get undressed.

When he wakes this afternoon, he has a drink and a sandwich while we wait for a police car to take us back to Lakki. He is very subdued and a little tearful. Fraser comes by to give him a man-hug and the tears start for real. Fraser just holds him tight and I join them. All three of us shattered by shock and relief. We break at the policeman's knock on the door. Lots of snivelling and not a little sheepish laughter. Tears and laughter, what we all needed.

At the Port Police HQ, the questioning starts again. I know some of the story from what Andy told Jess. What I hadn't heard was the persona Shona adopted for the young girl: 'Helen'. 'Helen' insisted that she and Jude should keep their friendship completely secret *'because it was more exciting that way'*. He swears there was no sexual content.

'Helen' said that when her mother met him at the travel agent in Symi she would be wearing a large black sunhat and a light green dress. The colour of the dress is a give-away if nothing else. The mother said her name was Ariadne. Ariadne? He falters frequently.

'I'm really, really sorry, Mum… I thought she was bringing me to Leros to surprise you. I thought Helen was here.'

'It's OK, Jude, no-one's angry. You're being amazing.'

They went by ferry to Rhodes and the first thing they did was take a photograph of him sitting on a cannon. Then they went shopping. She let him choose some shorts and a T-shirt but picked out an Olympiakos football club cap for him. He didn't want to wear it because he preferred his Rangers one but she told him it would impress Helen so he should put it on straight away. She bought herself some jeans, trainers, a tunic, and a baseball cap. They both changed their clothes in the shop. No wonder Fenne didn't spot them at Kalymnos.

After that, they took a taxi to a hotel where they were expecting her. The receptionist asked for their passports but she said that they were in the luggage and she would bring them down later, when they'd unpacked. From what Jude describes, they were in a suite and had a bedroom each. They had a meal in the living room, and he watched TV. He had to go to bed early because they had an eight o'clock ferry to catch. She joked with him about not being able to keep a secret and said she'd look after his phone in case he was tempted. He wasn't happy about it and she became annoyed, told him he was ungrateful and should learn better manners, like *'please'* and *'thank you'*. So he handed his phone over. He never got it back. Every time he asked, she joked with him then offered him something like a Coke or an ice cream.

Next morning, they caught the ferry. Shona had booked a private berth where they stayed except for going on deck to take a photograph at Kos.

'It was dead boring, so it was. She made me listen to a Harry Potter Audible book I heard when I was about seven.'

That explains bypassing Symi without Jude noticing. When they went on deck to take a photo, Jude didn't know it was Kos, just that 'Ariadne' wanted another one to show his mum and her daughter, Helen, when they got to Leros. When they got off at – he can't remember the name – the officer suggests Kalymnos and Jude nods recognition then continues, saying Shona pointed out a taverna, told him to go on ahead and she'd meet him there. So they'd appear to be travelling separately to the port police? Clever. With an Olympiakos cap, Jude could have been mistaken for a Greek lad, and Shona would have been unrecognisable in jeans and a baseball cap.

When Shona arrived at the taverna they took a taxi to another posh hotel. She played the same game about passports, telling Reception she'd bring them down later. Jude was allowed to go to the beach on his own but had to promise not to speak to anyone. He also had to promise to stay in sight of the hotel terrace and be back by six. This time they had adjoining rooms. They ate in Shona's room, then he had to go to bed. He heard her go out later and tried his door, but she'd locked it. There was nothing he understood on television so he had to go on listening to Harry Potter until he fell asleep.

I am furious that she did such a dangerous thing. What if there had been a fire? Why spend a night on Kalymnos instead of going straight to Leros? A last night of freedom?

Next morning, Jude says, Shona unlocked his room and told him to get showered and dressed and wait for her. When she was ready, they left the hotel in another taxi and went to a smaller place where they did some food shopping at a little supermarket then had breakfast at a taverna by the beach.

'I think she'd had a lot to drink because she had a headache and she was bad-tempered,' he says.

Oh dear, familiar symptoms of his mother's, I wonder? It does sound, though, like Shona had been on the booze the night before, given my recent experience of her.

At the taverna, she took another photo of him for their travelling diary, says Jude. That would have been the one with Telendos Island in the background. Then, after breakfast, they got on a smaller boat near the taverna. So that *was* how she did it, the small ferry to Leros from Myrties. I was right about her paying attention all the time that day at Xerocampos.

When they got to the next island, a man was waiting for them with a motorboat. They put on lifejackets and Ariadne/Shona 'drove' for a long time before putting the anchor down and sharing a picnic. Then they went on, eventually anchoring again and, after another meal of bread and cheese, spent the night on bunks down in the cabin, sleeping in their clothes on the twin berths. Shona woke him while it was still dark and told him to put on his lifejacket. She double-checked that he had it on properly before they went on deck. I recognise from this that she didn't mean him any real harm.

They waited for a long time and noticed all the cars on the road round the bay. He wasn't worried about anything because he thought it was all part of the surprise – but the surprise was on him when he felt a thump in his back and landed in the water. The launch took off and he panicked until he heard us shouting from the shore and saw someone dive in and start swimming towards him.

'I didn't know it was Uncle Fraser, though. Respect! We should be on the telly in, like, a psycho-thriller, and I could get to act me.' He doesn't know how near the truth he is.

The interview lasts about ninety minutes. It's been recorded and we have permission to leave Leros so long as we stay in the Dodecanese for the next couple of weeks, or so, to be available for further questioning. We may have to go to Athens, but nothing is certain as yet. As we leave, several of the staff shake Jude's hand and tell him 'Bravo!'. His ego expands visibly.

Jess is waiting at the hotel when we get back from Lakki. She has a selection of the coolest gear available on Leros for Jude to take his pick. First thing he wants to do, though, is go swimming. After being abandoned to the sea about twelve hours ago, he wants back in! I decide if normal is what he wants, normal he shall have. We call and meet Fraser and Donald on the beach at Pandeli.

FRASER

I am a hero. I admit not a lot of thought went into my lifesaving display; I hadn't gauged how far out Jude was – must have been at least seventy metres away – or the state of the water, far choppier than I thought. Back onshore, an ambulance waited to drive us to the hospital, the regular one. Annie and Jess arrived with Donald and Jim. The medical staff allowed the two girls in before checking us over.

We're just half a day from all the drama. Shona's in custody with the Port Police. Annie, Jess, and Donald are on sun loungers. Alexis is working. Annie's given me permission to be lovable Uncle Puke, a "normalisation process", she said. I don't know whether that's insulting or not.

After my imitation of Byron swimming the Hellespont last night, Jude's thrashed me racing the length of Pandeli bay. We slosh out of the water and sit under an umbrella at the beach bar. I've no idea how he's dealing with his whole experience.

'How you doing, pal?' Deep sigh.

'I'm, like, such an eejit, Uncle Puke. I thought she was this girl Helen's mother. But now I know there wasnae a girl at all. It was her on Snapchat all the time, Ariadne.'

'Who?'

'The one who kidnapped me. But she knew lots about Mum and me. That's really freaked me out.' I wasn't expecting this. Apart from confirming that nothing of a sexual nature happened he's been reticent about his time with Shoonagh/Shona. I don't push.

'You're not an eejit, Jude. She's a very devious – I mean, dishonest – woman. She fooled your mum for years.'

'Aye but Mum's – Mum. I should know about stuff.'

'Your mum's a psychologist, you'd think she'd know a thing or two, eh? But you're right, she didn't understand about Shona for a long time.'

'She worked it out in the end, though, didn't she?'

'Yes, she did.' He stares into the brown fizz.

'Tell you what, Uncle Puke, that Ariadne – she's dead rich. Awesome hotel we stayed in at Rhodes. The other one was OK, too.'

'You don't say?'

'Aye. At Rhodes, we had a bedroom each and a living room and they brought us our breakfast up. You could have anything you want. I had sausage and chips.'

'Attaboy. None of this yoghurt and fruit nonsense. Anything else about her? Apart from being minted?'

'Well… she was OK most of the time, but she was dead crabbit about my manners.'

'Your manners?'

Unbelievable. What is the woman? Mary Poppins on acid?

'Aye. Like my grandma. Made me say *'please'* and *'thank you'*– for *everything*. Even while we were on the motorboat, she said to tell Mum she had to learn to give instead of just taking and to be grateful. Can I have another coke, Uncle Fraser?' It's *Uncle Fraser* when he wants something, sly wee bastard.

'Sure thing, pal.'

Annie appears and attaches herself magnet-like to Jude, having forgotten that lovey mothers repel thirteen-year-old boys.

'Get off me, Mum! I'm no' a kid!' Even so, he can have anything he wants. Without saying *'please'* or *'thank you'*.

So, Shona/Shoonagh/Ariadne's a stickler for etiquette? Bet she didn't ask the Coastguard boys to say '*parakoló*' and '*efharistóh*' when they caught up with her this morning. As soon as they'd got Jude and me ashore they were off after her. Those boats can go up to forty knots, easily outrun the little putt-putt she was on. Once the searchlights were nosing her into shore and the megaphone started, you bet she did as she was told.

FIFTY THREE

ANNIE – Evening, Friday. Leros

At Jude's request, we have dinner at a pizza place with Fraser, Jess and Donald. I text Alexis but he doesn't show up. Jim is still with Shona at the Port Police HQ. Because the kidnapping happened at sea, she comes under their jurisdiction. It's likely she'll be transferred to Athens soon.

Jude's pooped and glad to go back to the hotel when the meal ends. The other three saunter down to the beach for a drink. It has to be a first, Jess spending time with two adult males, neither of whom fancy her. Donald is here for me, he's made that much clear. With Fraser, it would almost be like committing incest. Come to think of it, Jim hasn't shown any interest either. Maybe he's gay? Hadn't considered that. How unlike me.

I let Jude use my iPad to download a few games. His phone went with Shona. The hotel doesn't have Sky and the only English-speaking programme we can get is BBC World News. I watch it for a bit to see if Jude's kidnap is on it, but it's all about racist attacks in the UK following the referendum, Theresa May and Angela Merkel discussing Britain leaving Europe, and office workers being rounded up by the police after a failed coup in Turkey. Is Turkey not a good place to go on holiday any more? Everything is profoundly depressing. And then, of course, there's Donald Trump. At least he'll never get elected. That would just be too absurd.

Jude laughs out loud, snorting a few forbidden words. I don't want conflict right now, but –

'What? What's going on?'

'Nothin', just a load of garbage from Ariadne.'

The little sod has only been into my messages. For once, I forgive the intrusion because what he's found makes a lot of difference for Shona. It hadn't occurred to me – stupid! All my messages from the iPhone are recorded on the iPad. And the last text from Shona is there, the one I couldn't read because the phone screen was smashed. It says:

Boy in the colour of golden apples offered to Poseidon. You know where. Be quick. Ariadne xx

He and I gabble about what it could possibly mean. Shona told Jude to call her Ariadne. Time I looked up the name. We Google it. Wikipedia says she was the Cretan princess in love with Theseus who killed the Minotaur. That rings bells. Poseidon, we know, is god of the sea, which is where Jude ended up. But *'in the colour of golden apples'*? Does that refer to Jude's skin tone? We do a search for *'golden apples'* – and it turns out they're (probably) oranges, the ones that Hercules had to gather as one of his tasks.

''Course,' says Jude, 'she might have meant orange for the lifejacket?'

'Bloody hell! You're right!'

Jude preens like a cartoon cat. 'Elementary, my dear Mother.'

Was that last text a warning about what was going to happen? If so, it puts a whole new complexion on Shona's behaviour. She never intended to harm Jude and didn't anticipate her last text wouldn't get through. I will certainly share this with the Port Police.

Not surprisingly, after the excitement, it takes a while for me to settle the super-sleuth. But he's so shattered, just the effort to keep himself awake is the last straw. I am exhausted, too, but excited by the mythology link. Helen, the bogus girl on Snapchat, is easy; in Greek mythology, the most beautiful woman in the world, stolen from her husband King Menelaus by Paris which caused the Trojan War. No guessing why Shona would choose her. But Ariadne? It says that she told Theseus to trail a thread to help himself escape the labyrinth after killing the Minotaur. They sailed away together to Naxos but instead of marrying her as he'd promised, he deserted her there.

The story has other endings, but I suspect Shona may see this one as a metaphor with Theseus embodying the lack of respect and appreciation she feels she deserves. The need for attention and admiration is symptomatic of Narcissistic Personality Disorder and very strong in Shona. No wonder she identifies with Ariadne.

I find an alternative ending to Ariadne's story that's much jollier; Dionysus, *'the god of the grape-harvest, winemaking and wine, of fertility, ritual madness, religious ecstasy, and theatre'*, found her on Naxos, fell in love and married her, after which she ascended Mount Olympus as his wife and a goddess. I'd go with that version. Then an Olympian thunderbolt strikes me as I recall Shona's list of affairs that day at Xerocampos: a naval officer, a minor royal, a wine producer and a theatre impresario – none of them named. The first two embody Theseus and the others, Dionysus. Shona thinks she's goddess material.

A low achiever who was unloved by her parents, less valued than her brother and was abandoned, childless, by her husband; did Shona see me as another person who never appreciated her? Facts:

1) She helped me decide to have my child whom I then denied her.
2) I failed to thank or even contact her after I went back to Scotland.
3) When we were in touch later, I talked mainly about myself.
4) I attracted her childhood crush, Donald Mudie (who went sailing on Loch Fyne with Jim – hardly a royal like Theseus but posh enough).

5) Instead of going to Patmos with her, I chose to be with Alexis, the man who prevented her from working with refugees.

No wonder I became a focal point of everything negative in her life. I decide not to analyse the *'fertility, ritual madness and religious ecstasy'* aspect of Dionysus right now. I'll leave that to Peter. My head's aching enough for one day.

Alexis is on voicemail. Don't know what to tell him except it was an interesting day, remind him that I leave for Symi day after tomorrow and could he call? He's not blanking me, I'm convinced of that. Work must be taking all his time. How many more poor souls have arrived on Leros while my attention's been on Jude? Hundreds, probably.

Sitting by the open window with a beer, I'm glad of time to clear my thoughts. In my dreams, though, my mind goes on working and I wake in the early hours knowing what I must do.

FIFTY FOUR

FRASER – Leros

It's been a long day. We've all spoken to Clair. I'm looking forward to seeing her face for real instead of it just fading into my thoughts on a regular basis.

Pizza and booze, added to the relief we all feel, makes for a certain state of relaxation. Even so, Annie bows out early to get Jude to bed. Jim McCandless hasn't joined, he's spent the day with the Port Police and talking to the British Embassy in Athens. His sister's mental state complicates everything – now there's an understatement. Down in Pandeli, no-one's more surprised than me that Donald Mudie and I seem to be getting on. Perhaps because Jess is providing a sparky, scatty sideshow. Despite our tiredness, we take her up when she suggests a nightcap at the late night place.

A late night bar is the last place I expect to see Alexis, working the hours he does, but he lopes in around ten thirty. Does he know Annie isn't here? An old beardy guy and a not-so-old bird follow him. Jess being Jess hollers across from our table. I get the idea that Alexis doesn't really want to introduce everyone, but he can't not. The Father Time dude is his dad and says to call him Philo. Like the pastry? And the woman is his Aussie girlfriend, Gretchen. After downing a swift Amstel, Alexis takes an envelope from his shoulderbag.

'Look, Fraser, I only came for a drink to please my dad. I'm shattered and I must get some sleep. I was going to take it to the hotel tomorrow but since you're here… Can you make sure Annie gets this, please? She mentioned Maggie and the missing seven years. I assume you know about this? My mother did some local research for me, emailed it across. There's information about Maggie's family in Mechelen and the surrounds.' Jess is blown away.

'Oh, wow! Can I read it, Alexi? Maggie was my great-aunt.'

'Ah – there's a personal message for Annie in there, too, so I'm sure she'll pass on the material about your great-aunt.' He gives me his hand and rises to go.

'Fraser, I'm glad everything's worked out so well. You must be very relieved.' Worked out so well? What does he think's been going on? A game of hide and seek? Donald rises, thanks him and shakes his hand, Jess does a kissy kissy. He says '*Kalinίchtas*' to Dad, Gretchen, and all round then ducks out into the night.

It strikes me that the whole performance has been a bit final. I need to get something straight but I'm not clear what.

'Excuse me, all. I – er – I forgot to tell Alexis – '
And I shift out of the bar after him. He's stopped on the harbour's edge, to light his pipe.

'Alexi.'

'Fraser?'

'Was that goodbye? Is that the last we're going to see of you? I mean *any* of us?'
He pays a lot of attention to drawing his pipe. How would Clair deal with this? Let him talk. But he doesn't, so I do.

'Can I ask you something?'
Great start, Einstein, now what? He's waiting.

'Do you – Do you think you – I mean, is Annie…?'

'What?' OK, Uncle Puke, this is going well. Right. Ask an open question.

'It may be none of my business but – d'you think you and Annie are long-term?' To which the only answer can be yes or no. Oh, well done. Very well done. One I'm counting, two I'm counting, three I'm counting… he breaks it on five.

'You're her brother. It's natural that you should look out for Annie, so it *is* your business – in a way.' He stares out to Aghia Kiriaki Island. I have to tilt my head to look at him. The light from his pipe pulsates slowly several times. I'm just about to prompt him when he continues… speaking as though I'm in the remedial English class.

'Annie is an extraordinary woman and a beautiful one. Inside and out, as they say. I've become very – *fond* of her over a short period of time. But we – she and I – have to come to terms with our situation.'

'But'– I don't like the *'but'* or the *'coming to terms'*. His English is precise, maybe too precise. It gives him away.

'Sounds like you're dumping her, pal. Is that the 'personal message' in yon brown envelope?'

'Look, Fraser –'

'Is it because of Jude getting rescued? Another Western tourist child getting the publicity? Aye, we talked about that, Annie and I, back on Rhodes.'

'Annie is aware of the problems, she'd be the first to understand that NRH can't be compromised.'

'What? You mean she embarrasses you – you and your precious charity? Because of what she's been through?'

'I wouldn't put it quite –'

'You *are* dumping her. In a *wee note*? You may have sacred principles and a bloody halo, but your spine's baby turds. You know what? Annie's better off without you –' Time to head off. 'Forgive me if I don't give her your regards.' And because I can't resist it –

'Fannybaws!'

Fannybaws?

Then I feel it's not enough, so I swivel and take a swing at him. From my height it can only be an uppercut but it connects satisfyingly with his nose. His hands fly up to his face hiding what I hope will be a very bloody hooter. And his pipe skitters off the quay into the water – pffsh!

I have a feeling I just lost an argument. Wish the drink wasn't on me. I tank back, unsteadily, to the bar, hoping the giant isn't following Jack down the concrete path.

Philander, followed by Gretchen, pass me, presumably on the way to minister to the blessed Saint Alexis. Obviously, the minor fracas was lit well enough to be a sideshow. Philander bawls a well-known Greek obscenity at me and Gretchen spits a popular Anglo Saxon one. Inside, Jess and Donald are on their feet. Jess continues the trend set by Philander and Gretchen.

'Fraser, you are such a dick! What did you do that for?'

I snatch up the brown envelope.

'That. That's why I did it. He's only dumping her.'

I start to pulp it. Donald stops me.

'Fraser, that's Annie's property.'

He takes it from me.

'Whatever's in it is hers. Poor sweetheart.'

He seems genuinely upset for her. Looks like his marriage really is over because he's giving a good impression of genuinely caring for Annie, despite her fling with Alexis. Obviously, the stuff about London wasn't too strong, either. We only heard about the time she spent with Shona/Shoonagh in any detail. There must have been a lot more before. As her brother I sort of did and didn't want to know. It's funny and desperate that she hadn't a clue about the Zizou nickname. After all these years she's discovered even that was a lie. And now she's about to discover she's been with a Flying Greek Dutchman. I'm so sorry – and angry – for her. Let's hope it really is "*Andio Alexis*" for the rest of us.

Thankfully, the Pandeli night has swallowed the Dutch Bastard, Philander, and Gretchen. Maybe he's been honest with them and they've decided he deserved it. The bar shows no sign of closing, so we order another round. The brown envelope on the table has a presence all of its own.

FIFTY FIVE

ANNIE – Leros

While Fraser Jude-sits, I am at the Port Police HQ. I have spoken to Jim McCandless who has approved my request and, should his sister react positively, agreed to be an observer. All we need now is for the Port Police to sanction the meeting and provide supervision. As Jim and I wait, they are boundlessly polite. The offers of coffee and cake keep coming while I compose and recompose the questions I want to ask his sister, Shoonagh.

Jim can tell me very little other than she remained silent for the entire day, yesterday, responding only to offers of food and drink, and those with just a shake or a nod of her head. Police Authorities and the British Embassy in Athens are aware of the situation and it is certain that she will be taken there for interview by a psychiatrist and offered legal representation within the next few days. The only question is when, precisely? Another case of my friend, Shona, having no control. This will exacerbate her symptoms.

Where she does have control, however, is whether and when she will allow me to see her. I expect either to be refused or to be kept waiting for a long period. Come lunchtime, Jim suggests we retire to a taverna and wait. The Port Police have our numbers. Ironically, we end up at the same place where Shona and I sat after the outing to the War Museum – when she copied Jude's number from my phone. I mention this to Jim. He is not surprised.

'As I said in Rhodes, Annie, Shoonagh is an unusually intelligent and resourceful woman. Why this was never recognised when she was younger says something about her schooling.' While he's speaking I'm thinking Attention Deficit Hyperactivity Disorder in addition to the Narcissism diagnosis. Add to that Boarding School Syndrome and I come to the conclusion that Shona/Shoonagh never stood a chance. There but for fortune… Then I wonder if I was in a better position than her from the time I arrived with Rosemary and George? Only I know the answer to that. OK, OK, OK! What I don't know is… the answer.

There are several alerts on my iPad which I now have the space to look at. One is from Alexis. The other four are from Jess. All messages of support. I have heard from Alexis several times since Thursday night. What I need, more than this, is to see him. Is he being tactful in staying away or does he feel superfluous? A nasty shadow lurks, telling me this is all too much for a new relationship. *'But he's older than me, he should be more…!'* I'm not sure what it is that little Annie yowls. *'He may be older,'* snaps grown up Annie, *'It doesn't mean he owes you anything, even after a couple of shags'*.

Jim's phone rings, a few brief words, he clicks off and says, 'Royal summons.' We're three minutes' walk away. I wonder what awaits us. Will she be handcuffed? That would make matters a million times worse.

A policeman shows us up to an empty interview room where we sit at a table. After some ten minutes, the door opens and Shona/Shoonagh is led in by one officer and followed by a second who remains, officially, 'at ease'. Her handcuffs are unlocked and she takes a seat opposite us. Her hair is tied back but she goes through the motion of tucking it behind an ear. She is calm and behaves with dignity, despite the uncharacteristic jeans and T-shirt, and sits with her hands folded in her lap, waiting for one of us to begin. It's my responsibility, I have requested this.

'Thank you for agreeing to meet me, Shona – or would you prefer that I call you Shoonagh?'

She nods, graciously, half-smiling.

'Jude is well.' No reaction. No point in asking how she is, or is there?

'How are you?' She makes a small gesture taking in the room and policeman. I try again.

'I wondered if you would like to talk about what's happened over the last four days, Shoonagh?' We wait. It seems she doesn't. I thought I was prepared for silence, but now I don't feel so confident.

'Is there anything you would like to tell me?' No reaction from her. I feel a tiny flutter of what could be anger and try to suppress it.

'Shoonagh, you were very kind to me once, in London. But after that you stopped being kind, did some things that…' I've forgotten how I was going to phrase it so plough on with the next part of the 'script' I've prepared.

'Did my actions have anything to do with your negative view of me? Or my lack of actions?' She is not ignoring me, is definitely listening. I glance at Jim and receive a look of sympathy. I lean towards her slightly.

'Was it because I never said *'thank you'*?' For the first time, there is eye contact. I have not seen the strength of her intelligence before, it awes me. More than that, there is a controlled awareness. And – is it pity? Or contempt? I persist.

'It would be helpful if you could give a reason… please?'

She gives a short laugh, more 'Huh!'. I'm way off text now but driven on.

'Shoonagh, what happened to Eloise?' Jim looks up abruptly; this is the first time he's heard mention of my friend. Having started, I can't stop.

'Something happened to drive her away. What did you say to her?'

She raises her eyebrows. 'I said nothing to Eloise.' I steel myself and hold her look. Eventually she speaks –

'But I did have a word with Jean-Paul in Toulouse. Mentioned that he had a rival, and let him believe it was the rival calling.'

She impersonated me to Eloise's fiancé? It's all making horrible sense.

I feel sick with anger and loss. It doesn't matter, now, exactly what she said. That damage can never be repaired. But how did she find him when I failed to trace Eloise?

'Rosemary was very forthcoming about your friendships. But she was – an innocent – unlike her friend, Blanche, who saw what you were up to. And Blanche spoke excellent French. A few phone calls…'

The evening at the taverna – her French was rapid and fluent.

'You were Blanche?' Blanche, my mother's drinking friend…I'd always assumed she was Rosemary's age, never asked. Is there no area of my life this woman hasn't invaded?

'And who do you think settled your rent, Annie? Not poor little Eloise, surely? No, I did. I wouldn't have wanted little Jude homeless. Aren't you going to say *'thank you'*?'

Her audacity is breath taking. *Stay cool, Annie.*

'Why, Shoonagh? Why have you done all this?' She leans forward, her brow creased, as if she's asked herself the same question.

'I didn't want to, Annie. I just thought you needed to learn.'

I remember '*teach and learn*'. While I try to process my feelings she turns to the policeman and holds out her wrists to have the handcuffs replaced, regally, as though they are a reward – a right, even. Shoonagh has come to the end of a cycle that centred on me. Did it damage her life more than it did mine? My impulse is to go to
her, hold her hand, tell her that her life can get better. But I hold back, because that may not be true. She is led to the door which opens to reveal other waiting officers. As she passes through, Shoonagh pauses briefly, turns to me.

'By the way, he's married.'

FIFTY SIX

FRASER – Rhodes 2016

That Sunday evening, we all packed into the toy plane for Rhodes. I'd texted Clair to let her know our plans. Jude was back to normal enough to start whining for a new phone. Apart from that, we were a subdued group. Stress is knackering and we'd all had enough of it. Jim stood us a hotel for the night on account of the trouble his sister had caused. I decided it wasn't charity it was blood money.

From the moment I saw it in the distance, I knew that outline, silhouetted against glass doors. She was waiting for us on the front steps. Her kind of surprise, a good one. Walking up the path of shame I kicked myself over and over again for the meathead I was to have lost her. I can feel my eyeballs pricking, now.

Jude wellied ahead, almost knocking her off her feet. The rest of us joined them for a Harkin-Buchanan group hug while Big Banker 1 and Big Banker 2 stood aside, looking like the tools they were.

As we entered that marble time warp of a hotel, all I could think was… 'Symi, Guildford, Kilachlan, even Florida. Anywhere she is…'

ANNIE – Symi 2016

The blue-black sky comforted me. Sitting at Clair's place, glass of whisky in hand, overlooking Pedi Bay and hearing an Iranian family chatting and able to laugh, I allowed the relief to flood in. It was hard to believe the last ten days actually happened. All but the change of date and I might have pretended they hadn't – except they had. It wasn't just the date that was different, though.

There was an atmosphere between Jess and Fraser. They'd barely looked at each other let alone spoken from the time we left Leros till he hiked straight off to his place. Strange time to have a moody. Clair returned from saying goodnight to Jess, made me her priority, flopped onto the lounger next to me, close enough to snuggle up to. She snuggled back.

'Annie, just let go. Plenty of us to catch you.'

I relaxed into the rhythm of her breathing. I woke a while later. Clair was gone and there was a blanket over me. Through the wrought iron table the moon cast a shadow of the envelope from Alexis onto the flagstones. It contained information about Maggie's early life and, by his text, I knew there was something more for me. I hadn't found the right moment to open it, wanted to give the information about Maggie the space it deserved. No, not entirely true. I was afraid of what he was going to say. That photograph of him and the woman at Philander's, then Shoonagh's "He's married" punctuating my every other thought, just like Alexis's "flirting our pants off" remark did. I'd known Donald was married when we were having our 'dates', so if Alexis *was* married, why should I have a moral reaction to it? And since marriage wasn't on my agenda, why did I have an emotional response? I'd had a premonition that I was falling too far, too fast after our first night together. Maybe it was the ridiculous notion that Leros completed my puzzle, just because it looked like a jigsaw piece? Sure, I had found out about Shona/Shoonagh. But were there any other answers for me? It was so ridiculously simplistic, I knocked it out of my head.

I reached across for the brown envelope. Inside was another, a white one with my name on it. I ran my nail under the flap and took out a letter.

FIFTY SEVEN

FRASER – Leros. June 2019

I finish the mineral water and we say goodnight to the gang. Another long day in a succession of long days. I can almost hear my bones creak. We both have scooters parked on the roadside.

'I'll just drop in on the family on the way. Only be ten minutes,' I tell her.

'Sure. I'll go to bed and wait for you.'

'Don't make promises you can't keep. You'll be snoring in three minutes.'

'I don't snore.'

'Allow me to differ.'

She takes off, well aware that I'm lying when I say ten minutes. Annie's place is the opposite side of Pandeli Bay which is why I'm sure she'll be asleep by the time I get home.

Puttering up the road from Platanos, I look out to Aghia Kiriaki. It fair makes your heart dance, the moon above and the pearl shaft on the water below it. Takes me back to that night at the bar. Near enough breaking someone's nose is not the best interview technique. To be fair, I didn't know at the time I was a candidate but, well, here I am, Area Director of Nederland Redden en Helpen. No thanks to my drinking habits at that shameful moment.

I park up and halloo going through the front door. It's after ten, but school holidays so everyone will still be up. As I go through the kitchen a small missile thunders into my legs.

'Aagh! I'm being attacked – help – help!' I sweep up the mini-assailant. 'Gotcha, Rosie Posie!'

My niece chokes with glee. 'No, Unca Poo!'. I swing the offending bundle upside down and back again as I go on through to the balcony.

Annie looks up from her laptop. 'Thanks for that, Fraizhe – now I'll never get her to sleep.'

'Good to see you too, Mighty. Where's Jude?'

'Gaming with Andy.' Sure enough, the flickering light of a video game lights his bedroom window upstairs. As I collapse onto the cane sofa, Rosie wriggles off my lap and sits next to me with her pop-up book.

'Read me, Unca Poo!'

'In a minute. Folks get off OK today?'

Annie sighs with relief. 'Not before time. The heat was really getting to Rosemary. Think George would have liked to stay, though – or take Rosie with him.'

'Pretty full house with Andy here, too?' I don't know how she does it, three extra people, a toddler, a teenager and a pretty full time job.

'Bursting at the seams. Not sorry that the lads are away to Symi on Thursday. A few days of heaven. Then I'm up to Lesvos.'

'And himself?'

'Oh, who knows. See him there or here or – somewhere…How was your day?'

It's been as difficult a day as most. We spent a lot of it at the hospital with a Syrian guy who'd lost his whole family. Most to the war, then his wife and daughter on the crossing from Turkey. So numb he couldn't remember who or where he was. Fenne coaxed him to say a few words.

She and Annie are mates. Met the first time Annie was over here and the whole Jude thing happened. Whatever Annie saw in her, I did too, plus a whole lot more. Fenne brought out the adult in me, got me off the booze, helped me become, well, better. And somehow, we manage to work and live together and never tire of it. Never thought it could happen after –

Annie breaks into my thoughts.

'If anyone can get through to anyone, it's Fenne. Alexis always said her Arabic was better than his. But it's not just that.'

'You're telling me?'

'Fair point, well made'

'Unca Poo!'

Annie takes over. 'Ssshh, Rosie, let me talk to your Uncle Puke. Then he'll read to you.'

We cover the hotspot, the latest arrivals, distribution, all the sadly usual. I read a bit of 'The Little Prince' to Rosie then kiss her baby curls, hug my sister and shout Kaliníchta to the lads as I go.

My phone pings.

'Still awake. Hurry up.'

'Hold that thought. On my way.'

And I putter back around the bay to the apartment on the Vromolithos Road where Fenne is waiting for me.

ANNIE – Leros. Two days later.

'Clair – hello. How are you? How's your mum?'

'Hello, darling – I'm fine but afraid Mum's a bit touch and go. Jess has been an absolute star, caring for her, running around doing messages, keeping the social circle up to date and just – well, being with her.'

'When you say "touch and go"…'

'Ahm – to be honest, more "go". She's away with the fairies most of the time, the dementia and the morphine.'

'Oh God, so sorry, love. How awful for you – well, for her, for you, for Jess.'

'Comes with the territory. Life stops and life goes on. How are you?'

'Doing OK. The folks went home the day before yesterday. We've got Andy staying with us across from Symi at the moment, so Jude's happy. The pair of them are out on the prowl for unsuspecting young beauties as we speak. Then off to Symi together tomorrow.'

'Fraser?'

I'm cautious in my response. Clair is well over him, I'm sure. But he's in another relationship and she – actually, I don't know where Clair is on that personal level. We have little opportunity to talk girlie stuff.

'Different man. Still off the booze. This job's the best thing that's ever happened to him.'

'And the lady?'

'Fenne's good for him, too.'

'I'm glad.' She genuinely is. 'Afraid I'm not going to make Rosie Magdalena's name day this year. Monday, isn't it? Got anything planned?'

'Not really, at her age it's more a chance for the mums to get lashed on Prosecco.'

She lets go and laughs. 'Well, hope you get the little something we've sent in time. Kids' clothes are absurdly adorable over here so JJ and I got a bit carried away.'

It's their generosity that's absurd, I tell her – 'That mean I'll have to heave out another we'an to get the wear out of them?'

'Don't involve me in this. Up to you and your man.'

'Never going to happen. JJ is next in line as a baby machine.' I turn the spotlight on Clair. 'Speaking of men, how's Mechelen Man?'

'Examination has proved we cannot possibly be related. I may have to make up another excuse.' Said with unbearable smugness. Mechelen Man, aka Daniel, encountered on a 'Maggie research' trip to Belgium, has the social conscience of Gandhi, and the wit though not the personal inclinations of Oscar Wilde. Her perfect man. I am not a one to tolerate coyness. Or double entendres. '*Examination*'?

'Cut the crap, Harkin, you fancy the –'

'Kalinichta, Annie mou, love to you all.'

'Kalinichta, Clair mou. Back atcha.'

Jude and Andy have been cock-a-hoop at the idea of the ferry ride from Leros to Symi left to their own devices, so more than a little sulky when they discover this morning that Neféli will be chaperoning them on her way down to visit her sister in hospital on Rhodes. Sets my mind at rest. Rosie and I go for a juice and a coffee at a table by the water in Lakki. Same table I sat at with Jim while we were waiting for Shona's summons. Marijke from NRH calls.

'Hi, Annie. Just wanted to hear how you're doing, and to tell you we've found a great translator. Speaks Arabic, Kurdish, and Farsi. She has your number and she'll meet you on Lesvos.'

This is very good news. The last one suffered from burn out. It never occurred to me that a job like mine existed, but it's so obvious that people in trauma need counsellors, therapists and psychologists. On top of mastering Greek and applying for residence, I'm in ongoing training to deal with PTSD, bereavement and, something I never had, rape counselling. Finding a translator with the sort of vocabulary I need to understand or express isn't that easy, especially when feelings, mental states, metaphors used to describe them, and cultures are all so different. Sadly, a lot of men won't share their problems with me, so it helps to have a male translator. And sometimes, men don't want their women to speak to me. I wear a hijab when necessary and abandon it if the mood feels right.

'Thanks, Marijke, that's great. I'll look forward to meeting her.'

'Alexis plans to get there by Friday, but you know what it's like – what he's like.'

We share the joke. Aside from his mother, his ex-wife and I are probably the two women in the world who know him best. So civilised, the Dutch. I've learnt a lot from Marijke.

November 2019

Rosie lies sleeping in my arms as we sit atop the world, overlooking Pandeli Bay. The air is cool and blustery so we're indoors by the window. Jude's doing homework, under duress. At sixteen, he's become a Greek god, speaks the language like a native and excels at sports. Little Falairy, Rosie's name day gift, chews happily on an old sandal. Named so after my little Auntie Mary song rewrite 'Umpty Lairy, Tatty Falairy…', she isn't a Westie, but she is white and fluffy. Losing Jack and Tatty so soon, one after the other, meant making readjustments; they were another link with Maggie gone.

I haven't engaged with the birth parent search. Yet. May do in future but, with the change of home, of job, and becoming a mother again, I have enough filling my life. When Jude's ready, maybe.

Visits to Lesvos and Chios have been, as always, hard work, heart breaking, rewarding. Same here, too, on Leros. With so many people 'warehoused' in Turkey and Greece, one of the EU's less humane decisions, the big fear is infection sweeping through the camps. It isn't just mental illness that can be a silent killer.

There's no sign of incoming refugees at the moment but a winter crossing isn't ruled out. If I get a call, I have any number of sitters for Rosie. A voice echoes up the stairs.

'Yássas! I'm back with the pizzas!'

'That's your daddy, Rosie.' I whisper, and tousle her darkening hair.

Perhaps I should explain, at this point, what was in the letter from Alexis that I opened on my return from Leros to Symi three years ago:

'Dearest Annie

Here are some notes from my mother regarding your friend, Maggie, in Mechelen. She talked with a few people and gleaned some anecdotal information, better than Google or any ancestry website could offer. They will provide reading for a less stressful time.

But, before you share it with your friends, you and I have a reckoning. By the time you receive this, other priorities will have arisen in your life. Here are mine.

You are the most extraordinary woman I have ever known. If I were ever to let you slip from my life, I would be an even greater fool than I judge myself to be now. What I know also is that 'now' is not our moment. Politics and the needs of others dictate it. They may have dimmed enough within a year or so for us to be together. It is my dearest wish that we could be, and that you will consider it. I await your reply.

With my thanks and – yes – love

Alexis'

What could a girl do? Especially when Rosie made her presence felt.

As he enters the room with a pile of pizza boxes, my phone rings. I can't reach it.

'Could you answer it, Alexi mou?'

Dropping them on the table, he picks up. Jude bounds in, slavering at the pizza smells.

'Hello…Annie's phone…Oh, hi, Jim, yes it is…'

It will be Jim McCandless, Shoonagh's brother. He calls to give updates on her progress for my professional as well as personal concern. Despite her stalking me and nearly killing my dogs – and then my son – I still spoke on her behalf to the Greek and UK courts. The dogs didn't die and she'd warned me Jude would be pushed overboard, but my smashed phone stopped me from knowing. After extradition from Greece she was detained in a medium-security mental health unit but, having 'engaged' with her treatment, she transferred to a low-security no go area, and the terms of any volunteering restricted her to 'no public contact', which limited her to a very few areas. So, she's been working in the office of an animal charity and, it seems, doing well. I sense, though, that Shoonagh won't be that focused or meek for long. Alexis has been silent for a while then –

'Ah –'

That 'Ah' hits me in the solar plexus.

He turns to me.

'Shoonagh didn't arrive at work this morning. And Jim's car's been stolen.'

Jude freezes with a pizza slice half eaten. 'Oh, shit.'

'It's been recognised on camera in Dumbarton. Does that mean anything to you?'

It does. She's fair travelled today, Dumbarton's on the A82, just north of Glasgow. That means she could be going to her granny's old home in Lochgilphead or…Dunstaffnage, where Rosemary – where Mum and Dad live.

'Give me the phone, Alexi!... Jim –'

Το τέλος

Thank you for reading Jigsaw Island. If you would like to donate to the charities who have helped and informed in the writing, please see:
Aegean Solidarity Network Team at https://asnteamuk.org/
Refugee Support Devon at http://refugeesupportdevon.org.uk/

One of the many people who gave me their time, advice and shared experience was Alaa. I met him through Refugee Support Devon. He has become a dear friend. His story moved me as it will you, should you care to read it. What follows is truth, not fiction.

ALAA'S STORY

Alaa is from Syria, born in Damascus in 1988, and started school in 1994. He had his own flat in Damascus and dreamed of studying to be a lawyer. Damascus was a liberal and tolerant city where Muslim and Christian lived side by side with no problems. The Arabic spoken in Syria is very pure and unaffected by dialect. In 2012, when the war started, the family relocated to Daraa province, moving around a lot of villages to find a place to stay. Alaa has a brother, who was living in Greece at the time we first spoke, a married sister and a half-brother were still living in Daraa along with his father.

Alaa moved to West Bikar Shtoura, Lebanon, in 2013 where he lived in a partly built high-rise building that was open to the air (no outer walls). Even so, he had to pay rent. There was poor sanitation – no running water. Alaa paid to renovate and put in sanitation. His brother joined him after one month and remained in Lebanon until January 2019.

In Lebanon, refugees had to pay ground rent for a tent, wherever they were. He kept hoping that he could go back to Damascus but this was not possible as he would have faced compulsory conscription into Assad's army. This would also prevent him from going back today. He was to stay in Lebanon until the end of 2016. While there, he worked with a designer colleague who produced artwork on vinyl for advertising on vehicles. Alaa became very proficient at this and enjoyed the work.

He sent for his elderly, disabled father (an amputee who walked with crutches) to live with him in 2014. He had been living with Alaa's brother in Syria and returned there for six months on the death of his own brother, Alaa's uncle. While he was away, the Lebanon border closed – it was controlled by Hezbollah, and the military refused to allow Alaa's father back in. They had no sympathy for his situation and even stamped his passport blocking him from ever returning to Lebanon.

Alaa was very upset as he had been hoping to build a new life in Lebanon. He heard that a lot of Syrian people were travelling to Germany from Lebanon. He tried to leave in the summer of 2014, but Lebanon wanted a fee to allow him to leave because his visa had expired. He had to pay $200 US rent per month. All the time he was trying to work and to borrow money. Eventually, he had to leave Lebanon because he was afraid of being deported to Syria. He left Lebanon on 1 January 2016, paying a fine of $600 US to Lebanese Immigration. He had saved $1,000 in a year. The flight to Turkey cost him $400. He arrived in Istanbul, where he stayed with a cousin who located a smuggler – whom they met in a square in Istanbul and who agreed to take Alaa from Turkey to Greece for $700 US. He had to borrow another $1,000 in order to continue his journey. He and other escaping refugees were driven overnight in a van from Istanbul to a secret location on the coast near Izmir. There were 30 adults and about 40 children – and Alaa met a friend from Syria. By this time it was February.

The boat the smuggler provided was an inflatable with an outboard motor that was clearly too small. Alaa had bought a life jacket for about $20 US. They set off in a rough sea with metre high waves at around five a.m. The journey would take 4-5 hours they were told. They didn't know exactly where they were heading, only that they would arrive in Greece (it was to be Lesvos). The smuggler told them which way to head but they went off course because of the bad weather. The boat was 'driven' by a Kurdish refugee, a friend of the smuggler, who was given free passage for undertaking the task. (Alaa was to meet the man later in France.)

The passengers were screaming, crying and most were very seasick. After a while they saw a helicopter and were waving and calling for help. They saw a Greek ferry boat and tried to attract its attention. But there was a larger refugee boat and the ferry chose to help them. Eventually they saw land, but they didn't know if it was Greece, just hoped that it was.

A coastguard boat arrived. It wasn't big enough to take anyone on board but tried to shelter them from the worst of the waves by staying broadside ahead of the dinghy. After about 30 minutes, a second boat arrived and helped guide the dinghy to shore. The coastguards were very kind and sympathetic. When they reached the beach there were volunteers waiting – who told them to stop the motor and waded into the sea to help them. Everyone was soaked in seawater and cold. They were given blankets (remember this was February and, even in Greece, chilly) and fresh water. The Greek authorities sent a bus, which arrived about 10 minutes after they'd landed, and transported them to Lesvos camp – caravans for families, tents for others. Given food, coffee and drinks they felt more secure. Alaa felt huge relief after thinking he was going to die at sea.

That afternoon, everyone went to the police point in the camp to register details and fingerprints. Syrians were accepted as genuine war refugees – consequently, those who weren't pretended that they were but had lost their papers.

Registration meant that the refugees had permission to stay 6 months in Greece. After remaining in the camp for four days Alaa took the 12-hour ferry to Athens with thousands of other refugees.

In Athens, the police told them that the border with Macedonia was shut. Despite which, people tried to find smugglers to take them to the North of Greece. (It was not possible to move on from Greece to another country within the EU because refugees had to claim asylum in the first country of entry. Macedonia the state – now North Macedonia - was not in the EU. Consequently, Greek Authorities would not prevent refugees from crossing the border – it was N Macedonia preventing the crossing.) Eventually, 60 people, all Syrian, boarded a bus that took 14 hours, all on side roads, to get to Idomeni camp. This unofficial camp had had no government assistance for services, and refugees were dependent on themselves or non-profit organisations who offered assistance. The police arrested everyone on the bus 15 km before they arrived and took them to Kavala camp, run by the Greek military on a disused airport.

People were given tents (8 to a tent) and provided with water and sandwiches around 1 a.m.. The tents were pitched on wet grass, 2 blankets each. On the first night, they slept about 4 hours because they were so cold and wet. After the second day, they heard from Idomeni camp that it was possible to cross the border. Alaa and some others took a taxi to Idomeni to get a stamp on his 'Leave to remain' (remain in Greece) document; regulations meant that the driver had to drop them 5km from the camp and they had to walk the rest of the way. On reaching the camp, they learned that 200 people were being allowed through per night. The number allocated to Alaa was 4,500. This meant a 23 day wait and Alaa was disappointed but resigned to it. But the border into Macedonia closed before he was able to cross. He did, however, have the 'Leave to remain' stamp.

There were approximately 50,000 people in Idomeni camp. Alaa stayed in Kavala until May. The food was bad, the sanitation poor – people got sick. There were some doctors and sometimes they could give out paracetamol. That was all. It was 10 days after he first arrived that Alaa could have a shower. He heard that there was a hotel two to three kilometres away. A Syrian friend of his sharing the tent spoke good English so the two of them decided to go to the hotel and ask to pay for a shower. The hotelier agreed to a 10 minute shower for €6. Thereafter, the two of them used it every 2/3 days and also had a coffee and Alaa used the WiFi to contact his brother in Lebanon, cousin in Turkey and friends and volunteers.

Volunteers from overseas met at the hotel as they were not allowed into Kavala military camp – some were from Totnes, which is why Alaa ended up in Devon. Some were from Palestine and had come to support refugees as they could empathise with their situation. There were Spanish volunteers, too. Alaa made friends with volunteers and offered to go into the camps to identify the neediest people who were overlooked – those who weren't able to queue or unable, for other reasons, to take up anything on offer. He would accompany volunteers at night and go to individual tents in Idomeni and ask people how they were. Because he spoke Arabic and English, he was able to assist non-Arabic speaking volunteers. He was able to identify women who were on their own, or who had children, or disabled people. He could then direct the right people to assist them e.g. a Palestinian woman to offer sanitary products to women. Because of their culture, which made them quite shy in contrast to Western behaviour, many of the women were very reluctant to ask for help in any way.

Meantime, the border to Macedonia kept opening and closing. From March to May, Alaa helped volunteers preparing food and, while doing this, he made more friends from Germany and France. The uncertainty over whether the border would open remained and if it did, they didn't know where they could go on to.

Eventually, around 1 May, Alaa got a bus at Thessalonika and went back to Athens. His friends had left ten days earlier, including a friend's sister and children to look for a smuggler/forger to help them to Northern Europe. The Greek Ministry of Migration Policy says: "The only way that an asylum applicant may legally travel to another European country is through the procedure of the Dublin III Regulation, within the framework of family reunification. While being asylum applicants, you cannot travel to the rest of Europe, unless there are serious, proven health reasons that require your immediate transfer abroad".

As Alaa couldn't provide such a reason, he borrowed more money from his cousin and looked for a forger so that he could buy false documentation and get a plane out – but when he found one, the man wanted €2,000 for a fake passport and Alaa didn't have enough. He tried to buy a fake EU ID card as they cost only €40 and, as Greece is in the Schengen area, it meant that he could travel within Europe. With the first fake Italian ID he was trying to get to Switzerland but was arrested as he entered the airport and cautioned by the airport authority. The forger then got him a French ID card and he attempted leaving at the same airport. This time he got past the airport entrance and checked in his luggage – but at the boarding gate the woman spoke to Alaa in French and all Alaa knew to say was 'bonjour' – also, the ID said he was 40 and, at that point, Alaa wasn't yet 30.

The third time he tried was with an Italian ID card and again he was caught at the airport entrance. He was now famous in Athens Airport! So he caught a bus to Thessalonika to try leaving from the airport there. It was his fourth attempt, this time with a German ID. He was caught. His fifth attempt was with an Italian fake ID again. He managed to get to the check-in desk and there, the woman spoke in Italian. Alaa didn't know any Italian so just said 'Roma'. She smiled and said "Have a nice trip".

He got onto the plane keeping his luggage on his lap and pretended to be asleep in the hope that no-one would speak to him and he would give himself away. There was a scary moment when he was asked to put the luggage in a locker, but it was stowed away without incident. The flight was to Berlin. There were two other Syrians with three children on the plane. The woman was the sister of the friend who'd left the camp ten days before Alaa. Like him, she was very nervous because she had a fake ID card. Her husband was waiting for her at Berlin airport. Neither she nor Alaa were stopped on arrival. They were relieved because now they were in the Schengen area, they could travel freely within Europe. The woman's husband assisted Alaa with taking a bus to the city centre where he looked on the street for Syrian people. Alaa stayed one night in Berlin with friends of the husband. He asked about seeking asylum there but was advised to go to France or UK. He received help to buy a ticket from Berlin to Paris through friends and, the following, day took a plane to Paris, arriving at night and transferring to a bus for Calais. Again, he was helped by a fellow Syrian, this time, a woman visiting her son who helped him book the bus ticket.

Alaa arrived in Calais at the end of May and stayed in The Jungle until 1 October. During that time, he kept trying to hide in lorries leaving either from there or from Belgium. He slept in a park in Brussels for 40 days and was constantly arrested by police or beaten up by drivers – who were all angry with refugees. Once he hid for 3 days in a lorry and was discovered at Zeebrugge.

There were problems in the street with the French. Belgium wouldn't give asylum. In Germany it would take two years. He preferred to come to England because he'd heard English people were kinder.

Lorry etiquette was important: Refugees were all very careful not to soil the lorries, using bottles and condoms to urinate.

Once, he hid at night – the next day, three of them were found, one a man in his 50s. Russian drivers beat them up. Police came to help them but didn't arrest the Russians because the Syrians were there illegally.

His last chance was to catch a freezer lorry with a 17-year-old from Alaa's home village whom he'd met again in France. At four a.m. the police checked the lorry but only one side of the load – Alaa and his friend were on the other. They arrived in Dover and the lorry drove off. At 9 p.m. when the lorry stopped they started knocking on the door as they were freezing. His phone battery was down to 4%. The driver heard them but was afraid to open the door. Alaa sent his location to his cousin in case he died – then dialled 999. After two or three minutes, the police managed to track the phone – the police came and stopped the lorry and opened the door. Alaa and his friend were very faint because, by this time, the oxygen was very poor.

The police checked their documents and luggage, gave them water and let them recover then put them in a police car. The driver was being questioned by the police but Alaa explained that the driver hadn't known they were there. The driver was very grateful. The police let him go. Alaa and friend were kept in a cell overnight where an interpreter with an Iraqi accent spoke to them in Arabic. They were then taken to a holding centre where Immigration was contacted.

Because of aid workers from Devon, whom he met in the camps in northern Greece, Alaa decided to head for Devon. There, he was welcomed by Refugee Support Devon who helped him settle in the area. Being Alaa, he was soon volunteering help to other refugees arriving.

Alaa was concerned about his younger brother, Bilal, who was still in Lebanon. He had been working in a laundry there. When another laundry opened, the owner wanted Bilal to work for him. Alaa's brother didn't want to change jobs, so the owner went to the police and told them that Bilal's papers had expired. On 1 December 2018, the immigration police arrested Bilal and took him away; Alaa was frantic, trying to locate him. Bilal was missing for three days, after which he was taken to a local police station. The problem was that Bilal's visa had expired five years earlier (it was $200 per month for a visa extension but necessary also to have a guarantor).

Friends went to the police station to bring food, drink and clothing for Bilal but had to bribe the police to see him – food, cigarettes or money (usually $20). They also had to bribe the police to release him on around 20 December. During his imprisonment, a friend of Alaa's visited him and decided to find a smuggler to help. Bilal was granted a 'Leave to remain' card lasting 30 days, during which time he had to find a guarantor. The police told him to return, however, on 2 January to renew his card. He queued with other Syrians and, when he went into the office for his interview, was made to sign a document. He didn't know what it was but discovered that it was a deportation document. He was very anxious and rang Alaa.

The friend who had visited Bilal passed on the smuggler's number but Alaa didn't have enough to pay him so had to borrow money, again, from friends to help his brother. Consequently, Bilal was able to get to Turkey and stayed for 20 days in Istanbul with the Syrian network of friends. He decided to get to Edirne near the norther border with Greece by bus. He hid in nearby Iskender for two days then walked to the Greek border. Bilal was with three friends. They met a woman who had two young boys of three years and seven months whom Bilal helped carry across the border. After this, they walked for four days to Thessaloniki, from where they took the night bus to Athens.

Bilal managed to reach the UK in Spring 2020, obviously a very happy reunion for the two brothers. Their sister and half-brother are still in Syria.

Alaa has found work and a place to live in the UK. Whether he will ever be able to study Law is uncertain. Whether either of the brothers will ever be able to return to Syria is equally unknown; it will never be while Assad and his political cohorts are in power.

ACKNOWLEDGEMENTS

My thanks to the following people for sharing their knowledge, experience, without which I could not have written Jigsaw Island:

Alaa, for sharing his refugee experience.
LEROS: Takis Varnas, Eglantine Lobstein, Jo Finn, Anne Tsakiriou, Christina Tsakiriou
Dimitris Stamatelos
SYMI: Andrew Davies, Symi Solidarity
ATHENS: Captain Demosthenis Botsis, Commander Hellenic Coastguard Service
UK:
Sue Way, Homeless Projects Manager, Church Army
Charity Opolot, Education, Employment and Training Worker, Church Army
Trupti Desai & Tameem Shaaban of Refugee Support Devon
Dr Michael Humphreys, Dr Catherine Pollard, Dr Elizabeth Osborn
Leigh Watson, Kristen Cope, Rachael Kerr
Editor Greg Rees for his knowledge and patience
Dr Jenny Kane for her inspiration and encouragement.
Mike, Ellie and the staff of The Ship Inn, Teignmouth for helping with publicity.

Martyn Stead, for his unswerving support, practical help, and love.

Jigsaw Island was originally crowdfunded through Unbound Publishing. Circumstances dictated cancelling the project but I thank Unbound for its faith in the novel. Beyond that my deep gratitude to the following people who were kind enough to pledge – listed in order of pledging.
Martyn Stead, Veronica Spink, Sue N Williamson, Angela Pridgeon, Ian Doyle, Nick McVernon, Sue Redpath, Bill Dixon, Ricky Lonmon, Kate Walker, Mark T C Arnold, Jeannie Reid, Alex Scotchbrook, David Tucker, Julian Cope, Andy Charman, Una Allman, James O'Malley, John Schluter, Michael McVernon, Alison Crowter, Bob Clowes, Naomi Stolow, Edgar Coble, Pam Jordan, Sarah Braine, Margaret Taylor, Veronica Pitts, Victoria Stead, Deborah Cranston, Claire Payne, Glenn Aitken, David Silver, Michael Gaunt-Edwards, Jon Stead, Katherine Reynolds, Gill Newton, Cat Widdowson, Anne Williams, Ros Steen, Stephen Yershon, Debbie Singleton, Gail Smith, Janet Dowling, Susie Smith, Jill Doyle, Allison Justus-Smith, Anne Cater, Janet Davies, Ian Featherby, Rita Adam

AUTHOR

LYNNE MCVERNON grew up in Surrey, went to Wimbledon School of Art, read English Literature at the University of Reading, trained as a theatre director and directed across the UK for twenty five years. Her first novel, TERRIBLE WITH RAISINS, also featuring the Greek islands, was published in 2013. JIGSAW ISLAND takes the story forward.

www.lynnemcvernon.com

Made in the USA
Middletown, DE
04 January 2021